AF490672

ASHES
and
RUINS

Love, War, and the Home Front

K. LANG-SLATTERY

Published by Pacific Bookworks, Laguna Beach California

ISBN: 979-8-9862013-0-6 (hardcover)
ISBN: 979-8-9862013-1-3 (paperback)
ISBN: 979-8-9862013-2-0 (Kindle/mobi)
ISBN: 979-8-9862013-3-7 (epub)

Subjects: 1. World War II / 2. Germany 1934-1940 / 3. London 1939-1943 / 4. The Blitz / 5. Rationing in WWII England / 6. Enemy Aliens in WWII England / 7. Jews – German – WWII / 8. Daily life – London – WWII

Library of Congress Number: 2025920506

Cover design by Cole Waidley
Interior book design by Lorie DeWorken, MindtheMargins.com
Edited by Lorraine Fico-White, Magnifico Manuscripts, LLC

The Kiss photo image, courtesy of Louise Stokheld
Crown Graphic by iStock.com/Anton Tokarev
Locket image by iStock.com/horiyan
Letters image by iStock.com/Bjoern Wylezich
Daisies image by iStock.com/kolesnikovserg
Cover background image: Firemen at work in bomb damaged street in London, after Saturday night raid, circa 1941, New York Times Paris Bureau Collection. Provided to Wikimedia Commons by the National Archives and Records Administration, Image modified by Cole Waidley.

DEDICATION

I dedicate this book to all mothers and daughters who face the world together. And most especially to my own daughter, Erin Slattery, who has always been my companion and friend. Her smile brings light to my life.

TABLE OF CONTENTS

Book One—ASHES

Book Two—RUINS

Book One

ASHES

"Moved by the understanding that purity of the German Blood is the essential condition for the continued existence of the German people and inspired by the inflexible determination to ensure the existence of the German Nation for all time, the Reichstag has unanimously adopted the following Law, which is promulgated herewith."

Law for the Protection of German Blood and German Honor, The Führer and Reich Chancellor, Adolf Hitler, September 15, 1935

CHAPTER 1

Spring 1939
Memories

CLARA HELD THE DELICATE necklace in the palm of her hand and wondered how she would be able to part with it.

She knew that what she was about to do was dangerous. She looped the necklace over her fingers and allowed it to catch the early spring sunlight coming in the windows. A perfect pearl hung suspended in the center of a platinum triangle from which a string of smaller pearls and tiny diamonds dangled. A gift from her mother on her wedding day twenty-five years before, the necklace was far dearer to her heart than the simple diamond engagement ring her late husband had slipped on her finger the evening their marriage had been brokered at her father's bank.

Her lips pressed together, she carefully folded the keepsake into a square of waxed butcher paper and slid it into the open seam of her granddaughter's soakers. The packet lay flat between the inner absorbent knitted wool and the outer layer of rubber. With the threaded darning needle waiting for this task, she closed the seam with tiny, careful stitches. She would not allow the Nazis to get their hands on one of the few things she still had from her mother.

She held up the mended soakers. "George, do not wash these without removing what I've put here," she said.

Her son-in-law sat in the armchair and cradled his infant daughter in the crook of his arm. "Don't worry. We won't even put them on her until we get near the border."

Clara tucked the soakers into the nappy bag and returned it to the foot of the baby's pram. She held out her arms. "Let me hold her one more time before you go."

George straightened his long legs and stood up. "Give her a last cuddle," he said. "I'll go get our luggage and see if I can hurry Edith up. If she doesn't come down from the attic soon, we'll miss the train to Frankfurt." George shook his head. "This is the second time she's disappeared into the attic. I have no idea what she's looking for because she won't tell me."

"Don't worry. It was a special place for her when she was growing up. More of a children's retreat than the storage space it is now." Clara smiled at George. Though it wasn't the first time she had spent time with him, during the four days of his and Edith's visit, Clara had come to trust her son-in-law. "I'm sure she's feeling a bit nostalgic. Maybe she's rummaging about looking at old photos or simply sitting and remembering happy times in the attic."

"I'm sure your right, Mrs. Lang. But she seemed agitated when she went to the attic an hour ago."

Clara watched George go into the bedroom and close the door. Edith had probably left the repacking until the last minute and now her husband would be forced to throw everything into their suitcases. *No matter,* Clara thought. Enfolding the baby in her arms for these final moments was the only thing of importance. She nuzzled her nose into the infant's neck and kissed her full cheeks and smooth forehead. The child smelled of talcum powder and that indescribable aroma of young life. She remembered holding her own infant children and was surprised to feel a tingle in her ample breasts, almost as if they could still release milk.

Her other grandchild lived far away in California, and she had only seen photos of her. This was the first grandbaby she had been able to hold, kiss, and snuggle. And now, her darling little Hazel must return to England with her parents. Clara felt a tear slide down her cheek, and, swallowing her sorrow, she gently laid her forehead against the baby's knitted blanket. She would have ample time to weep later.

She heard the clatter of footsteps coming down the stairs from the upper floor. Edith burst into the room. Fragments of dust clung to her hair, and the skirt of her traveling suit was askew.

"I couldn't find what I wanted," she said. "Lots of stuff has been moved since I was up there last." She stamped her foot and Hazel twitched in Clara's arms. "I can't find my old keepsake box anywhere."

Clara reached out and straightened her daughter's skirt. "Are a few trinkets so important?"

Edith checked behind her before she whispered, "I wanted a last look at my school-girl diary. And some old letters I'd saved. Letters from the man I loved back then." She glanced toward the bedroom door before continuing. "But, Mutti, I couldn't find them."

At that moment, George appeared from the bedroom, lugging their suitcases. "What letters?"

"Nothing, George. Only a few letters from a childhood friend. Everything up in the attic is all moved around and half the stuff belongs to Dr. Weiss and his wife." She glanced toward her mother, her eyes pleading and brimming with fear. She then straightened her expression and turned to her husband. "It doesn't matter, really. Just a silly thought. I hope I haven't made us late for the train."

George carried the suitcases toward the door of the apartment. "I'll take the luggage down, then come back for you and the baby," he said as he passed near them.

Clara folded back the satin pram cover and lowered Hazel into the sturdy, German, baby carriage. "How pretty you are in your lovely pram," she said. "I love to see you there." Clara felt lucky to still have plenty of money after the sale of both family homes. She had been able to buy the best carriage as a gift for the baby.

Edith grasped her mother's arm and pulled her close. As they embraced, she spoke softly in Clara's ear. "Please, find my diary and the letters. Being back in Germany has opened my eyes. Things are much worse than I thought. Nazi flags everywhere and anti-Jewish signs and graffiti on every building and shop. And the newspapers. Such awful headlines and the despicable notices and political cartoons. Suddenly, I've realized that my old diaries could be dangerous for Charlie."

Clara was puzzled. "Charlie? Who—"

"Mutti, remember when you and Vati made me stop writing to my friend . . . the Aryan man?" Her voice was low and insistent. "Well, we didn't stop writing . . . or seeing each other. I wrote about him in my diary, and he sent me love letters! Please find them. Most will need to be burned . . . for his safety. That's why I was trying to find them, but now I'm out of time and I need your help."

Clara only half grasped the import of what she was being asked to do. She stroked her daughter's cheek. "Don't worry. Tell me. Where did you hide them?"

Edith's words tumbled out. "Under Granny's dresser. In one of your old stationery boxes. . . . I think it was marbleized."

"Yes, I remember seeing one of those old things some months ago. I'll find it." She took hold of her daughter's shoulders with both hands. "Tell me what you want done with whatever's in that box."

Edith glanced back toward the door before continuing. "Please check everything before burning it all. Maybe there are a couple of letters from Charlie you can bring for me to keep as a remembrance. I don't mind if you read my diary before it's reduced to ashes. If you read it, my words will have a second life. When we are together again, we can compare our memories of happier days."

Clara nodded. "I'll find them," she said. "And I'll bring what I can. Whatever seems safe to carry."

Edith backed up and stared at her hands, avoiding her mother's eyes. "There is one unopened letter that haunts me still." Her voice trembled, and her fingers touched her mother's sleeve. "I wish I had read it. Perhaps I would have done things differently these last few years. Please be my eyes and heart. If it's safe, bring that letter to me when you come."

"Yes, my darling. I'll bring what I can." Clara enfolded her daughter in her arms again and kissed her cheek. "We'll be together soon," she whispered. "I promise."

George's heavy footsteps on the stairs announced his return. "We must go," he said as he entered the apartment.

Clara clasped Edith's hand. "Our visit was too short, but I'll see you again before Hazel learns to walk."

Edith grabbed her mother's arm. "You must come sooner than that! Please, Mutti, it gets more difficult every day. Why do you continue to stay here?"

Clara was not ready to explain to her daughter why she remained in Germany. It was too new and too personal. "I'll come," she said. "But there's official paperwork I must do before I can leave. So many taxes to pay and clearances from the police. And I still have things I want to ship to California and to you in London."

"Shipping stuff isn't important." Edith's voice was stern, and her eyes demanded attention. She picked up her hat and pinned it over her short bob. "My brother and I both worry about you. He wants to see you again before his visa for the United States is issued. You must come soon."

Clara sighed. She simply wasn't prepared to leave yet. "I'm only a widow woman," she said. "Besides being Jewish, I'm of no significance to the Nazis. If I keep out of their way, I will be safe." She remembered saying similar words to her son Herman when he left for England five months earlier. So far, she had been right.

George stepped forward and touched Clara's arm. He towered over her, and his face was serious. "Please, don't linger, Mrs. Lang. The air in Germany is filled with hate. You will always have a place to live with us. We can guarantee you and so can your brother Bruno. You'll be safer in England. If war breaks out . . . if Germany and Britain go to war . . . Well, you won't be able to come easily after that."

"Yes. Yes, you're right. But Chamberlain is still intent on keeping peace. Maybe his diplomacy will succeed. Don't worry about me. I have my newly stamped passport and visa. I promise I'll come before it expires." She jumped at the tooting of an automobile horn in the front yard. "That's the taxi," she said. "You must go."

George lifted the infant out of the pram and settled her into Clara's outstretched arms, then he and Edith together trundled the heavy, folded pram down the broad staircase. Clara followed behind. Before relinquishing Hazel to her mother, Clara kissed the baby's forehead, then her nose and both her tiny hands. "Goodbye my sweet girl," she whispered.

With one hand, Edith lowered the veil of her hat over her face. George stood tall in his English worsted suit. Once on the train, they would speak only English. They must appear to be nothing more than an English couple on holiday. It had been agreed that Clara should stay home; for safety's sake, she would not accompany them to the station.

Clara watched through the curtains as the driver settled the pram and the two suitcases into the boot of the taxi. George held the passenger door open. With Hazel in her arms, Edith turned for a last look at her childhood home. She seemed to know she would never see it again. She waved her hand toward her mother standing in the shadows of the entryway, then turned and slid into the back seat. George folded his lanky frame into the seat beside her and pulled the door shut. The driver started the engine. Clara watched as the taxi drove out through the gate onto Bernhardstrasse and away. All the tears she had held back for the last few days escaped and streamed down her cheeks.

One step at a time, she climbed the stairs to her small apartment, the two rooms where she now spent her days. No longer was she mistress of the entire house. No longer could she sit on January afternoons surrounded by potted ferns and warmed by the winter sunlight that flooded through the wall of windows of her beloved enclosed porch. The dining room with its crystal chandelier, the parlor where her grand piano had once reigned in splendor, the modern kitchen where Cook clanged pots on the gas stove, the bedroom where she had slept with her husband for twenty years—all were now off-limits.

Yet, Clara knew she was fortunate. Herr Doctor Weiss and his wife had paid a fair market price for the home, not the insulting amount that was usually offered for Jewish homes these days. Unmentioned in the written sale contract but promised by the couple, Clara was allowed to live in a few of the upstairs rooms for as long as she wanted. Herr Weiss had a separate apartment designed and built to include the tower room with its view of the street and Edith's old bedroom with its adjoining bath. A kitchenette was tucked into what had previously been a linen closet. It was a comfortable space for a woman living alone.

The entry hall, with its majestic stairs to the upper floor, was technically part of the Weiss home now and Clara knew not to linger there. Once in her private rooms, she walked to the tall, curved windows of the tower and opened the draperies. The view stretched beyond the front yard, over the trees and lake of the

English Garden park, all the way to the train station in the hazy distance. Edith, Hazel, and George would be arriving there soon. Clara wiped away her tears with the heel of her hand. She refused to succumb to depression; it was what had killed her husband.

She settled in her chair and reached for her knitting basket. The jumble of yarns and long pointed needles stared back. There was no half-finished project to work on. What could she make with no ideas, little yarn, and even less initiative? She walked over to the kitchenette and opened a cupboard, then let the cabinet door close with a bang. She bent to the small electric refrigerator. She had made potato pancakes for Edith and George that morning and the cold remains congealed on a glass plate. She walked into the bedroom. It would be a relief to sleep in her own bed again after four nights on the couch. She lay down, her head on the feather pillow. Three minutes later she sat up, jumpy and unable to relax. Edith's whispered request haunted her thoughts.

The stairway to the top floor and the attic itself were mutual territory, shared by herself and the Weisses. She tiptoed up the wooden stairs and stepped into the dusty space, closing the door noiselessly behind her. She jerked the chain and the three ceiling lights flickered on. The attic was filled with boxes belonging to the Weisses, as well as her remaining furniture, pieces that didn't fit into the apartment and weren't worth shipping to America or England. Recently, Clara had spent many hours among the things in the attic. *Why hadn't Edith asked her for help sooner? Was she afraid of George's reaction if he discovered her girlhood crush?*

At the far end of the attic, the windows from the top of the corner tower allowed slanted rays of sunlight to gild the space. A few old cushions still leaned against some crates under the window. Clara closed her eyes and remembered the days when her two eldest, Friedel and Edith, had entertained friends in that sunny spot, their favorite teenage hideaway. Later, Herman had come here to curl up and read his adventure stories in a place free of the bullying he experienced daily at school. Now, the attic had become a place of memories, and she knew where most mementos hid.

Clara clearly remembered pushing several smaller things under the ornate, guest room wardrobe. She shoved away a stack of boxes filled with linens and monogrammed underwear from her trousseau and bent down to investigate the dark space underneath the wardrobe. Far back, among the dust balls, she saw the green swirls of marbleized paper dimly breaking up the black gloom. She got the broom leaning in a corner and lay on her stomach. With the long handle, she nudged the box closer so her fingers could grasp the edge and tug it forward.

Clara brushed off dust and cobwebs clinging to the box and walked over to the light by the window. She twisted the catch and peered inside. A small notebook, a white diary, and two stacks of letters, each bound with a frayed satin ribbon, filled the box. A tiny paper envelope glued to the bottom revealed a gold key hidden inside. This was the secret stash that Edith had been desperate to find.

Clara lowered herself to one of the crates under the tower windows. She settled the stationery box in her lap and stared at the contents. Her fingers played with the ribbons that tied the letters. Edith had asked her to read everything before destroying anything. But where should she begin? If she read the diaries first, perhaps she would better understand her daughter's youthful emotions, joys, and concerns. She would tackle the private letters later.

The diary was covered in white leatherette and had a tiny lock. Clara remembered when Friedel had given it to his sister for her birthday not long before he left for America.

"Try to include a sentence or two of English with each entry," he had said after she opened the gift. "You must practice English to be ready to leave if it comes to that."

Edith had slapped his shoulder playfully. "Don't worry about me, brother," she said. "I'll practice my English so I can come visit you when you're rich and famous."

Clara arranged the pillows so she could rest her back against the windowsill. She fit the key into the diary's lock. With a squeak, the key turned, and the latch snapped open. Her daughter's handwriting started off carefully, then gradually slanted and dipped in a way more familiar to her mother.

CHAPTER 2

The Diary

May 9, 1934

I am seventeen! I can't believe it! Friedel gave me this pretty book with its pages edged in gold for my birthday. I've never had a diary before, and I never cared to write about my life. It's my brother who loves to write.

Still Friedel is the best brother! And the diary is a lovely gift. He has always been the family golden boy. According to Rikka, I'm the one who deserves coal in her stocking. How I hate her, even if she is my sort-of, very-distant cousin.

When he gave the diary to me, Friedel told me to stay alert. Germany will get worse every day, he said, and suggested I should keep a record of everything. Of course, he also told me to write in English!

Easy for him to say. I'm not as good at foreign languages as he is. But I'll try a sentence or two. Next time . . .

Maybe keeping a journal will help me sort out all the angry feelings I have these days.

June 5, 1934

I have forced myself to open this diary and write again. Everything is changing so fast. I guess my brother is right, I should record it. But I mostly just want my life to be like it used to be. My happy school days ended last year, but I still had to go to class. So unfair!

At least now I've officially finished gymnasium. Of course, I wasn't allowed to take the graduation exam. No Jews allowed for that important event. Without the exam, I will not get a certificate. And I am barred from applying to university, too. Marlisa and I had planned to go to nursing school together, but that dream is over. What will my life be like? Everywhere I turn something else is off-limits to Jews.

Friedel will soon leave. We are all nervous waiting for his visa and immigration papers to arrive from the US Embassy in Berlin. He has steamship tickets to sail on the SS Bremen on July 12 and is desperate not to miss his ship! The Bremen can cross the Atlantic and deliver him to New York in less than five days! I wish I could fit myself into his suitcase.

Clara looked up from her daughter's words. The pale sunshine coming through the dusty attic windows warmed her neck like a comforting, hot-water bottle. She closed her eyes and remembered how eager her eldest son had been to leave Germany. His dreams of university had been shattered when he was denied access to the qualifying exams.

"Why should I be labeled a Jew?" he said. "I'm no more a Jew than I'm a Christian or a Muslim."

He'd been so angry. Clara remembered how he had ranted.

"If I can't go to university, I may as well leave this benighted country. At least in America, I can be free."

With his father's blessing, he left soon after his nineteenth birthday.

Clara tucked a loose strand of hair behind her ear and returned to Edith's diary.

June 6, 1934

I have only one friend now. Marlisa, my best friend since kindergarten, still comes to the house to visit. These days, she only comes after dark. She sneaks in the kitchen through the back door. She's brave, I guess. And she loves Cook's lebkuchen. Maybe the sweet and spicy smell draws her all the way from her house.

Sometimes, I wander the streets by myself. I long to rip down all the signs that say, "Jews not welcome here." They make me want to scream.

I have felt like screaming for more than a year. Ever since the first of last April when there was the national boycott of all Jewish businesses. The SA marched in the street and into our yard. They threw rocks and rotten potatoes at the door to the basement where Vati stores his leather inventory. Vati has been in a black mood ever since that day. He returned from a business trip to see the mess in the yard. Besides that, his shirt was torn and his hat smashed. He said he was set upon by hooligans at the train station.

I forgot that Friedel told me to write English sentences. Here is my first effort: *Rotten potatoes smell worse than vomit.*

June 8, 1934

Summer is here, for sure. Today I gathered up my courage and went to the public swimming plunge at the river. There are none of those nasty signs at the river. Not yet, anyway.

The water is clear and cold and lovely for swimming laps. I went back and forth until I was exhausted. All the kids who used to be my friends sat together under a tree. They looked the other way when I walked up. Nobody even nodded or said hello! I'm persona non grata. I turned away and shut my ears to their laughter and whispers. I found a grassy spot behind a hedge far away from the group. I lay on my blanket, read my book, and pretended my ex-friends were invisible.

June 10, 1934

Father is so unreasonable! Last year, he forbade me to go out on Saturday evening to the youth promenades. I used to love walking around the town square arm in arm with my girlfriends. We would flirt like crazy with the boys. But Vati said no more. Not as long as the Nazis are in power and the Hitlerjugend roam around and cause trouble. He never liked me going anyway. I'll bet he was pleased to have an excuse like the Nazis to forbid me my greatest pleasure. I miss it so much! Of course, my so-called friends ignore me if we pass on the street after school. They wouldn't walk with me at the promenade now anyway. Sometimes I wish I were a crying type of person. I need a good cry!

English sentences to please my brother: *Friedel waits for his US papers. My younger brother, Herman, rides his bicycle. I sit home alone.*

June 15, 1934

I'll bet Friedel is glad to be leaving. He can't go to university and his friends don't come around anymore. He used to be one of the most popular boys in school and, for sure, the smartest. His friends spent hours with us in our family's attic. I loved being teased by them. Now they are nowhere to be seen.

English: *Friedel reads and writes all alone in the attic.*

June 18, 1934

Friedel's US visa and his immigration card arrived today! He is ecstatic. We only have three more weeks left for the family to be together.

English: *My brother is leaving soon for his big adventure! I will miss him.*

June 20, 1934

Vati finally agreed with me about something. I begged him to allow me to go to the domestic school in the fall and get a practical certificate. If I cannot train to be a nurse, I will need to have some other skill. I've always loved clothes and Grossmutter taught me to sew. As a kid, I spent hours in the kitchen watching Cook prepare dinner and even helped her sometimes. I told Vati that I wanted to be a dressmaker or a cook. He agreed that getting a domestic certificate might be a good thing for me.

I told Vati that once I get a certificate, I will leave Germany like my brother. He only grunted, but it was a positive grunt. I know getting a visa for the United States is more difficult every day, and I could be waiting a long time. If I have domestic training, I can apply for an English permit to work in service. That's easier than getting a US visa. When I explained this to Vati, he told me I'm not as dumb as I often act. That's his idea of a compliment.

Domestic service is quite a step down for our family, but Vati signed my application to the school.

My English sentences are: *At my new school, I will learn to make lebkuchen. They will be as tasty as the biscuits Cook makes.*

June 29, 1934

Finally, something wonderful has happened! Marlisa called and said I must come with her to the promenade. She wanted to do something with me before she left for nursing college. She declared she didn't care what the snooty Nazi girls said because she'd be gone soon.

I snuck out the back door when Vati was in his study. Marlisa and I strolled around the square, our arms linked, ignoring all the sidelong glances. We flirted with the boys and one of the cutest ones offered to escort me home. Imagine how brave he was to do that!

I told him he probably shouldn't as I'm one of those tainted Jews. I thought my words quite smart, but Hanz said it didn't matter to him. At my front gate, I told him my father forbade me to go out at night and without Marlisa to walk around with, I wouldn't be at any more promenades.

I probably won't see him again. Sooo sad!

English: *Hanz is cute. He held my hand when we walked home.*

June 30, 1934

Last night, I must have stepped on that stupid creaking board as I tiptoed up the stairs.

Naturally, this morning, I was called on the carpet. Vati is home for the weekend after his weekly business trip selling leather. When I came down for breakfast, he was at his study door and waved me inside. He stood in his usual you're-in-trouble pose, his hands clasped behind his back. Cousin Rikka, always at my father's side, sat enthroned in her special armchair. Her beady eyes glared at me. Naturally she got her two pfennigs in first. Where had I been last night that I came home so late?

Vati spoke in his no-nonsense, tell-the-truth tone. He demanded to know where I had gone.

I tried to explain, but Vati grabbed my arm so hard it hurt. He had a rolled-up newspaper in his other hand, and I thought he might hit me with it like he used to when I was little. But he only told me I was grounded for two weeks. No swimming at the plunge. No walking around town. I'm not even allowed to go to Grandmother Lang's. He gave me the lecture again about always being on my best behavior and staying away from young people in the Hitlerjugend.

The whole time, Mother was in the parlor playing the piano. I could hear the soothing notes in the background as Vati issued his verdict. Later, she joined me in the breakfast room and sat down next to me as I nibbled a piece of toast. She put her arm around me and kissed my cheek. She promised we would go to the cinema when my punishment was over.

I know Mutti is frightened of Vati when he gets angry, and she hates Rikka as much as I do. But what can we do? Vati and Rikka are always cozy together, à la tête-à-tête. They are the king and queen of the house. My poor mother is like a servant in her own home. The only thing she has control of is deciding what Cook will prepare for dinner and when the maids will beat the rugs.

Without her music, I fear Mutti would be a ghost. When she plays her violin in her room at night, it makes me want to cry, the sound is so sad. Mostly she plays the violin when Vati is spending time with Rikka in her room.

English sentence: *Rikka is a devil wearing women's clothing.*

Clara stopped reading the diary with a shudder. The English sentence revealed the depth of Edith's feelings about Rikka. She had understood that Edith and Hugo's cousin were like oil and water, but now she realized her daughter had sensed more about Rikka's role in the family than she had realized.

CHAPTER 3

An Arranged Marriage

CLARA HAD ALWAYS KNOWN that her husband was more interested in the lavish dowry that came from her family than he had been in her. He had never loved her, and to be honest, she had not loved him. She had simply married him at the insistence of her wealthy and old-fashioned parents who were eager to see her settled before she was labeled a spinster. She was the fifth daughter to be married, with two younger ones yet to go, and her father seemed to be running out of good suitors.

Clara soon realized that Hugo's rough, domineering personality would be uncomfortable to live with, but for the first few years they had at least been compatible. His need for heirs and his normal male urges had been enough to bring her the wonderful gift of children.

After the birth of Friedel and Edith, Clara believed that her family was complete and that she and Hugo had established a semblance of balance in their relationship. She loved being a mother and Hugo traveled often for his business, sometimes as far as Italy, buying leather and selling it to cobblers and shoe and handbag factories.

During the week, when Hugo was away, Clara could do as she pleased in the substantial home built with her dowry money. She pursued her music and continued her girlhood hobby of photography, developing her own photographs in a closet converted into a darkroom. Trained as a kindergarten teacher, she opened a small preschool in their home, the children attending during the week when Hugo was most often away.

On the weekends, she played hostess to her husband's many friends from the local theater and his social club. She enjoyed the intellectual stimulation of these company evenings, the delicious meals prepared by their cook, the lively conversations, and the varied and interesting company. Sunday evenings were enjoyable, too, when Hugo's relatives who lived nearby—his uncle, his sister with her husband, and Hugo's mother—gathered for dinner around the long dining table. Clara's dowry had protected Hugo's business from the worst effects of inflation and the economic depression. He often repeated his belief that because people always needed shoes, the family leather business would remain profitable, even during dire times. Clara had been content, if not happy.

In late 1919, when she unexpectedly realized she was pregnant again, Clara was thrilled. After Herman was born, she was instantly devoted to the infant with his blue eyes, brown curls, and captivating smile. But, in the middle of the night, when the baby was only a few months old, Clara woke to a gripping pain in her belly. Nausea surged through her. When she tried to get to the bathroom, she collapsed on the floor. She could do little more than curl into a ball and moan. Her body felt hot, but she was racked with chills. When the baby cried to be nursed, she could not even lift her head.

Hugo, roused from his snoring slumber by the baby's cries and his wife's agony, called the doctor who diagnosed an acutely inflamed gall bladder. As she was rushed to the hospital for surgery, Clara worried about her three young children. Who would care for them while she spent weeks in the hospital recovering?

Hugo solved this problem by asking his cousin Rikka to come all the way from her parents' home in Erfurt to stay while Clara recuperated. It was a strange solution. Rikka had spent little time with the older children and had no experience with infants. One of Hugo's two sisters, both of whom had more experience with children, would have been a more sensible choice. His younger sister, Gusti, lived in town and knew the children well. Yet, it was Rikka who Hugo asked to come and help.

Clara returned from the hospital to find Rikka comfortably installed in the tower guest room where Hugo now spent hours keeping her company. When Clara began to feel better, she had suggested it was time for Rikka to return to her parents' home. Hugo informed his wife that his cousin would stay—he enjoyed her company. Besides, she no longer wished to live with her parents who nagged her constantly to find a husband.

"She will be a help with the children," he said.

Slowly, one step at a time, Rikka managed to change Clara's life. First, she demanded that the kindergarten be closed. The young students were too noisy, which aggravated her migraine headaches. Then she claimed that the smell of photo chemicals caused her to feel nauseous. Hugo demanded Clara get rid of her darkroom. Without the creative element developing her own photos offered, Clara gradually took fewer and fewer pictures, her camera growing dusty on the shelf. She was left with only her music as comfort and distraction.

Worst of all, Rikka interfered with the children's discipline, monitoring their behavior during the week and reporting it all to Hugo. Freidel was the heir apparent, the family favorite. Rikka was hesitant to interfere with his comings and goings. Besides, he seemed not to care what she said and simply carried on. Herman was the baby the whole family, including Rikka, adored. Later, as he grew from toddler to schoolboy, he learned to avoid confrontation with Rikka by staying quiet and out of sight. But Edith, the middle child, was a girl, and a girl with spirit. Rikka's treatment of Edith made it clear that she believed the girl needed discipline and a strong hand.

Clara used affection and trust to raise her children, but Hugo preferred corporal punishment coupled with intimidation. As the children grew older, he used home detention, which he termed "house arrest," for any infraction of his strict rules of behavior. In this regard, Rikka was his collaborator. Gradually, Clara had little to say regarding her own children. Hugo was the man of the house. He listened only to Rikka and no longer consulted Clara about family or business matters. She was as much under Hugo's thumb as her children were.

Clara wondered how she and her children had endured those years in an autocratic household. *Perhaps it prepared us to silently endure these Hitler years,* she thought. *So like the gradual loss of rights and escalating indignities, I endured under Hugo's rule. This is a concept worth pondering . . . but later.* Now she was more interested in continuing to discover the heart and soul of her daughter. Clara picked up Edith's diary again and continued reading.

July 1, 1934

The worst news! I feel like a murderer. Hanz got beaten up! Because he walked me home!

Marlisa telephoned this morning and in a whispery voice told me all about it. A gang of Hitler Youth set on him when he went to play soccer yesterday. They beat him awfully. He is in the hospital with bruises, a sprained wrist, and a broken nose. He will forever have a crooked nose because of me. Hanz's sister called Marlisa and told her to warn me to stay away from her brother or she and her friends would beat me up, too.

Marlisa said she was glad she was leaving town and could start all over with new friends. That idea made me sad. What a mess! It almost makes me glad to be on house arrest.

English: *Marlisa is still my friend. Hanz's sister is dangerous.*

July 7, 1934

I am so bored staying home all the time, but I guess it's better than being beaten up. Good thing I like to read novels. I can drift into the story and pretend I am anywhere else but here. As I can't go out to the library, I've had to search my brothers' bookshelves. Herman only has boys' adventure stories. Friedel loaned me his copy of "Siddhartha." Amazingly, I really like it. Better India than Germany!

Mutti tried to teach me a simple duet on the piano. She ignored my mistakes, but I saw her wince every time I hit a wrong note. Friedel invited me to come in his room and watch him sort his stuff. Now that's boring! He filled boxes with his poetry notebooks, his precious books, and other keepsakes. At the end, he added his childhood lederhosen. I saw him rub his hand lovingly along the stiff leather of the short pants and stroke the embroidered suspenders. He really loved wearing those old-fashioned breeches as a boy, just like I loved twirling the full skirt of my dirndl.

It's all to go into the attic. I wonder if he'll ever see that stuff again.

To add drama to my days, Rikka smiles evilly when she sees me. When Vati returned home on Friday from his business trip, he was in a foul mood. At dinner he grumbled that anti-Jewish propaganda is turning long-time customers against him. Many refuse to buy from him now and one of his oldest clients in Munich locked his shop and put up the closed sign when he saw Vati walking down the street with his sample bag. He says he's tired of the stink-eyed stares.

English: *I am bored and sad and hate writing these silly English sentences. I can't wait for domestic school to begin.*

July 10, 1934

Friedel left for America today. His two allowed (by Vati!) bags were packed so full he had to sit on them to make the latches click shut properly. He said I can keep his copy of "Siddartha" and gave me one of his empty notebooks with a funny poem written on the first page.

The whole family, including Rikka, went to the train station to say goodbye. Mutti was crying even though she knows leaving Germany is the best thing for him. I was crying, too, and Herman hugged him so long, Friedel finally had to pry him loose. Vati shook Friedel's hand and, in a low voice, said to make him proud. Tomorrow night my brother will be in Bremerhaven boarding the ship for America.

English: *My brother travels to America. I stay in Germany where Nazis march in the streets shouting Sieg Heil!*

July 14, 1934

I wish I were anywhere but where I am . . . stuck in Meiningen . . . always looking over my shoulder for a bully SA thug or an SS officer.

Yesterday, my house arrest was over, and I walked to the plunge. Luckily there are still no anti-Jewish signs in the swimming area. The sky was robin's-egg blue. Not a cloud anywhere. Well, that's the sky. Life on earth is filled with clouds and swastikas.

I went to my grassy area behind the hedge and stretched out to read. I kept my nose in my book. I'm reading "The

Dream Room." It's a story of romance and art and music, so
I love it.

Mutti kept her promise and we went to the movies
this afternoon. We saw "If I Had a Million." I wish a dying
tycoon would give me a million dollars! I'd leave Germany
immediately and take Mutti and Herman with me. Gary
Cooper is sooooo handsome! He makes me swoon.

English: *I do not have a million dollars or a boyfriend. I
used to be always happy and busy with my friends. Now I
am always alone.*

July 17, 1934

Friedel is in the Mid-Atlantic, by now! Most likely he's found
a pretty girl on the ship (or she has found him)! He draws
girls like bees to honey.

Herman sulks around the house because all his friends
are in the Hitlerjugend, and he's not allowed to join. He
keeps pestering me that we should go to the swimming
pool together. A thirteen-year-old brother is not my idea
of good company, but I gave in because he sounded so
pitiful. Surprisingly, he is easy to be with. He had one of
his adventure novels to read and didn't jabber constantly.
Still, I told him to find his own entertainment for the rest of
the summer.

English: *I miss my older brother. My younger brother is
a nuisance.* (I had to look up that last word in my German-
English dictionary.)

Clara lifted her head, stretched, and rubbed her neck. She knew that Edith had been close to Friedel, and it was natural that she had taken his departure hard. As the oldest, he had been ringleader for the three children, helping them find a safe space in their home of divided adults. Her children had each been so very different . . . one from the other. Friedel, imperious and intelligent, funny and creative, was the beloved leader the other two followed. Edith was the mischief maker, a rebel, and a saucy jester. She was the attractive target who deflected Rikka's arrows from her siblings. And Herman harbored a deep and steady current that longed for adventure under his quiet and mild nature. Clara thought that perhaps she was the only one in the family who noticed her youngest's dreams—to the others he was just a lovable little boy.

The extreme changes in Germany had broken up the triumvirate and left Edith without the comfort of her older brother. Clara sighed and turned back to her daughter's diary.

July 20, 1934

We haven't gotten a letter from Friedel yet, but he must be in Chicago by now, all cozy with our American relatives. School begins next month. I guess there will be other Jewish girls because my enrollment pushed the Jewish percentage over what's allowed. Vati had to apply for a special dispensation for me based on his service at the front during the Great War. How stupid! Vati was angry and embarrassed that he had to prove he was a loyal citizen. But he did it.

July 25, 1934

Vati's Laws for living under the Nazis:

1. Only go out when it is important to do so.
2. Walk straight to your destination.
3. Be proud. Don't look left or right.
4. Don't do anything to attract attention.
5. Never smile at a man in a uniform. This includes the SA (especially), the SS, or the local police.

July 28, 1934

Today I broke the first of Vati's laws and the fourth one, but not the others.

I went to Meir and Son to get new socks and underwear before the fall term starts. I didn't have to go. I have plenty of socks but most of them have holes in them, and I hate darning! Besides, I love wandering around the store aisles examining all the pretty things.

When I got to the department store, there were two SA Brown Shirts standing near the entrance. They asked everyone why they would go into a Jewish store. A few people ignored them and went inside anyway. Most shoppers turned away and walked down the street like they had made a mistake.

When the Brown Shirt asked me, I flipped my long, blond braid over my shoulder. Because I need panties, I said. I gave him a cheeky stare. His eyes bulged out and his mouth hung open. Before he could get over his shock, I strode past him and into the store.

But I couldn't relax and enjoy the sample perfume counter or the fashion displays. When I left, the same SA guy recognized me. This is what we said to each other.

Him: Hey, girlie. Why do you shop with these thieving Jews?

Me: Because I'm a Jewish girlie. Can't you tell?

I flipped my blond plaits for good measure.

Him: Sound of throat clearing and then *phtooey!* (him spitting)

Vati would be proud of the way I walked away, head high, without turning around. But he would be very angry with me for talking back. It was probably dangerous, and I've vowed to be less reckless in the future.

English: *Where will people shop if they can't go to Meir and Son?*

August 3, 1934

Our old president Von Hindenburg died yesterday. Vati swings between deep depression and towering rage. He says that Hitler was leading the president around by the nose for the last year anyway. Now there is no one to slow down Hitler and his followers.

August 8, 1934

Friedel has been gone almost four weeks. I miss him terribly. My favorite thing was to hang out in the attic with my brother and his friends. He always called it our private children's kingdom. Whenever I was upset about Rikka's nastiness, Friedel told me I was queen of the Children's Kingdom, that Rikka had no power there.

My only solace is the swimming plunge at the river. The cold water and physical exercise lift my spirits almost as much as my brother's poems used to.

English: *I am reading, "The Murder at the Vicarage" in English. It is a struggle because I must look up lots of words. I love the terrible Miss Marple! She is a smart busybody.*

August 19, 1934

We finally got a letter from Friedel. He has arrived in Chicago and is working in the basement of our second cousin's department store. He says it's hot and humid and he hates being inside all day. He also says he's changed his name to Fred because it's more American. I'm going to practice referring to him as Fred. I wouldn't want to embarrass him when I visit him in Chicago.

English: *Next week domestic school will begin. Will I find new friends there?*

⸺ ॰⸺

Clara remembered every one of the letters her older son had sent. They dribbled in, months between each one, and they were all addressed to his father. She had poured over the words, trying to get a sense of his new life in America. He was so determined to fit in, yet the name change had been difficult for her to accept. She supposed that if she ever made it to America, she would have to get used to calling him Fred.

She shifted and stretched out her legs in an attempt to get the kinks out of her back. At almost fifty, sitting on the floor among cushions was not as comfortable as it had once been. *I really should move downstairs,* she thought. But instead, she turned again to the diary.

⸺ ॰⸺

August 26, 1934

I am surrounded by country girls, the not very bright, and a few Jewish rejects like me. This school is a gathering ground for those who have nowhere else to go but still hope for a brighter future. Most of the students come from the surrounding towns and villages. The school emphasizes the domestic arts—cooking, sewing, ironing—even how to stoke the furnace and raise yard chickens. Academics are not neglected. We also take either French or English, German culture studies, and household accounting. After graduation, we are expected to enter service. I'm hoping for something more elegant than scullery maid. I dream of becoming a seamstress creating gowns for wealthy debutantes. It might even be more fun than my lost future as a nurse.

Honestly, I love learning the stuff I used to watch our servants do. When I was a child, we had Cook, three maids, the gardener, mother's seamstress, and father's chauffeur. Now we only have Cook and one maid who sings Hitler's "Horst Wessel" song under her breath while she dusts.

August 30, 1934

Including me, there are three Jewish girls at school. We are an odd bunch.

First there's Rachel. She is pretty in a timid way. She is thin, wears glasses, has dark wavy hair, and speaks in a whisper. Her fingers continually twist the ends of her cardigan or fiddle with her hair. I wonder if she was always so nervous, or if she's like that now because she's been bullied. I think she's smart, but it's difficult to tell as she seldom speaks.

Gertrude (we call her Gerti) is tall and buxom. She already wears her dark red hair in a grown-up style pinned on top of her head. She reminds me of Mutti's sister Ida, and I can't imagine her getting bullied. Gerti's family lives in Suhl where my cousins live. Her father is an attorney, and her mother is a friend of Cousin Hilda. Gerti's life has changed in the same ways that mine has and now, instead of going to university to study languages, she will end up as some rich family's housekeeper.

And then there's me: Edith, a girl easy to describe. Very short, pink-cheeked, long blond braids. The image of a German girl on a Nazi poster. I used to be full of smiles and a great flirt. I had a can-do attitude and always saw the bright side of things. Lately, I find all these skills difficult.

We three Jewish girls are friends because we're at this school for the same reason. We need to find work and the best professions are closed to us in Germany . . . though I'd choose Gerti as a friend in any case.

In the first weeks of the term, I quickly made friends with other girls besides Rachel and Gerti. If I remember to be lighthearted, my jokes and antics are popular. After all, everyone needs a good laugh now and then, especially these days. Of course, the Aryan girls only talk to me at school. If we pass on the street after school, they keep walking.

English sentence: *School is school. Assignments, homework, and friends. It will be boring to write about. Maybe I will stop writing.*

September 10, 1934

I was so wrong. Stuff does happen at this school and it's the same stuff that's happening everywhere. After only two weeks of good times and new friendships, all that fell into ruin . . . and again because of Nazis!

Two Hitler-loving sisters, twins, have come to the school. They were in my class at secondary school. They are MEAN and total dummkopfs. I heard they failed the Abitur exams and now they can't get into any academic higher school. Hitler preaches that a German woman's place is in the home and those two probably think getting a few domestic skills will help them find a Nazi husband. They enrolled late because they were in Nuremberg with their family for the big annual Nazi rally. They keep telling everyone how great it was. Parades, searchlights that reached to the clouds, bands, and huge swastika flags. Ugh!

As soon as the sisters realized that there were three Jewish students, they started saying nasty things about us. They intimidated the other Aryan girls with Nazi slogans and Heil Hitler salutes. They persuaded everyone to boycott us or they'd report to their father, a big somebody in the SA. Last week's friends no longer sit with us at lunch or work with us on projects. I HATE those sisters!! They have ruined everything!

September 12, 1934

The boycott continues at school and escalates by the day.

The two Nazi sisters (I refuse to write their names out), have all the other girls in thrall. Gerti and I have nicknamed them the Brown Twins—brown like their League of German Girls uniforms and their father's SA uniform. An ugly color for an ugly organization!

Anyway, the Brown Twins make a point of ignoring Gerti and me, but they torment poor Rachel. Yesterday, they purposely bumped into her table in cooking class and knocked over her mixing bowl. Cake batter splashed across the floor. The instructor saw the twins bump the table, but she yelled at Rachel for wasting ingredients and making a mess. So unfair! I stood up and raised my hand to object, but Gerti pulled me back down into my seat. I felt the hiss of her breath in my ear when she told me to stay out of it.

September 18, 1934

I wish I hadn't listened to Gerti last Friday. On Monday morning, Rachel wasn't in cooking class. And she didn't come this morning, either. Fräulein von Braun, the headmistress, came into class and informed us that Rachel had withdrawn from the school because her family was moving to Holland. Fräulein is strict and walks like she has a broomstick up her backside (like a Von anything should). Usually, she's fair and the girls respect her. It's villainous that she pretends not to see what the Brown Twins are doing.

I won't let them intimidate me! No matter what Gerti says.

English: *Nazi girls don't scare me. I will stay in school and get my certificate.*

Clara felt ashamed that she hadn't understood that Edith had endured bullying at the domestic school. She vaguely remembered her daughter being more subdued than normal but had assumed she was simply preoccupied with her new studies.

With a guilty pang, Clara realized she had been too preoccupied with her own problems. She had been coping with Hugo's ever-present short temper and moodiness. Of course, Rikka was still demanding and self-centered and hadn't noticed that most of their help no longer came to the house or that Clara was now doing much of the housework. Clara found the remaining maid, a young woman who sang Nazi songs while she did her chores with half-hearted nonchalance, increasingly difficult to supervise. Often, the girl had to be reminded to dust, sweep under the furniture, or scrub the tub. Sometimes it was easier for Clara to do herself what the maid neglected. Certainly, Rikka never offered to help.

At the time, Clara had not considered Edith's change in behavior a problem, and her daughter had never shared her troubles. In the evenings, Edith often helped Cook in the kitchen with washing up, scrubbing the counters, chopping vegetables, and making gravy—whatever Cook needed. Clara remembered the comfortable sounds of her daughter and Cook talking in the kitchen as they prepared supper together.

Still, Clara felt bad that she had not known her daughter was experiencing trouble at school. She remembered her own girlhood filled with friends, dances, trips to Switzerland, and a plethora of household help so she never had to do anything except study and sit chatting with her sisters. That was the kind of life Edith might have had if the Nazis hadn't changed everything.

Clara remembered that Edith had seemed happier later in the autumn. She hoped the diary would soon show the change hadn't been a construct of her motherly imagination. Edith's mood was certainly lighter in the next entry, but it was not quite the change Clara would have wished.

CHAPTER 4

Charlie

September 22, 1934

I have a secret! A wonderful thing happened today. I have a
new friend!

As usual, I went to the swimming area this afternoon. The
water was like ice! I wrapped my blanket totally around me,
even over my head. I'm sure I looked like a plaid penguin as
I waddled past a couple of ex-friends who lounged in their
usual spot. I sat on the grass near the hedge and hugged my
knees to get warm. My throat felt tight as I thought of all
the friends I used to have . . . girls I had played hopscotch
with, boys who had pulled my braids. Now they are gone
to university. The few still in town turn the other way when I
walk by. I no longer exist for them.

I was about to leave when a guy came striding across the
grass toward me. I rested my cheek on my knees and closed

my eyes and hoped he would go right past. But his footsteps stopped in front of me. His voice was deep. I'll never forget our strange conversation. He asked why I sat alone. A pretty girl like you, he said. Not very original.

I thought he must be slow if he couldn't see what was so plain. I lifted my head and told him, No one sits with me because I'm Jewish. These were my exact words, and I thought this would send him scurrying away. But he didn't move. He stood in front of me, the sun shining over his shoulder. The bright glare hurt my eyes. I had to raise my hand to shield them. I could only see the man's dark silhouette.

I'll not forget what he said next.. Did I ask what you are? he said. I'm no Nazi and I don't care about that!

I was dumbfounded and couldn't think what to answer. I hoped he would walk away but instead he asked if he could sit down with me. Now I was convinced he was either dumb or reckless. Well, reckless is better, I thought.

I shook my head and told him it would probably be better for him NOT to sit with me. I couldn't stop the saucy words I added. If he stayed or went, it made no difference to me. Now I was the one being reckless! It's terrible what a girl starved for friendship will do.

He lowered himself to the grass nearby and half reclined with his long legs stretched out and his weight on his elbows. He stared across the river at the flowing current. It felt strange. I watched him out of the corner of my eye to make sure he didn't do anything scary. He was so relaxed that it made me feel nervous in a good way.

He was lit by the sun and finally I could see what he looked like. Tall. (I'm always attracted to tall boys.) Clean-shaven, with a long, thin nose, blue eyes, and light-brown hair combed away from his forehead. He reminded me of Gary Cooper. In his own way, he's also quite swoonably handsome. He wore a warm, knitted sweater, a pair of loose trousers rolled up at the bottom, and slip-on shoes without socks. The seat of his trousers was damp, like he had swim trunks underneath.

After a long silence, he turned and introduced himself. Charlie. He asked if I was allowed to tell him my name.

I said my entire name: Edith Marie Pauline. He made a joke about a long name for a small girl. Again, not very original! I asked if he was new in town because he certainly didn't know who's who or how to behave according to our country's new rules.

He told me he was born in Meiningen, and his parents still live here. He said he's been away for ten years. First, to study engineering at the university in Berlin and now he has a job there. Recently he started coming back for monthly visits because his father is old. I figure he must be thirty years old himself! Way too old for me! I should be more careful about who I let sit with me. But if he's not worried about sitting with a Jewish girl, I won't worry about sitting with an older man.

He asked me what I do. I told him I was a student at the domestic school. Reckless again, he asked if he could walk me home. Again, I told him he better not.

But he repeated his request, and I thought, Why not? He doesn't seem the type that a gang of Hitler besotted youths would beat up.

I led him along my secret path through the park to our back gate, avoiding Bernhardstrasse. What an odd pair we must have seemed . . . me wrapped to my chin in a woolen blanket and him strolling in his damp summer trousers. We paused on the bridge over the remains of the medieval mill ditch and looked down into the rushing water. He asked me why I seemed so sad. Without thinking, I told him that I missed my brother who had gone to America and about my troubles at school. He told me to ignore bullies and small-minded girls. His advice sounded like Vati's, but oddly easier for me to hear.

When we reached the back gate, he asked if he could write to me. That surprised me! Without a moment's thought, I said yes and gave him my address. Now, I wonder . . . What if he's an SA spy? Perhaps I am too trusting. But I need a friend, even just a pen-pal. I don't want to burden Mutti with my troubles. She has enough of her own. ~~Friedel~~ Fred is too far away. Herman is just a schoolboy and has his own problems. I only see Gerti at school. Marlisa almost never writes. Only one postcard since she left. I am desperate to have someone to talk to!

English sentences: *I'm not used to writing so much. My fingers hurt. I have a new, very handsome, friend.*

So this is Charlie, Clara thought. This was the man . . . the Aryan man . . . who Hugo would forbid Edith to correspond with, the man who would later send her love letters that would need to be burned.

It was obvious, at least at their first meeting, that Charlie was respectful and didn't take advantage of a young girl without friends. She wondered how long before this man wanted more than conversation. She would only find out if she kept reading.

September 27, 1934

Just as I had about given up, another postcard from Marlisa came today. No return address again. I telephoned her house to ask her mother where I could send a letter.

Frau Kirsch was like a stranger on the phone. She told me not to write Marlisa . . . that it would only cause trouble. Then, in a whispery voice, she said not to call again and hung up on me without another word.

My entire body shook. I had to wipe away hot tears. I never used to cry, but this year, tears come to me without warning. Mostly they are tears of anger.

How could Marlisa's mom be so cold? Was this the same woman who used to make us sugared mint tea when we played tea party when we were eight? Who tucked us in and told funny stories when I slept over when we were ten? The same woman who picked us up from the movies when we were thirteen and took us to get ice cream at the Sächsischer Hof?

October 2, 1934

Gerti has left school! I don't blame her. With Rachel gone, she and I were the new targets of the Brown Twins' bullying. She couldn't stand it anymore. She plans to go to England on a work permit. Gerti is a great cook, and she will probably get a position as a scullery maid or cook's helper. She promised to stay in touch and reminded me that I can always contact her through my cousin who is friends with her mother.

Things have been so awful at school that I keep forgetting to add an English sentence. I get plenty of practice in English class. Now I can even write a complex sentence!

October 4, 1934

Wow! I got a letter from Charlie! Lovely!

I like the way he writes! So friendly and relaxed and full of questions and tales of his activities in Berlin. He sent an address and asked me to please write to him.

English: *Who needs Marlisa? I have a pen pal!*

October 6, 1934

I wrote my first letter to Charlie yesterday. I wrote how much I enjoyed his words and getting his letter. Then I told him about Gerti leaving and how all the boycotting evil from the Brown Twins now falls on me alone. After I'd finished, I reread it. My penmanship was messy in some places and my words a jumble, so I carefully rewrote the entire letter on fresh stationery. I hope he finds my writing good enough. I don't want him to think of me as a silly schoolgirl.

October 12, 1934

School is no fun without Gerti. I must slog through my classes alone. I keep my head down, do my assignments the best I can, and don't answer back when the twins taunt me. I want a certificate!

October 16, 1934

I got another letter from Charlie! I must make sure nobody at home sees his letters. If Rikka gets her hands on one of Charlie's letters, she'd hurry to report to Vati. Then I'd be in all kinds of trouble.

Charlie will be visiting his parents this weekend and we will meet on Saturday afternoon. Here is what he wrote: I can't wait to see the pretty face of Edith Marie Pauline! I am excited.

English: *I can't wait to see Charlie!*

October 20, 1934

I am blissful. I haven't felt this happy for months and months.

Charlie and I were together all afternoon. We sat on the grass by the river for more than two hours and talked and talked. He told me all about his work and life in Berlin. He can't stand all the Nazi banners. He says there are still secret cabarets in the city where one can listen to jazz music, which he loves. He told me all about Benny Goodman and Count Bessie, not actually a count he said, but an American Negro who has his own band. Can you imagine!

Charlie saw a No Jews Allowed sign on a Berlin park bench that had been defaced with a black swipe of paint. It was a small resistance that gave him hope. I wish I could have seen it! Charlie is against National Socialist ideas. When will Germans come to their senses? he says. I wonder the same thing.

Charlie walked me to the back gate again. He asked if he could hold my hand—to keep my fingers warm. Charlie is like a big brother, a best friend, and an advisor, all rolled into one handsome bundle. Too bad he's so much older or I'd make him my boyfriend instantly!

We made a plan. He will use blue envelopes for his letters so I can spot them easily when the mail comes. He promised to write every week!

English sentence: *Charlie is my new best friend. When I am with him, I forget to be nervous and depressed.*

Clara stopped reading and rubbed her eyes. Edith's raw teenage angst touched her heart. Her daughter had suggested she read the diaries before destroying them and with that permission, she had handed her mother a gift. Clara had been given the rare glimpse of her daughter's journey to womanhood. She wondered if Edith had been reaching out, pleading for understanding, casting her mother as a confidante because she had no other friend to truly trust.

Clara's nest among the boxes and pillows was warmed by the golden glow of the afternoon sun. She leaned her head back and thought of Albert. Could he be the friend she needed and longed for? Edith's young experiences of love with Charlie were a surprising window into unimagined possibilities.

CHAPTER 5

Albert

Clara's first meeting with Albert had been only three months before. After Kristallnacht, she had begun to suffer from headaches painful enough to require a nap with a cool cloth on her forehead. She had also experienced several bouts of sweating and heart palpitations. She knew she needed to get a medical evaluation, but her regular doctor now refused to see his Jewish patients. She shared her distress with her landlord Dr. Weiss, a pediatrician.

"I think you need a doctor who has more experience with adult problems than I," he said and suggested she go see his friend, a Jewish doctor and a colleague from earlier days. "You will like Albert Fiedler," he said. "Dr. Fiedler is kind and gentle. He is a certified internist who specializes in gynecology. And he's learning a lot these days about the illnesses caused by stress and fear." Dr. Weiss explained that Dr. Fiedler had returned to Meiningen recently when his patient list in Berlin dwindled to zero. Now he saw Jewish patients in his home office in the Jewish section of town.

A few days after Herman left for England, Clara experienced another severe headache accompanied by a bout of palpitations. It was past time to take care of herself. She called the number Dr. Weiss had given her, and Dr. Fiedler answered the phone himself. He apologized for having no receptionist or nurse but said there was the advantage that he no longer had many patients either. "I can see you tomorrow anytime," he said. "Any time in the afternoon. When would you like to come?"

The early March day was chilly as Clara walked through the town center, past the church and the center square, and down the narrow, cobblestone streets of the old town. The doctor lived in a comfortable apartment on the second floor of an older, stone building not far from where her mother-in-law's home had been. His living room was homey with dark wood walls, a Persian carpet, a couple of armchairs, and an overstuffed sofa covered in amber velvet. A painting of a German country scene hung over the fireplace and an upright piano stood against one wall. In another corner, a Chinese folding screen partially concealed an examination table and a tall, white metal cabinet.

Dr. Fiedler positioned an armchair near the couch and motioned for her to sit. "Let's talk as friends, shall we? I no longer have a desk to sit behind, and this suits my temperament better anyway." He brought her a glass of water, without asking, and settled himself in the large armchair. "What troubles you, Frau Lang?" he asked. "How can I help?"

Clara told him about her headaches and palpitations. He asked when her symptoms had started.

"In November, about the same time as the pogrom," she said.

"But my son was hiding in my apartment, and I was trying to get him out of the country as fast as possible. I ignored my problems and concentrated on getting him safely away."

"Very understandable," he said. "But now you are here. Tell me, what your life is like otherwise . . . compared to a few years ago."

"I shouldn't complain," she told him. "I am better off than most Jews these days. For now, I am stable financially, have a comfortable place to live, and all three of my children are safe, one in America and two in England."

"And you? What support do you have here? What of your husband? Or friends?"

"I've been a widow since 1935," Clara said, her voice low and hesitant. "Hugo's younger sister, Gusti, was a friend, but she immigrated to Peru with her husband in January. My husband's uncle still lives in Meiningen. I speak to him occasionally, but we're not close. I was raised in Nuremburg, but most of my sisters and brothers—there were quite a few and I was the third youngest—live in America or England now. The older generation—my parents, aunts, and uncles—have passed away. My best friend from before is the wife of the Chief of Police. As you can imagine, we're not friends anymore. I've applied for a US visa, but we all know that could take years. My daughter lives in London with her husband and a new baby. They've urged me to come but I don't want to be a burden. Arriving without funds . . . I guess I didn't want to think about leaving until my youngest son emigrated. Until Kristallnacht, he had been in no hurry. He left only three days ago for England and is staying with my brother who lives in the countryside near London."

The doctor cradled her hand in both of his, his glance deep and direct. "Frau Lang, many of my patients these days suffer from unexplained symptoms like yours. I'd like to check your heart rate and pulse and a few other things before I make a full diagnosis." He stood. "I have no assistant, as you know. In order to make my women patients comfortable, I use my mother as a ladies' companion when I need to do an exam. If that's okay with you, you can go behind the screen and undress while I get her. You will find a hospital gown on the examination table. Is that okay?"

Clara agreed to this strange procedure. The gown, similar to the gowns she had worn during her surgery many years before, was clean, though patched in several places. She sat on the table, her short legs dangling over the edge and waited, wondering what the doctor's mother would be like.

Dr. Fiedler returned, pushing an elderly lady in a wheelchair. Her pure white hair was swept back into a simple bun. Her legs were bandaged, and her eyes were filmed with cataracts. "Mutti, this is Frau Lang," the doctor said.

The old woman reached out her hand and laid it on Clara's knee. "Don't worry, my dear," she said, her voice quivering. "My son is the best doctor in town. He is loved by all his patients. I can see well enough to protect you, though I'm confident no protection is needed."

The examination was quick and thorough. After it was over, Dr. Fiedler explained that he would take his mother back to her room while Clara dressed. They would talk again in the living room.

Once settled, Clara on the sofa and Dr. Fiedler in his armchair, he explained his diagnosis in a confident way. "I found no physical problems. Perhaps a bit of elevated blood pressure, but nothing more. I suspect that you are suffering from anxiety and stress. This can cause headaches, heart palpitations, as well as loss of appetite, insomnia, and many other symptoms." His dark eyes held her gaze. "I am going to prescribe a calming tea. I will give you a small bag of it to start, and you can get more from the herbalist who has a stall at the Saturday market. Besides that, you can take aspirin when the headaches are painful. But the tea is best." He made a few other suggestions of ways to reduce stress. "Though, these days, it's almost impossible to escape it entirely." He paused a moment and then took her hand in both of his. It was a comforting thing to do, and it felt very natural. "Frau Lang, do you have any special things you like to do that help you feel calm? Like painting or reading or music?"

"I love to knit, and I play the violin," she said. "I used to play the piano, too, but it was stolen."

"Ahh . . ." The doctor's sigh showed he understood. "I also like music. I play the cello. Music can calm the soul better than almost anything else." Only now, he released her fingers, and Clara missed the warmth of his touch.

"Yes, my violin has been my companion since childhood." Clara remembered how playing it when Rikka and Hugo were together in Rikka's room had helped her get through the evenings. But she had come to associate the violin with sadness and hadn't played it lately.

"Frau Lang, there is a group of us, mostly amateurs, who meet here to enjoy playing chamber music together. Mutti plays the piano when she is up to it. She knows the keyboard by heart and manages quite well even with her poor vision. We have a flutist, a woodwindist who plays both the oboe and the clarinet, and a young lady who is a virtuoso on the mandolin. And myself, of course, on the cello. We are all Jews, and we must keep the gathering small so as not to attract attention, but we have been wishing for a violinist. Would you be willing to join us one evening? We meet on alternate Wednesdays."

The idea of meeting with a group of other Jews seemed a little risky, but a music group—that held a great deal of appeal. "Yes," Clara said, "Let me think about it. Maybe one day I can join you."

"Call me anytime and I'll let you know when our next evening together will be. If you can come, I'll put out another chair." He stood and, once again more professional, he reached out to shake her hand. "It has been a pleasure to meet you, Frau Lang. I hope the tea helps. Don't hesitate to call me if you have any questions or other medical concerns." He grinned. "But if you call about coming to our little music group, you must call me Albert. At the group, I'm simply Albert, not Doctor Fiedler."

Remembering all this, Clara leaned her head back against the pillows and closed her eyes. The first time Albert had held her hand in a personal way formed an indelible memory in her heart. It was on the night she first joined the music gathering.

For two weeks she had drunk the grassy tea Dr. Fiedler prescribed, a mixture of chamomile, mint, and lavender. She had experienced no more heart palpitations, and her headaches were fewer and less intense.

One morning, she picked up her violin for the first time in several months. She plucked the strings and slid the bow across them. A sad sound filled the room. She ruffled though her stack of sheet music and found a copy of "Hungarian Dances." As she played, she forgot her worries, but her sense of loneliness was heightened by the lively tune. *This is a piece that should be played with others,* she thought.

As if it were a sign from above, she realized it was Wednesday. She wondered if the music group would be meeting that evening. The doctor answered his phone on the second ring.

"Hello, Doctor." She hesitated, then said, "Albert . . . I mean Albert. This is Frau Lang. I'm calling to ask if your chamber music group is meeting tonight and if so, might I join you?"

"Yes, absolutely. You're in luck. Tonight is the night. I'm pleased you called." His voice held a note of gaiety and fun that she had not heard for a long time. "I will put out an extra chair for you, Frau Lang. We begin at five. Will that suit you? I know it's early, but we must finish before curfew when the SA gangs start roaming the streets."

"Yes, I'll be there," she said. "And please, if I am to call you Albert on music nights, you must call me Clara."

The afternoon had turned gray, a cold wind tossing the branches of the trees in the English Garden. Knowing it was difficult to find a taxi driver willing to transport Jews, Clara decided to walk despite the turn in the weather. She chose her dress carefully, a flattering pale blue with pearl buttons. She bundled up in her best coat, the one with the fox collar, and pulled on her kidskin gloves. Finally, she pinned her favorite hat, which sported a grosgrain ribbon and a lace half veil over her coiled braids. When she checked herself in the mirror, she realized she might be overdressed, but she didn't care. She hadn't dressed up in ages and she was pleased to have this occasion. She grabbed her violin case, strode out of the house, and turned toward the town center.

By the time she arrived at the doctor's home, her toes, fingers, and ears were icy. She was glad Albert opened the door quickly and she could step inside his warm vestibule.

"Oh, my dear Frau Lang, you are cold. Surely, you didn't walk all the way."

She smiled at Albert's concern. "Actually, normally, I like the cold. As a girl, I loved to ski. But I must admit, the air was chillier than I expected. And remember," she said, "you must call me Clara tonight."

Albert helped her take off all her outer layers and hung them on the hall tree. "Come. We are all in the parlor."

Clara followed him into the comfortable living room where the other guests stood near the fireplace or sat on the davenport. The men rose to greet her.

"This is Clara," Albert said. "Finally, we have our long-awaited violinist." He introduced the others in turn.

Jakob was tall, with a beard and a balding head ringed with a fringe of unruly dark curls that hung over his collar.

"Jakob plays the flute," Albert explained. "His music ranges from angelic to pan-like. He is also the scholar of our group."

Jakob nodded his greeting and smiled shyly. His shoulders were slightly stooped, as if he had spent too many hours bent over the Torah.

"Bernhard plays both the oboe and the clarinet. Whatever is needed," Albert said. "He also serves as our coordinator and conductor. He used to be the first-chair clarinet in the Frankfurt Symphony Orchestra, but, of course, not anymore. He's the only professional musician among us."

The man was round, sturdy, and barely taller than Clara, his sandy hair parted in the middle and slicked down with pomade. He reached out his hand and shook hers heartily. "Don't let that introduction intimidate you," he said. "I'm more of a Bernie than a Bernhard. That's what you must call me. Bernie."

Albert's mother was seated at the piano, her fingers playing lightly on the keyboard. "You've met my mother, of course," Albert said. "Mutti, Frau Lang . . . Clara, has joined us this evening. Do you remember her?"

The old lady swiveled her wheelchair to face Clara's direction. It was obvious that she saw little more than blurs. "Yes, of course, I remember. Welcome, my dear. You must call me Trude. We are all on a first name basis here." She stretched out her arm toward a young woman who had remained silently by the piano while the other introductions were made. "This is Eleanor. Her fingers make the mandolin sing like an angel."

The young woman stepped forward and extended her hand to Clara. "It is a pleasure to meet you," she said. Her fingers were long and narrow, her nails trimmed and manicured. It was as if she thought of them as part of her musical instrument. She reminded Clara of her niece, Renata, slender, calm, and self-assured, with a short dark bob and glittering brown eyes.

Bernie and Albert were setting up a semicircle of straight-backed dining chairs and an assortment of music stands around the piano.

"Come. Let's start and see how Clara works into our group." Bernie waved each musician to a specific chair and handed around sheet music. "Clara, are you familiar with 'Clair de Lune?'"

How smart Bernie was to start off with this slow and beautiful piece that almost every musician knew. It was perfect for integrating a new member into the group. The evening passed too quickly. They worked on the Debussy and at the end, tried a short piece by Bach. Albert's mother's fingers on the piano were light and expressive. Her arthritis and blindness seemed to disappear—she was young again as her hands danced over the keys. Each player contributed a special tone to the music, and Bernie was expert at working through difficult parts and coordinating Clara into the group.

At the end of the evening, Albert brought out a tray with tea and a glass saucer of honey cookies. The group sat around the room, sipping from their teacups, for only a few minutes. Then, one by one, they stood, said their goodbyes, and quietly left. Seeing the evening was over, Clara stood to leave, but Albert touched her shoulder.

"Wait a moment," he said. "We must go one at a time or the SA will think we have been engaged in a political meeting. Wait until everyone else has left, and I will escort you." He stood and peeked out between the drawn curtains to the street. "It's begun to rain," he said. "I have a patient who still has a car. I'll call him. It is far too wet to walk home . . . and too late as well."

Albert insisted on riding with her to make sure she arrived safely. "Who knows what can happen, these days," he said. In the car, he took her hand in both his, like he had that first day when she had come as a patient. "May I hold your hand as a friend?"

he asked. "It is a gesture I learned as a doctor to calm agitated patients, but tonight I want to hold your hand because it calms me. With all the changes in our world today, even a man can feel nervous and unsure. But when I am with you, I feel a wave of calmness enter my soul."

Clara hardly knew how to respond. Albert had revealed his vulnerability without a hint of shame or embarrassment. It was a glimpse into a man's heart that Hugo had never once revealed to her. She squeezed Albert's warm, strong hand. "It is the same with me," she said, her voice barely audible. "This evening has brought me solace." She wasn't sure if it was Albert or the night of music that had made her feel so light.

When they arrived at the gate in front of her house, he opened his umbrella and walked her to the front porch while his friend waited. They stood only a moment by the door, light rain pattering on his umbrella.

"I hope you will join us again in two weeks," he said. "Your violin made our little group complete—a true chamber music ensemble. And I believe that getting to know you will make me complete again."

Clara smiled at him and said, "I will come again." She turned, unlocked the door, and stepped inside. From the open doorway, she watched Albert hurry across the front yard to his friend's car. As she walked through the foyer to the stairs, she wished she dared to skip like the young girl she felt in her heart.

Now, as Clara thought back, she realized it had only been a couple of months since the first time she joined the music group. Whenever they met, Clara was there. The group had become her main—perhaps her only—pleasure. As she gradually prepared to emigrate, anticipation of the time with Albert after the others left kept her going from day to day. Getting to know this man had become the reason she was no longer eager to leave.

Thinking of Albert reminded Clara of Edith's descriptions of Charlie in the diary. Her daughter had found a special friend, and now Clara had, too. She resettled herself against the pillows and began to read again, instantly transported from 1939 back to 1934.

October 26, 1934

Today I came close to disaster! I had to stay late at school to clean up a mess caused by one of the Brown Twins, which she had cleverly made to look like I was responsible. When I got home, Rikka was coming down the stairs to check the mail! Just in time, I grabbed the blue envelope and stuffed it in my blouse. So close! I took it up to the attic to read.

October 29, 1934

I haven't been very steadfast about writing in this diary. I've got letters to write now—one or two a week. And a real person to tell my feelings to, not just these blank pages. I told Charlie about the diary. How it sometimes feels like a chore. He says I should write in it as often as I can. It doesn't have to be every day. Think of it as a journal, rather than a diary, he said. A place to keep notes and ideas and important events, like my own historical record. I like his idea.

November 2, 1934

Another letter from Charlie. Besides him, I have no friends at all. The mounds of homework and projects at school keep me too busy to weep. Charlie says I should concentrate more on improving my English if I plan on emigrating after I get my certificate.

English: *Sometimes I want to stay in Germany because that's where Charlie is.*

Clara ran her finger down the page and skimmed the short entries. Some were simply notes about assignments at school or bits about life at home or the weather. Whenever a letter arrived from Charlie, Edith noted it and surrounded his name with drawings of hearts and daisies. The longer entries were usually about significant events that deeply affected her daughter. Clara slowed down and read these carefully.

November 7, 1934

Something amazing happened at school. One of the older
girls finally had enough. I guess she got tired of watching the
Brown Twins pick on me.

Yesterday, one of the sisters snuck over and turned up the
oven where my bread was baking. The classroom filled with
black smoke and the smell of burning. This older girl, Ilse,
who mostly ignores both the boycott and the sisters, had put
her loaf in the same oven because it was ready to bake at
the same time as mine. Now her bread was black, too. She
was so angry! She threw her blackened loaf in the bin and
marched over to the sisters. Enough! she yelled. Stop this
stupid tormenting of Edith. That's what she said. We're here
to learn and that's all we want to do, she shouted and glared
at the twins.

The other girls in the kitchen shuffled their feet. They
stood back waiting to see what the sisters would do.
Amazingly, the twins stalked out of the room and didn't
come back till the end of class. Not another word from them.
They simply tossed their overcooked loaves in the bin on top
of Ilse's.

Today, no more hazing. No more boycott. In cooking
class, Ilse sat next to me. She whispered that she would
make sure my problems with the sisters end. But remember,
she said, this doesn't mean I'm your friend.

English: *I wrote to Charlie about Ilse. He will be glad that
I have an ally.*

November 16, 1934

Every week a blue envelope arrives from Berlin. Either on Thursday or Friday. I rush home from school on those days to check the post. The same evening, I write Charlie back, and I forget about journal writing.

November 18, 1934

A few girls at school are talking to me again. Ilse came to me yesterday when we were assigned a joint project in cooking class. She said she wanted to partner with someone eager to work hard and do things correctly.

English: *In the dressmaking class, I'm sewing myself a new frock. It has a V-neckline and is made of velvet, the color of wine. I can't wait to wear it for Charlie.*

Clara remembered that dress, so grown up and elegant. It foreshadowed what a fine seamstress Edith would become, but it also seemed to herald her daughter's transition into womanhood. Clara remembered how Edith had strutted and swayed her hips each time she wore the frock. And, Clara remembered, it was about this time that Edith had started to use lipstick and had begun wearing her braids wrapped around her head like a crown of gold. As a mother, Clara was unsure she was prepared for the next diary entries. As she read the first line, she knew something new was on its way.

November 24, 1934

Charlie and I kissed! I must write it all out. I'll never forget a single detail of this special day. It will be a long entry. Most likely my hand will be aching before I finish.

Yesterday, Charlie and I met at our special place near the hedge. The plunge is closed for the winter so no one else was around. Charlie brought a thermos with hot chocolate. We took turns sipping out of the lid. We were cozy and warm, all wrapped up together with my plaid blanket. When the cocoa was gone, Charlie asked for one more taste. And he kissed me! His lips were soft and warm and sweet with milk. It was the best kiss ever! But only one kiss! I wanted more. Chocolate kisses are the best!

We held hands as we walked to my gate, and Charlie begged me to meet him again on Sunday. He would tell his parents that he had to return to Berlin on the noon train so we could meet in the afternoon after he goes to church.

Today at noon, Charlie waited for me at the bridge that crosses the Werra River. We walked all the way up the hill to Schloss Landsberg. Most of the time the castle is empty and mysterious because the owner travels back and forth to America. We discovered a secret nook between the garage and the back garden wall where Charlie kissed me again. More than once this time! His hands never strayed from my shoulders to my breasts. I wonder if he longed to let his fingers go there as much as I wished they would. My breasts tingled in their loneliness. He called me his delicious Edith, and said he is aware of how young I am, and he will never pressure me.

We barely made it back in time for him to catch the last train to Berlin.

English: *Charlie smells like lavender. It is either his soap or his shaving lotion. The smell is divine!*

Clara sighed and rubbed her temples. Her daughter's friendship with Charlie had clearly turned romantic. For a brief moment, she thought of cautioning Edith. She had to shake her head to clear her mind. She needed to remember that all this had happened almost five years ago. What was done was done. She returned to the diary.

November 30, 1934

I am busy at school with projects. I know I am neglecting this journal. When I take up my pen, I only want to write to Charlie. Am I falling in love? My heart beats like mad when I see one of his blue envelopes in the post. I am numbering each one. I keep the blue letters with this diary in a box under my bed. Today's letter was his seventh!

English: *I will try to write in the journal more often. Charlie says short entries are better than blank pages.*

December 14, 1934

What a disaster! Vati found Charlie's letter today.

Father is traveling less because his business is falling off. Most of his regular customers refuse to buy from a Jew! Of course, he is in a nasty mood and is often at home during the week. Today the mail came when I was still at school. Of course, Vati noticed the Berlin return address.

The minute I walked into the house, I knew I was in big trouble. Vati stood by his office with the blue envelope dangling from his fingers. He slapped the letter against his thigh and pointed me inside his study. The only good news was that he was alone—no Rikka in sight. Seems she had one of her migraines. Sooooo very (not) sad.

Anyway, I stood in front of my father's desk and waited for the thunder. Vati thrust the letter toward me. He demanded to know who wrote to me from Berlin.

My heart dropped to the pit of my stomach. I pressed the letter against my chest. I could barely speak, and my words faltered. A friend. Only a friend.

Vati ordered me to read the letter out loud. Now my heart dropped all the way to my shoes. My fingers shook and I almost dropped the envelope as I pulled out the pages.

Thankfully, Charlie followed our agreement to keep his words beyond reproach in case a letter was discovered. He mentioned the Schloss and sharing hot chocolate, but nothing about our kisses. When I finished reading, I was able to breathe again.

Vati's anger was no more than I expected. His voice was cold. Wasn't I forbidden to walk out with boys? Why did I persist? And now a boyfriend from Berlin! Vati's voice thundered in my ears. When his explosion was over and he was finally silent, his breath came in angry huffs.

I cast about for something to say that might calm him. He's not a boy, I told my father, and I'm not a little girl anymore. I felt like stamping my foot, but I didn't. Then the words tumbled out. Charlie grew up in Meiningen, I told Vati. I met him at the plunge. He's a local boy and his parents still live here. He works in Berlin. He's educated . . . an engineer with a well-paying job. Besides, he's only a good friend, nothing more.

I thought this information would calm my father, but I had miscalculated. Vati demanded to know how old Charlie was. Then his eyes narrowed. He had latched onto the word engineer. He sputtered as he asked about his job. Then came the inevitable words: If he has such a good job, he must be an Aryan. Am I right?

I looked at the floor and mumbled the one word that spelled disaster. Yes.

Vati pulled the letter out of my hands, ripped it into shreds, and tossed the precious bits into the fireplace.

House arrest was inevitable–the duration of my punishment was the only thing in question. I suppose it could have been worse. I am restricted to home and school until the first of the year. And, of course, forbidden to correspond with Charlie! No more letters! Vati's final words chilled me. This must stop! Think, girl, it is dangerous for your friend, too.

I ran to my room and threw myself on the bed. My hands stung and I was surprised to see bright-pink, half-moon fingernail marks on each palm. I had clenched my hands into tight fists, but I didn't feel the pain until I was in my room.

As I write this, I hear Vati yelling at Mutti in their bedroom. The sounds rumble across the hall, but I can't understand what he's saying.

～ꝰ～

That afternoon was clear in Clara's memory. Hugo had stormed into the bedroom. She was in her dressing gown, pinning her long hair into a roll and wondering what to wear for dinner. When he burst into the room, she turned from her mirror. Her husband's face was florid, his eyes ablaze. *What now?* she remembered thinking. It didn't take much to get Hugo upset back then.

"Did you know your daughter is exchanging letters with an older man? An Aryan, no less! Is she crazed?"

"I had no idea," Clara said, her heartbeat rapid at this news. "Surely, it's not good and she needs to be discouraged."

"Discouraged! She must stop this foolishness immediately." Hugo paced the floor, his hands clasped behind his back. "I've given her house arrest until after the holidays," he said. "She is not allowed to go anywhere other than school."

Clara nodded. This was Hugo's preferred punishment since the children were too old to be whacked with a folded newspaper.

She hoped there would be nothing more. *She would talk to Edith later,* she had thought. But Hugo continued.

"House arrest won't stop Edith this time. It never has and her folly could affect us all," he said. "I will write the man. I copied out his return address. He must be told to cease and desist! He must stop writing to our daughter."

Clara could well imagine the imperious letter Hugo would write in his current state. *No good will come of that,* she had thought.

"Hugo, let me write the letter," she soothed. "A mother's touch may be more effective than a father's demands. You said this man is an Aryan. We must tread gently. If we write too full of righteous anger the man could turn on us . . . as you said . . . angry interactions with an Aryan could have ramifications for our entire family."

Hugo stopped pacing and considered his wife. "You may be right," he said. "You write the letter. But you must be firm. Do it tonight and I will mail it first thing in the morning."

CHAPTER 6

Love

January 5, 1935

No letters from Charlie since before Christmas. I'm sure Vati
has ripped them all up.

With the holiday over, he has gone off to meet a Jewish
shoemaker in Erfurt. He must get some new leather orders,
or his business will go bankrupt. I can tell he is worried.

But, for me, my father's absence brought a wonderful
surprise—a blue envelope! I stuffed it deep into my pocket
and ran all the way up to the attic before I dared read
Charlie's words.

He said Mutti had written to him. She told Charlie he
must stop writing to me because it was dangerous for us
both. But she suggested he could send a farewell letter right
after the New Year. She knew father would be away on
business and Rikka, father's spy, would be at her yearly visit

to her sister. I love this week! And I love my mother. I must thank her for her kindness to Charlie.

At the end of the letter, he wrote, Do you want me to stop writing? If you want me to stop, I will.

I want him to keep writing! Charlie is the only one who keeps me sane. I must find someone willing to be a secret mail carrier.

January 6, 1935

I have talked to Grandmother Lang's maid. She is a widow and a romantic soul. She used to tell me stories about falling in love with her husband when she was no older than I am now. Granny is heavy and old and can't go downstairs to pick up the mail, so Berta always does it. I have sworn her to secrecy. I told her to keep a lookout for the blue envelopes at the end of each week. She can bring them to the market plaza on Saturdays when she shops for Granny's weekly lunch with Vati. I will meet her every Saturday at the vegetable stall.

I've told Charlie to address his letters to Berta Pauline Lang. I can't wait for the first letter via special courier.

English: *Berta and I are excited, but we must be as calm as spies in a Hollywood film.*

January 26, 1935

When I arrived at the plaza today, Berta stood near the vegetable seller's stand. She shifted nervously from one foot to the other. I had to ask her if a letter had come before she remembered to pull it from where it hid under the potatoes in her basket. I grabbed the treasured blue envelope and pushed it into my coat pocket.

Inside the Church of Our Lady, I sat in the back pew. My fingers were clumsy as I ripped open the envelope. The letter was short. I know the words by heart.

Dearest Edith, I hope this reaches you in time. I will be in Meiningen on 26 January. Please meet me at our special spot at 11:30 in the morning. I long to hold you in my arms again!

It was close to 10:00 when I dashed out of the church. By the time I reached home, my heart thrashed in my chest like a caged animal. Mutti was playing the piano in the parlor. I gave her a huge hug. She looked up, puzzled by my show of affection. But she smiled and kissed my cheek before she turned back to the keyboard.

I told her I had to go to school this afternoon to help one of the teachers. I hate to lie to Mutti, but I need an alibi. I will be gone all afternoon.

In my room, I put on my new velvet dress. I just finished it yesterday. Because of the cold weather, I had to cover it up with my winter coat. I tiptoed down the stairs and made sure not to step on the creaky one. I left through the kitchen, grabbing an apple from the fruit bowl, and snuck out the back gate.

Charlie was waiting. The footprints where he had been pacing were green in the frost-coated grass. I ran to him, and he encircled me in his arms. Bliss!

Maybe it was the danger of our forbidden meeting. Or the cold January air. We clung to each other like lovers. I put my hands under his coat to keep them warm. Charlie's gloved hands encircled my back, then clasped my rear and pulled me even closer. Despite our wandering hands, it was too cold to stay outside.

We half ran around the English Garden, taking back alleys, to the little café near the Bahnhof. We thought it would be safe so far from my neighborhood. We scrunched together in a back booth. Even the café was cold. Freezing wind blew inside every time a customer entered or left. Charlie ordered a bowl of spaetzle soup, and we took turns dipping our spoons into the rich broth laden with twisted dumplings. Charlie cut up my apple with his pocketknife for our dessert.

When it started getting dark, Charlie hailed a taxi for me. He had to return to Berlin early the next morning, so sadly, no Sunday kisses! He promised to write to "Berta Pauline." He kissed me before he put me in the taxi. I can still feel the warmth of his lips as I write this. Our secret meetings are heavenly!

English: *Charlie did not see my new dress, but he touched it.*

February 2, 1935 – Our mail plan is working!

English: *Berta is always nervous when she brings me a letter.*

February 5,1935

This term we have a new German culture teacher. Herr Kirsch, Marlisa's father! He used to teach history at the Gymnasium but has been demoted to domestic school. I wonder what he did.

Herr Kirsch must teach the class with a Nazi slant. I wonder if he hates it, too! It's all Hitler and race theory and more Hitler stuff. Class meets for the first two hours of the morning on Wednesdays, which totally ruins that day. First a stiff-arm salute and a loud, Heil Hitler! I refuse to say those words, but I move my lips and pretend. My salute is more at half-mast than up. Herr Kirsch never seems to notice. Still, he sticks to the new Nazi textbook. He drones on and on while the Brown Twins and a few others sit at rapt attention.

Herr Kirsch used to be friendly and full of smiles when I visited Marlisa. Now, standing in front of the classroom, he seems a different man, stern and serious. He refuses to make eye contact with me. Perhaps he's afraid of losing his job entirely. Maybe Marlisa and her mom are afraid, too. I can't blame them. Listening to the Hitler party line every Wednesday makes me depressed and nervous the entire day.

English: *Tomorrow I will skip class. Maybe Mr. Kirsch won't notice.*

February 8,1935

I skipped German culture class and when I passed Herr Kirsch in the hall on Thursday, he didn't say a word. Next week, I'm going to ditch again.

Oh, no! Clara thought. The last words Edith had written sent a chill up her spine. This latest folly would not lead to anything good. Again, she wished she could go back in time and warn her daughter to be more careful—to think before she acted. Yet again, she had to remind herself that whatever would happen had already happened. She shuddered and began to read the next page.

February 9, 1935

Today was a blue letter day! Charlie says he falls asleep remembering my smile and my chilly hands on his chest. He says these memories of me bring lovely dreams.

February 16, 1935

Charlie's letters are the only joy in my life! He says he's found a place where we can meet without freezing. He said he can't tell me where in a letter, but it will be safe and warm. I can't wait to see Charlie's secret hideaway. Only a few more days until Saturday.

English: *I will wear my wine-red dress again. I hope it makes Charlie drunk with love.*

February 23,1935

I am in love! Charlie and I met in the English Garden. It is a wonderland of snowdrifts. His kiss was mint sweet as if he had just sucked a breath lozenge. We romped about like children, throwing snowballs and making angels on a hillside of unblemished white. When we were out of breath and our fingers numb from the cold, he led me to a narrow lane behind the train station. He put his arm around my shoulders and covered my eyes with his hands. I filled my lungs with the toasty aroma of his leather gloves. The sweet smell of his lavender soap. The odor of damp cobblestones, earth, and ashes. The warmth of his body pressed into my back as he led me along. The sting of cold air against my lips and cheeks. The blackness behind my eyelids and the gentle pressure of his hands. The lingering taste of mint on my tongue from his kiss. I could feel it all. My senses are alive when Charlie is near.

Charlie guided me. First some turns, then a step up and we climbed five stairs. I heard a key turning in a lock, the creak of rusty hinges. He gently nudged me over a threshold. His chin touched the top of my head. His arms were around my waist. Open your eyes now, he said.

We stood in a tiny room. A narrow bed pushed against one wall. A table with two chairs. A three-drawer dresser. The room was clean, the bed neatly made. A man's jacket hung on a wall peg. Shelves filled with books lined one wall and a multipaned window looked out across roofs toward the tree covered hills. A rough stone sink and a little cast-iron stove with a pail of coal next to it filled a corner of the room.

Charlie's warm breath whispered against my neck as he apologized for the simple hideaway. I turned in his arms, kissed his cheek, and declared it was lovely. He pulled off my wet gloves, scarf, and heavy coat. Then he nodded toward the table. Sit, he told me and bent to light the stove.

Charlie said the room belonged to a school chum from his elementary days. Though their lives had taken different directions, they had stayed in touch. He wouldn't tell me any more details, and he warned me not to ask questions. It was best for his friend and for me not to know too much.

We stood shoulder to shoulder with our open hands extended toward the stove to catch the warmth of the flames. Charlie filled a kettle with water from the pump and set it on the burner to make tea. We sat on the bed propped up against an array of pillows and drank from mismatched mugs. When the tea was gone, Charlie wrapped his arms around me and kissed my lips—one of those long tender kisses that warms my entire body. I didn't want to stop kissing. We slid down, our bodies touching shoulder to toe. We explored secret places, his hand stroking the burgundy velvet of my dress. Those strong hands found their way underneath to touch the silkiness of my slip. My body felt like it was floating in Champagne, the bubbles nibbling at my breasts, my nipples, and my inner thighs.

Suddenly I realized where we were heading. I didn't want him to stop, but I didn't want to go further, either. I found the strength to still his roving hands and sat up straight. He leaned back against the pillows and gazed deep into my eyes. His voice was husky when he spoke. What did I want? he asked.

I wasn't even sure myself what I wanted. I'm still not certain. All I know is I must wait until I am sure. I struggled to find the words to explain . . . how I've always imagined my first man would be my husband on my wedding night. I asked him to forgive me. Maybe I'm a silly child. But I wasn't ready to give up that romantic dream.

Tears streamed down my cheeks. He gently wiped them away with his thumb. He was very tender as he soothed me. He said it was OK. He put one hand on my cheek and asked me to forgive him. He took out his clean handkerchief and wiped away my tears. He ran his thumb down my cheek and along my jaw until he cradled my chin in his palm. Did I want to leave? he asked.

No . . . I didn't want to leave. I suggested we both sit up. Was he OK with only kissing and cuddling? He assured me kissing was more than enough. We made a pact. No laying down on the bed! No touching under our clothes. We set the pillows and our coats against the wall and used the bed like a couch. He kept his arms around me, but mainly we talked. Finally, Charlie said his friend would be home soon. He had promised to use the room no more than two hours.

Charlie said he trusted me not to peek. I kept my eyes closed as he guided me down the stairs and across the rough cobblestones. Footsteps approached. I wrapped my scarf up over my mouth and ducked my head. Someone brushed past and I heard Charlie whisper, Thank you, my friend.

I can't believe I wrote all this! I must hide this book and Charlie's letters somewhere Vati will never look. I think the attic is a better place than under my bed. I will be on house arrest for the rest of my life if my father discovers them!

Clara lifted her head and realized her heart was beating rapidly in her chest. It was unsettling to read her daughter's intimate words, to realize how close Edith had come to losing her girlhood. But it was the vivid description of the sensation of floating in Champagne that had caused Clara's heart to pound. She had never felt anything of the sort, had not even imagined it possible, yet she suddenly longed to know the feeling of effervescence nibbling at her breasts.

She rubbed her eyes and shook her head to dispel the sense of shame that gripped her gut . . . to think of such things when reading her daughter's diary was verging on lewd. She must be more careful about allowing her own needs to melt into her daughter's words.

February 27, 1935

Happy days!

— I love Charlie and he loves me.
— I no longer go to German culture class. Wednesday mornings, I visit Grossmutter Lang, or I sit on a pew in the Church of our Lady and read.

— Herr Kirsch has never said anything about my absence.

— Most of the girls in school talk to me.

— The Brown Twins ignore me.

— Ilse and I are friends, though she won't admit it.

— I am reading "The Murder at the Vicarage" in English again and this time it is easier.

At home, things are not quite so rosy.

— Vati is constantly worried and depressed. His business is terrible! After supper, he and Rikka retreat to her room to offer each other comfort.

— There have been no cheerful dinner parties for more than a year, and the adults are all moody and missing their social life. (This problem I can understand!)

— Rikka has lots of migraines, which makes her meaner than usual.

— Mother plays sad songs on her violin almost every night.

— Herman mopes around and spends hours in the attic. I can smell cigarette smoke trickling down. He complains that his school chums have deserted him, even Otto, his best friend since third grade. Of course, he's miserable.

— Worst of all, a great deal of Mutti's silver service was stolen. The thief (or thieves) seemed to have known exactly where the best stuff was stored. We are all sure the culprit was the maid, who has not shown up for work since the theft. Rikka is livid because the thief poured ink on her latest embroidery project. I guess whoever it was knew Rikka, too! The police refuse to investigate. The policeman told Mutti that Jews didn't need fancy silver!

March 1, 1935

I read Charlie's latest letter over three times before I stashed it in my secret hiding place in the attic. His words are like poetry.

When we kiss, the touch of your eyelashes on my cheek resembles the caress of butterfly wings. That's what he wrote!!! I fear he'll grow bored with my constant childish complaints about school and life at home. Will he keep loving me?

March 9, 1935

Charlie wrote we should hide the rest of mother's silver in several different and totally new places. He wants to help, but really there is little he can do to make things better for us. He says he wishes he could kiss my tears away. I miss him every day!

March 10, 1935

Vati didn't go to his mother's house for lunch today. He phoned her and said he wouldn't go near the town center because Meiningen is celebrating the 10th anniversary of the local Nazi Party. The market and the streets are decorated with flags and garlands, and the mayor's committee built four temporary towers, one at each corner of the plaza. It's quite disgusting how fervent some people can be. The Führer is expected to show up tomorrow for the celebrations. The town Nazis are excited. When Vati read the morning paper, he threw it down and stomped on it. He spent the rest of the day in a foul mood.

March 11, 1935

Ha! Ha! Hitler didn't show up! He probably went to his villa near Berchtesgaden instead. Soooooo sad!

March 16, 1935

Berta has resigned!

This morning, she handed me Charlie's letter and announced it was the last one she would carry. She explained that Grossmutter almost caught her stuffing the letter in her shopping basket. Berta said that except for my Granny's poor eyesight, she would be unemployed, and I would be on eternal house arrest. Berta can't risk losing her job, especially now that Vati gives her extra money to clean for us three afternoons a week. He refuses to hire another Aryan maid! With so many worries, I barely have energy to write here. But I must make an effort.

English: *I need another safe mail carrier for Charlie's letters. I will die without them!*

March 18, 1935

Yea! Ilse has agreed (reluctantly) to be my secret letter person. She lives in a rooming house, and Charlie can write there. She will bring letters to me at school. I promised it would only be for a few months till the end of the term.

March 20, 1935

Herr Kirsch is my hero today!

When I arrived at school, he waited for me in the hall. He motioned me into his classroom and closed the door. I was sure I was finally in trouble! He said nothing, only pointed to the grade book open on his desk. I peered at the row after my name. Every square for the last two months was marked with a check to show I had been in class. In each space where an assignment should be recorded, he had written a passing grade. He stood near the desk and gazed out the window. He never turned toward me, but I heard him say he refused to be the one to deny me a certificate when so much else is being denied. He warned me not to get caught by the headmistress because he wouldn't be able to protect me then. It's good to know Marlisa's father remains inside this stern man who now wears a National Socialist armband.

March 23, 1935

Another blissful Saturday!

Charlie and I spent hours talking and cuddling in our cozy, borrowed paradise. Charlie brought sandwiches and a thermos of hot chocolate. I love it when he kisses the sweet foam off my lips. It was difficult to resist reaching under his shirt to touch the warm skin of his chest, but we kept to our plan. If he isn't allowed to touch under my skirt, I can't touch his chest. Finally, to cool our passion, we got up and stood at the window looking across the roofs toward the hills. I could see lingering patches of snow under the trees. But summer is coming! In some sunny areas, there are dots of blue and yellow, probably crocuses, which always say warm weather is on its way. Charlie whispered against my ear. I will remember his words forever. . . I long to marry you. Would you have me? One day? When we can figure out a way . . .

I stood on my tiptoes and kissed him. Yes. One day . . . , I answered. Then I buried my face in his chest and breathed in his lavender smell.

This is the last time we can use the room. Charlie's friend is nervous about his landlady finding out that a Jewess is spending time there. I wonder—does a single loyal person exist anywhere in Germany? Charlie says not to be upset. The days will soon be warmer, and we can meet in the park again. Worse news is that Charlie's visits home may be less frequent and shorter. His firm has a huge, new project and he will be very busy. No more Sunday kisses! How will I survive?

I love Charlie with my whole heart, but I wonder if we will ever be able to marry. The way things are and with Charlie being Aryan, I know Vati would have apoplexy at the idea.

March 29, 1935

Ilse brought me a letter! I hid in a stall in the school lavatory and read it two times. Naturally, I was late for sewing class and Frau Winter made me stay after class to bag up heaps of fabric scraps to take to the paper mill. But I don't care! I have a letter!

April 2, 1935

Friedel (I mean Fred) has his birthday today. My brother is twenty! In his last letter, he complained about the freezing Chicago winter. He said icy winds blow off the lake constantly. He wants to go west to the land of oranges and flowers!

English: *Fred rides a horse through a forest of cactus. (I wonder, can you call a lot of cacti a forest?)*

April 5, 1935

Charlie is part of the architectural team that will design and build a whole village, dorms, and stadiums in Charlottenburg before the 1936 Olympic Games. With such an important project in the works, his firm has turned up the pressure for him to join the National Socialist Party. So far, he has been able to stall. He says he will concentrate on being the best and most indispensable engineer on staff. Yea, Charlie!

April 10, 1935

Charlie's letter today was too short! No poetic sentences . . . I can tell he is stressed.

April 15, 1935

Herman turned fifteen today!

Mutti planned a special dinner for him, but the evening was spoiled when Vati asked my brother what his birthday wish was. Herman announced he wanted to quit school, and Vati exploded. He refuses to allow it. Herman was almost in tears explaining how he was constantly picked on for being a Jew. He told Vati that he's given poor marks even for his best work when he used to get high grades. He must sit at the back of the class. No one will talk to him, and he's not allowed to participate in sports programs. He is totally shunned. I understand how that feels!

Vati is so inflexible! He demands that his son stand proud and be strong.

Herman tried to argue. He said the law says he can leave school at fourteen and now he's fifteen. That should be enough standing strong. But arguing with Vati is hopeless.

He yelled at Herman that he must stay in school. Mutti cringed in her chair. Of course, Rikka agreed with Father.

April 18, 1935

Charlie has promised to be in Meiningen the weekend before my upcoming nineteenth birthday so we can celebrate together. He wrote he will NEVER join the Nazi Party. I think this is as dangerous as saying he loves me.

April 25, 1935

A stranger—an Aryan, of course, a full-blooded German with connections to the SA—has bullied his way into the business that has been in Vati's family for three generations. He has pretty much taken over and now Vati has little to do. This Aryan is selling all the leather neatly stored in our basement. Vati gets only 5%, but at least it's getting sold and he says he's lucky to get any amount.

April 28, 1935

Charlie was here! I had to calm him down because he was upset about all the red and black Nazi banners hanging from the buildings surrounding the Market Plaza. It's for a Nazi event for the Hitlerjugend. All the city schools will be closed on Tuesday for a ceremony and speeches. Herman and I have agreed to stay home together. We will inhabit the Children's

Kingdom in the attic and read and play cards all day.

Charlie worries about us being seen together. For my birthday, he insisted we go somewhere that we are strangers. He knew a guesthouse in Obermassfeld-Grimmenthal with a good restaurant, so we went there for lunch.

Grimmenthal is a cute town with an old city gate and fields all around. The Werra River runs through the town, too, like in Meiningen. I easily passed as an Aryan in my fur-collared coat, with my blond braids wrapped around my head catching the sunshine. Charlie held my elbow and steered me right past the sign in the front window that read, "Jews Not Welcome." The dining room was dark wood and shadows. We slid into a corner booth with high wooden sides. The waitress was full of smiles when she came to take our order.

The rouladen was delicious! The beef was tender, and the filling had the perfect tang of mustard and pickles with salty bacon. Our forks touched as we shared a slice of apple strudel for dessert!

After lunch, we walked around the village and through the fields covered in yellow, lavender, and white wildflowers. The sweet, honey-like scent of the flowers attracted hundreds of bees, and the breeze was filled with their buzzing. In the shade under the town gate, we exchanged hungry kisses. Kissing can be a special kind of exploration. Who knew?

It was almost dark when the train brought us back to Meiningen. I had to hurry home so I wouldn't get in trouble. I was so full from lunch and kisses, I could hardly eat Cook's dinner.

This morning, I longed to see Charlie and I did something I'd not done before. I went to the train station hoping to catch a glimpse of him when he came for the early train. I stood in the shadows near the entrance. When he arrived in a taxi, I stepped into the sunlight. We only had time for one quick kiss. He whispered in my ear, My beautiful, brave, and crazy sweetheart.

I love the way he talks!

English: *My memories of this weekend will fill my heart until Charlie returns next month.*

CHAPTER 7

The Devil Within

Pale sunlight filtered through the attic window and fell on the pages of Edith's diary. It was difficult for Clara to remember that her daughter's words were written four years before. They felt so immediate to her, so appropriate to what she was experiencing in 1939. Edith was right when she wrote that joyous memories could sustain you. Clara was discovering this as she collected her own radiant memories in a secret corner of her heart.

She had not eaten since morning and the edges of hunger nibbled at her stomach. She returned the diary to its box, carried it downstairs to her apartment, and set it on a side table.

She rummaged through the refrigerator. The cold potato pancakes still held no appeal. She pulled out one thing and then another until she found a half empty container of pickled herring in sour cream, one of her favorite snacks. She dumped the contents onto a saucer, buttered a thin slice of dark, pumpernickel bread, and poured herself a small glass of Schnapps. She settled into her armchair with the meal beside her and picked up Edith's diary again. Her daughter's words sent her back to 1935 when life still seemed to be a night terror from which one would soon awaken.

April 30, 1935

Vati is in a nasty mood today because a new law prohibits Jews from flying the German flag. I don't understand why he cares. He only flies the flag a couple of times a year anyway. When I asked why he still wants to be so patriotic and German, he answered, I am German! It's not about wanting to be . . . I simply am. Vati fought for Germany in the Great War and came home from the front with typhoid! He believes that should be enough to prove he is a patriotic German.

English: *Father says he is German. Hitler says he is not.*

May 2, 1935

Only three more weeks and I will have my certificate!

I can't wait for it all to be over. First, our written exams for the academic classes. Then the special lunch and cooking class oral exams. The sewing and tailoring classes will present a fashion show to showcase our work. We will be handed our certificates at the ceremony that same afternoon.

May 6, 1935

Unbelievable! I have been chosen to be the master of
ceremonies for the student fashion show!

All the students are working together to plan the event.
Most of the girls (everyone except for the Brown Twins
and two of their sycophants) agree that I'm the best one for
the job! They say I'm funny and they want the show to be
lighthearted. We needed a theme and there were lots of
ideas. Finally, it was narrowed down to me dressed as a devil
or a witch. I can't help but wonder if the girls like the idea of
a Jewish girl, dressed up as something evil. I prefer to think it
is their macabre sense of humor, which I share. I told them I
prefer to be a devil. We will vote next week.

Ilse and one of her friends will model my projects as I
won't be able to. I must run the show!

May 9, 1935

Today I am nineteen years old! At dinner, Vati didn't ask
me what my birthday wish was. He announced that he had
secured a place for me to work for six weeks at a Jewish
children's holiday camp and then I will attend an advanced
seamstress school in Aschaffenburg. It will be fun to spend
some summer days at the children's camp with my cousin,
Renata. But I will miss Charlie!

I am grateful Vati has set up the dressmaking school and
post-certificate training for me. However, I dread staying with
my father's sister, Aunt Martha, in Aschaffenburg.

Naturally, I didn't hint to Vati that I'm no longer eager to leave Germany (and Charlie!).

May 10, 1935

Today I received a beautiful birthday card that Charlie painted himself. Butterflies and bees and crocuses in ink and watercolors. I didn't even know Charlie was artistic! He also wrote a lovely poem inside. It's only three lines. Charlie says it is Haiku, a special kind of Japanese poem he's always admired. I will keep this card forever!

May 13, 1935

The school fashion show will be called Lucifer's Favorites. I'm not sure it makes any sense, but it allows me to dress up like the devil, rather than a witch—a character whose traditional hooked nose and moles would be too much like the poster depictions of Jews for my taste. I might have had to resign if that was the choice.

For the final exam in cooking, our class has planned a meal we are confident will be delicious. Everyone hates the orals after lunch because the teachers ask all kinds of tricky questions to get students to make a mistake. They tell us working under pressure is part of being a cook in a wealthy home. I wonder if Cook has felt pressure working for our family. I hope not.

May 20, 1935

I think I've started a rebellion. I hope it doesn't all go wrong.

I kept thinking, What if I put sleeping powder in the instructor's coffee at the luncheon? Would they get too sleepy to ask complicated questions? The idea made me laugh. I whispered my joke to Ilse. But Ilse is so bold, she latched onto it and told a couple of her friends. The idea traveled like lightning and soon most of the girls in class were giggling and saying, Edith is such a mischief!

By the end of the class period, Ilse had convinced everyone we should do it for real! Not the Brown Twins, of course. Ilsa glared at them and warned that they best be quiet. They are the minority on this.

After school, Ilse and I went together to the chemist. It was the first time I had done anything with her outside of school, and I was giddy with excitement. We even rubbed our eyes with coal dust to look like we hadn't slept in days. We hung our heads and tried to be somber. We told the chemist what we wanted, and he went to get it. When Ilse had the packet in her hand, we were so relieved we ran out of the shop. Oops! We forgot to ask the dosage! If we put too much in the coffee, the teachers could fall dead asleep! That would be unfortunate.

May 29, 1935

Written exams today. I made up my answers on Herr Kirsch's exam because I hadn't read the text or been to class in ages! I wrote lots about Hitler and how great he is for every question.

The accounting exam was easy and I'm sure I did well.

The English exam wasn't as difficult as I expected, but I should have written more English sentences here. I think reading "The Murder at the Vicarage" helped.

English sentence: *The terrible Miss Marple improved my English vocabulary.*

May 30, 1935

The practical exam in cooking was more than we expected! Luckily, I'm still here to write about it.

Ilse and I put about half the powder in the coffee pot and took it to the teacher's table. The teachers drank coffee with their lunch and kept sipping during the group evaluation. Naturally they found a few things to complain about, too. My spaetzle could have been lighter. Ilse's sauerbraten in gingersnap gravy earned raves, but the Brown Twins lost a point because their streusel cake was overbaked and dry. I guess they set the oven too high!

After a short break, it was time for the orals. No area of food preparation was off-limits. I watched anxiously for the teachers to start yawning. I hoped they would get sleepy before it was my turn.

Fräulein Becker began to squirm in her chair, then she stood up suddenly and hurried out of the room. After she returned, Frau Schröder got up and left. By the time I was being questioned, the teachers only asked short, easy questions. They seemed in a hurry to finish. Not at all sleepy! After the last student was quizzed, Frau Wagner said we should clean up the kitchen. Then she and the others hurried out of the room.

While we were cleaning, one of the Brown Twins crept into the hall to check on her beloved Frau Wagner. When she came back, she was livid! All the teachers were in the toilet! Ilse and I tried to suppress our giggles. The twins glared at us and one of them asked in a hiss what we put in the coffee. Ilse told her to calm down. It was only sleeping powder. Maybe the teachers were allergic.

Personally, I suspect the chemist tricked us on purpose and gave us a laxative. Maybe we overdid the coal dust and droopy faces. Or perhaps he recognized me as a Jew and decided to teach me a lesson. I hope the teachers don't think the lunch gave them food poisoning!

May 31, 1935

Another big day at school! This time everything went beautifully!

My devil costume was black from neck to toe. (We didn't have enough red stuff to make a full red outfit). Black blouse, black skirt, black stockings, black shoes. The only red spots were my horns (sewn to a headband) and my tail. The girls made me a super devil's tail out of empty wooden thread spools, painted red, strung on twine, a triangle of red cardboard at the end. They sewed it to my waistband. I loved swinging my tail around and looping it over my shoulder.

The girls strutted down our makeshift runway modeling their frocks. The audience laughed at my commentary and the way I danced about and swung my tail. I turned the black, Jewish devil into a frolicking kitten. The audience loved me! An SA officer from a nearby town was in the front row next to our headmistress. He laughed uproariously at all my silly antics.

As soon as I had my certificate in hand, I was eager to leave. But Fräulein Von Braun pulled me over to meet the jolly Nazi. He shook my hand and patted me on the back. If he only knew! My blond braids and blue eyes had made a fool of another Nazi!

Ha! He insisted I pose with him for a photo. He pulled me onto his lap and I dared not refuse. A Jewess disguised as a devil, I slung my red tail over my shoulder and grinned at the camera. I hope it will be on the front page of the local paper tomorrow. In the rear of the auditorium, the Brown Twins glowered.

Mutti had been in the audience earlier, but when the photo taking was over, she was gone. I'm sure she was shocked to see me fawned over by a Nazi. Lucky thing Vati was out of town.

⁓

Clara remembered how she had left the festivities without greeting and hugging her daughter. She had been upset by the irreverent gaiety of Edith's devil character, and when she was encouraged to sit on the SA man's lap, Clara had stood abruptly, almost knocking over her chair, and hurried from the room.

In the street, she paused and inhaled several deep breaths to calm herself. Indeed, like Edith, she was relieved Hugo was out of town and unable to attend the graduation. If he had been there, she was sure there would have been a scene . . . likely he would have pulled Edith off the stage and out the door long before her performance was finished.

Clara returned to the diary. Even a description of stolen kisses would be better than more about Edith's reckless behavior with a Nazi.

～∾～

June 1, 1935

Today was bittersweet. Charlie and I met, but we knew it would be a long time before I would be in Meiningen again. We tried to make the day special.

We hiked out Landsberger Strasse and up the hill to the ruined castle on the ridge. No fear of running into my overweight father on that steep hill! Cook had packed lunch for me. She suspects I'm meeting a boy, but she has no idea who and, anyway, she would never tell.

White, puffy clouds floated through a glorious clear sky. As we walked, we made a game of inventing names for the soft, white shapes. Flowers blanketed the hills, turning them into golden eiderdowns of daisies, poppies, and dandelions.

Bees busily buzzed from flower to flower. I picked a daisy and began plucking off petals. He loves me. He loves me not. He loves me. I've enjoyed this game since I was a kid. As always, it ended up with he loves me. I waved the last petal and grinned at Charlie.

Daisies are always right, he said. We joined hands and walked through the flowers, swinging our arms high into the air.

By the time we arrived at the top of the hill, we were hungry and thirsty. We found a shady spot to rest. We leaned against a fallen log, and I opened the sack with our lunch. We picnicked on Cook's fresh-baked bread slathered with chopped ham, butter, and pickles. We had kisses for dessert. Too soon, our solitude was broken by the sound of voices. We gathered up the remnants of lunch and disappeared into the trees, a magical forest of dappled light and moving shadows. We found a few wild strawberries, and they were our second dessert. The breeze smelled of pine. Sparrows hopped from tree to branch collecting dry grass and moss for their nests. We made our own nest from pine needles in a nook behind a boulder. So romantic! Charlie licked strawberry juice off my chin. His third dessert!

Soon our kisses were deep and passionate. For a moment I forgot about staying a virgin until our wedding night. Charlie stopped kissing me and asked if I wanted to stop. I told him I wasn't sure what to do. He suggested we walk around the crumbling remains of the old castle. Better to wait until I'm sure, he said. Now, as I write this alone in bed, I wonder, am I too naive? I love him so much. I wonder what I'm waiting for.

He took me by the hand and led me to a little shrine among the rocks. Candles in jars surrounded an image of the Virgin Mary. Charlie crossed himself in front of the icon. I asked him why he did that. Was he Catholic? He laughed and said, Of course.

That's why he goes to Mass with his parents on Sundays. What a dummkopf I am! He lit one of the candles to keep me safe while I am away. He looked at me with sad eyes and promised I would be in his heart every moment we are apart. He squeezed my hand and kissed my cheek..

We walked down the hill slowly, making our day last as long as possible. Our fingers were like they were part of the same hand, so tightly were they locked together.

I am going to miss Charlie something awful.

The sound of her cuckoo clock tweeting six times brought Clara back to 1939. Dusk gathered outside the window, and the street-lights on Bernhardstrasse blinked on. Clara pulled the heavy drapes across the window. She set her empty plate in the sink, poured herself another glass of Schnapps, and settled back in her comfort-able chair. She was grateful for her daughter's permission to read the diary—a rare gift from a daughter to her mother. The story of Edith's growing love for Charlie spoke directly to Clara as a mother, as a woman, as an echo of her own desires. She continued to read and was drawn back into her daughter's life.

CHAPTER 8

Changes

June 5, 1935

Renata and I are at the children's home. It's a special summer camp for Jewish children whose parents are trying to arrange immigration somewhere. Anywhere! So many Jews are getting frantic about leaving. At the camp we try to give the children a happy summer while their adults go from embassy to embassy. Some have joined the Zionists and learn Hebrew. They dream of traveling to Palestine. Some take classes in Spanish or try to improve their English like me. They apply for visas to the US, Canada, Argentina, Cuba— anywhere in the Americas.

I am assigned mostly housekeeping duties here at the summer home. The director says she doesn't want the children to get attached to me as I must leave in the middle of the summer. I help the cook, which is enjoyable. I scrub laundry in the basement and mop floors, which I don't like. Renata will be here the entire summer, so she is assigned to oversee a group of children. Lucky Renata!

My cousin and I are fortunate our fathers found this place. I hadn't realized until my cousin told me that Vati and her father paid for us to be here! They negotiated a discount because we are old enough to help with chores and childcare. I can't believe Vati would pay for me to work! I guess he wanted me out of town this summer. I wonder why he thought it was so important. Did he suspect I was still seeing Charlie? Or was he worried about all the Nazi activity in our town? Meiningen is a hotbed of Brown Shirts and SS these days.

June 19, 1935

Finally, a letter from Charlie! I hid the blue envelope in my bra and read it in the toilet stall after hours. I'd love to tell Renata about my love, but I don't dare. My cousin is an honest sort. She might tell her mother, Aunt Ida. Then it would surely get back to my mother who is as close as a twin to her sister. Best to keep it all a secret. But I ache to have someone I can talk to. Letters are not enough.

June 26, 1935

It is tedious here. Hours scrubbing linens and kids' dirty knickers. I love the children and feel sad for them, but they

are a terrible amount of work. I wish I could do more fun
stuff, like Renata. After their afternoons in the fresh air, the
children always eat better at supper, and the dining room is
filled with chatter from their high spirits. I'd like to go with
them and sing marching songs as we hike through the forest.

July 3, 1935

Another letter from Charlie today! His letters always lift
my spirits. Late at night, when Renata is dreaming, I read
Charlie's letter over and over by flashlight.

English: *I keep my precious letters in the bottom of my
suitcase.*

July 12, 1935

I am home in Meiningen. Vati is dead! Mutti sent me a
telegram and said to come home immediately.

Vati died suddenly from a heart attack. I have been
crying off and on all day. The funeral is tomorrow. Vati wasn't
always kind to me, but I loved him anyway!

I sent a telegram to Charlie. I hope he can come to
Meiningen while I'm home!

July 13, 1935

The morning was dreadful. I suppose all funerals are
dreadful, but this one was especially so.

We had to bury Vati in the Jewish section of the cemetery! He will hate being there. I picture my father in his coffin, pounding on the lid, and shouting, Not here! I'm German. Not here.

Berta and Great-Uncle Martin struggled to help Grossmutter Lang up the hill to the burial plot. Vati's casket was already down inside the grave. The gravedigger waited nearby with his shovel. Mutti begged the old man for a chair for Granny and he grudgingly brought one from his shack. Moaning and crying, Granny sat down heavily. Her wide bottom overflowed the wooden seat. It's a miracle she made it up the hill.

Great-Uncle Martin gave the eulogy. He talked about Vati's many wonderful qualities, most of which I had seldom seen. Obviously, he saw his nephew through different eyes. We all sweated in our black clothing, each swallowed by our individual sorrow. Aunt Martha, always stoic, held a lace handkerchief to her nose and sniffed. Aunt Gusti swooned against her husband's shoulder. Mutti, dark circles under her eyes, simply looked exhausted. Herman stood with his arm supporting Mutti, constantly clearing his throat. Cousin Hilda and Fritz brought along Gerti from Suhl. She stood next to me and held my hand when I began to weep. Of course, Rikka, her sister beside her, stood at the head of the grave. We were a pitiful group.

Mutti tossed the first clod of dirt on top of Vati's coffin. When I threw my fistful of dirt, I wanted to jump into the grave. Vati had been like a rock for me. Hard and uncomfortable, but always there. He always tried to make me better. Life is too, too grim, and I don't know how I will go on without my father. Then I glimpsed Charlie. He stood back in the shadows under the trees, directly across from me so I would be sure to see him.

Charlie came! He held two fingers against his wrist, a signal for when to meet.

Back at the house, Cook had prepared Vati's favorite lunch. We stood around and filled our plates with ham and potato salad. I was too nervous to eat and kept an eye on my watch. When I could stand it no longer, I announced I needed fresh air. Gerti offered to come with me. I hated the hurt expression on her face when I told her I wanted to walk alone. I wish I could tell her why! She is leaving for England soon with a work permit. We probably won't see each other again.

In the hall, the sound of Mutti and Rikka arguing came from Vati's office. I've never heard that before! Their words were muffled by the thick door. Rikka's sister sat alone in the parlor, twisting a handkerchief. I rushed past her. Charlie waited for me!

He stood in the shade of a Linden tree. He silently encircled me in his arms and pulled me to his chest. I could feel his heart beating through my blouse and his shirt. He stroked my hair and kissed my forehead. He whispered that everything would be OK. He loved me, and I wasn't alone. How calm he made me feel!

When I returned home, Rikka was nowhere to be found. I asked Herman what happened, and he shrugged. He had seen her leaving with her sister, both lugging suitcases. That was all he knew. Good riddance! One positive thing has resulted from Vati's death. It seems Rikka is gone! I hope for good!

Clara had been reading Edith's diary since early afternoon and now it was evening. She rubbed her eyes and massaged her temples. She would never forget those days four years ago, immediately before and after her husband's death.

For several weeks the house had been quiet. Edith was away at the children's camp and, as she did every summer, Rikka had been visiting her sister. Before the woman left, Clara had overheard Hugo and his cousin exchanging angry words. She had not been able to hear much through the closed door of Rikka's bedroom, but she had heard the words "leave Germany" and "emigrate," and then Hugo's voice shouting, "No! Hitler will not chase me away from my homeland."

For the entire summer, Herman had been almost invisible. He spent most of his friendless hours in the attic or riding his bike around the countryside. Clara was pleased when her son chose the outdoors as she was a firm believer in the uplifting quality of sunshine and fresh air. It distressed her that Hugo spent most of his days holed up in his study with the shades drawn, his erratic moods as dark as his room. He never traveled during the week anymore, and he had refused to work for the usurper Aryan.

"Let him figure out how to sell the remaining leather on his own," Hugo grumbled.

One evening after supper, Clara was surprised to hear a knock on the front door. Hugo answered it quickly, as if he had been expecting this late-night caller. She left her piano to go into the entrance hall to see who had arrived. Hugo's friend, Dr. Weiss, greeted her with a cheery, "Hello, Frau Lang." But Clara detected a note of nervousness underneath his greeting.

"Conrad has come for a short social visit, to share a cigar and a brandy," Hugo said, as he ushered his friend toward the study.

Clara had no desire to join in a masculine tête-à-tête. "I'll leave you two to visit then," she said. "Let me know if you need any-thing." When she climbed the stairs to retire an hour later, the men were still in the room. She could hear the rumble of their low voices through the door, the tones indicating a serious discussion.

The next day, Hugo seemed calmer. Less his usual argumenta-tive self, he was sunk deep into his own private thoughts.

On Saturday, Hugo phoned his mother and told her he would be unable to come for lunch, that he had a headache and would take a nap. Clara had made plans to go to the cinema with Hugo's sister Gusti but offered to stay with her husband in case he needed her. He waved his hand dismissively.

"No, go along and enjoy the movie," he said. "I don't need a babysitter. I'll be all right." And so, she had gone. Of course, she realized staying wouldn't have made any difference, but still she felt guilty to have left him alone.

When she and Gusti returned from the cinema, Hugo was sit-ting in his favorite chair in the glass-walled, plant-filled Winter Garden porch. Clara's first thought was that she was glad he had come into the sunlit room and was no longer in his cave-like study.

Thinking he was napping peacefully, she and Gusti walked on kitten feet. As they passed the door to the conservatory, Clara smelled a curious acrid odor.

"Wait," she said. "I smell something."

Dangling from Hugo's hand was the stub of a burning cigar. The red embers touched his fingers, and his flesh was charred. Hugo was peacefully relaxed, his eyes closed, but he was not breathing. On the table next to his chair, a small metal tray held a few ashes. An empty pill bottle lay on its side. As she snatched the small bottle and stuffed it deep in her pocket, she heard the sharp intake of Gusti's gasp behind her. Clara stared at the relaxed face of her husband. *What about "standing strong?"* Clara thought. Hugo had abdicated his role as an example by doing the opposite of what he demanded of their son.

The days that followed were a haze. Telegrams to Friedel, Edith, Rikka, and Aunt Martha, and phone calls to other family members, to the undertaker, to Hugo's lawyer, to Dr. Weiss, and to their family physician, who only came by as a brief formality. She had to go to the city hall in person and sign papers regarding the cause of death. "Heart attack," she wrote as the doctor had instructed. Then she decided to add "due to Nazi persecution, boycotts, and the loss of his business." She didn't dare write "possible suicide," which would be disloyal to Hugo's memory and might trigger a police investigation, but she had at least testified to part of the truth on his death certificate.

The funeral was as pitiful as Edith had described. Certainly, Hugo was buried in a place that would not allow him to rest in peace. All his adult life, Hugo had avoided friendships with Jews and now, of his Aryans friends, only Dr. and Frau Weiss were faithful enough to attend the burial. No other of his countless previous friends and business associates dared to come to the Jewish cemetery. She had noticed the one unfamiliar man standing in the shadows of the nearby trees. Clara now understood he was Charlie, and he was there, not for Hugo, but for Edith.

Later, back at the house, while the meager group of family members shared stories of her husband, she had not noticed Edith's disappearance. She had been concentrating on the task of removing Rikka from her life.

When Rikka stood up from holding court on the sofa and announced she would go to her room for a nap, Clara stopped her. "Rikka, please join me in Hugo's study first. There is an issue we must discuss."

Rikka followed reluctantly, her sister trailing behind. At the door, Clara stayed the sister with a gentle hand on her arm. "Please wait in the parlor," she said. "This does not concern you, and it will go better if Rikka and I can manage quietly on our own."

In preparation for this talk, Clara had rehearsed over and over. She had removed Rikka's special chair from the room leaving no comfortable place for her to sit. Only Hugo's oak desk with its oversized chair and two straight-backed side chairs remained in the study. Clara saw Rikka's face change as she took in the new arrangement. She seemed to sense that it did not bode well for her, and she glared at Clara.

Clara took a deep breath and began what she had practiced. "Cousin Rikka, you have long been a special companion to Hugo, but he no longer needs you and I certainly do not. You came into my home fifteen years ago and stole my husband from me. Now, I am finally able to take back my rightful place."

Rikka tried to interject. "Clara, it was your husband's wish, that I—"

"No! Do not interrupt. I am in charge of my own home again. It is no longer your home. I do not want you here. Not for even one more night."

"Surely, you don't mean to kick me out today. Not on the same day that my cousin has been laid to rest!"

Clara could hear the anger and emotion rising in Rikka's voice, but it did not weaken her resolve. She was determined to do what she should have done years ago. Hugo could no longer stand in her way. "I will give you this afternoon to gather your personal belongings, your clothing, and other personal effects. If you mean to stay in Meiningen tonight, you should call the hotel and see if they have a room for you and your sister."

Rikka's expression was defiant. "There is my dresser and the chaise lounge, my bedding, and the stained-glass lamp, all gifts to me from Hugo. They are mine and I will have them. How do you mean for me to arrange for their removal if I must leave today?"

Clara sighed. She had anticipated this. "What do I care for some items of furniture that my husband gave to his mistress?" She heard Rikka's sharp intake of breath, but the woman did not deny the term. "Mark the items that are yours and send a van to pick them up within the week. I want nothing left here to remind me of your relationship with my husband." She turned and walked toward the door. "I hope never to see you again, Rikka. You are no longer part of my family." Clara walked across the hall and up the stairs to her room. She took her violin out of its case and began to play Mozart's Requiem.

As she remembered this scene now, four years after it happened, she felt pride. But she also felt the shame of having let Rikka dominate her life for all those years. Why had she endured it? Was it the gradual, almost imperceptible, way Rikka had commandeered her rights? Or was it her fear of Hugo and her blind acquiescence to the conventions of marriage? She felt that she had allowed herself to be abused. She would not let this happen to her again.

The sound of Dr. and Frau Weiss returning home for the evening brought Clara back to the present. She closed her eyes and took a deep breath. These memories, like Rikka herself, agitated her. Perhaps reading Edith's diary would help her to calm down again.

July 14, 1935

I will not return to the children's camp. The dressmaking school starts soon. I will go directly to Aschaffenburg. At the funeral, Aunt Martha let me know she had received a letter from Vati the week before he died. He had written that she must watch me closely, especially my mail. She said she took her brother's warning seriously. Seems like my stone remains with me. Vati's reach extends beyond the grave.

July 18, 1935

A van came today to pick up Rikka's belongings. Mutti says she no longer lives here. She has moved to her sister's home, and they plan to emigrate. I didn't even ask where. Wherever she goes—good riddance.

I have been repacking my suitcase. Out go the shorts, sundresses, and walking shoes. In go pretty blouses, skirts, and dresses, especially my wine-colored velvet. A seamstress must dress well. I will be in Aschaffenburg until mid-December. I hope to learn a lot while I'm there. A seamstress job will be more pleasant than working as a nanny. I've had my fill of dirty children's linens.

Herman does not have to return to Gymnasium this fall. He is ecstatic! Cousin Hilda told Mutti about a business school near them that teaches typing and accounting. She says Herman can stay with them and help at their hardware store to earn pocket money while he attends classes.

July 25, 1935

Madame (that's what we call the master seamstress) is a Jewish lady. She started this school last year. It's a small school—only the mistress, two assistant instructors, and a dozen students of varying degrees of Jewishness. We are all here for the same reason. We want to learn to be dressmakers. Madame says dressmakers are needed everywhere but time is of the essence if we want to emigrate. Her classes are intense. She teaches advanced sewing techniques, garment fitting, and pattern making.

I found another student, Marlene, who has agreed to be my letter carrier. Charlie can mail letters to her boardinghouse, and she will bring them to me at school. Marlene is gutsy and likes the idea of being a lover's go-between.

Living with Aunt Martha is unpleasant. I have my cousin Max's old room which is OK. Aunt Martha has never been easy-going and now she is like the Gestapo. She watches my comings and goings and checks the return address on all my mail. She'll only find letters from Mutti!

August 9, 1935

Marlene delivered a letter from Charlie today!!! During lunch break she asked what he wrote, and I read her a little section. But not all! I hope she doesn't get too nosy.

August 18, 1935

I got a letter from Mutti with shocking news. At least it was shocking to me. Before he died, Vati began arrangements to sell our house. Mutti said she had half expected something of the kind. The good news is that Vati's friends, Herr Dr. Weiss and his wife, bought it. They insisted on paying a fair market price even though they could get it much cheaper. Most Jewish homes are snapped up for one-third their value. At least some Germans don't take advantage of our difficult times. But such honest people are the exception.

August 24, 1935

I have two letters from Charlie! They go with me to school tucked into my corset (more secure than my bra!). At night I sleep with them and dream of his kisses.

Last night, I lay wide awake remembering Charlie's caresses. I was jarred out of an imagined kiss when the bedroom door squeaked. Aunt Martha crept in like the spy she is. I didn't dare breathe or move. She went through all the shelves of my cupboard. She flipped the pages of my books. I know she was searching for letters! But they were safe under my pillow. My journal was hidden away under my mattress.

Today during lunch break, I sewed a kind of cummerbund with a pocket. I can wear it under my clothing. Charlie's letters will be safe next to my body day and night.

August 30, 1935

Vati really tried to solve a lot of problems at the end. It's almost like he knew he would die soon.

Mutti wrote that Vati begged Dr. Weiss to consider converting a portion of the house into a small apartment for our family. Now that it's only Mutti, Dr. Weiss has agreed to the idea. He and his wife won't move in until after the apartment is completed. Mutti says they are not in a hurry and have given her a year. They are beyond kind.

English: *Herman is living in Suhl now and attending business classes.*

September 3, 1935

I have four letters from Charlie in my special belt. They keep
me warm at night.

I love dressmaking! I am so busy I forget my loneliness
for hours at a time. I have friends here and real clients
come in to get dresses made. They look through catalogs
and point to what they like. Then we help Madame and
her assistants with the fitting, cutting, and sewing. Mostly
we are making traveling suits for Jewish ladies leaving
Germany. One lady came in and selected wool for a suit.
She and her husband had applied for a Canadian visa.
She returned two weeks later to select a lighter fabric and
ordered a summer frock because now her family will go to
Shanghai. I told her I have a great-uncle who went there a
few months ago.

Besides our work with clients, we must make a dress
for an assigned classmate. It is the end of term project and
without it, Madame says we won't earn a certificate.

Writing in this white book feels a bit childish these days
and I'd rather write to Charlie in what little time I have.

September 15, 1935

Horrible!! Full-page spreads fill the newspapers declaring the
latest Nazi laws. A whole set of new statutes was announced
at the annual rally at Nuremberg. Jews have been stripped
of German citizenship and all the rights of citizens. We are
now only "subjects of the state."

None of us could concentrate today. The newspapers were passed around the workshop. Anger and fear swept the room. When I read the Law for the Defense of German Blood and Honor, I ran out to the balcony and doubled over. I sunk down into a ball against the wrought iron railing. I could not control the great gasps that came from deep inside. I was afraid I would be sick. Marriage and extramarital intercourse (yes, those were the words right in the newspaper) are now forbidden between Jews and German citizens (or related blood—whatever that means). Anyone who breaks this law can be punished by a prison sentence with hard labor. Oh, my darling Charlie! Whatever will happen to us?

There was also nonsense about Jews being forbidden to employ German women under the age of forty-five. I suppose that is to protect young Aryan innocents from licentious Jewish men. I thought of Cook. Luckily, she is fifty, so Mutti won't lose her right away.

When I was able to pull myself together, I went back into the workroom. The girls were arguing about who was a Jew and who wasn't. One girl said her mother was Aryan and she had been baptized a Catholic as a baby. She was sure the laws wouldn't apply to her. She sounded a bit smug.

When Marlene saw my red eyes, she looked scared. She asked me in a low voice if Charlie is an Aryan.

The law doesn't say anything about letter carriers, I told her. I begged her not to desert me and assured her that Charlie is only my friend. We have done nothing that would be illegal. Not yet, anyway.

Finally, Madame stopped all the speculation. She told us getting the certificate was imperative now. We should all think seriously about leaving Germany. She even suggested that if we stayed, there was a silver lining. Jewish families would need to hire Jewish maids and cooks and seamstresses now that they could no longer employ German girls. I couldn't help but think that Jews are poorer every day, so few will be hiring anyone. Madame probably wanted to give us a ray of hope, but her comment seemed a bit tasteless.

October 3, 1935

Two letters from Charlie. The first dated September 16 and another the next week, after he got my hysterical letter. He promised that no law can make him stop loving me. His words are salve to my broken heart. You have become half of me and I'm not a whole human without you, he wrote. Wow!

Charlie says we need to be careful now wherever we are, not just in Meiningen. He thinks Mutti might help us meet. I need to remind him how dangerous that would be for her. He must forget that idea. I would never ask her to be part of our dangerous secret.

A sense of relief flooded through Clara as she read this entry. Perhaps Edith had begun to learn caution. Her daughter's secrecy, a result of Hugo's strictures, had become a survival asset. Clara was grateful that she had considered her mother's safety, too. It was true that, though the Weiss family were friends who went out of their way to provide Clara a safe place to live, their attitude could have easily changed if she had helped a mixed, Aryan-Jewish couple, even if half that couple was her own daughter. Thankfully, Edith had resisted asking her mother for help. As a result, for over three years Clara continued to enjoy the unusual privilege of living openly in an Aryan home, protected by her friends.

⚬

October 15, 1935

Once this journal had a few lighthearted entries. When I first met Charlie. When I was the fashion devil. These days it feels more like a chronicle of life falling into ruins.

My partner for the dress project has left for France. Her mother is Aunt Martha's friend. Aunt says they refused to stay in Germany as non-citizens. Her friend was eager to go, saying they would not wait until their passports were ripped from them. Naturally, Aunt doesn't think that can ever happen.

Now that I am without a sewing partner, I asked Madame what I should do with the fabric I had already cut out. Her answer was short. Find another partner and remodel the dress. Madame is as nervous as everyone else, which makes her impatient with what she calls inconsequential problems. Now Marlene will get two dresses. That's the best way for me to thank her for passing me Charlie's letters.

November 15, 1935

The girls from mixed families can stop wondering if the
September laws apply to them. It's all been spelled out in
an adjunct issued yesterday. There are even charts in the
newspapers! Naturally, I'm a Jew. Lack of religious belief
means nothing. All four of my grandparents were Jewish by
blood and were part of a Jewish community. That sets my
fate in Nazi stone. Anyway, I've had no doubt regarding my
status since I was forbidden to take the Abitur exams.

Our poor little Catholic girl is now officially and legally
classified as a Jewish Mischling of the first degree. It's
better than being a full Jew, though the term Mischling is a
derogatory word that means half-breed. But watch out! If she
marries a Jewish man, she will automatically be demoted to
being a full Jew and immediately lose her citizenship. We told
her to stay away from cute Jewish boys! Madelene, whose
widowed, half-Jewish mother raised her alone after her Jewish
father was killed in the last war is naturally fully Jewish like
me. Three Jewish grandparents is all it takes. The Nazis are
meticulous; they've made a rule for every possibility.

December 8, 1935

Charlie constantly declares his love for me, though now he
puts it in code. He writes I saw two butterflies kissing, and
I know that means he loves me. I say nothing about love
or kisses or missing him in my letters. My code words are
"remember the daisy." But I worry someone might figure out

what we mean. I keep imagining my Charlie in front of a court of law, proudly declaring his love for me. He would surely end up in prison moving rocks. I couldn't bear that, even if I were piling stones right next to him. But the Nazis would never allow us to be imprisoned together. The Jewess would be separated from her lover. All this gives me nightmares.

My seamstress days will soon be over. I will be home in Meiningen with what's left of my family (and Charlie!) in time for the Christmas holiday.

December 18, 1935

I am home. I received my seamstress assistant certificate, though there was no graduation ceremony. We all thanked Madame, wished each other luck, and hurried home. Madame is closing the school and moving to Paris where she has been offered a job in one of the fashion ateliers.

Madame was right about Jewish families looking for Jewish nannies. I've found a job in Erfurt through an ad in the Jewish newspaper. Starting January 1, I will be caring for two boys whose Aryan nanny had to leave. I warned Frau Klein that I don't know how long I will be able to stay. She says she fully understands but right now they are desperate.

Mutti is going through papers and trinkets, children's clothing no longer used, and labeling furniture with tags that say, "Sell", "Keep," or "?". I'm quite proud of how Mutti is managing on her own. I see an independent quality emerging. She is energized by her ability to make decisions without looking over her shoulder to see what Vati or Rikka will say. I wish I had known this side of her earlier. She will manage fine if I leave for England soon. Now it is only my love for Charlie that keeps me here.

December 25, 1935

Christmas dinner was a sad gathering with only Mutti, Herman, and me seated at the dining table. We nibbled on goose wings, red cabbage, and potatoes. We asked Cook to join us for dessert, and she emerged from the kitchen carrying a frosted stollen on Mutti's crystal platter. The sweet cake, redolent with spices, nuggets of dried fruits and nuts dotting each slice, cheered us up. The yeasty taste reminded me of past holidays. I told the story of finding coal in my stocking when I was ten and later, a new doll under the Christmas tree. This year, there is no decorated tree in the parlor, yet Herman insisted we sing "O Tannenbaum" holding hands around the dinner table.

CHAPTER 9

The End Begins

December 28, 1935

This morning, before Herman returned to Suhl, an uninvited guest came to the house. My brother heard the loud knocking first and hurried to the door. I was right behind him, half hoping it was Charlie but knowing it couldn't be. An SS officer was on our front porch. He stood like an apparition dressed in a full, black uniform. The two crooked lightning bolt symbols on his collar glinted in the winter sunlight. He had come to steal Mutti's piano!

My legs shook uncontrollably the entire time he was in the house. He ordered Mutti to have everything ready to be picked up by a van in three days' time. When he left, Mutti turned to her beloved piano, sat down, and began to play so fiercely I worried she would crack the keys.

Clara could feel her blood pressure rise as she remembered the SS officer who had requisitioned her beloved piano. They called it requisition, but, in reality, it was theft.

She had heard the loud knock and had walked toward the entry, but Herman, younger and faster, opened the door while she still stood halfway between the salon and the vestibule.

The officer strode into their home without an invitation. "I've come to see Frau Lang," he declared, and his cold eyes settled on her.

Clara nodded. "I am Frau Lang," she said. "How can I help you, sir?" She hoped he did not notice how her hands shook.

"Where's your piano?" he asked.

"Just in here. In the salon." Clara gestured toward the room that was the heart of their home.

The man strode forward, past Clara standing in the wide entry to the salon, his eagle glance inspecting the paintings on the wall as he went. Herman and Edith trailed several paces behind, unwilling to leave their mother alone with an SS officer. In the salon, Clara watched in dread as he ran his fingers over the glossy finish of her grand piano.

The officer's eyes turned hard. He stood with his legs spread and his hands behind his back as Hugo used to do. He had not removed his hat when he came inside, and he didn't take it off now. Though he had no horse and had arrived in a car, he carried a riding crop and, when he began to talk, he slapped it against his leg. Clara found him terrifying, but she was determined to appear calm. He would not see her fear.

"I understand you need to get rid of this piano," he said, his voice imperious.

Clara straightened her back. "No, sir," she said. "The piano is not for sale." She tried to control the quaver in her voice.

The SS man ignored her words and continued to talk. He knew the house had recently been sold. "Wherever you go now," he said, "a widowed Jewess will have no room for a grand piano."

Clara's legs felt like jelly, and she made an effort not to wobble. She absolutely refused to faint. She straightened her back and stood as tall as her almost one and a half meters allowed. "I will keep my piano for now," she said. "Though the house is sold, the new owners will not move in for another six months. I will not sell my piano before then. Perhaps you would like to come back in June or July to check if I am willing to sell then."

"You are mistaken, Frau Lang! I will have the piano now. My wife wants to learn to play." He slapped his riding crop against his boot and continued. "A van will pick up the piano on the afternoon of December 31. It will be a lovely New Year's surprise for her." He looked around and appraised the room. His fingers caressed the cloisonné vase filled with pine branches and holly berries that stood on the lid of the piano, and he nudged the oriental carpet underneath with his crop. "I will direct the movers to get the whole ensemble," he said. "Make sure everything is prepared for transport in three days." With two fingers, as if it were trash, he lifted Hugo's picture off the piano and dropped it onto the armchair nearby. "You can keep the photo," he said, and a sneer twisted his mouth.

Clara realized there had been no offer of money and there would be none. The SS man stalked toward the front door without turning his head or closing the door as he left.

Edith and Herman watched him go, holding each other back as he strode past them. They watched the officer get into the back of a black sedan in the drive. As soon as the car was out of the gate, Herman wrenched free from his sister's arms and ran. Clara heard the loud slam of the back door as he left the house.

Edith stood, seemingly immovable.

"We can relax now, darling," Clara said. "He's gone." She turned and walked to her piano, her fingers caressing its shiny surface. She sat on the bench and began to play a powerful and dramatic coda from one of Beethoven's symphonies.

Edith gently picked up her father's picture and set it back on the piano. Without a word to her mother, she turned and climbed the grand staircase. She stayed in her room and did not come down for dinner. Herman was gone for three hours and missed his train to Suhl.

Clara shuddered at the memory of that day. She had been thankful that both Herman and Edith would be gone before the SS van arrived.

∾⌒

December 29, 1935

Glory, Glory! A day with Charlie. We have not seen each other since my father's funeral!

I saw his tall figure as I walked across the snow-covered

English Garden. He waited at the door of the old stone chapel and pulled me inside. He tucked my hands into the warm spaces under his arms. My breath came out in misty clouds, but Charlie soon warmed my lips. I was frantic to make up for all those months without his kisses.

Charlie laughed at me. Slow down, he said. We have all day and need to find someplace warm. Nowhere in Meiningen will be safe from prying eyes. Charlie declared we must go to a place where no one knows us. My blond braids will protect me.

At the station, I sat on a bench in the waiting room while Charlie checked the schedule. I wrapped my woolen scarf around my head and looked at the floor. Soon Charlie returned. He didn't speak, but, right in front of me, he stumbled. He reached out to steady himself on the bench where I sat. Without looking at me, he dropped a ticket on the seat. I was quick to grab it up and hurried to the public lavatory. A round-trip ticket to Eisenach! A long train ride each way and a space of three hours in between!

We had to act like strangers. I lingered in the WC and near the newsstand. Charlie sat in the waiting room, his face hidden by a newspaper. When the train came, we boarded separately. After the train was well out of the station, Charlie came forward and sat down next to me. Good morning, Fräulein, he said. May I sit here? We were like spies in an espionage movie.

It was lovely to be with Charlie again. But I was so nervous! I kept checking at every stop to see if any new passengers were in uniform. We held hands under our spreading coats. At Eisenach, we ducked into the first restaurant near the station.

Once we settled in a booth, Charlie pushed a narrow box wrapped in gold paper across the table. Inside was a dainty gold locket on a chain. My heart skipped a beat to see it. It was oval with delicate scrolling decoration. Inside, he had fitted a tiny piece of paper with a heart drawn in red ink. He told me he feared a picture of him might be dangerous, but he wanted me to know I had his heart. He fastened the locket around my neck and tucked it under my sweater. Beneath the table, he caressed my fingers with his own.

The waitress told us how to find the town cinema. It was the only place we could hope for some privacy. In the dark, with only the flickering light from the screen, we felt safe enough to kiss. I blocked out the newsreel with its marching soldiers and declarations that the race defilement laws would save German blood from pollution. The film was a story of a Nazi spy hero. I whispered in Charlie's ear that we could learn some good tips on being secretive. A woman sitting nearby hissed for us to be quiet. I heard her mutter that we should be ashamed, kissing in public. What a Nazi crone! We felt so uncomfortable that we left before the film ended.

On the first half of the ride back, we sat with our heads together. We both knew the next months would be difficult. It's too dangerous to meet in Meiningen, or anywhere we might be recognized. Finally, when we no longer needed to hide from my father, we must hide from the German police.

I don't want to jeopardize my new employers, so Erfurt is out, too.

Charlie worried our coded letters could be deciphered. Phone calls would be risky as, most likely, the police listen in. Telegrams could be a problem for the same reason. We decided we would still write regular letters, but very carefully. To make matters worse, Charlie will have an intense work schedule until the summer. We have arranged a code that he will send me by telegram if he has a free Saturday. Two travelers by chance at the same village train station at noon. One thing we know . . . neither of us is prepared to stop being in love!

By the time the train pulled into the Meiningen station, we sat in separate cars. Tomorrow morning, I travel to Erfurt and begin my new job.

This is the last page of my pretty, gilt-edged diary. I still have the notebook my brother gave me as a goodbye gift, and it will make a fine journal. Writing no longer feels childish to me. I need to keep a record of my love . . . and of the terrible changes!

English: *I'm glad I won't be around when Mutti's piano is hauled away.*

Clara closed the white diary and rubbed its smooth cover. She imagined that she was stroking Edith's cheek. It seemed strange now that only two days ago she had seen her daughter as little more than an affectionate and spirited young woman who sometimes made poor decisions. She had not understood the plethora of things her daughter had seen and experienced. As mother and daughter, they had both allowed too many things to go unspoken. After reading the diary, Clara had a better understanding. Edith was more than simply impulsive. She was brave, emotional, open-hearted, determined, and, yes, funny. She was no longer simply a daughter to be loved unconditionally. Clara had glimpsed a strong and passionate young woman, a person of immense value, a mentor even, and someone who might become her confidante.

Clara laid down the diary and picked up the plain blue notebook. Inside, the pages were ruled, like a school essay book. The first page held a poem in her eldest son's handwriting. Though it was humorous, seeing it brought tears to her eyes. The next pages were filled with Edith's slanting cursive. Clara knew 1936 would be a difficult year to read about and the pages would end abruptly.

<hr>

January 4, 1936

The Kleins are wonderful people to work for, but like all Jewish families these days, they live under storm clouds.

The two boys are cute and well-behaved, though they miss their other nanny and tell me what she would do and how I must do the same. Werner is seven and quite serious. He used to attend the city school, but his mother says he came home crying every day and was too nervous to learn to read. Now he goes to a new Jewish school and is finally learning. Engle is five and is truly an angel, the same as his name. He goes to kindergarten at the same school two mornings a week.

Frau Klein is more a friend than a boss. Her husband is an orthopedic surgeon at the city hospital. They are both consumed with arrangements to emigrate. Dr. Klein applied for a work-study visa to England as a physician, but he was declined. They also applied to the United States but have given up hope that an American visa will arrive in time. Frau Klein has several cousins who live in Pretoria. So, they have applied for visas to South Africa, which they hope will be faster. I've told Frau Klein that I'm considering going to England, but I need to get a UK work permit, which is easier with an actual job offer. She encourages me to start the process immediately.

I am torn. I feel like two people, one who wants to stay and one who wants to flee. When I'm not reading Charlie's letters, I mostly want to flee. Most nights when I lay in my bed alone, I want to weep. Our love has been declared forbidden. It is too cruel!

January 6, 1936

Mutti sounds almost gleeful in her latest letter. She described how she "prepared" the piano for the movers. She is a bit of a resister in her own quiet way! I am proud of her. Where was this strong Mutti when Rikka was around? I could have used her then. But I ripped up her letter. If the house is raided, always a possibility these days, a letter like that might send her to prison. I must tell her to be more careful!

Clara looked up from the blue notebook. The last few lines had hit like a blow to her chest. Had she failed her daughter all those years? Had she been a poor model of womanhood? There had always been love between them, but it seemed Edith had reached adulthood before she could say she was proud of her mother.

Edith had carefully omitted any details of what her mother had written in the letter. Clara remembered what she had done and how elated she had felt. Without a thought, she had written everything to her daughter.

The morning before the van was to arrive, Clara had carefully cut two of the piano cords—one bass string and one treble string—and loosened a few tuning pins. She did not dare disturb more. It was important for the instrument to seem okay the first time it was played. Next, she had spilled ink on the oriental carpet so there was a dark, uneven shape and few splashes of black near the fringe. Finally, she had tapped the bottom of her beautiful vase with a hammer until a crack appeared and two pieces of enamel fell out.

When the van arrived, the stupid sergeant who came with it to inspect the goods noticed nothing amiss.

The memory of what she had written in that long-ago letter filled her with fear and shock. How had she dared to write so boldly of her vandalism of the piano? She would never write such words now. She was sure there were watchers everywhere. Letters written innocently by Jews had occasionally led to arrest and imprisonment. Her words could have gotten her arrested even in 1936. Now, three years later, she knew enough to be more cautious.

They had all written freely back then. In earlier diary entries, Edith had been casual about her criticism of the Reich and had mentioned things Charlie told her about his negative attitude toward the Nazi Party. Besides that, there was the issue of her daughter and Charlie, an Aryan man, continuing their romantic relationship even after the Nuremberg Laws came into effect. It was clear to Clara that Edith was right. When she finished reading the diary and the letters, she must burn them both to ashes. It would be too dangerous to do otherwise.

Clara picked up the notebook to finish the chore she had taken on.

January 23, 1936

I have written to Hilda Myer and asked if she knows an address where I can write Gerti in England.

Germany is getting worse every day. If Charlie and I cannot be together . . . If we are forbidden to marry, I must leave. I can only hope Germany will come to its senses before Charlie forgets me.

I have my passport still and Germans don't need visas for England. But I must have a work permit to live in Britain and earn wages. The Nazis want Jews to leave Germany, but first they steal all our money, turning even the richest into penniless immigrants. I'll need a job to survive. I cross my fingers that Gerti knows a family who might hire me.

February 20, 1936

Yea! I got a letter from Gerti! She is working for a wealthy family in London where she is the downstairs maid. She says the upstairs maid is Lithuanian, the butler and the housekeeper are Scottish, and the cook is German (but not a Nazi, Gerti promises).

Her employers need what they call an au pair . . . not a nanny exactly, she said. I would be expected to help with the children (there are two girls, ages eleven and thirteen) and assist the housekeeper occasionally, especially before parties and such. She said the job would only be for room and board and a few shillings of pocket money. I think it's a good start. Gerti has recommended me! The family asked me to write with my qualifications and send a small photo. If they like my letter, they will apply for a work permit for me.

Frau Klein, who went to school in England as a girl, will help me with the letter, though it might mean she will lose me.

March 3, 1936

The Klein's home is in upheaval!

Dr. Klein returned from the hospital in the middle of the afternoon. He has been fired from his position as head of orthopedic surgery. In fact, he will no longer be allowed to practice at the hospital. A new law says no Jewish medical doctors can practice at government hospitals!

Doctor and Frau Klein have closed themselves into his study. Their voices seep out from under the door, and the boys know something is wrong. I suggested a walk to the park, but Warner refused to leave the house. We spent the rest of the day in the nursery playing Chinese checkers. Engle is too young to understand the logistics of the game, but he likes jumping the marbles around the star-shaped board.

After the boys were in bed, Frau Klein explained everything to me. Dr. Klein will turn his study and the parlor into an office to see patients. She said he studied to be an internist in medical school before he changed to orthopedics. He can easily switch back to treating stomach ailments and kidney stones. She will be redoubling her efforts to find a place where they can immigrate. She encouraged me to make plans to leave Germany as soon as possible. Meanwhile, we must keep the boys quiet when patients are in the house.

March 10, 1936

I got a telegram from the Atkinsons in London. They want me! They said to send back if I accept, and they will start the paperwork for my permit. I telegrammed one word: Yes!

March 15, 1936

Another telegram. Permit started.

The Kleins are now taking French classes three evenings a week. Maybe they will go to France

March 23, 1936

A long letter from Mrs. Atkinson. The permit process could take a month, but her husband has requested that it be expedited. She seems to believe he has influence with the labor board. They will arrange my transportation. She wants me to start work by the end of April.

I am excited. I can't wait to leave this dreadful country! Except for Charlie. I must see him one more time. It's been almost three months!

April 4, 1936

I am back and forth, up and down. The boys are skittish with my mood swings and all the changes. Doctor is short-tempered, sitting in his home office all day. Patients come only in fits and drabs. Soon Frau Klein will be unable to pay me. I will have to leave.

I have been thinking a lot about Charlie. He is madly working to help finish up the firm's part of the Olympic complex. If I want to see him before I leave, I must go to Berlin.

Why did I turn Charlie away and insist on remaining a virgin? I was so naive! I'm probably one of the few girls my age who is still innocent. In her letter, Gerti hinted she is sleeping with her Swedish boyfriend. If I can get to Berlin, I must convince Charlie. If only it weren't a crime now! What a fool I've been!

I will be twenty soon. Woman enough to decide what to do with my own body. He is my first love! He MUST be my first lover. I need that memory before my life changes forever.

April 15, 1936

Everything—I mean everything—went wrong last weekend. I wanted to surprise him. A childish idea that backfired.

And I chose the worst weekend to go to Berlin! It was Easter and Charlie was in Meiningen! It never occurred to me that Charlie would go home without telling me. Seems his father had to have surgery and was in the hospital. He managed to get off work because of the holiday and his father's illness.

When I got to his apartment in Berlin, his landlady offered to let me stay in Charlie's rooms until he returned on Sunday evening. She guessed I was the young lady he wrote to so often and said it was time he got engaged to such a pretty, German girl.

I stayed, though I was constantly nervous. The busybody landlady kept coming in to talk to me. Did I want dinner? Would I join her for tea? She assumed I was Aryan, but I felt like I had the word Jewess tattooed on my forehead. Sunday afternoon came and went. Still no Charlie. The landlady was concerned, and I was scared to stay with her any longer. What if Charlie didn't return? What if the landlady realized I was Jewish?

I called my older cousin Lisa, who lives in Berlin. It was a risk, but I hoped she wouldn't ask questions. She's only half-Jewish (now a Mischling) and she lives alone above a little bookstore she owns. Of course, when she realized I was in Berlin, she insisted I come to stay with her. In the evening, I telephoned Charlie's landlady. She said Charlie had called to say his father would be coming home the next day and he would stay to help get him settled. He was upset when she told him I had been there. He told her that if she heard from me again, she must tell me to stay until he returned.

Lisa heard me crying and I blurted out everything about Charlie. I thought she would understand. I was so wrong! She called me crazy and a little fool. Didn't I realize that society and its rules were different now from when her parents fell in love? She demanded that I return to the Kleins the next morning. She declared that if I left during the night, she would call my mother and maybe even the police. I didn't believe that last bit, but I didn't want Mutti to worry, so I did what Lisa demanded.

In the morning, she took me to the station, bought a ticket to Erfurt, and watched as the train inched out of the Bahnhof. I jumped off at the next stop. I phoned Frau Klein to say I had an appointment at the British Embassy in two days and needed to stay on. It was a lie, but I didn't care. I took the tram back into the city and found a hotel where I rented a room. When I called the landlady, she said Charlie had phoned only moments before. He was on his way back to Berlin on the midnight train! I told her I would come by the first thing in the morning and to please put a note in Charlie's room that I would be there before he went to work.

I barely slept. I was at Charlie's place before 7:00 in the morning. Charlie gave me a big hug right in front of the landlady and then led me inside his rooms. He wanted to spend the day with me. He had phoned his employer and told the boss he was still in Meiningen.

He took me to Grunewald Park. We wandered through the trees and found a café for coffee and pastries.

When I told Charlie I had only been to Berlin once before when I was about eight, he said we should go to Potsdam. It would be peaceful there and we could relax. On the tram, we passed near Charlottenburg. He pointed through the trees at the almost finished Olympic buildings and the half-built stadium. He seemed proud to be part of the project. But he said he would be fired if anyone found out he was skipping work to be with me. I kissed his cheek to let him know I appreciated the risk. The people on the tram smiled to see happy lovers. I bet they wouldn't smile if they knew I was Jewish.

In Potsdam, we walked all around the Sanssouci Palace, through the gardens and around one of the lakes. All the time, I was talking. First, I told him about my job in London and that I would be leaving before the end of April. He hugged me tightly and said of course I must go. England would be safer for me. He would stay loyal until my return, no matter how long it took. Maybe he could even visit me there. Finally, I told him I was finished with being a little girl who thought virginity was important. I was a woman now and I wanted to make love to him. I never should have waited so long.

Charlie protested. It was OK. He didn't mind waiting until we could marry. He didn't want to hurt me. It was too dangerous, especially now. But I kept talking. I declared I would be devastated if he didn't agree to make love to me. I even had a room in a hotel. I longed to lie naked next to him. Please, please, you must make love to me before I leave for England, I begged. I declared that I wouldn't be able to bear it if he didn't. I even got down on my knees in Sanssouci Park to beg him. Finally, he agreed. Yes, he agreed! We laughed all the way to the tram lines. He kept his arm around my waist the whole time we rode toward the city. I felt wonderfully free being in Berlin about to make love to the best man on earth. My mood was like the name of the place . . . Sanssouci— without worries—carefree. Carefree! What a joke!

When we got to the hotel, I went to the desk to get my key. Charlie followed me to the elevator. Suddenly the quiet lobby echoed with the words, Wait, Fräulein. Stop! The clerk came out from behind the counter and hurried toward us. Whatever did he want? He seemed embarrassed as he explained that Charlie couldn't go to the room with me. He would have to wait in the lobby.

At first, I couldn't understand what he meant. Why must he wait? I had paid for the room. I needed his help. He was my tutor, and I needed to study. Good lies, I thought. But not good enough.

The clerk was very formal. Regrettably, he informed me, the management does not allow men on my floor. I had rented a single room on the ladies-only floor! The clerk glared at me and then at Charlie. In a loud voice anyone in the lobby could hear he said, this is not a brothel! I stood speechless. I was so angry! Tears stung my eyes. Disappointment engulfed me.

Charlie stayed composed. He asked if there was another room available, a double room perhaps, another floor.

But the clerk's voice was haughty. He informed Charlie that every room was booked. Besides, he told us, as my papers indicated I was a Hebrew, unless Charlie carried Jewish documentation, he could not allow us to share a room. On pain of arrest, he said. I was humiliated! I will not stay here, I declared and ducked into the elevator when the doors opened.

While Charlie waited downstairs, I went to the room and grabbed my valise, stuffing my pretty nightie underneath my other clothes. I returned the key to the clerk and turned to leave. Wait, he said again. He told me I owed for that night as it was after check-out time. I slapped down the required marks and turned my back on him. Charlie calmly took my suitcase, and we walked arm in arm out the door.

All my pleading had been for nothing. I felt totally stupid—like a child. We were both disillusioned. The feeling of romance evaporated into mist. Neither of us had the strength to look for another hotel in the busy city. The clerk's warning frightened us, too. It seemed we had nowhere we could go. By unspoken agreement, we headed to the train station where I bought a ticket on the next train to Erfurt.

We spent our last hour together in the darkest corner we could find, huddled against a stone column. Charlie tried to distract me. He pointed out how all the Nazi, antisemitic posters had been taken down to impress the many foreigners who would soon be arriving for the Olympics. He thinks that maybe the games this summer will turn the country around. Hitler even agreed to let Negro and Jewish athletes compete. But I doubted it would make a difference in the long run. I don't give two figs for the Olympics or Hitler right now, I retorted. I only wanted him to hold me.

Charlie wrapped his long arms around my shoulders and kissed my forehead and my neck. His breath brushed my ear as he spoke words of reassurance. Everything would be OK. Our love would weather the separation. He said that it was God's will.

I was so unhappy that I forgot Charlie's religious beliefs. I lashed out that I didn't believe in God and that, if there is a God, he is ever so cruel. When I saw the pain in Charlie's eyes, I felt bad. But I refused to take it back. Still, he repeated over and over that he loved me and would wait for me until Germany regained its sanity.

I told him, Don't wait! This is the end. I am leaving the country. You must forget me! I shouted. I meant it, too. He's thirty-three! He will be an old man before Hitler dies. How could I ask him to wait for years, to give up any chance of family and happiness? I told him I would start fresh in England, and he must not wait. He must make a life for himself. That is what I intended to do. My face was wet with tears and the front of Charlie's jacket was soaked from my weeping. He touched the locket I wore under my blouse and said I must remember his heart is always with me, no matter what happens. Those were his last words to me.

When it was time to board the train, he lifted my bag to the top step and grabbed my hand one last time. As the train began to slowly move forward, he lifted his hand and placed it on his heart.

I found a window seat and peered through the glass. Charlie was on the platform, waving and waving until I could no longer see him.

The final thing that went wrong . . . the Kleins were full asleep when I arrived. I had to bang on the front door of the darkened house. Dr. Klein was paralyzed with fear when he opened the door. He stood in his pajamas, his robe untied. His shoulders slumped with relief when he saw it was only me. He let me in without a word and relocked the door.

I'm exhausted from reliving the most terrible days of my life. My fingers ache from writing and my heart aches from loss. I think this is the longest entry in my journal, and it may be the last.

CHAPTER 10

A Möbius

CLARA PUT DOWN EDITH'S diary and cradled it in her lap. She had read for so many hours her eyes ached, and she rubbed the bridge of her nose. Had her daughter been wanton to want one night of love with this man who obviously adored her? She knew that as a mother, she should be shocked, but she was not. She realized that she was sad for Edith. Perhaps a last night of intimacy and pleasure would have made Edith less eager to jump into the arms of the Englishman she would meet later.

Clara knew her own longings colored her response. Like Edith, she must leave Germany. Like Edith, she hesitated because of a man. Her new relationship with Albert was too sweet to give up and she longed for that special night her daughter had missed. She wondered if Albert would take convincing like Charlie had. Would she, too, have to beg? Their relationship had moved quite quickly from friendship into something more. Perhaps it was the times, days filled with uncertainty and fear for the future, that allowed her daughter and herself to feel so deeply. She realized that she, too, was eager to abandon her long-held ideals of chastity.

After the first chamber music meeting, Clara had been to four more music evenings, and each time, Albert insisted on escorting her home. On the second evening, he called his friend again, but two weeks later the group broke up earlier than usual and he suggested they walk.

The April evening was mild, the sky was clear and speckled with stars. A full moon lit the streets with silver. Albert held her hand the whole way.

"Even on this lovely spring evening, you will be cold by the time we arrive at your door if I don't keep your fingers warm," he said with a chuckle. "If only I could hold both your hands at the same time and still walk."

Clara had to smile at the image of Albert trying to walk while holding both her hands. Would he walk behind her, kissing her neck as they passed into a shadowy space? Or would he have to walk in front of her, walking backward so he could face her as he talked? No, that way he would surely trip.

And they did talk. The walk through the streets of Meiningen could be drawn out to last almost an hour—an hour that Clara came to treasure. There was much to share, so much to know about each other. They had both lived a full life—years and years before they even knew of each other's existence.

Albert told her how he and Dr. Weiss had been gymnasium friends and had gone to university together. When they had both decided to study medicine, they found themselves together again in Berlin.

"I fell in love with a girl there, too," he said. "She was the daughter of one of my professors. She was beautiful and kind and radiant with smiles, and I married her as soon as her father allowed me." Albert was subdued as he continued. "Sadly, our lighthearted days did not last long. We tried to have children, but God saw fit to withhold that blessing. Perhaps he does know best. When Emily was only thirty-two, she was diagnosed with cervical cancer. Her suffering lasted less than a year."

Clara murmured her sorrow for him. Albert explained how the experience had led him to study gynecology and turn to that specialty.

"Perhaps," he added, "my blessed Emily, led me to you." He told her how he had stayed in Berlin, stayed in touch with his in-laws, and worked at the city hospital as head of gynecology. When he was fired in 1936, he had established a private practice, and many women patients continued to see him. But gradually his patient list shrank. Last year, when the law restricted him from treating Aryan patients, he decided to move home to Meiningen and was pleased to discover that his gymnasium and medical school friend lived and practiced in their hometown.

"Was it difficult to leave your practice and all your friends in Berlin?" she'd asked.

"No, not like you'd expect," he said. "By that time, all my patients had left, most of my friends had vanished, and my in-laws were packing to leave Germany. Besides, my mother needed me. My stepfather had recently passed. My own father died when I was five, and my stepfather was the man who raised me. He was a kind man, and I loved him. My mother and I could mourn together. And as you see, her health is fragile. As we know, getting an Aryan girl to help is no longer allowed. And Jewish women who might be willing to care for an old woman are all emigrating. Eleanor does what she can. Mother adores her, but even she is seeking a way to leave. She is the guardian of her younger brother and must think of his safety."

"What about you, Albert? Do you think of emigrating? Moving to a country where you can fully practice medicine again?"

He shook his head. "I do think of it. I can't deny that. I have made applications and am on the waiting list for the United States. I have a number with six digits!" He laughed. "I'll be seventy before those numbers come up. Anyway, my mother needs me. I am her only child. She has no one else. As a doctor, I know her life is nearing its end. Moving now would disrupt her final days. And I will not leave her to die alone." He sighed. "Perhaps a few months, a half-year at most. Then I will leave if I can find a place that will accept me."

Clara was touched by Albert's honesty. He did not mind sharing his vulnerable side. But he could also be funny in an endearing way. Perhaps it was his sense of humor that attracted her most. And he had that wonderful doctor's trick of listening fully, holding her hands in both of his.

For her part, Clara shared stories of her childhood in the luxury of her Nuremburg family home. Her father was the heir to a family of wealthy bankers who moved with the elite, and her mother's family was even more highly placed in the Jewish community. Growing up, she and her sisters and brothers lacked for nothing. Her uncles were friends of the literati and intellectuals.

She was encouraged to study music and go to university. She had been nurtured by a close family of aunts and uncles, cousins, and nine siblings, including three older brothers and six sisters, four older and two younger. Albert was in awe of such an ample childhood.

"It must have been wonderful," he said. "I was always alone as a child."

"All my brothers are more than ten years older than I, almost adults by the time I was in grammar school. My three older sisters were kind, but they were preoccupied with their own lives. We three younger girls were inseparable. We became a bit of a sisters' club. We all went together to boarding school in Switzerland where we learned to ski and speak French."

He asked where her sisters and brothers were now. She told him about her oldest brother moving to London as a young man, even before the Great War, and how she had brothers and sisters scattered around the world—London, New York, Chicago, even Paraguay and Brazil. They had all emigrated. She was the last of her family remaining in Germany.

Clara found it easy to tell him troubling and intimate stories when they were walking side by side. That was how she revealed her imperfect marriage and the intrusion of Rikka. It was while they walked that she told him about the days after Kristallnacht when Herman hid in her apartment. Albert explained how he had escaped arrest because he had gone that morning to consult with Dr. Weiss about a sick child he was treating. He had stayed for two days in the doctor's basement and sent a message to Eleanor to check on his mother. It was funny to think now how close they had been during those three fearful days, he cowering in the basement and sleeping in the back seat of his friend's Opel Olympia and Clara on the second floor protecting her youngest son.

But they didn't talk only about their past. They shared their love of music, especially the Romantic composers like Brahms, Liszt, and Chopin. They talked of books, and sometimes, they talked of their plans. Albert encouraged her to go to England to be with Edith and Herman and her brother.

"But I'll miss you when you're gone," he always added. "I am fully content when we are together."

When they parted, it was always close to, or after nine, the hour when Meiningen's evening curfew for Jews began. She worried that he would not make it back without being spotted by a policeman or a group of roving SA men.

"Don't worry," he said. "I'll show them my doctor's papers and say I was visiting a patient."

The last time they had been together, a few days before Edith's visit, he had looked out the window of his apartment at the dry street and the clear sky.

"April showers," he said and, as they left, he had grabbed his umbrella from the stand near the door.

Clara laughed. "The sky seems wonderfully clear to me," she said.

"Nevertheless, I'll bring my umbrella in case we need it."

She couldn't fathom why he was in such a gay mood about the possibility of rain. But he was right, they did need it. When they got to the alley near the mill ditch, a place where they often lingered, he opened his umbrella and held it between where they stood and the sidewalk. Albert put his free arm around her waist and eased her toward him. For a heartbeat they paused, their eyes and lips so close Clara could feel his breath on her cheeks.

"May I?" His voice was tender. His lips were the same. The kiss lingered and when he released her, she was breathless. "I've been wanting to do that for days and days," he said.

"Please, again," she whispered.

It was not far from there to her house, but on the front porch he opened his umbrella again and between the wide black circle and the heavy oaken door, they kissed a second time.

"I will remember your lips in my dreams," he said. "Enjoy your visit with your daughter. I'll see you in two weeks. Yes?"

Clara nodded and slipped into the house. She couldn't wait until she was upstairs. This was one night she didn't want to run into the doctor or Frau Wiess in the hall. When she closed her door behind her, she leaned against it and let out her breath. She had never felt like this before. Never. Not even on her honeymoon. She remembered thinking, *So this is what falling in love is like.*

Now it was quite late. She set Edith's notebook on the side table. The cuckoo bird had chimed twice more while she read and daydreamed. Clara was exhausted. There was only one more diary entry to read. Then she would go to bed. Charlie's letters would have to wait until the morning.

April 27, 1936   One last entry and then into hiding!

My bags are packed. I am in Meiningen and tomorrow I will catch the train to Frankfurt. From there to Calais in France.

Mrs. Atkinson sent tickets for the ferry and the London train, as well as the actual work permit, which is secure in my purse next to my passport. I am nervous and excited and scared, too.

My brother Fred has written one of his infrequent letters to Mutti. He will leave Chicago, he says. He wrote that he refuses to endure another sweltering summer or freezing winter in Chicago sitting on a stool in the basement writing letters in answer to customer complaints. The orange groves of California beckon him. He says he intends to settle by the Pacific Ocean. He and I are on the move, not together, but in unison.

My diary days are over. I will journey to a new life in a new country. Despite the disappointing fact that I remain a virgin, I am a grown woman and must make my own way without the support of a father, a mother, a brother, or . . . my greatest love.

I will miss Charlie in the deep corners of my heart. I will never forget him, not for as long as I live. I will never take off the locket he gave me. His heart will always be next to mine. I have resisted writing to Charlie again. Oh, Charlie! That last hour at the Berlin Bahnhof will be my final memory of my first love . . . my always love. The wound is too raw to reopen it and there is nothing more to say. I must leave him behind, though he is the best part of my life.

I will hide all Charlie's letters, including the one that came to Erfurt the day before I left, which I do not dare open for fear of losing my nerve.

My journal, both the pretty, white diary and this notebook,

both gifts from my brother, will be hidden in the dark recesses of the attic, our once-upon-a-time Children's Kingdom. I hope, someday, when Hitler is dead and gone, to return and reread this chronicle of three wonderful and terrifying years. Maybe, I can even share the story of Charlie with <u>our</u> grandchildren.

Goodbye Charlie. Goodbye journal. I will celebrate my twentieth birthday in London!

The morning after reading Edith's diary, Clara sat at her small dining table, nursing her second cup of coffee. She stared at the two piles of letters tied with ribbon. She could not bring herself to begin reading them. She didn't know why she felt reticent. Would they be even more revealing than Edith's diary? These were love letters to her daughter from a man, a man she had never met, a man who was not her daughter's husband.

Clara closed her eyes. Edith had suggested she read them. No, not suggested—begged. She must at least find that special birthday card Edith had mentioned in her diary, the one she wanted to keep forever. She would save this memento if nothing else and bring it to her daughter. Perhaps there were other special sections she could save, perhaps a letter or two that would not cause any trouble with George. If nothing more, she must skim the letters so that she could determine which ones might be safe to take to London. Her own new romance made her hyper-aware of the importance of the special memories of falling in love. And there was the unopened letter, the one Edith had asked her to find, to read, and to bring to her if it was safe to do so.

The letters waited. Clara slowly untied the ribbon. The letter on the top bore a postmark of October 1, 1934, and #1 was written in pencil on the envelope. She checked Edith's diary for the mention of Charlie's first letter. This was surely it. Edith had stacked them in order and even numbered them. She need only look at the ones that Edith deemed significant enough to mention in the diary.

She flipped through the stack, past the early letters, until she saw the gap in December 1934 when Hugo had prohibited their correspondence. She opened the first letter from 1935 and saw it was filled with declarations of love and the pledge to keep writing if that was what Edith wanted. Had she and Hugo driven the couple to define what they meant to each other? Had they made their forbidden love even sweeter because of its heightened danger?

Clara located the letter dated February 27, 1935, with the line, "When we kiss, the touch of your eyelashes on my cheek resembles the caress of butterfly wings," exactly as Edith had described it. Charlie was a man falling in love. She set that letter aside.

For a while, in April and May the letters were quite short and she only skimmed a few of them. Clara found the letter where Charlie declared he would never join the Nazi Party. That one most certainly must be burned.

The letter postmarked May 6, 1935 was a different shape . . . square, rather than rectangular and the envelope was lavender rather than blue. She gently extracted the birthday card. Hand-painted flowers, bees, and butterflies formed a heart shape on the thick white paper. The card was more beautiful than she had imagined, the colors of the design vivid, and the inked lines fluid and graceful. Clara was enchanted by the work of this artistic engineer. She opened the card and read the poem.

Blossom petals fall,
Honey scented. Bees buzzing.
Your lips like nectar.

Clara had to wipe away tears before she could slip the card back into its envelope and set it aside. She almost stopped going through the letters at this point. She had found two beautiful letters to save for Edith. Perhaps it was time to simply burn all the rest. But the unopened letter waited at the bottom of the pile. Edith had asked her to read it and bring it to her if it posed no danger to Charlie or herself.

Toward the bottom of the stack, the letters were no longer numbered, but they were still arranged in order. The final letter had no number, and its flap remained glued in place. Clara held it in the palm of her hand, weighing its substantial thickness. She hesitated. Should she do what Edith could not? This letter could contain anything . . . a passionate goodbye, a gentle breakup, news of being fired or questioned by the SS, or a declaration that he would follow her to London and she must wait for him. Any of these possibilities would be devastating to Edith and the new life she was building. But her daughter had whispered that this letter haunted her. She had begged her mother to read it. Clara's fingers loosened the envelope flap without her willing them to move. She spread the folded sheets on the table and her eyes fell on the words forming a message more intense than any she had anticipated. His handwriting curled and flowed.

My dearest, beloved Edith Marie Pauline,

You have woven your way deep into my heart, and I regret that I could not grant your request when we were together in Berlin.

You declared you would be devastated if we didn't make love. You begged on your knees in Sanssouci Park that I must make love to you before your departure for England. You wept as you declared your wish for me to be your first lover; that you needed the memory to hold in your heart. And I agreed. I promised you we would make love and then it couldn't happen. Again because of a rule not of our making.

I would not break a promise to you, my love. I hope you will allow me to grant your wish now, if not in action, at least with words.

Come with me, my darling, to a room, a better room than the one on the singles' floor. Still, it is a small room, an intimate place with a wide bed, an en suite bath, and a sofa for cuddling. We sit on the sofa as we sat those few times on the narrow bed in our secret garret hideaway. Can you feel my arms around you? My hands wander to caress your breasts, soft and full like doves nestled in my palm. My heart overflows with the joy of touching you. This time we do not stop. My hands have found that warm patch between your legs and you moan.

"Wait," you say. How often have I heard this before?

*This time, it is only for you to stand and unbutton your
blouse, unhook your bra. Your garments fall to the floor,
the silk pooling around your feet. Your blouse, your bra,
your skirt, and your slip—all of it falls. Only your panties
remain as you stand in your glory and turn to me. My
heart drums against my ribs. I rise and lead you to
the bed.*

"I would kiss you everywhere," I say, "and lower—"

Clara slammed down her hand to cover the writing. She could
not read any more. She would not. She closed her eyes and inhaled
and exhaled slowly. She was sure this letter surpassed the love
letters of romantic poets. Yet she could not read further. And she
could not take it to Edith. If George discovered these erotic words
written to his wife, irreparable damage would be done to their
marriage. She must not even describe Charlie's words when she
told her daughter about this last letter.

Clara was compelled to check the closing. What if Charlie
ended with a plea for a future together, some final hope of being
reunited? If he did, would she even dare to tell her daughter? Still,
she needed to know, if only for herself. She turned to the last page
and read:

*Dearest Edith, please keep the memory of our love close to
your heart for all your days.*

*You told me not to wait. That you will start fresh
in England. And you should. Yet, my soul will allow no
alternative other than to wait for you until Hitler has*

passed from our memory, until we might be together again freely.

When this time of terror is over, I will find you, wherever in the world you are. If I am lucky, you will not have married. If I am unlucky, I will simply let you know I still love you and then leave you in peace. You are the love of my life. Remember, you have my heart. Wear it always close to your own.

Yours forever, Charlie

Tears streamed down Clara's cheeks as she returned the pages to their envelope. She gathered up the pile of letters and took them to the fireplace. A few logs left from the winter half-filled a copper bucket on the hearth. She crumpled up yesterday's newspaper, set the twists of paper in the fireplace, and placed the logs over them. Then she selected a long match from the spill vase on the mantel and struck it against the bricks of the hearth. It didn't take long for the paper to flare and the dry wood to begin to glow. Once the flame caught, she began to tear up the letters. Piece by piece, they were given to the fire until there was nothing left but ashes. The final love letter was the last to go into the flames. As she watched the edges of the paper curl and blacken, a sob ripped itself from her throat. She covered her face with her hands and wept.

Clara clutched the diary and notebook to her chest. They would remain safe for a while longer. She placed them back into the box and set the one letter she saved and the painted birthday card gently on top. In her bedroom, she shoved the box far back on the bottom of her wardrobe.

Fresh air would help rid her head of the smoke and the dreams and the emotions. She grabbed a sweater and strode across the street to the English Garden, so near and yet another world with its rocks and grottos, its lake, and a small wilderness of trees and brambles. The sky was clear with only a few puffy clouds floating across a perfect blue. Birds chirped in the trees. It was full spring. A lilac bush drooped with purple blossoms, the heady floral scent floating on the breeze. Banks of bright-yellow daffodils lined the paths.

Clara remembered the hikes she and Edith had enjoyed on their vacation to Switzerland in 1937. Edith had been working diligently for a year in London. Her letters were cheery, filled with tidbits about the English family, the other German young people she met at parties, and walking in the park on her days off. Twice, she went to visit her uncle, Clara's older brother, and his wife at The Wilderness, their estate in the country near Wimbledon. She wrote that she liked Bruno, but his wife Nelda was a chilly sort. Edith's only struggles seemed to be speaking English with ease. She said she understood her employers well enough, but she lacked confidence speaking. She complained that the children teased her about her heavy German accent. She wrote that she was working on building her vocabulary by listening to news and commentary on the English wireless and even watched variety shows from the BBC on the family's new television set. She said she repeated what she heard on those English shows over and over and gradually her English was improving.

After three months, Edith had found a job that paid better wages, this time as a downstairs maid. She shared an attic room in the house with another maid and saved as many shillings as possible.

"I'm earning a whole pound a week!" she had written.

Along with the change of job, Edith appreciated having a variety of different English voices and ways of speaking to listen to and imitate. After a year, her spirit restless, she had given notice. She was eager to find an even better job where she might have her own room.

Clara had written to invite her daughter on holiday while she was between jobs. "I have the money," she wrote, "and you deserve a vacation after working hard for a year with no complaints. Please return home for a few weeks. I've been invited by my cousin Dora to her home in Bavaria and you could come with me. We will tramp the hillsides and enjoy the fresh air. There should be no SA men about to bother us there."

And Edith had come. They had spent their days outside breathing in the free mountain air, and each evening, they returned to Dora's chalet with bouquets of wildflowers to grace the simple meals her cook prepared. Edith had chatted about her days in London but had never mentioned missing anyone or anything in Germany. She had certainly never mentioned Charlie.

When Clara returned to the apartment after her walk in the English Garden, she searched her desk for the letters Edith had written from England over the last three years, most of which she had saved. With her newfound understanding of her daughter's heart, she wanted to read a few of them again.

She brewed herself a cup of the herbal tea Albert insisted she continue to drink.

"Three times a day, without fail," he had instructed.

Edith's letters were written on thin, airmail paper, the envelopes edged with red and blue stripes. She spread them out on her table. She had not been as meticulous as her daughter and they were all in a jumble, but she found the letter sent after their return from holiday.

CHAPTER 11

Letters from London

May 15, 1937

*Dearest Mutti, Thank you for the lovely Bavarian holiday!
And let Cousin Dora know how much I enjoyed the relief
from the daily grind of work in London.*

*I had no idea where I would sleep the night I returned
to the city or how I would find my next job. I stowed my
suitcase at the left-baggage at King's Cross station and went
straight to the nearest Corner House restaurant. There are
rows and rows of tables filled with all manner of workers.
Everyone sits around and chats and exchanges news and
job leads. Wednesdays are the best as most domestic
workers have that day off. Luckily, it was Wednesday!*

*Right away, I saw a couple of girls I knew. I told them
I had just returned from Germany. A million questions
flew my way! Finally, I was able to ask if any of them*

knew a place I could lay my weary head for a few nights. Sadly, all of them lived in shared servants' quarters. No guests allowed!

I was about to leave and try one of the other Corner House restaurants (there are several in London), when a girl I'd never seen before leaned over from a nearby table.

"Du kannst bei mir bleiben," she said. Yes, in German!

She said she had a couch where I could sleep and invited me. When I told her I had left luggage at the station, Sophie (that's her name) said we could retrieve it on the way to her flat.

Her bedsitter was a tiny attic room. That night, she brewed a pot of strong coffee on an electric hotplate, and we sat at her rickety table sipping from chipped mugs. I liked her right away.

Then something strange happened. She put a record on her phonograph. I expected upbeat jazz or soothing classical music. But NO! The Horst-Wessel-Lied blared forth. "Die Fahne hoch" and so on. Sophie sang right along with it, marching in place. I couldn't believe I had landed in the nest of a Nazi sympathizer!

But I don't stand for any of that stuff in England. I stood up and told her, "I'm Jewish and I hate that song."

I expected her to kick me out the door, but Sophie is full of surprises. "I invited you and now that you're here, you listen to this," she said. Should I gather my things and run out the door or sit back down? I was so baffled I stood there open-mouthed until the song ended. Sophie *calmly returned the German platter to its cardboard jacket and put on a Tommy Dorsey record. She sat back down at the table. As if nothing odd had happened, she asked if I would like another biscuit!*

I've been here three days now and Sophie hasn't played the Nazi anthem again. I think singing that song was a weird way for her to show me that she was in charge in her apartment. It didn't sit well with me when it happened. But now that I know Sophie better, I realize she has a quirky sense of humor and loves the unexpected.

Strangely, I like her a lot. She is kind and her impulsive ways can be a lot of fun. Though her daybed is lumpy, it's big enough for me. She's invited me to stay until I find a job. I want a position that comes with a room . . . or better yet, with a wage that will allow me to get my own bedsitter.

Give Herman a hug for me when you see him next. I'm glad he has applied for his US visa. Now it's a waiting game. When will you apply for yours? Soon please!
Love you to pieces, Edith

This letter had made Clara laugh the first time she read it, and she smiled after reading it again. Edith had developed into a gifted storyteller and her command of English had grown.

Clara rifled through the letters in front of her. Sophie, who worked as housekeeper for an artist, helped Edith secure a place with a friend of her employer, a cartoonist for the *Daily Mail* who Edith claimed was well-known to London newspaper readers.

Sophie and Edith occasionally went out to dinner or the theater with the two friends. This didn't seem quite proper to Clara, but she shouldn't have worried. That relationship turned out to be little more than a platonic friendship to pass the time. The trouble came from somewhere else.

Clara searched for the letters dated December and the beginning of 1938. The one from shortly before Christmas was filled with nostalgic memories of childhood holidays and descriptions of the Yuletide decorations in London. Edith wrote that she loved having her own furnished room, a couple of girls downstairs were planning a Christmas Eve party, and she had bought a new red dress to wear.

"It's stunning," she wrote.

This wasn't the letter Clara wanted to find. It must be the next one with the early January postmark.

January 6, 1938

Dear Mutti, Happy New Year! I hope you enjoyed your Christmas day with Herman. The holiday party I mentioned in my last letter was smashing. There were plenty of nice fellows to chat with and lots of dancing.

I spent most of the evening with two brothers and a third "bloke" (that's English slang for a guy). They had two girls with them, too, and we all became a kind of group. One of the brothers had no date, and he stuck by me like glue. He's a magnificent dancer and we danced together constantly. I'll bet we were comical. He is extremely tall . . . like a good fourteen inches taller than me! He's handsome, too. Kind of dark and exotic. He's lots of fun and super at paying compliments, like how gorgeous I looked in my red dress.

I had a little decorated tree upstairs and I kept trying to slip away to light the candles. Whenever I was about to leave the party, the tall fellow (his name is George) asked me for another dance. A bit after midnight, I couldn't stand it any longer, so I invited the group to come see my Yule tree. We all trooped up to my room, and they politely oohed and awed. They were so nice, I offered them a piece of the stollen you sent me. (It is delicious!) But we were pulled back to the party by the music that drifted up the stairs. We danced until dawn.

George and his brother work for the post office installing new telephone lines. They share a room in a house in Richmond, not far from Kew Gardens. The family who lets them the room invited them for Christmas dinner and said they could bring a friend. George invited me. I'll bet the family didn't expect a girl he had only met the night before! After dinner, George insisted on escorting me back to my place. There were no taxis or buses working on Christmas night, so we had a long walk halfway across the city. By the time we reached my neighborhood, we were like old friends.

I guess I have a boyfriend now. Anyway, George wants to be my boyfriend. He's already asked me to marry him! Can you imagine? I told him to stop asking—that it was

way too soon. Don't worry, I know better than to marry a
man I've only known for two weeks.

    Mutti, come to stay in England. We could share a flat.
I know you would be uncomfortable with Aunt Nelda,
but, I'm sure, your brother Bruno would help out a bit
now and then. He is quite kind (in contrast to his wife
who is almost as bad as Rikka!).

    Please think about it. If war starts, it will be too
late to emigrate! The English are expecting war if Hitler
doesn't stop talking about lebensraum, and you know he
won't stop till he's grabbed whatever he can.
    Love and hugs, Edith

With the clarity of hindsight, Clara knew more happened than
Edith was comfortable writing to her mother. In her next letter,
Edith shared details of a new housekeeping job she had taken at a
large estate in Surrey, south of London. She wrote of days off spent
with George riding about in a motorcycle with a sidecar.

Clara found the letter she was searching for. As she reread it, she
remembered how the words had once sent her immediately to the
phone to inquire about airplane tickets from Frankfurt to London.

March 8, 1938

Mother, I need your advice—and I need you!

    George keeps asking me to marry him! He asks me
morning, noon, and night. He says he won't stop until I
say yes. I don't know what to do. Please Mutti, come to

London for a week. I need you to meet him. I need your opinion . . . will he be a good husband? I do like him a lot, he's got a responsible job, and he's masses of fun, but I'm not sure I'm ready to be married. And I miss you! Please say you'll come.

My new job is fine, but I like living in the city better than Surrey and have given notice. I will return to London in a few days. Please come visit! I must see you! Edith

Clara had telegraphed Edith that she was coming. Three days later, she was on the train to Frankfurt and then on the plane to London. Luckily, in 1938, it had been less complicated to travel back and forth from Germany to England. She needed only a short-term, visitor's visa and to leave her cash and valuables in Germany.

The trip to London was her first time on an airplane. As soon as she and the other passengers were settled in their comfortable seats, the steward came down the aisle and gave everyone cotton balls.

"Stuff them into your ears," he said. "It gets loud."

Within minutes, the deafening roar of the propellers and their engines vibrated through the metal of the fuselage. The plane taxied down the runway, and Clara watched the asphalt speed along under the huge wheels. Suddenly, as the plane lifted into the air, she felt the strange sensation of being pushed down into her seat as if by a giant hand. The airport and surrounding fields disappeared under a gray blanket of clouds, and the cabin turned frigid. Clara wrapped her coat tightly around herself, glad for the fox collar and the rabbit fur lining of her gloves and boots. Over the channel, caught in an updraft, the plane bounced and lurched, and she grabbed the armrests. The steward came around again, this time offering blankets, cups of strong, hot tea, and hard, ginger candies to suck.

"To combat nausea," he said.

Clara closed her eyes and inhaled deep breaths. She would think about seeing her daughter and meeting George, the persistent boyfriend. Once the plane had cleared the Channel, the steward came around again, this time with small triangular ham and cheddar sandwiches and more cups of tea.

Her brother Bruno's car and driver met her at the airport to take her to the guesthouse where he had helped Edith secure a room for their visit. Bruno sent his regrets that business didn't allow him to see her that day, but she and Edith must come out to The Wilderness for lunch on Sunday. She hardly knew her brother, who was fifteen years older, and she anticipated the pleasure of spending time with him.

Clara checked into the rooming house, and the manager led her to a corner room with windows overlooking Baker Street below. The room was cozy, with two beds, a wardrobe, and a matching, Chintz-covered armchair and settee in front of a coal-fired heater. The toilet was only two doors down the hall and a room with a bathtub was at the far end. In one corner of their room, a folding screen partially separated a dressing space. There was a washstand with a porcelain water pitcher and a bowl, both painted in a blue willow pattern. A straight-backed chair held a neat stack of folded towels. Clara collapsed onto the settee and stretched her short legs toward the heater. She could not keep her eyes open and drifted into sleep.

CHAPTER 12

Edith's Choice

CLARA DOZED FITFULLY. WHEN she opened her eyes, only forty minutes had passed. Outside, dusk was falling across the city. She walked to the windows and, before she closed the drapes, she watched the traffic in the street below, the headlights of cars and buses moving in a steady flow. A light knock sounded against the wooden door, and she opened it. Her daughter stood on the threshold, wrapped in her coat, her face flushed from the night chill and her travels. Curls of loose hair poked out from the woolen scarf wrapped around her head and neck.

Edith dropped her suitcase and threw her arms around her mother. "Oh, Mutti, I'm glad you're here. I've missed you so!"

"Darling girl, you wrote and I'm here." Clara embraced her daughter. "Come in now and rest a moment. Then we need to find a place to eat. I'm starving."

Edith swept in and the previous peacefulness disappeared. Her words tumbled out and filled the room. "Mutti, there's a comfortable pub not far from here. They have the best steak and kidney pie. You'll love it. I must freshen up. What a scramble to get here. I had to work until past three this afternoon to get all my work done before I left. My employer was kind, but I like working in the city better. I'll find another job after our visit. We're to join George at the pub in an hour. I can't wait for you to meet him."

"So soon? We're meeting George tonight?" Clara was disappointed. She had anticipated a few days to visit with Edith and learn more about this man before she came face to face with him. But the girl seemed to be in a hurry.

"Yes, tonight. I hope that's okay. I want you to get to know him. He won't stop asking me to marry him. I need your advice. How can you judge without meeting him?" She drew in a deep breath and continued. "Tomorrow night, too. He'll meet us after work tomorrow, too."

Clara sighed. "I hope we'll have time to go out to The Wilderness this weekend. Bruno has invited us for lunch on Sunday."

Edith stood at the washstand and splashed her face with cool water, then blotted it with one of the fresh towels. "I don't know," she mumbled. "Maybe . . . The main thing is for you to get to know George."

As she remembered these events more than a year later, Clara was certain she would never forget that night and the following days. She had carefully observed each detail of meeting George. If he wanted to marry her daughter, he deserved her full attention.

Her first impression was that he was unfailingly polite. He waited for them in the cold, outside the restaurant, and opened the door for them. He was so tall that it seemed like he was bowing when he leaned over and said, "I am pleased to meet Edith's mother." He pulled out her chair so she could sit, addressed her as Mrs. Lang, and asked what she would like to order.

"Shall we start with a glass of lager?" Edith said. "It's somewhat like beer, Mutti. I think you'll like it."

"I think that's an outstanding idea," Clara said. "We all need to relax a bit."

George grinned at that. "Lager is perfect for first meetings," he said. "The flavor of ale is strong, and the effect is even stronger. One might get too relaxed."

The light, bubbly lager produced the desired effect. Clara enjoyed speaking in English again after years of mainly writing the language in correspondence to her son in America and now to Edith. George was an easy and fluent talker who proved willing to reveal himself in flowing words. He told about growing up in India where his father had worked for the British East India Company.

"My brother and I were sent to England for boarding school when I was ten and he was twelve. I haven't been back," he said, "though I feel as attached to India as I do to England." He mentioned his work stringing new telephone lines and installing communication systems. He talked of the joy of bumping down country lanes with Edith in the sidecar. "I'm careful." he said. "I wear goggles and a helmet, and I bundle Edith in the sidecar with a blanket. She has a helmet, too, and so many woolen scarfs that you can only see her eyes." He paused, his gaze tender. "Don't worry. We don't go out if it's raining or snowing. It'll be more pleasant in the summer. Then we might even take a weekend and go to Brighton."

While he talked about the motorcycle trips, Edith fidgeted. She couldn't seem to settle down. And Clara noticed she didn't gaze at George with lingering, love-filled eyes, though they were relaxed together and genuinely affectionate. When only a dab of gravy from the steak and kidney pie was left on her plate, Clara asked him why he was so sure he wanted to marry Edith.

"On Christmas Eve, I fell for her instantly," George began. "She was beautiful in her red dress with her hair caught up in a glittery band. And can she dance!" Both he and Edith laughed then, and she put her hand on his arm. "But what got me the most was when she invited us up to see her Christmas tree. She was joyous when she sang her German song and offered us a slice of Christmas cake." He sighed and put his huge hand over Edith's, which lingered on his arm. "I know it may seem strange that I want to marry her when we've only been together a few months. I'm twenty-seven," he said, "and I'm ready to settle down and have a family. We enjoy a lot of the same things . . . dancing and jazz and weekend excursions. And though I'm a British citizen, I was raised in India. In a way, we're both immigrants." He paused, as if to let his thoughts catch up to his speech. "I know I can often be moody. I try to keep that side of me under wraps. Edith helps me without even trying. She is so full of life . . . She simply makes me happier." He added in a more formal tone, "Mrs. Lang, I love your daughter. I make enough to support us . . . not fancy, but comfortable. The more I know her, the more I'm positive I want her to be my wife because . . . well . . . because she makes me a better person."

Back in their room, Edith sat on the edge of her bed and pulled off her shoes. "What do you think, Mutti? What about George?"

"Edith, I need time to contemplate. I'm totally exhausted. I've been on a train and crossed the Channel on an airplane. And now this . . . meeting George, not to mention a few glasses of lager." Clara stepped behind the folding screen, unzipped the side of her dress, and lifted it over her head. "Please give me until morning. We can talk at breakfast."

"But, first impressions, Mutti? What was your first impression?"

Clara sighed. "He's a charming man and he seems sincere. Yes, I like him. And, yes, he is certainly tall." She emerged from behind the screen in a long, flannel nightie, crawled into one of the single beds, and pulled the covers over her head. "Now let me sleep," she mumbled.

When she awoke in the morning, Edith, still wearing her slip, slept soundly in the other bed. Clara dressed and went downstairs to ask for breakfast in their room. The manager prepared a tray with coffee, buttered toast, two boiled eggs, and several rashers of bacon. When Clara returned with the tray, Edith rolled over with a groan.

"Good morning. See what I've got for us." Clara set the tray on the end of her bed. "Breakfast in bed, if you like."

Edith sat up, wrapped the blanket around herself, swung her bare legs over the side of her bed, and groaned again. "Coffee. That's what I need." Clara handed her a cup and she took a few sips, then set the cup on the nightstand. She seemed a bit green as she stood and dropped the blanket. "Be back in a jiff," she said and hurried out of the room.

Clara fluffed her pillows up against the headboard, placed the tray where she could reach it, and leaned back against the cushions to sip her coffee. Edith didn't quite seem herself. When she returned, Clara patted her bed. "Come, sit over here. We can talk and sort everything out."

Edith brought her coffee over and sat on the edge of her mother's bed. "Mutti, I don't know what to do. George is set on marrying me. He won't let up. He's fun to be with, and most of the time he's thoughtful. I like him and all that."

"What is it that makes you hesitate?" Clara asked.

Edith nibbled on a triangle of toast. She sipped her coffee. "I'm not sure," she said. "I'm not sure I want to marry so quickly. I'm not sure I love him. Right now, I'm not sure of anything. I wanted you to meet him before I say yes . . . or say no . . . or, better yet, continue to say nothing. Please tell me what you think. Would he be a good husband?"

"I like him," Clara said. "I find I like him quite a bit. He's polite and he seems to be genuine in his feelings for you. But you know, dearest, I don't have experience with real love. I'm not sure I know what makes a good husband." Clara carefully cut off the top of her boiled egg and scooped out the soft yolk with her spoon.

Edith lifted her egg out of the cup and rolled it around in her palms, then put it back without cracking it open. "Should I say yes to George, Mutti? Please help me."

Clara leaned back against the bed pillows. She needed to be careful. "Edith, I can't tell you what to do. It's not my decision to make. If I tell you not to marry him and you never find anybody else who loves you as much, you'll not forgive me. If I tell you that you should marry George and the marriage goes wrong, then you'll blame me for that. You must decide this for yourself.

You need to let your own heart and head lead you, not mine." She reached over and caressed her daughter's shoulder. "Whatever you decide, I will support you." She swung her legs from under the covers. "Come, get dressed now. Let's go for a walk. The sun is out."

Edith rose and went behind the folding screen. Clara asked her if she would like a pitcher of warm water so she could wash.

"Please, yes," her daughter had said, and Clara went to fill the pitcher and brought it back to the room.

"Here you go," she said as she poured warm water into the washbasin. Edith, stripped down to her panties, lifted her arm and sponged the length of her side and up under her breasts. Clara noticed that her daughter's breasts were full and firm, her nipples dark. Perhaps she imagined it, but her tummy had a slight bulge, too. And there was her quick departure to the WC earlier.

Clara sucked in her breath. "You're pregnant," she said. "That's what this is all about, isn't it?"

Edith quickly grabbed a towel and held it in front of her body. "Mutti, I didn't mean for you to find out like this. I haven't told a soul. No one except George. I was going to tell you later."

"How much later?" Clara gathered up Edith's blanket from the bed and tossed it to her. "Here, put this around yourself again. We have more talking to do." She strode to the settee.

Edith followed, the blanket tangled around her legs, her head down. Tears hung on the edges of her eyes. "I was going to tell you this morning. Only I had to find out your impression of George first." Edith turned to face her mother. "Mutti, I don't want to get married because I'm pregnant. Not because of that! He would always blame me." She blinked several times to keep the tears from overflowing, then sat up straight. "After only three months, I don't know George well enough to decide if I want to spend a lifetime with him. And I don't want to have a baby with a man I can't fully commit to. Maybe sometime in the future . . ."

"But Edith, this problem won't wait. You're pregnant now."

"Don't worry, Mutti. I've made up my mind to get rid of this baby. I have everything arranged with a midwife who does such things in her home."

Clara was shocked. "An abortion? You mean to get an abortion?" She grabbed Edith's hands. "It's dangerous. It's both dangerous and illegal. What does George say about all this? Is this why he's willing to marry you?"

"Oh, Mutti! George has been asking me to marry him since way before I realized I'd even missed my period. He says this makes no difference and he will go along with whatever I want. I told him I am determined to end the pregnancy."

She had implored George to run the motorcycle, with her in the sidecar, into a ditch and shake the baby out that way. "We tried it, too," she said and lowered the blanket to reveal a greenish-purple bruise on her shoulder. "All I got for my trouble were bruises and a week of neck pain."

"Please listen to me." Clara tried to make her voice firm. Any wavering would reveal her conflicted emotions. "You can come back to Germany to have the baby. I'll help you."

But Edith shook her head, making her short curls swing. She would never bring a new life into Germany, a country filled with hate. Clara asked why not marry George? "He has a good job, and he loves you," she reasoned. But Edith was adamant that she would never marry because she had to. She didn't want to trap a man into marriage, even one who had already proposed. Who knew what future argument might result in blame being thrown back at her.

Clara suggested adoption and Edith burst into tears. "How could I live knowing I had a child out in the world, a child I would never know, who I had given to someone else to raise? I'd rather die than know I had deserted a living, breathing baby," she said between sobs.

"With a backstreet abortion, you might get your wish. You could die, you know." Clara knew this was harsh, but she had to make sure her daughter realized the danger.

Edith nodded. "I don't care! I'm willing to take the risk."

Clara sighed. She had always known her daughter to be stubborn and reckless. She asked Edith about the cost. Wasn't it terrifically expensive? Edith told her George had given her what he could, and she had borrowed the rest from her friend, the cartoonist. "I didn't tell him why. And I'll pay him back," Edith said, "Even if it takes a year of scrimping."

"Why didn't you ask Bruno for money? My brother has plenty to spare."

Edith rolled her eyes. "Mutti, seriously? I couldn't."

Clara understood Edith's hesitancy. She did not know her brother well and had no idea how he would react. He had emigrated to Britain when she was ten and she had seen him only a few times since then. Clara knew Bruno occasionally helped Edith, but she was also aware that his wife clearly did not welcome an influx of her husband's Jewish relatives, regardless of the situation in Germany. Besides, confessing the need for an abortion to any male relative would be shameful and embarrassing. Nelda, cold and straight-laced in the best of times, would be scandalized and shun Edith forever.

Clara felt a surge of angry tears prickle her eyes. She had plenty of money back in Germany. If she were able to transfer her reichsmarks to England, she could pay for a safer abortion for her daughter. There were always doctors willing to help a young woman in trouble if enough money was offered. She remembered a married cousin with three young children who had discovered she was pregnant again weeks before they were about to emigrate. Her cousin had been able to have an abortion safely in a doctor's office. But Nazi law made it illegal for Jews to take money out of the Reich, thus she had none to give her daughter.

Nothing Clara said would change Edith's mind. She would not return to Germany. She would not get married. She refused to carry the pregnancy and give her baby away. Emotionally spent, mother and daughter sat huddled shoulder to shoulder.

When Edith spoke, her voice was determined. "I have an appointment tomorrow for the procedure." She wiped tears across her cheek with the heel of her hand. "I'm going to do it! I'm afraid and all, but I'm going." She squeezed Clara's hands and tears welled up again. "Will you come with me, Mutti?"

"Yes, of course I'll go with you. But I doubt they'll let me come in." Clara held back her tears. "Get dressed now. We need to walk. I need to feel the sun. We've said everything there is to say."

They talked little the rest of the day. They filled the silence with sightseeing along Baker Street. They wandered the aisles of the huge Marks and Spenser department store. They nibbled at sandwiches in a tearoom but left more on their plates than they ate. They sat silently on a bench in the park, throwing crumbs to a few hungry pigeons.

Dinner with George was a desultory affair. "Edith has told me all about her problem and her appointment tomorrow," Clara told George, while they waited for their dinner order.

Tears filled George's eyes. "I'd marry her tonight if she'd let me," he said. "But she is determined to end the pregnancy. No amount of pleading changes her mind, and, believe me Mrs. Lang, I've tried."

Clara understood. She had tried, too. After that, George had little to say. He picked at his food while Edith and Clara stared at their plates and moved the mashed potatoes around with their forks. When the waiter came to collect the plates, Clara felt a twinge of distress to see the waste going back to the kitchen.

When they reached the lobby of the guesthouse, George held tightly to Edith's hands and pleaded to let him come with her in the morning. But she shook her head.

"My mother will be with me," she said. "That's all I need. And please don't come around here until my mum calls and says it's all right."

George kissed her. He ran his fingers through his hair and seemed about to speak again, but he simply hung his head, turned, and walked away down Baker Street.

The next morning, Edith and Clara went by cab to the East End. The taxi stopped in front of a red-brick house in need of paint. Clara asked the cabbie to come around to pick them up in two hours. She hoped this would be enough time. Mother and daughter stood together on the front stoop, and Edith rang the bell, the sound echoing dully beyond. The door opened a crack, and a tired face appeared in the narrow space.

"Which one of you is here for our services?"

"Me," Edith said, her palm on her chest, holding her heart in place.

"First name?"

"Edith," she whispered.

"Only you can come inside."

"But she's my mother." Edith's voice was so low Clara barely heard the words. She understood the response that came through the half-open door.

"If you're old enough to need this place, you don't need your mum. I imagine she wasn't with you when you got yourself into this trouble."

Clara hugged Edith tightly. "You can change your mind, you know," she whispered.

"Hurry up before you attract a copper. No lingering on the doorstep. Come in or go away." The woman was getting impatient.

Edith walked through the door "What about my mum?" she mumbled.

The old woman pushed Edith into the dark hallway and stuck her head out the door. "You can wait in the pub 'round the block," she said. "Come back in an hour and a half. But no waiting on my doorstep." She pointed to a newsstand at the corner. "Wait there until you see your daughter come out." Then she closed the door in Clara's face.

Clara went to the pub and sat at a table near the windows. When the barkeep came around, she ordered a cup of tea. He seemed to be used to nervous women biding their time in his establishment and brought the tea. But she couldn't sit still. She needed to move. She circled the neighborhood, up one street and down the next, then back again. Finally, when she could walk no more, she went to the newsstand and looked across toward the red building. Nothing. No one. She glanced at the display of daily newspapers on the stand.

On each front page, huge letters declared in various ways:

GERMANY ANNEXES AUSTRIA!
HITLER VIOLATES THE TREATY OF VERSAILLES!
AUSTRIANS WELCOME THE NAZIS!

Clara gasped, her knees sagged, and she grabbed onto the side of the newsstand to steady herself.

The vendor rushed around his stall, bringing a wooden crate. He set it upside down and held her arm to help steady her. "Here lady. Sit down before you fall. It's rotten news for sure."

Clara collapsed onto the wooden box. Her hands trembled. "I can't bear it. Not today,"

"Are you waiting for someone, too?" he said and cast his eye toward the door where Edith had disappeared.

Clara could only nod silently. Her chest heaved and tears flooded her cheeks.

"Don't worry, Missus. The midwife is experienced. I'll help you watch out for your young lady."

When Clara felt she would be unable to sit quietly another moment, the door finally opened, and Edith emerged. Clara rushed across the street, the news headlines forgotten. Her daughter's face was pale, her eyes dark and rimmed with red. Her lower lip was bruised, and she wobbled a bit on her feet.

"Mutti," she said, her voice weak and low. Clara embraced her and they walked slowly together down the stairs and to the newsstand where Edith sat on the crate until the taxi returned.

Edith barely made it to their room where she collapsed on the bed. Clara hovered over her all afternoon. She laid warm compresses on Edith's stomach and rubbed her back. She changed the bloody pad the midwife had secured between her legs. Though Edith was bruised, Clara was relieved to see she wasn't bleeding uncontrollably. Later in the evening, after sleeping most of the afternoon, Edith was able to swallow half a mug of hot broth, which the manager brought to the room.

That night, Edith's forehead was warm, her face damp, her sleep fretful and filled with dreams. Clara moved the armchair close to her bed and dozed, waking often to check on her daughter. She clearly remembered that sometime in the darkest part of the night, Edith mumbled in her sleep.

"Hold me," her daughter had moaned. "Charlie. Charlie. Hold me."

At the time, Clara had not understood why she didn't call for George.

The next morning Edith was better, physically, though she remained emotionally drained and unreachable. She buried herself under the covers and slept most of the day. She continued to bleed, but it seemed little more than a heavy monthly cycle. Twice she sat up to nibble on crackers and sip more broth, but she was soon exhausted and fell asleep again.

Clara asked the house manager if she could use the phone and called her brother to explain that Edith was ill, and they wouldn't be able to come for lunch the next day. Missing this rare visit with Bruno was impossibly sad, but caring for her daughter came first.

That night, Edith again tossed and turned, but her forehead was cool, and she didn't call out in her sleep.

On the third day, Edith managed to sit up for more than an hour. She was suddenly hungry and ate several pieces of buttered toast, two boiled eggs, and later a large bowl of porridge studded with raisins. She leaned against the bed pillows her mother had wedged behind her back and sipped a cup of strong English tea laced with milk. Clara sat at the foot of her bed and touched her daughter's knee.

"I'm so sorry I wasn't allowed to stay by your side when you went to the midwife," she said. "I feel like I failed you."

Edith enclosed her mother's hand in her own. "No, Mutti. You didn't fail me." she said, her voice low. "You've been right beside me when I needed you most. I was so relieved to see you afterward. Most likely it was for the best you weren't inside to hear me screaming and screaming."

Clara sat silently, allowing her daughter the space she needed to talk. Edith described how they put her feet up in metal hooks and tied them in.

"I felt vulnerable laying there with my legs spread and my arms strapped down, too," Edith said. "A helper told me they had no ether or chloroform. She warned me it would be painful, but no warning could have prepared me. She put a kind of stick into my mouth and told me to bite down and not scream. And the damned midwife—sorry Mutti. She told me not to cry or they would send me away. When she began with her cold instruments, pain seared its way inside me. She said it was a good thing I'd come as early as I did, or it would have been worse. She told me she had to work slowly to be sure she got it all and that I must lay still without moving. Mutti, it was terrible. It felt like she was taking the baby out in pieces!" Tears trickled down Edith's cheeks and dripped on the sheet as she talked. "I couldn't help myself. I screamed and screamed." After the worst was over, the helper had taken her to a dark room with a cot and told her to rest. "A few minutes later I saw her walk down the hall with a bundle of bloody sheets." Edith covered her face. Her shoulders heaved. Finally, she continued. "When the woman came back, she made a quick check between my legs, replaced the pad, and said, 'Well, you're not hemorrhaging. You can go now.' She walked me down the hall reciting instructions to keep my feet up for a few days. No lifting, no running around, and no 'shagging,' as if I would want to do that again for a while! It was like this was an everyday thing for her, but it wasn't for me. I was ever so glad to see you when I walked out the door."

Clara put her arms around her daughter, and they held each other in silence, both of their faces wet with tears. "You shouldn't have had to go through all that," she whispered. "No one should have to endure such agony." Clara remembered thinking how important money was for a woman's safety. Wealthy women could find a real doctor to help at such times. These backstreet, illegal abortions were the only option for poor women and unmarried girls who made a mistake. And now, because of Nazi hatred, her daughter, the granddaughter of a millionaire banker, was one of the servant class in London. She kissed Edith on the forehead. "Shall I telephone George now? He must be worried."

Edith breathed in, a deep, shuddering gasp as if to fortify herself, then nodded silently.

That evening, George arrived with a bouquet of flowers. He sat by Edith's bed, held her hand, and kept repeating he was sorry, that he should have been there. He stayed for several hours, allowing Clara time for a bath. She leaned back in the warm soapy water and felt the last few days' tension ease from her back. Then she remembered the newspaper headlines. And the wireless news spewing out reports of Germany's annexation of Austria. One never knew anymore what Hitler would do next. The situation could change rapidly. She must return home. Her youngest son was still in Germany. Clara felt the muscles in her neck tighten again when she thought of Herman. She stepped out of the tub and reached for the towel.

When she returned to the room, Edith was curled up asleep and George sat in the armchair gazing at her, his eyes filled with tenderness. At Clara's request, he came to sit with her on the settee.

"George, I must go home. I dare not stay longer." She explained that her airline ticket was in two days. She must return. Herman and her elderly, ailing mother-in-law, who had only a loyal maid to help, needed her. "You got Edith into this mess," she said. "I've cared for her as long as I can. The difficult days are over. Now it's your turn." George promised he would ask for a couple of days off so he could stay with Edith. He would find a room for her near his work, a place where he could easily watch over her until she was strong again.

Clara returned to Germany knowing that she was leaving her daughter in loving hands. The marriage question remained unanswered.

CHAPTER 13

Kristallnacht

HER MIND FILLED WITH the memories of fourteen months before, Clara sat in front of the pile of letters on her table and sorted them into chronological order. Most of what Edith had written after the events in London was easy to remember. George did as he promised. He had set her up in a single room, a bedsitter near where he worked in Richmond. Each evening, he came to the flat, laden with food and sometimes flowers. Edith didn't say that he slept over, but Clara was sure he did. Edith wrote that he was a devoted caregiver and continued to beg her to marry him. "*George is trying marvelously to convince me what a splendid husband he will be, and he has almost persuaded me,*" she wrote.

Clara found the one-page letter that had arrived the week after Easter and reread it.

April 17, 1938

Dear Mutti,

George and I have tied the knot. He has been so very attentive. Really the best and I couldn't say no to him any longer. I know he will be a good husband and provider.

We got married two days after I said yes, on the Thursday before Easter, April 14. We went to the Chelsea Council Chambers and an official said the necessary words. I am now Mrs. Collett, George's wife. I will forever be sad that you weren't with me. I only had Gerti and Sophie to stand with me. Herald, George's brother, came to support George. Afterward, we all went to a pub and got sloshed.

George has found us a small flat in Chelsea where we will set up housekeeping. For now, that will be my full-time job.

Please say you are delighted! I think I've done the right thing. George loves me and that's more than half of it.

Hugs, your daughter, Edith

The news had been bittersweet. Clara was sad she hadn't been able to see her daughter as a bride and worried that Edith had married for little more than George's persistence and her need for love and security. Yet she was hopeful that George's love would be a strong foundation for their marriage.

Clara took the sorted letters back to her room and stashed them in the bottom of her wardrobe next to the box holding Edith's diary. That piece of old furniture was becoming the repository for memories. Clara wandered around the small apartment and touched her favorite things—the porcelain duck from Copenhagen, the small, silver, openwork basket, a tall vase decorated with lavender hollyhocks, which had belonged to her mother.

The day after Clara received the letter from Edith about her marriage, Hugo's mother had died quietly at home. The maid telephoned with the news when Clara had her fountain pen in hand and was writing to congratulate her daughter on her marriage. She had quickly added an invitation to come home for a honeymoon and choose anything she wanted from her grandmother's jewelry and collection of small treasures.

"I'll pay for the trip," she wrote. "Don't worry on that account. Do be sure to get yourself on George's passport before you come. You are married to a British citizen now and travel on his passport as his wife will be safer for you."

With her mother-in-law gone and Edith settled, Clara knew it was past time to apply for a visa. If she had to leave Germany, she would go as far away as possible. *When war comes, and it surely will*, she thought, *England will be in the midst of it. Better to go to America and join Friedel.*

She took the train to Berlin and stayed with her niece. First, she had to have a professional photo taken and wait for it to be developed, then two long days of standing in line at the US Embassy waiting for her turn, followed by several stressful hours of meticulously filling in all the paperwork, and finally an interview. She was exhausted at the end of the tedious process, but her application for a visa was stamped and filed. She still had to get sponsorship from someone in the United States who would guarantee her financial support, but she was sure that either Friedel with his wife or her sister Ida would be able to provide the needed affidavit. Clara knew that her visa application would trigger close surveillance by the Gestapo, as well as the German Foreign Exchange office monitoring her bank account. In the future, she would need to be extra wily and cautious.

Two weeks after she returned to Meiningen, another wedding announcement arrived in the mail, this time from California. Scrawled on thin airmail paper, her oldest son wrote that he had married an American woman, and they were expecting a child in the fall. With the help of his father-in-law, he had written, they were building a little house.

It will be within walking distance of the Pacific Ocean,
in a beautiful town known as the home of artists. I have
planned a balcony where Bonnie and I can stand and listen
to the waves. We have our own gum grove (that's a stand
of Australian eucalyptus) at the back of the property. If
you rub their leaves between your fingers, they emit a
camphoraceous aroma similar to rosemary.

With both her oldest children married, each setting up homes in faraway places, Clara knew she should dispose of the furniture stacked in the basement storage area. Dr. Weiss and his wife, who had lived in the main part of the home for over a year, had recently suggested they would like to convert the large space back to its original purpose as a garage where they could keep their automobile. Clara also needed to sell her mother-in-law's house and its furnishings quickly.

Clara finally admitted to herself that Friedel and Edith would never return to Germany to raise their families. She had quite a bit of money left from the sale of the home to the Weisses and would have more from the sale of Marie Lang's home and furniture. None of those Reichsmarks were of any use except in Germany. Though her account with the Deutsche Bank was now blocked and she needed permission from the Foreign Exchange office to make withdrawals, she would find a way.

A few weeks before, in the end of April 1938, new laws mandated that Jews must register all real estate and valuable property and that the government had the right to seize it at any time. She determined to use her money to ship furniture and other family treasures to California and London. The cost would be exorbitant, but what did it matter? She would not leave all that money and beautiful furniture for the Nazis to take as their own.

Clara asked Dr. Weiss to write out an official invoice for monthly rent that allowed her to withdraw larger sums from the bank, and she began to carefully control her spending on food and other daily needs.

Even before Edith and George arrived for their honeymoon visit, Clara began the project. She put the Lang Shlundgasse Street home on the market. She went through the rows of furniture in the basement at Bernhardstrasse, a space once filled with the beautiful leather of Hugo's business, and tagged each piece for either California, London, or for sale. She ordered several large crates and hired packers to come to the house and prepare the furniture for shipping.

When Edith and George arrived, they walked through the old Lang home where Hugo had been raised and his mother had lived until her death. Edith selected a few special things easy to fit in their suitcases.

"Choose some larger things if you like," Clara told her daughter. "I'll see to the shipping."

Edith had learned to sew on her grandmother's treadle sewing machine, and it remained in the sunny corner where, as a girl, she had made small, drawstring pouches and doll clothes. She ran her hand along the shiny black machine.

"You must have it," Clara said. "You're an accomplished seamstress now and you need your own sewing machine."

George stared longingly at the white refrigerator that stood in the kitchen. He didn't dare ask for such a heavy piece of machinery, but Clara saw his glance.

"I don't care how heavy it is or how exorbitant it is to ship. It's better to use the money for that than to leave it for the Nazis to claim." She opened the refrigerator door to show George the small compartment that made ice cubes in a metal tray. "It's a marvel," she said. "Hugo bought it for his mother less than five years ago. George, I'm sure you can fix the electrical plug to make it work in England. Shall I ship it to you?"

Edith stood next to her husband and touched his shoulder. "Can you imagine? Making our own ice rather than paying for it to be delivered and watching it melt away."

George nodded and turned to his mother-in-law. "If you can manage to ship this beast, I'll make sure it works," he said and squeezed Edith around her waist. "Glad I got that pay increase,

Shorty. We may need a larger flat to make room for so many treasures."

George and Edith only stayed four days, but Clara had no time in 1938 to cry over their departure.

The cherrywood breakfast room furniture and inlaid bedroom set Hugo had bought right after their marriage were swaddled in packing kapok and wood shavings and shipped off to Friedel in California. Clara cheerfully counted out the Reichsmarks to pay the packers and the shipping company. Naturally, the Duetsche Bank was happy to withdraw the exorbitant amounts for the ordinary tax, the Jewish special tax, and the Jewish supplemental tax from her account and forward it to the German government.

As promised, George found a larger flat nearby and Clara had crates prepared to send to Harcourt Terrace, London. Besides the sewing machine and the glass cabinet she loved, Edith would receive drawing room furniture, including a settee, a sideboard, two chairs, and several side tables. The refrigerator was crated up and shipped separately. An overstuffed couch and the huge banquet table were too big for the London flat or her son's California seaside cottage, and Clara sold them, along with most of her mother-in-law's furnishings. All went for a pittance to one of the scavengers eager to snap up anything from Jews who must divest themselves of their possessions before they fled Germany.

By summer, with most of the furniture gone, Clara began to sort through paintings and household accessories. She shipped most of the paintings to California, along with the second-best silver crafted with an "L" over crossed ribbons on the handles, fifteen place settings of Rosenthal china, as well as a few masculine trinkets including an old ship in a bottle, a Munich beer stein, and a silver inlaid briar pipe, all of which had belonged to Hugo's father. Edith would get the silver candelabra, a couple of paintings, glassware and crystal, and the other half of the set of Rosenthal china. As long as the money lasted and there were things of value left to ship, she would keep the crates going across the English Channel and the Atlantic Ocean. Her possessions would end up in Edith's basement flat or travel across the vast North American continent or through the Panama Canal and up the Pacific Coast to California. She was determined to leave nothing for the Nazis. She knew that the shipping and packing companies reported all Jewish shipments of goods out of the country. The Gestapo kept track of shipping orders, home sales, and anything that indicated a Jewish family was preparing to emigrate in order to ensure the collection of the astronomical Reich Flight Tax. She could not procrastinate for long.

In the middle of these frenzied months of sorting and shipping, Clara received news from Edith that she was pregnant again.

I wish it hadn't happened so close on the heels of that earlier experience, but somehow I now feel more prepared to be a mother and George is simply giddy with joy. And I know you will be elated! Soon you will be a grandma twice over! I only regret that I will not give you your first grandbaby. Fred's Bonnie will beat me to it! What irony!

Now alone in her apartment in 1939, the scents of spring wafting through her open window, Clara's thoughts drifted back to the previous autumn. Most of her furniture had arrived at its far-flung destinations and was being used by her older children. Things seemed to have calmed down and she was used to the restrictions on her life. She didn't go out except to shop and enjoyed the quiet days of fall knitting baby sweaters and little booties. Herman came from Suhl to visit her on alternate weekends, and she always enjoyed his visits. They talked about traveling to America when their visas came through and agreed to watch for any Nazi policy that would demand a fast escape to England.

Then Kristallnacht exploded. During the early morning hours of November 10, 1938, the unequivocal warning that Herman must flee came with smoke from the burning synagogue and the shouts of angry crowds in the street.

Clara remembered that November morning vividly. She was still in her dressing gown, braiding her hair, when her son appeared at her door with tales of his cousin's arrest by SA goons. He told her that when he crossed the bridge into Meiningen on his motorcycle, he had seen black smoke rising from the old town. They both knew that, as a young male, he was doubly vulnerable to arrest. The disappearance of Great-Uncle Martin and the phone call from Gusti, whose husband had been dragged to jail in his pajamas, confirmed their fears.

"No one . . . nobody can know you're home and no longer in Suhl," she told her son. "It must be a secret." On that day, the long weeks of Herman hiding in her apartment began.

Herman was restless. He paced the rooms or huddled in the window seat, staring out at the English Garden across the street. Clara, forced to act normally to protect him, continued to go to town to buy groceries, past the greengrocer and butcher shop, which both displayed signs that read "No Jews will be served," to the pitifully stocked grocery in the Jewish neighborhood where smashed windows were crisscrossed with tape, swastikas and Nazi slogans defaced the walls. An acrid smell lingered in the alleyways and a pall of smoke hung heavy in the air. Afraid her letters would be opened and read by the SS, she wrote lies to Edith, saying Herman was roving the countryside on his motorcycle and had so far evaded arrest. When the letter from California with pictures of her first granddaughter arrived, she was unable to rejoice.

Weeks later, news from family told of the gradual release from Buchenwald of men who had been arrested. One morning, they learned that Martin was home and the next she heard from Gusti. Her husband was back, though very ill, and they would flee to Switzerland immediately. It was time for Herman to come out of hiding. On instructions from the police chief, whose wife, Katrina, had been Clara's best friend, she had shaved Herman's head down to stubble so he would look like he had been in prison along with most other Jewish men. She was determined to get Herman safely out of the country, and her son finally agreed. He would leave Germany, American visa or not.

While Herman filled out an application for a transit visa to the UK, Clara wrote letters, one after another. She wrote to her son in California and to Hugo's cousins in Chicago. They must find a way to help, to offer sponsorship to expedite Herman's American visa.

Next, she wrote to Bruno in London. For her son's safety, despite her unease regarding Nelda's attitude, she must ask her brother for help. She took up her fountain pen and slowly began the letter.

> *"Kristallnacht has made it imperative for Herman, my youngest son, to leave Germany. He has applied for a transit visa for the United Kingdom, and he must travel as soon as it and his updated passport arrives."*

Clara rubbed her temples and tried to think of something that might soften the English sister-in-law she had never met.

> *"He will need a place to stay for only a short time, only until his US visa is issued. Edith and George are expecting a new baby any day and their apartment is small. Would it be possible for Herman to stay with you while he waits? Please speak to Nelda. Perhaps she will agree."*

Clara signed the letter and blotted the ink. She wished she remembered the proper way to pray.

Within a week, Bruno's telegraphed answer came:

Send Herman. Nelly has agreed.

In early February, Herman's German documents arrived in a thick brown envelope. Inside was his exit visa and his new pass-port. Herman hated the ugly red "J" stamped on the first page of his passport to designate the carrier was Jewish. Even more, he detested the false name of "Israel" that had been substituted for

Ludwig, the middle name Hugo had given him at birth. His British transit visa arrived a few days later. There was nothing left to do besides pack, get a clearance from the local police, and pay the exit taxes. Herman was excited to begin a new life. He would be near his sister and before long, he would be an uncle.

The night before Herman left, Clara prepared a special dinner and tried to make the event a celebration. If she kept busy, perhaps her tears would not fall until he was on the train the next morning. They opened an expensive bottle of wine Hugo had saved too long. With her first sip, her mouth puckered. The wine had gone to vinegar. Herman laughed at the sour taste on his tongue.

"Mutti, Germany has gone sour, too," he said. "The Nazis will cause trouble even for widow ladies. Promise you'll join Edith and me in England as quickly as you can. Forget shipping all this stuff and come."

Clara promised her son she would leave Germany when her paperwork was in order. She had yet to submit her passport to get it stamped with the large red "**J**." She promised she would take it to the police station the next day.

"Until you join Edith and me in London, we must write," Herman said. "I'll write in English, like my sister and brother do."

Clara had touched his cheek. He was her baby, and now he was leaving, too. "Yes," she said. "We will all write in English. It has become our new family language."

The next morning her son was gone, and she was alone in Germany.

She was alone with her headaches, her palpitations, and her worries. And then she had met Albert.

CHAPTER 14

Spring 1939
Love Before It Ends

After the visit from Edith, George, and the baby and the following days of emotional intensity while she read Edith's diary and Charlie's letters, Clara felt headachy and depressed. She could not seem to gather enough energy to get out of bed. Even frequent cups of herbal tea didn't help. When the phone rang, she wished she could ignore it. It was probably more woeful news. But Albert's voice greeted her.

"How was your visit with your daughter?" he asked.

After she had told him that all went well and little Hazel was a darling, chubby baby, he reminded her that the next evening would be a chamber music evening.

"I've missed you," he said. "I can't wait to hear your sweet violin . . . and walk you home, of course."

Instantly, Clara's headache vanished. The anticipation of Albert's kiss was like a strong tonic. As she looked forward to being with Albert again, the revelations of her daughter's diary and letters swirled around in her mind. Edith had longed to give her-self to her first love. *Perhaps,* Clara thought, *the value of chastity is overrated.* Her mind kept drifting to the imagined sensations of Albert holding her skin to skin as they lay between silky sheets. *What would that be like,* she wondered. She must not wait too long. Time was running out.

The next evening, she and Albert walked together in the blue summer twilight and Clara spoke about the experience of read-ing Edith's diary. "It was like my daughter was speaking to me across the years," she explained. "She begged me to find the hid-den box. She asked me to read the letters and the diary. Often what she wrote shocked me . . . in a good way. Though reading her boyfriend's letters felt intrusive. I only skimmed those." She paused. *Should I really share the next part?* she wondered. Then she plunged ahead. "The last letter . . . that was the most difficult, but Edith had asked me specifically to open it. I only read the first page . . . and the last. That letter was so very beautiful and inti-mate." They had reached the dark space near the water channel where they liked to linger. Albert embraced her and kissed her neck. "The letter was like erotic poetry," she whispered into his chest, ". . . so explicit it . . . it made me long for you to do the things Edith's man friend described."

Albert tightened his arms around her. His voice was low and gravelly. "How I would love to be with you, my darling. I long for more than kisses." He was silent for a moment and seemed to gather his courage to speak again. "I have not felt this way since I was a young man and a new husband."

"I've never known this feeling. Not even as a bride. Please, can we arrange a special evening for the two of us? I long for it with all my heart."

"I will figure out something." His voice broke before he continued. "If you assure me that is what you want, I will make it happen."

Clara held Albert's eyes as she answered. "Reading my daughter's diary and Charlie's letters gave me a new perspective. I don't want to let my chance for true love slip away. Especially during these uncertain times, Albert. Who knows what will happen next? I want to follow my desires, to experience life fully before it's too late."

As they continued toward her home, they talked of the logistics of arranging a time together. There were difficulties. The hours after each music night were too short. They both wanted more time together. They did not want to be rushed. Neither of them thought his apartment, with his mother in the adjoining room, would be proper. And Trude could not be left alone for more than an hour or two, especially in the evening when she ate a light meal and needed help preparing for bed. Perhaps Albert could arrange for Eleanor to come in one evening and keep her company.

"If you come before Dr. and Frau Weiss get home from their office and stay late, they wouldn't notice," Clara said. "At any rate, I'm allowed to have guests. They never said a word when Herman was there all those weeks."

"Don't worry about Dr. Weiss," Albert assured her. "He has proven a loyal friend. If I meet him in the foyer, I'll explain that I'm on a professional visit. He won't say a word to anyone."

Clara could see his grin in the light of the streetlight.

"I'll see what I can arrange with Eleanor. One evening next week? Or sooner?" The question hung in the air as they stood at her gate.

"Yes," she said. "Yes. Call me after you talk to Eleanor." On the porch, Clara stretched to her full height and kissed his cheek. "I wish you could come up tonight," she murmured.

"Soon, my love." Then he turned and walked down the steps. At the gate, he paused and turned back toward Clara, who remained on the porch gazing after him. Albert raised his hand in a gesture of promise.

Clara was filled with anticipation as she waited for Albert's call. When it came on Saturday morning, he seemed as excited as she felt.

"Eleanor said she could come the day after tomorrow," he told her. "I can be with you by three in the afternoon. Is that too early? I can come later if you prefer, but I told Eleanor I have a meeting with my lawyer and then dinner with friends. I must leave during business hours." For a moment he was silent, but then his warm voice continued. "I feel like a teenager making plans to sneak off with a girlfriend. Please say three is okay."

"Yes, of course, three is wonderful. I'll prepare a light meal and chill a bottle of wine. Would you like that?"

"Yes, I imagine we'll both need a drink to calm down," Albert said. "Herbal tea might be better." She could hear his chuckle over the phone line. "But I like the idea of wine," he added.

"Till Monday then," she said and gently placed the receiver on its hook.

Clara stood near the phone table and closed her eyes. She imagined this was how Edith had felt when she planned to meet Charlie. She had no memory of herself ever feeling like this as a young girl. The flood of new emotions made her jittery.

She went into her bedroom and stood in front of the mirror. She had never been slender and in midlife her waist had thickened. In the last few years, she had managed to drop a few pounds, but her tummy was no longer firm. She always wore a corset to keep it from jiggling under her dress. What was she thinking? Was she daft to consider taking a lover when she was almost fifty?

Clara removed her dress and corset and stared at her body in only her undergarments. Was this what Albert would see? Even Hugo had not seen her like this since she was in her twenties, during their honeymoon. After Freidel was born, he seldom came to bed until she was in her long nightgown and tucked under the covers. His urges arrived in the dark and spent themselves quickly as he grunted and sweated above her. After Rikka arrived, all intimate interest in his wife had disappeared.

Clara sat on the end of her bed. Her memories of lovemaking were faded and joyless. She remembered a few moments of pleasure in the first weeks with Hugo, before he went off as a soldier to the war. By the time he returned, weak with typhoid, she was pregnant. Moments of pleasure between them never returned.

Surely it would be different with Albert. He was unlike Hugo in every way. She had no doubt he would be a kind and affectionate lover. Clara tried to imagine what it might be like to lie in bed with a man who cared for her. She rubbed her temples with her fingers. *I have no frame of reference,* she thought.

She stood in front of the mirror again and removed her underwear. Never had she inspected her nakedness like this, certainly not accompanied by imagining a man touching her. Her skin remained smooth around her hips and neck, though her tummy sagged slightly and was edged with small white scars that appeared after her first pregnancy. Her heavy breasts had begun to droop, their nipples large from nursing three babies. How could she imagine Albert would find her body attractive? She must find something pretty to wear to bed. Albert must not see her like this.

Clara slipped on her dressing gown and rummaged through her drawers. All she could find was her everyday nighties, winter flannel gowns, and cotton shifts, none of them new. She remembered the box of linens and undergarments stored in the attic. The sheer cotton negligee she had worn on her wedding night would be in that box. Perhaps it would fit. She dressed without bothering with the corset and climbed to the attic. The negligee, with its matching peignoir, was at the bottom of the box. She held the sheer batiste gown up to the light. The neckline was edged with lace and tiny embroidered roses danced across the sleeves and yolk. She had only worn it a few times and then packed it away.

Back in her room, Clara slipped the nightdress over her head. It was tight across her chest and abdomen and the too-small armholes caused the flesh of her bare arms to bulge. The side seams were ample enough that she could let them out, but the bust would still be tight. It pushed her breasts downward and flattened them. The flowing peignoir, with its open front, fit better. Perhaps she could wear it without the nightie. She wondered if that might be too risqué. She would wash and iron them both and see what happened. There was dinner to think about. What should she make? And she must put a bottle of wine in the refrigerator.

Clara busied herself the next day with preparations. She cleaned the apartment, baked a small, streusel cake, and washed the trousseau negligee set. The following morning, she left early to do her shopping. She gazed longingly into the fishmonger's window, past the sign warning Jews to stay out. She settled on buying only fresh produce available to anyone in the open market. She filled her basket with thick white and green asparagus, a few new red potatoes, small bundles of chives and parsley, six large hen's eggs, and several handfuls of plump red strawberries. At the end, she added a wedge of cheese. Back in the room, she sliced and chopped, boiled the potatoes, and arranged all the prepped food on a tray covered with a tea towel. She set her small table with a linen cloth and the only silver she still possessed.

She would spend the last two hours preparing herself. First, a long soaking bath to calm her nerves. Well before three, Clara was dressed and waiting. She sat in her armchair and sipped a cup of herbal tea, careful not to drip any on the front of her best summer dress. She ran her hand across the white silk dotted with small blue circles. She liked the feel of it under her palm, slippery and enticing. She sniffed her wrist to breathe in the scent of jasmine she had rubbed there. She touched her hair and fingered the hard nubs of her diamond earrings. When her cup was empty, she could not sit any longer. She walked over to the windows and gazed out to the road. Her cuckoo clock tweeted three times. She stopped the pendulum with her finger. Tonight, she did not want to hear the chirping of the passing hours. She looked out the window again.

Albert was coming through the gate holding a bouquet of flowers. Her heart fluttered as she hurried down the stairs and opened the front door before he knocked.

Safely inside her cozy flat, Albert laid the flowers on the table, wrapped his arms around her, and pressed his lips to hers. They kissed more deeply than ever before. A sense of safety and abandon gripped them and they only pulled apart when they were both out of breath. Clara laid her face against his chest and closed her eyes.

"Please give me a moment," she whispered. "We have all afternoon and evening together."

Albert sighed "I lost my head." he said. "Please forgive me."

"It's all right. I think we're both nervous. I know I am." She extracted herself from his encircling arms. "Let me put the flowers in a vase," she said and turned toward the sink.

He stood behind her as she filled a vase with water and arranged the flowers. "I'm afraid I will want to keep touching you. You must simply slap my hand if it's too much or too soon," he said with a chuckle. His arm lightly encircled her waist, and she turned around to face him.

"Okay, but no more kissing for a while," she said. "Now, let's open the wine and relax together. I want to savor the moment."

Clara poured two glasses of wine and motioned for him to join her on the love seat. They sipped slowly, strangely at a loss for conversation. Desperate to talk normally, Clara asked about Eleanor. How long would she be able to stay with his mother? Did he think she suspected anything? These questions only accentuated the purpose of the evening.

"Ask me about something that has nothing to do with tonight," Clara said. Albert asked if she had any news from her son in California or new letters from Edith or Herman. Gradually they were able to talk together in the familiar way they were used to.

When their glasses were empty, Clara rose and filled them again. Albert followed her to the table where the bottle stood by the vase of flowers. He laid his hand on her shoulder and turned her gently toward him.

"I must kiss you again," he said. "Please say I can."

In answer, she lifted her face and nodded. His lips were warm and insistent. She felt them slide from her lips to her ear to her neck and back to her lips. His tongue tempted her to open her mouth and let him in. Unknown sensations traveled from her lips to the tips of her breasts and down to her stomach. She had never felt these stirrings before. His fingers cupped her breast as he continued to kiss her. She grasped his hand and held it there. "Please, come see my other room," she whispered and walked slowly to the bedroom, keeping his palm next to her heart.

Albert surveyed the room. "I will remember this place always," he said.

Clara began to undo the pearl buttons that fastened the front of her dress. He stopped her fingers in their task.

"I must know you want this," he said. "I must know we are together on this."

"I think I would never forgive myself if I didn't allow this to happen."

"Then, let me help you," he said. His fingers pushed hers away and continued down the front of her dress, loosening the pearls from their buttonholes as he went. "Relax, my Clärchen, and let me love you the way you are meant to be loved."

Hours slipped away, their clothing in small heaps around the bed. Later, Albert in his shirt sleeves without tie, jacket, or trousers, Clara in her silk dress without the stiff stays of her corset, they sat propped against the headboard and finished their second glass of wine. Suddenly feeling the rumblings of hunger in her stomach, Clara suggested supper. She heated the potatoes in butter and made two asparagus and herb omelets. They sat comfortably on the settee and nibbled the simple meal.

Clara curled against Albert, her knees tucked under her like a girl. She certainly did not feel like a girl. The warmth and knowledge of being loved as a woman filled her and she could not stop herself from smiling. Albert was peaceful and relaxed, his legs stretched out toward the fireplace. His hand rested on her thigh in a gesture so intimate it filled her heart with joy.

"You are a beautiful woman, Clara." He stroked the silk of her skirt. "I'm glad we found each other. Before I met you, I never believed I would love another woman. Now, here I am, almost sixty, and I have found you."

"And I you." She reached for his hand and held it in both of hers. "Albert, I feel the days ticking by. To have found love during such a time, when we could easily be torn apart any minute, it makes me want to weep." She placed his hands over her heart and held them to her breast. "Do you feel the wild beating of my heart? I am too full of joy to weep. I want to embrace each minute with you."

"May I take you again to bed?" Albert asked. "Perhaps we will do nothing more than lay together and talk. I am not young anymore and have no idea of what I am capable of these days. But I long to lie next to you, to hold you in my arms again before the evening is spent."

As they walked into the bedroom hand in hand, Clara saw the folded trousseau set on her dresser. She lifted it up and held the delicate bundle to her chest. "Wait," she said, "I want to show you something. Get under the covers and wait." When Clara returned, the drape of the embroidered dressing gown flowed around her ankles. Albert, propped up against a pile of cushions, watched as Clara turned slowly, her movement allowing the gown to open and reveal her bare legs and the sweet bulge of her tummy.

"Come here, my love. I believe I have more to give you."

After Albert left only minutes before the start of the city-imposed, Jewish curfew, Clara lay in bed, her sheer dressing gown now primly closed, her mind full of the evening's romantic moments. She could hardly believe that the night had been real. The cake and the cheese remained untouched, though she and Albert had nibbled strawberries in bed and kissed the sweet juice off each other's lips.

Clara understood that they would not be able to meet daily. She needed to keep her mind busy. She had sent her favorite necklace and several other pieces of jewelry home with Edith and George. She would go through the few things she had not yet shipped or sold, those things she had been unable to part with because of their memories. Whether she left or stayed, she didn't want Nazis to touch her jewels and keepsakes.

CLARA KNEW THAT SHE would eventually end up in America, living with her oldest son and her new daughter-in-law. She and Herman had both applied for US visas and that's where they would have to go when the paperwork came, Herman to Chicago under the sponsorship of Hugo's wealthy relatives and she to be sheltered by Friedel in California. Only Edith had opted for the United Kingdom and not applied for a US visa. Now her daughter was the wife of a British citizen—her life would be in England.

It was past time to gather up any remaining valuables, as well as photographs and small treasured knickknacks. She would prepare two crates, one to send to Friedel to keep for her, the other for Edith to help her remember her childhood family. Slowly, Clara walked through her home and the attic, selecting items from the shelves and boxes.

She carefully wrapped the porcelain duck, a Rosenthal snail with a fairy riding on its back, her mother's vase, and the small, silver filligree basket in tissue and set them in a crate surrounded by sawdust. A carved wooden candelabra brought back memories of vacations in Switzerland and it went in the California bound crate, too.

A new law forbade sending jewelry out of Germany, but Clara ignored it. She dropped her diamond earrings into the hollow stem of a brass candlestick and poured melted wax over them. Her emerald ring disappeared under melted wax inside the matching candleholder of the set. The two candlestands and their hidden gems went into the crate that would be shipped to London.

She brought down several boxes from the attic and went through them. One was filled with dozens of formal table linens, cloths and napkins in damask, cotton with inset lace, and simple monogrammed linen, most large enough for the huge dining table she had sold. They would make padding in the shipping crates, and she distributed the linens equally into both. Another box held monogrammed undergarments. The drawers and chemises from her trousseau were totally outdated, but she could not bear the idea of SA men touching these intimate garments, the embroidered underwear she had worn with such hope. The bloomers and chemises went into the crates. At the bottom of one storage box, she found a stack of tiny, crocheted infant jackets worn by all three of her children and a packet with her wedding veil carefully wrapped in tissue. Why had she saved that? She now had two granddaughters. Perhaps her oldest would wear the veil one day at her own wedding. Clara slipped the tissue-wrapped veil into the California crate. The infant shirts were divided equally between the two boxes. She tucked a few other small items deep between the linens. She retrieved the boxes of family photos she kept in a drawer of the sideboard. Those must go, too.

She went through the pictures one evening and divided them equally. There were old photos of cousins and aunts, pictures of Hugo with his theater friends, pictures from her honeymoon and trips to Switzerland, snapshots of the children, pictures she had taken herself and a few studio portrait shots. She put one packet of photos in each crate, surrounded by table linens. At the last minute, she took down the picture that hung on her bedroom wall. It was a photographic composite of portraits of all her brothers and sisters in a row, her own young face staring out on the right side of the long, horizontal picture. She wrapped it in several linen napkins and laid it in the California crate.

She had walked up and down from the attic to her rooms and to the basement garage countless times over several days. She was exhausted as she surveyed her depleted rooms. Anything that was left would need to fit in a traveling trunk when she left or must be abandoned to the Nazis. Clara called the shipping company to come pick up the two last crates. The rates had doubled since her previous shipments, but what did it matter? These final two shipments would certainly trigger the total freezing of her bank account. Now it would be even more difficult for her to get cash for her daily use. Luckily, she had anticipated this. Through frugal living and always withdrawing the maximum amount of cash allowed, she had accumulated quite a stash which she kept well hidden in secret places around the apartment.

Clara recognized that she should leave. But outside her window, the chirping of birds and the floral scents wafting from the English Garden filled her with hope. How could she leave Germany now when the promise of summer drifted in the air, and her heart was filled with love? Hitler and his henchmen seemed far away, especially if she didn't read the newspaper and kept her wireless tuned to classical music. In the evenings, rather than listening to the news, she played her violin. When her instrument was on her shoulder, her chin tucked into the chinrest, and her arm guiding the bow, she would think of Albert and remember the feel of his kisses.

She attended the music evenings at Albert's house, anticipating the walk home. Their conversation during their walks revolved around when they could be together again at her apartment. One more time, he had been able to find an excuse to ask Eleanor to come for the evening and sit with Trude, though most of his visits were only for the afternoon hour while his mother napped. They listened to music on the wireless or lay cuddled in bed discussing a possible future. Albert would not consider leaving while his mother lived.

"But you must go quickly," he said. "I have applied for a US visa and a British transit visa, and I will follow as soon as I can."

Clara insisted she would wait a while longer, perhaps his mother would improve, and they could all leave together.

"No, my love," Albert said. "That is a false hope. And I cannot wish her to die sooner." When her transit visa from the United Kingdom arrived, Clara could not bring herself to leave Albert behind . . . not yet. Regardless of their doubts about a future or perhaps because of them, their love grew each day.

One evening at the end of a chamber music gathering, Eleanor motioned Clara to one side when Albert went to get the tea tray. The men huddled together discussing the latest restrictive laws. Eleanor touched Clara's arm.

"I can see what's going on," she said, "And I'm thrilled to help. We must all grab what joy we can at times like this."

Clara felt shy and was unable to meet her glance. How could she admit to this young woman the fullness of her feelings for their friend? "We, Albert and I, are both grateful for the time you sit with Trude. You are kind to her . . . and . . . well, it gives us time."

Eleanor shrugged. "I'm glad to do it," she said. "I know what it's like to be in love. I'm engaged, you know." She held out her left hand where a small diamond glittered.

Clara's expression asked the unspoken question.

"He's gone now," Eleanor said in response. "He emigrated to Brazil with his parents last December. We should have married before he left, but it all happened so fast. Now I'm trying to get visas for my brother and me and he's trying to expedite things from Brazil. My brother is only twelve and I'm his guardian since my father died two years ago. I won't leave without Joshua."

Clara was concerned for Eleanor. "I'm sorry for your troubles," she said. "I hope it all works out for you."

"Thanks, but you know . . . Albert has been like a father to us for several years. And I can see how he loves you. That's all I need to know." She moved closer to Clara and continued in hushed tones as Albert walked by with the tray. "What I wanted to tell you is I would be willing to stay overnight with Trude if you want. I know Albert won't ask me, but I want you to know I can do it. Joshua could come with me. He loves Trude, too, and this apartment is larger and more comfortable than the tiny flat where we stay now."

"Are you sure?" Clara whispered.

"Certainly." Eleanor said. "I only wish I had been as brave as you before my Marko left."

That evening as they walked home, Clara told Albert about her conversation with Eleanor.

"Oh, dear, I thought I was being careful, making up stories about what I had to do." He stopped walking and enfolded Clara into his embrace. "This is embarrassing for me. She is like my daughter . . . a daughter shouldn't know these things about her father."

"Hush, Albert. Don't be silly," Clara said. "Think what I know about my daughter after reading her diary. And what I told you about my trip to London. These are unusual times, and life is topsy-turvy." She held both his hands in hers. It was a gesture she had learned from him, and it had become the way they both let each other know when they had wanted to talk about important ideas. "Do you think you and I would be together the way we are now if not for the extreme uncertainty of these times? Of course not. It is a small blessing amidst these days so fraught with upheaval and fear. We must embrace it. Please talk to Eleanor. I fear the certain end of our time together is near. I want to wake up with you beside me at least one morning before I must leave."

Albert, as usual, was true to his word. A day was arranged when Eleanor and Joshua would spend the night with Trude.

Albert arrived with his comb, toothbrush, and a fresh shirt in his doctor's bag. Clara greeted him at the door with a glass of wine, cheese, and pear slices piled on a plate. They rejoiced in the long hours ahead, languid hours passed in the sensations of lovemaking. In the end, Clara got her wish. They awoke together as a ray of morning sun filtered between the bedroom curtains. She rolled over and kissed his bare shoulder. "You are the husband of my heart," she said. "And I thank you for the bounty of love you have given me." Albert gathered her into his arms, and she was content.

The next day, everything fell apart.

CHAPTER 15

———

July 1939
Farewells

CLARA BASKED IN THE afterglow of her night with Albert, when the phone roused her from a sleep filled with pleasant dreams. The instrument had jangled five times before she got to it. "Hello, Guten Morgen." She hoped it was Albert. Almost no one else phoned her these days.

The low voice of her friend Katrina came to her through the phone line. "I am going to the market this morning at ten." Then the phone went dead.

It was their code.

Katrina had been her friend since their children were babies. Almost twenty-five years ago, they had both pushed prams around the central square and stopped to chat. Over the years, they became friends, as did their two eldest sons, Friedel and Hansy. While the boys played together, the mothers knit hats and children's sweaters, shared parenting tips, confided about their husbands, shared their interest in music and books, and offered advice on how to handle household help. Katrina's husband had been a police officer in those days. Now he was the Chief of Police.

The two women hadn't spent any time together for five years, not since Herr Mueller had joined the Nazi Party. At first, the women had exchanged occasional whispered words when they passed in the public square. Over the last few years, Katrina had not said a word if they met accidentally in a shop or on the plaza. She had only nodded and, occasionally, she dropped an encouraging note into Clara's shopping basket. Last year she had dropped a note that read:

> *"I will phone if there is danger that cannot*
> *wait for a chance meeting. I will say a time*
> *and place and you must be there."*

She had not signed her name, but she had added in tiny print: *"Burn this."*

This was the first time Katrina had called. The meeting was in exactly an hour. Clara, too nervous to eat breakfast, paced the apartment and drank two cups of strong coffee. Finally, sensing the worst, she went to the attic and brought down her suitcase. Then she pinned on her hat, put her coin purse in her pocket, her shopping basket over her arm, and strode out the door. The morning was warm, and the humid air made the cloth of her cotton dress cling to her back. By the time she arrived at the market square, beads of perspiration clung to her forehead. She had forgotten to bring a handkerchief and wiped the moisture away with her hand.

Clara went directly to the stall of a local farmer that sold produce. She knew this was one of Katrina's favorite vendors. But her friend was not at the stall. Clara turned slowly to check around the square and saw Katrina waiting on the other side, in the shadow of the church. Clara quickly selected lettuce and a small bunch of parsley, paid, and dropped them in the basket. She touched a plump tomato. It was as red as the background on a Nazi banner, but certainly sweeter. She sensed Katrina beside her.

"Don't turn your head," her friend said, her voice low and raspy. Clara felt her basket strain against her arm as Katrina stuffed a folded paper under the lettuce. "Now go home," her friend whispered.

Clara walked home as fast as she could. With the door securely closed behind her and the front drapes drawn, Clara unfolded the note and read the words her friend had scrawled on a scrap of paper.

You must leave. No later than tomorrow!
The police plan to evict all Jews from their
homes. You will be forced to live together in a
ghetto house in the old town. The orders have
been signed. I have seen the list of the ones to
be moved in three days. Your name is on it.
Beware, this is only the first step. Godspeed.
My heart is with you.

Clara picked up the phone and called Albert. When she heard his voice on the line, she could do no more than whisper, "Albert. Something's happened."

"Good morning, darling. I miss you already," he said. His voice brought tears to her eyes.

"Shush, Albert. Listen. There is news I must tell you . . . in person. Come to me soon . . . as soon as you can."

"What is it?" He paused and then said, "Are you ill, Frau Lang? Are you sick?"

"Yes, doctor. My heart is filled with pain. I need you."

"I will be there. When Mutti is napping, I will come to you."

While she waited for Albert, Clara began to rummage in her almost-empty drawers. She could not take everything. There was no time to ship a trunk. She had miscalculated. What she could not take she would ask Frau Weiss to donate to the clothing bank at the synagogue. She would be able to take only what she could carry in one suitcase.

She must appear to be going to England for a summer holiday, yet she knew she needed to think long term. There was no way to know how long she must stay in London before her US visa arrived. Herman had been there for more than four months. Her British transit visa would allow her to stay in England once she was safely there. It was getting out of Germany that would be the problem.

She had no time to pay the huge Reich Flight Tax, now as much as 90 percent of her assets, get an updated tax clearance certificate, submit a customs declaration, or file a certificate of dissolution of residence with the police. It must seem that she was simply going for a short visit with her daughter living in London. Luckily, her passport, newly emblazoned with the large red "J," had stamps to prove she was in the habit of traveling back and forth. She would take her most recent letters from Edith and Herman in case she needed proof of family in London. But she must be careful to hide her transit visa and her US verification of visa application.

Clara began to sort through her clothing. She would only take sturdy, practical things in good repair. She rolled up two sweaters and put them in the bottom of her luggage. Between the sweaters she stacked undergarments, including a corset, stockings, two pairs of gloves, and four blouses. Then she carefully folded two long-sleeved dresses, two summer frocks, and two skirts. She laid them carefully on top. Perhaps she could fit in another blouse and a light jacket. The special pockets in the lid held her dress shoes, as well as a pair of light slippers to wear indoors. With the extra blouse and the jacket added, the case was full. There were only small spaces between her clothing. She set aside her hairbrush and combs, her toothbrush, and a few other personal items to add later. She got the box of letters from the bottom of the wardrobe and placed it on the bed beside her open suitcase.

She went to the living room, lifted her violin from its stand, put it in its leather case, and placed it next to her suitcase on her bed. She would not leave her violin for a Gestapo officer to play. She would bring it with her, even if she had to carry it on her lap for the entire journey to London.

She took her winter coat with the fur collar and her largest leather handbag out of the wardrobe and laid them on the bed. This was all she would be able to manage. These things and the clothes she wore. As Clara stared at the items arranged on her bed, she heard a tap on her apartment door.

She had been distracted. This was the first time she hadn't waited at the window to watch for Albert's arrival and let him in the front entrance herself. She rushed to open her door.

"A maid let me in," he said and held up his medical case. "I told her you were ill, and she said to go right upstairs." He led her to the sofa. "What has happened? Are your children okay?"

"Yes, they're splendid. It's not that. Remember I told you about my friend? The one who's married to the Chief of Police?" She lifted the note out of her pocket where she had stuck it until she could show it to Albert. "She called this morning, and we met at the market. She gave this warning to me." She trembled as she held out the paper.

Albert's lips drew tight as he read the words and the lines on his brow deepened. "You must do as she says. You must go, my love." He drew in a deep breath that caught in his throat. "It is past time for you to go. We have known this, but our love made us test fate."

Clara felt the sting of gathering tears. "Albert, how can I leave you? Please find a way to come with me. We can bundle your mother up in blankets. She can travel in her wheelchair. There would be two of us to care for her. Please say you'll come. I will pay for the fare for us all. Train. Boat. Whatever!"

"Stop this now! You know it is impossible. We've talked about this before." Albert put his hand under her chin as if she were a child and he must make her pay attention.

Perhaps she was a child at this moment, a child unable to accept reality.

"Darling," he said, "I love you with all my heart, but she is my mother. I will not ask her to spend her last days in the struggle of travel and adjusting to a new home. She gets weaker by the day and seldom leaves her bed except to join the music group . . . her only pleasure these days." He wiped the tears from Clara's cheeks. "As her son, I will not leave her. As her doctor, I believe she will not finish the summer."

Clara gasped. "Is she so ill?" she said. "I hadn't realized. I must visit her."

"She doesn't like to show it to her music friends," he said. "But without the needed medication, she is in great pain." He leaned down and kissed Clara gently. "Do not try to visit. You must pack and leave tomorrow morning." He kissed her lips again. "As your lover, I promise to follow. No more than a month or two, I think. Perhaps they won't make a dying lady and her doctor move immediately to this ghetto building, this Judenhäuser. But if the Nazis are that cruel, which is what I expect, I must be with Mutti. This news makes it even more important for me to stay with her."

Clara nodded. She knew he was right, though she didn't want to acknowledge it. She threw her arms around him and wept. He held her until she could cry no more, then wiped her cheeks with his handkerchief. She stood up straight. She was determined to be strong as she faced the future. "Albert, you must go and warn our friends. They will need time to prepare. The police can't possibly gather every Jew in one day." They stood and walked together to the door, their fingers tightly entwined. "I must finish packing. And I need to arrange for my train and plane ticket. And send a telegram to Edith." Her eyes searched his. "Will you return tonight? I know you can't stay, and I don't think I could bear to leave in the morning if you did. But I must see you once more before I go. If you come, I promise not to cry." She opened the door and gently pushed him out.

When Albert left, she put her hand in her pocket and pulled out the note. *I must burn this,* she thought. She walked to the cold fireplace, the note firmly in her fingers. She took one of the long matches from the vase on the mantel, struck it against the bricks, and touched the flame to the note. The edges of the paper turned black, and a flame caught hold. She flicked the burning note into the fireplace. The paper flared, then disintegrated, leaving only a curl of black ash.

Clara made the necessary phone calls to the train station, to Frankfurt Airport, and to the telegraph office. Because she did not have all the necessary permits for emigration, she had to purchase a round-trip ticket to London with a return date the following week. She was lucky to get the last available seat on a flight from Frankfurt to London the next afternoon. The return ticket she would never use was easier. The agent informed her that the flight out of London next week was only half full. The expensive ticket, coupled with the Jewish travel tax, would deplete her stash of funds considerably, yet there was still a large amount of money in her Deutsche Bank account that she would probably never see again.

She brought her purse from the bedroom and inspected the inside. There was a place where the lining was loose, and she snipped the stitches of a nearby seam. She got her passport, the transit visa, and the US affidavit from her desk. One more time, she checked the card that confirmed she had applied for a US visa. She had been given #121,485 on the waiting list. The official letter that came with the card warned that the average wait time for her number could be as much as five years. It had been over a year since her application. She slipped the affidavit card and the transit visa in between the silk lining and the leather. Then with tiny invisible stitches she closed the seam. No matter what happened, she must never part with her handbag.

She put her passport in a pocket on the inside of her purse. She gathered her stashed marks from various drawers and secret hiding places and tied them into two bundles. One she put with her passport, the other she put in a leather money pouch she could buckle around her waist. There was plenty to pay for the train ticket and the plane ticket she had booked. She might even have more left over than she was allowed to take from Germany. She wished she could give the surplus to Albert to help any of their friends who needed it. But who knew what might happen between here and Frankfurt that would require a few marks to smooth the way.

She spent the rest of the afternoon with scissors, needle, and thread. She arranged her few remaining pieces of jewelry on the table in the living room. She would wear her diamond engagement ring and the matching wedding band. Their absence might cause suspicion. The amethyst brooch she wrapped in a silk hankie. She slit open the woolen layers of her coat's lapel and tucked the bundle inside, then stitched it closed again. She hid the matching amethyst and black opal ring in the other lapel. With the fur collar in place, the lumps were invisible. Two platinum stick pins, one with a pearl, the other filigreed, she pushed under the lining of the violin case.

Feeling hungry at last, she nibbled on pumpernickel and cheese. Finally, she entered her bedroom and took out the stacks of letters and the box that held Edith's diary. She would bring the single letter from Charlie and the birthday card with her to London. But they had to be well hidden. She slit open the lining of the summer jacket she had added to the top of her suitcase. She slipped the letter and the card inside, then closed the opening with tiny stitches. She selected one letter from her son and several from her daughter, making sure none of them included pleas to leave Germany. She stuffed them into her purse. She carried all the other letters and the diary to the fireplace. Slowly she tore them into pieces. She lit the paper scraps scrawled with words on words and watched them burn. The gold-edged pages of the diary curled prettily into flame, but the leather cover burned slowly, leaving jagged, singed remains in the firebox and an acrid smell in the air as the black smoke curled up the chimney.

Back in her room, she rolled up winter underwear, a pair of knitted mittens, and a woolen scarf, soft things that would be useful when the weather turned cold. She placed them around the violin in its case. If anyone questioned why she traveled with woolen under-wear in July, she would explain that it was to pad her violin.

The cuckoo clock had chimed patiently several times since she had begun her packing. It was almost dusk, and she had not heard from Albert again. She must keep busy. She inspected the clothing in her closet and selected a comfortable suit to wear on the plane. To the lapel of her suit, she pinned a black ebony broach that opened like a locket and held a picture of her sister Ida. She set aside all she would need for the journey, walking shoes, her corset and underth-ings, stockings, a hat, and gloves. Perhaps she could get away with wearing extra layers, perhaps two blouses, or three pairs of under drawers. She would decide later. Still Albert had not called.

She made herself a cup of herbal tea and put the remainder of the packet in her purse. She sipped the tea and closed her eyes. She could think of nothing else to do. She felt quite proud of how organized she had been. She wrote a note to Frau Weiss, then ripped it up. Better to write to her once she was safe in England.

At last, the phone rang, and she jumped to answer it.

"I'm on my way," he said. "Watch for me."

Clara stood at the window clutching the long drapes and watched the street. When his figure strode through the gate, she hurried downstairs to the front door and let him in. Without a word they returned to her apartment and closed the door. Albert clutched her to his chest.

"I'm sorry I'm late. I talked to as many people as I could. I told them about what will happen." He sighed. "Most believed me. Some didn't. When I went to warn Eleanor, I asked if she could sit with Mutti. She came, of course, but she said I must not linger more than an hour. She says she will flee with Joshua tomorrow and she must pack."

"Where will she go?" Clara asked.

"I don't think she knows. She simply doesn't want to get caught in a ghetto house. She fears they will never get away after that. I think she's wrong. The Nazis want to be rid of us, as long as we leave empty-handed. Anyone who gets the proper papers together and pays all the taxes will still be able to emigrate." He lifted her chin up and his eyes probed deep into her heart. "I'm counting on it, Clara."

Clara tried to be hopeful. "Eleanor and her brother are strong. Perhaps she can get to Switzerland. There are ways to get across the border, especially for young hikers."

"Ah, my pretty Clärchen. If only we were young enough to hike over the Alps."

His laughter turned into sobs. "You promised not to cry, but I didn't," he said. For a long time, they stood in front of the cold fireplace and held each other. He kept whispering, "I love you, Clärchen. I love you and I will follow you to the ends of the earth. Till then, we will write." With a moan he disentangled himself. "I must go. Eleanor will be frantic." He leaned down and covered her mouth with his warm lips. They kissed knowing they might never kiss again. To put the lie to that silent thought, he said one last time, "I will love you forever." He put his hand on her face and slowly slid his thumb along her cheekbone. "You are my heart, Clärchen. I will follow as soon as I can." Then he turned and walked out the door.

Clara had promised not to cry, and she had kept that promise. Her tears flowed only when he had closed the door, but she did not allow them to consume her for long. She needed to be at the station by 5:30 a.m. to catch the train to Frankfurt. She would eat something and drink a glass of schnapps. Then she would have a long bath and set her alarm for four the next morning.

Despite the schnapps and the bath, Clara could not relax. Most of the night, she lay perspiring in the twisted sheets and could not find rest. When dreams came, they were too real to count as sleep. She was at the front gate waiting for the taxi to the station before 5:00 a.m.

The train trip to Frankfurt seemed endless. When the sun came up, the day was warm and humid. She could not get comfortable on the sticky leather seats. She was glad she had decided not to wear two blouses. She had put on three pairs of underpants and, even though she felt warm and uncomfortable under her skirt, she was glad to have done it. It was one final thing, though certainly a small thing, she had done to defy the Nazis.

The taxi from the train to the airport was exorbitant and the driver demanded a large "Jewish supplement." When Clara entered the waiting lounge at Rhein-Main Airport, it was a relief to get out of the afternoon heat. But her anxiety far surpassed her exhaustion from the night without sleep and the long train ride. Her round trip ticket to London waited at the British Airlines ticket desk and she paid for it with the remaining cash in her purse.

At the German government inspection counter, she had to lay out all her baggage. One of the Gestapo officials eyed her winter coat. "Why bother with such a heavy coat in summer?" he said. "Let me take it off your hands."

Before he could reach out, she stripped the fur collar away from the coat, making the snap fasteners pop. "It's a gift for my daughter," she said. "She is even shorter than I and this coat will surely be too small for your lady." She offered him the fur. "Take the collar. Your wife can add it easily to a coat that fits her properly." The man reached for the fur with a smile and with a careless wave he indicated she could move on.

At passport inspection, she handed her documents and airline ticket to the official as directed. The man opened her passport to the identification page with the large red "J." She stood at attention in front of him, her violin case between her feet, her purse over her shoulder, and her coat across her arm. She held her breath. He raised his head, stared at her through squinted eyes, and asked if she had any gold with her. She shook her head. "No, sir."

The inspector held out his hand. "Your Jewish travel tax," he said. Clara placed the stack of Reichsmarks in the designated amount on the counter and the clerk grabbed them up. Next, he asked how much cash she was carrying abroad.

"Only ten marks," she said, which by this time was all she had left.

"What is the purpose of your trip to London?" he asked. "How long will you stay?

"Only a short visit to my daughter and to see my new grand-baby," she said. "You can see the return date on my ticket. I must return next week." She felt perspiration trickle from under her arm down her side. She put her free hand over the lump in her coat lapel, now clearly visible in the bright lights.

The officer stamped her passport, slammed it closed, and passed it and her plane ticket back without a word. Clara picked up her violin case and walked as rapidly as she could to the wait-ing area near the gate to the runway.

She sat upright in one of the chairs, her handbag and her violin case in her lap. The important thing was not to attract attention. The July heat seeped into the crowded room each time the doors to the hot tarmac opened. She folded her winter coat across the next seat and again laid her palm over the lump in the lapel made by her hidden ring. A short, bald, gentleman approached, the fringes of his tallit prayer shawl dangling below his suit jacket, and stood nearby, shifting his feet. She moved her coat to the top of the pile on her lap and nodded toward the empty seat. He fidgeted with his pocket watch, rubbed his hand over his sweating head, and crossed and uncrossed his feet. He seemed as nervous as she felt. When a loud voice came over the speakers announcing a flight to Paris, he stood and hurried to the boarding gate. Finally, the gruff German voice announced the flight to London. She gathered up her things and joined the line of passengers showing their tickets at the gate.

Clara walked with the others across the simmering asphalt, past the silver nose of the plane stenciled with the words "British Airways," and climbed up the steep stairs to the passenger cabin.

Her shoulders ached from tension. Strands of hair had come loose from her braids and straggled out from under her hat. Two rows of seats stretched ahead, the aisle between them full of passengers getting settled. The steward helped her find her place and she sank into the cushioned seat.

She looped the strap of her handbag over her shoulder and stood the violin case next to her knees. She folded her coat and laid it across the small table next to her. Her feet dangled three inches above the carpet and the efficient English steward brought her a footstool.

"I hope this will make you more comfortable, Madam." His smile was warm, though he quickly turned away to help other passengers.

Clara tugged off her gloves and tucked the errant strands of hair under her hat. She glanced around at the full cabin. A scattering of English businessmen occupied some of the seats, but there were several couples and two buxom ladies who could be sisters traveling together. More unusual, considering the cost and difficulty of securing an airline ticket, there were several families with children. Across the aisle from her, a mother struggled to get her toddler settled on her lap. Her husband held a crying infant against his shoulder and patted the small back in a vain attempt to quiet his tears. On her flight to London the year before, the plane had not been so crowded with nervous people carrying an excess of hand luggage. It seemed many others, like herself, were finally fleeing Germany.

The steward came down the aisle with his cotton balls. Clara knew to stuff them into her ears right away. Minutes later, the engines thundered to life, and the plane began to move forward down the runway. Clara waited for the feeling of straining against gravity as they lifted into the air. Her sadness was accompanied by relief as the silver wings of the plane whisked her away from Germany.

Clara's whole body relaxed as they rose above the low clouds. Once the plane had leveled out, the steward returned. On this July flight, he passed out plates of sandwiches layered with cucumber slices rather than ham and cheese. Of course, there was the welcomed, strong English tea. Despite the hot weather below, the high altitude turned the air in the cabin as cold as midwinter. Clara settled her coat across her shoulders and succumbed to her need for sleep. She woke to a sinking lurch as the aircraft began its descent. Far below, the White Cliffs of Dover passed beneath the wings, the pale, chalky stone reflecting the golden glow of the setting sun.

When Croydon Airport came into view below, Clara held tight to the armrests and prepared for landing. Gray dusk shrouded the surrounding green fields. The plane passed over a row of enormous hangers, then bounced as it hit the runway near a white circle painted on the tarmac.

At customs, officials waited patiently as she parted the lining of her purse and removed her transit visa. They had her sign an affidavit that she understood her stay in the United Kingdom was only temporary and that she would not accept employment while in Britain. Once that was done, they stamped her passport quickly. She found the appropriate counter, and, after a wait, her suitcase arrived. A porter carried it for her into the booking hall and set it down near the wall with maps showing British Airways flights and weather conditions at various airports. The room, which had been almost empty the last time she was there, was bustling with passengers coming and going. Unable to see through the scurrying crowds, she lugged her suitcase toward one of the benches that faced the central, wooden pillar with its clocks showing times around the world. She sank wearily onto the hard seat. Edith would have to find her.

Her head was heavy, and her temples ached. She needed herbal tea. She closed her eyes and rubbed the back of her neck.

"Mutti! Mutti, I'm here." Edith's clear voice reached her ears, and she lifted her tired eyelids. Her daughter enveloped her in the calming balm of a hug. "Mutti, hurry now. George has a taxi waiting outside and the baby is sleeping across his lap so he can't come in and help." She grabbed Clara's suitcase and pulled it across the tiles of the floor. "Come on, now. Let's go."

Clara picked up her violin case, her purse, and her coat and followed Edith outside. Her daughter waved to a waiting taxi and the driver hurried over, carried the suitcase to the cab and swung it into the boot. The evening sky of England arched overhead like a protective umbrella. Bright stars twinkled against the black velvet heavens and wisps of cloud passed across a half-moon. She had made it.

Book Two

RUINS

"Women's courage is the valour of endurance, of standing up to endless small difficulties, of putting up with things and making things do."

Rosita Forbes, *Women's Own*,
September 30, 1939

CHAPTER 16

The Last Weeks of Summer

WHEN CLARA AWOKE THE next morning, her limbs ached, her head throbbed, and her eyes were swollen from weeping the previous night. She could not seem to make herself get up from the narrow bed. The tiny room would be hers for the unknowable future. Besides the bed pushed against one wall, there was a side table with a lamp, a chest with four drawers, and a rocking chair. Her violin case and suitcase stood in the corner. She had not had the energy last night to unpack. That chore lay ahead. It wouldn't take long as she had little with her.

Her arrival the night before had been a roller coaster of emotion. First the relief of seeing her daughter and son-in-law and feeling safe. Then the pleasure of taking Hazel in her arms. George had relinquished the baby gladly. She stirred in her sleep, then nestled against her grandmother's bosom. Clara kissed the infant's head and breathed in the baby smell of her curls.

When they arrived at Edith and George's basement flat, her

son-in-law paid the taxi driver one coin at a time. Clara feared the long ride around the southwest edge of London to Harcourt Terrace had stretched his budget. George opened the gate and picked up her suitcase and violin.

He turned to Clara. "You best let Edith carry Hazel down, Mrs. Lang. The stairs are steep, and I'm sure you are tired."

With the baby in her arms, Edith stood to one side and watched as Clara carefully descended. At the bottom of the stairs, George unlocked the apartment door. He held it open and ushered her in with a sweep of his long arm.

"Welcome to your new home," he said. "We are both so pleased you are finally with us."

Clara peered into a long, dim, windowless hallway. *Such a dark space. It's like a cave.*

George flicked a switch and light revealed comfortable details. The pram was parked against one wall and four doors opened off the other side. At the far end, her German china cabinet stood prominently, filled with crystal glasses and the Rosenthal soup tureen in a place of honor. Nearby a door set with colored glass panes that glittered in the electric light led to what must be the sitting room.

George walked ahead and opened the third door on the left. "This will be your room," he said. "We didn't have much warning of your coming, but Edith cleaned it this morning." He set her cases in the corner.

Clara hesitated at the door. Edith stood beside her and put her hand on her arm. "It's your room," she said, "for as long as you need to stay."

George pointed to one corner. "On my first day off, I'll install a rod so you can have a place to hang your dresses." He took Hazel from her mother. "I'll put the baby in her cot," he said. "You two can relax."

Edith had pointed out the door to the loo, which was next to her small bedroom. "I'll fix a pot of tea," she said. "Come into the lounge through the glass door when you're ready."

There was a handbasin next to the toilet, and Clara splashed her cheeks and allowed the cool water from the tap to run over her wrists. After taking a few deep breaths, she walked into the sitting room and looked around. The space was comfortable with a settee and the two stuffed chairs that had once stood in her own parlor. Her side tables graced each side of a painted brick fireplace and a dining table, with a child's highchair next to it, filled a space near an open door that led to the kitchen. In an angled corner at the far end of the room, French doors revealed the dark night outside.

Edith came in with a tea tray and motioned to one of the chairs. "Come, Mutti. Sit down and be comfortable. This is your home now." When she set the tray on one of the side tables, her fingers caressed the wooden surface.

Clara could see the tabletop was cracked and stained from water damage.

"It arrived this way," Edith explained. "George says probably the Nazi customs inspectors poured water into the crate. He promised he would refinish it one day, but I told him not to because it reminds me why I left Germany." She poured a cup of tea and offered it to Clara. The first sip of the hot brew was like heaven.

George stepped into the room and reported that Hazel was safely tucked into her crib. "I'm off to the pub," he said. "I'm sure you ladies could use space to talk." He smiled at Clara. "I must leave for work early, but I'll see you again tomorrow at supper, Mrs. Lang."

The tea and splash had revived her, and Clara returned her son-in-law's smile. "If we are to live together, George, you must call me by my given name. Otherwise, you will make me most uncomfortable."

George nodded and clicked his heels together. "Goodnight, Clara." A huge smile stretched across his long, thin face.

Once her husband had left, Edith leaned forward. "I'm ever so glad you have finally come to us, Mutti, but why the sudden departure? What happened?"

"I got a warning." Clara's voice trembled. "From Katrina Mueller." She saw her daughter's eyes wide with amazement. She told Edith about the telephone message, the trip to the market, and the paper note stuffed into her shopping basket. "I almost didn't come away," she confessed as tears began to stream. "There was someone I didn't want to leave . . . a man. I should have told you sooner. . . . It was all fast and so unexpected to fall in love at such a time." She began to cry and covered her face with her hands. She felt her daughter's light touch on her arm.

"Mutti. Mutti. It's okay. Have you truly fallen in love? How wonderful!"

Clara sobbed and wiped her eyes with her handkerchief. "No. It's terrible. He can't leave Germany . . . at least not yet." Her shoulders heaved. "Oh, God. I'm miserable. He made me leave.

He promised he would follow, but I'm sick with worry. I can't bear to imagine what might happen to him."

Edith moved over and perched on the arm of Clara's chair, embracing her mother fully. Her concerned voice soothed. "He'll be all right, Mutti. We'll figure it out. Uncle Bruno will know what to do. Please, Mutti. Please." Clara leaned against Edith and allowed her pent-up tears to flow. Even when her weeping subsided, mother and daughter clung together, the quiet occasionally broken by the shudders of Clara's lingering sobs. Finally, Edith stood up.

"I think we need a glass of port," she said.

Edith poured the amber liquid into small, stemmed, crystal glasses. They both lifted their drinks, and Clara swallowed the heady wine in one gulp. Edith poured again and sat back down. "Tell me more," she said, "I need to understand." Between sips of port, Clara told Edith about Albert. All he meant to her. How kind he was. The music they shared. His ill mother. Their dream of a future together.

Edith had asked no questions, simply nodded and made encouraging sounds like "ahhh" and "I see."

As her story played itself to the end, Clara put her palms firmly on her knees and forced herself to calm down. "I must write to him and keep encouraging him to come to England. I can't see how I can go on without him."

Edith leaned forward and whispered. "Speaking of letters, dear Mutti. Did you find what I asked for? Did you find the unopened letter?"

Clara tried to appear calm. "I found it, Edith. But I burned it right away. It was too incriminating. If the Nazis found that letter, Charlie could go to prison."

"What did he say? Please at least tell me what he said."

Clara held her daughter's eyes. "Of course, he declared his love. He said he would wait for you, and he would marry you when the bad times are over." It was only a little lie and mainly a lie of omission. She wondered if she had said more than she should have. Would this scant bit of information do more harm than good? She hurriedly added, "As you feared, most of the other letters would be dangerous for him, too. I didn't dare to leave them lying about any longer. I burned them all, and your diary, too." Clara saw the tears gather on her daughter's lashes.

"Couldn't you save anything? A letter or two for me to cherish?"

Clara stood up. "Wait," she said, "I have one. And the birthday card with the Haiku." She went to her room and returned with her summer jacket. "Do you have small scissors?"

When Edith brought her embroidery scissors, Clara snipped open the seam and lifted the letter and the card free from their hiding place. Edith held them to her chest and her tears streamed in rivulets down her cheeks.

"Thank you!" She hugged her mother tightly. "I hope you get a letter from Albert. A letter that you can treasure."

"Will you show them to George?"

"No, Mutti. I can't. He doesn't know about Charlie, and I can't tell him." She pushed the letters into the opening of her blouse. "I've waited too long. And I've learned that George can be a bit mean when he thinks I'm flirting . . . well . . . I don't dare."

As Clara lay in bed the following morning, she remembered how she and her daughter had been caught in a jumble of emotions and how Edith had continued to pour the strong wine into her glass. That explained the morning headache. It was clear to Clara that she had needed a friend to confide in. She had been alone in Germany. And Edith, living in a foreign land with only her English husband and a few friends, had needed her mother.

Clara sat up, swung her legs over the edge of the bed, stood, and slipped into the loo in her nightgown. As she returned to her room, she heard Edith moving around in the lounge and the babbles of the baby. She carefully folded her travel suit, put on one of her summer dresses, and began to unpack. She had only arranged a few things in a drawer of the bureau, when she heard the doorbell chime. Edith's footsteps ran past in the hallway, then her clear voice.

"Herman. I'm glad you're here. We had quite a night and Mutti is only now getting up."

Clara rushed into the hall. Her sadness evaporated at the sight of her son.

The afternoon stretched pleasantly ahead. Clara reveled in having two of her children around her. *Why hadn't she come earlier?* But that question always reminded her of Albert and she had to shove back the ache in her chest that rose up. They played with Hazel, who was an adventurous crawler and had to be constantly guarded from sharp corners. They nibbled on sandwiches and walked in the back garden George had planted with day lilies, dahlias, and freesias. Herman insisted on hearing the story of her escape and her new friend Albert.

Edith told her that the British government considered war with Germany inevitable. They constantly issued directives advising the citizens of England to prepare for an invasion.

"Last fall everyone was issued pig-like gas masks that stink of rubber." Edith grinned and added, "We are told to always carry them with us, but there are none small enough for Hazel and the cardboard carrying case is ugly and mine is already worn through on the corners. I've stashed it away and I shan't wear it until I hear the alarm. And we are meant to keep a month's supply of food and to grow vegetables in our garden, but George refuses to dig up the yard while his flowers are in full bloom." She waved her hand toward the hall. "We're lucky to have the old stone-lined wine cellar off the hall. It will be a grand bomb shelter if war starts."

When George returned in the evening, he greeted Herman with a hearty shake and, with a hug and a kiss, gathered Hazel into his arms. "Bedtime, my sweet," he cooed and carried her to the front bedroom where her cot was nestled between the big bed and the wall.

"He loves putting the baby to sleep." Edith's voice brimmed with pride and love. "He recites nursery rhymes, sings a lullaby, and rubs her back until she drifts toward dreamland."

When George returned, Edith laid out a party meal. They opened a bottle of wine and toasted Clara's arrival and the pleasure of being together again. The meal lingered on as they talked about conditions in Germany, the travels of their widely flung relatives, and news from Friedel.

"Mutti, remember, he's Fred now." Herman nudged his mother as he spoke. "That's what you must call him when you arrive in California. He is proud and determined to be an American. He will be angry if you keep using his childhood name."

Clara knew her son was right. "Yes, from today forward he is

Fred to me. And you? How is your life with my brother and his wife? It must be magnificent living at The Wilderness."

"I like it well enough," Herman said. "Aunt Nelda has taken to tutoring me with my English, and we have become quite chummy."

Edith chuckled and rolled her eyes. "Sure glad she likes someone in our family, because she seems to hate me. I don't get along with her any better than I did with Rikka."

"Surely, Nelda's not as stern as that," Clara said. "And Bruno wrote that he loves your gay spirit. He's quite fond of you, I think."

"Well, he's a dear and I'm fond of Uncle, too." Edith smiled and gave a thumbs-up gesture.

George hugged his wife. "We're both fond of Mr. Kohn," he said. "And Edith is learning not to ruffle Nelda's feathers."

Clara couldn't help but smile. She turned to her son. "Must you go back to Kingston this evening? I haven't seen you for so long."

Herman told them that he could stay a few days. Bruno would come by after work on Tuesday to greet his sister and would drive him back to the estate. "On Monday I'll go with you to register with the local police and the German consulate. That way Edith won't have to drag the baby about in the pram and you can start to learn how to use the underground the way we common folk do."

George stood up, stretching his long arms until they touched the ceiling. "I'm ready for bed," he said. "I've been up since dawn. We have a serious workload these days setting up additional phone lines from one government office to another."

Clara had been having trouble keeping her eyes open. She wasn't used to that amount of conversation or wine. "Me too. You read my mind, George."

THE NEXT FEW DAYS passed too quickly. Herman chatted with his mother while she unpacked. They walked together around the neighborhood and through the huge park-like cemetery nearby. At night, he slept on a folding cot in the hallway. Over the weekend, George installed two rods across the corner of Clara's little room, one to hang her clothes on and the other for a curtain to close off this closet. Edith sewed the curtain and a new cushion cover for Clara's rocking chair, both in a matching, gayly flowered chintz. George cut a handful of late blooming freesias from the garden and brought them to her room in a jam jar. Their sweet floral scent filled her tiny space.

On Monday, Herman accompanied his mother to the German consulate where she was told gruffly that she must come back every month to keep her passport valid. Next, they went to the local police station to register, and she was issued her own gas mask in its cardboard carrying box. The next day, her brother Bruno's visit was too short. He had no idea how to help Albert and Clara hated that Herman must return with him to his Kingston estate, but her son seemed eager to go.

Bruno winked at her and whispered, "There's a young lady he has to keep an eye on."

Herman blushed. "She's a neighbor and an art student. I promised to pose for her . . . for a portrait class. Just a portrait." Now his ears were bright red. "I'll come again in a few weeks, Mutti."

The following weeks were both agony and adventure. Clara filled her days helping Edith with the never-ending chores of a housewife and mother. She and Edith listened to the wireless as they prepared meals in the kitchen, the German refrigerator humming in the background. In the morning and evening, there were news reports, weather forecasts, and announcements, and, in the afternoon, music programs and comedy shows. Clara scanned the daily newspaper for articles about conditions in Germany and Chamberlain's efforts to avoid war. The days were sunny and she enjoyed the freedom of long walks around the neighborhood without feeling fear. She wandered far past Harcourt Terrace, north to Earl's Court and South Kensington and south, toward the river, to Chelsea. She pushed Hazel in the pram around the green, shady trails of Brompton Cemetery and Redcliffe Square. In the evenings, after supper, she sat with Edith and George in the lounge or the garden. She knit baby garments and wrote to Albert. She avoided going to bed until she could no longer hold her eyes open.

Each night was an agony of worry. Was Albert in a ghetto house crowded with families or still at home? How was his mother? Was she hanging on to life? Clara had come to love Trude, and she hated to think of the old woman living her last days in fear. *When will it all be over?* she wondered. Clara lay awake for hours each night, her head filled with worries. When the long-awaited sleep finally arrived, it brought nightmares or dreams of Albert's kisses that set her nerve-endings atingle enough to wake her.

It was a hot summer and her little room had only one small window high in the wall. Most nights, she slept in only a cotton chemise, her sheet and blanket tossed to one side. Her headaches and palpitations returned, and she drank the herbal tea until the packet she had brought with her was empty. On Monday after the August Bank Holiday, Clara walked to a part of Earl's Court that was new to her. On a small side street, she discovered a chemist who carried herbal teas. She described the tea Albert had pre-scribed, and the chemist said he could easily mix it up. When she returned home with the new packet, she met the postman on the pavement in front of their apartment.

"G'afternoon, Mrs. Lang," he said. "I've only now dropped off your daughter's mail." He grinned. "That letter from Germany you keep asking about. It arrived today."

"Oh!" Clara gasped. She almost tumbled down the steep stairs to the basement in her haste. A beige envelope with a German stamp and postmark lay on the rug where it had landed after com-ing through the mail slot. She held the letter to her breast, hurried to her room, and sat on the edge of her bed, staring at it, her heart thumping. She ripped the envelope open. She recognized Albert's straight handwriting on the single sheet, but the words were not written with his favorite pen. The letter was in pencil.

August 20, 1939

My darling Clara,

I got one letter from you before we were moved to the building where we now live. Thus, I know you made it safely to your daughter's home.

Do not worry. I am well and Mutti is with me, though she is quite weak. The move was difficult for all of us but once we have settled in, we will be all right. We have many friends living close now. Mutti and I share a room. Bernie, his wife, and three children are in the room next to us. Your husband's uncle, Martin Lang, is on the same

*floor and I have met him. Such a small world we live in
now. Of course, I miss you and Eleanor and Joshua.*

Clara had been holding her breath and now she let it out with
an audible tremor. This meant Albert, his mother, and many others had been sent to a ghetto house for Jews. The good news was
that Eleanor and her brother had gotten away. There was little
more to the letter and much of the second part, which described
conditions at the old building where they now lived, had been
blacked out by censors. Thankfully, the postal inspectors had not
covered the new address where she could write to him. His words
blurred before her eyes as she read his final sentences.

*You are the light of my life, my dearest Clärchen. I
understand that with the correct paperwork and payment
of taxes, I will still be allowed to emigrate. I cling to the
hope that this will be true when I am able to say goodbye
to my mother. God willing, that will be soon as she begs
Him each day to allow her to leave.*

*My love flies to you across the water and through the
clouds.*

Yours forever, **Albert**

Edith stood in the doorway. "What is it, Mutti? You are as
white as a sheet." Clara silently handed her the letter, and Edith
read it. "But this isn't so grim. It sounds like he's okay."

Tears dripped from Clara's cheeks to the front of her blouse
and she looked up at her daughter. "But he's in a Judenhäuser!

Who knows what the conditions there are like? So many people together in one building in the old town. Whole families in one room. And Trude lingers. Even before I left, Albert was having difficulty getting the medication she needed and now . . . She must be suffering greatly. Surely, they have lost all their possessions to the Nazis. How will he pay the taxes?" She wiped the tears away. "I have no idea how I can help. Maybe his friend Doctor Weiss can loan him the money to pay the exit taxes." Her voice trailed off.

Edith's face had fallen, her smile of encouragement gone. She sat on the bed next to her mother and put her arm around Clara's shoulder. "For now he is okay," she said. "You must stay positive. And write to him at the new address. Perhaps we should contact the Central British Fund for German Jewry. They do what they can to aid Jewish emigres."

Clara spent the afternoon writing to Albert and the next morning she rushed to mail the letter. After she watched the envelope disappear into the postbox, she felt restless. She did not want to return to the basement where she would have to talk to Edith and put on an untroubled face for little Hazel. Clara paced the streets, up and down along Fulham Road, past the cinema and north on Gilston Road. She turned around at Saint Mary's church and walked all the way past Kings Road until she came to the Thames River. Across the water, a large swath of wild marshland stretched into the distance. She crossed over the bridge and found a bench that had a view of the fields and ponds. The leafy fronds of carrots and overgrown asparagus waved in a gentle breeze and the calming aroma of dried lavender drifted on the fresh country air.

Clara patted perspiration from her forehead with her hankie. She had walked too far in the heat. She was suddenly aware of the ache in her feet and legs. Her heart thumped against her ribs. *I must calm down*, she thought. She had spent the last few weeks drowning in waves of anxiety. Too often she had been reduced to tears. She knew that Edith was concerned about her. *I must get myself under control. All this weeping accomplishes nothing.* She had been strong and practical after Hugo died. She had been organized and resourceful as she packed and shipped all her possessions. She must be strong again. For now, she knew Albert was well. She must do what she could to help him. She put her hand in the small of her back and straightened her spine. She vowed to weep less and to stop being a worry to Edith and more of a support.

She found a bus on the embankment and climbed to the open upper deck for the ride home. She gazed at the streets as the bus bumped along the road. When she paid attention and cast aside her own concerns, it was obvious that the people of London were preparing for war. Blackout fabric was advertised for sale in shop windows. On one alleyway, a concrete shelter was being constructed against a nearby building. Workmen were busily painting the curbs in black and white stripes, and pedestrians hurried along the pavements loaded with packages, their gas mask carriers slung over their shoulders. The headlines on the daily papers at the newsstand announced Hitler's non-aggression pact with the Soviet Union, his continued buildup of troops near the Polish border, and government plans to begin evacuating children, pregnant women, and hospital patients out of London.

DURING THAT WEEK, EDITH decided they must finish the half-made blackout curtains that lay folded on the top of her sewing cupboard. Luckily, they had few windows, and most were small. They spent the afternoons while the baby napped with the thick black fabric strewn about the room. Edith's legs flexed constantly on the treadle, stitching the seams, while Clara hemmed the curtains by hand. The biggest one was for the double glass doors that opened onto the garden. Thursday evening, George put up a sturdy rod across the top of both doors and by the next day the heavy drapes were installed. They were none too early as a strict blackout began on the same night.

On Saturday, September 2, Herman came for another overnight visit.

"What a mess," he said when he arrived. "It took me hours to get here. All the buses and the underground are crammed with children, teachers, and families with kiddies in tow being evacuated to the country."

Edith hugged the baby to her. "I'm glad Hazel's too young to go on her own. I couldn't bear to be parted from her. And I won't leave Mutti or George, either, not when we're finally together again."

The family sat all evening listening to the dreadful news from Europe of Hitler's invasion of Poland. With a feeling of impending dread, they went to bed after midnight and regrouped in the dining room over morning coffee. George set out toast, jam, and boiled eggs, but the usual ample Sunday breakfast was notably absent. Edith, Clara, and Herman were too worried about what would happen in their homeland to care about cooking or eating.

They nibbled on the toast and listened intently to the wireless bulletins, which repeatedly announced that the Prime Minister would be addressing the nation.

At precisely 11:15 a.m., from the cabinet room on Downing Street, the voice of Chamberlain came over the airwaves.

"This morning the British Ambassador in Berlin handed the German Government a final Note stating that, unless we heard from them by 11 o'clock that they were prepared at once to withdraw their troops from Poland, a state of war would exist between us.

I have to tell you now that no such undertaking has been received, and that consequently this country is at war with Germany. . . ."

When the Prime Minister finished speaking, Clara clutched her son's hand. "We are both here on German passports." Her voice was edged with fear. "What will happen to us now?"

"It'll be okay," George reassured them. "You have family who will protect you—myself and Bruno. We're British citizens, and we'll vouch for you."

They were still gathered around the table when the air raid siren began to wail. Edith, her eyes wide, picked up the baby who sat contentedly playing with a squeezy toy on the floor nearby. "To the wine cellar," she called out and rushed into the hall.

CHAPTER 17

September to December 1939
We Are the Enemy

THAT FIRST SIREN HAD been a false alarm. For days afterward, people talked about the terror they experienced when the air raid siren blared so soon after hearing England was at war. Clara had, quite simply, felt deep relief when no bombs fell. She and Edith made a pact that when the next warning wailed, they would remain calm.

Within twenty-four hours, the radio announced that BBC television transmission was shut down for the duration of the war as it would interfere with radar. This was only of mild interest to any of them as they did not own such a newfangled and expensive entertainment box. The next evening, the wireless news announced that all visas of enemy aliens were cancelled, and German aliens would be called before tribunals to determine their danger to the nation. This directive hit Clara and Herman personally.

Less than two weeks later, Herman phoned to say he had received his notice to appear before the Kingston tribunal. The following day, Clara received her summons. She must come to the

Chelsea Council Chambers on her scheduled day and bring her passport, visa, and any letters or affidavits she could gather that would vouch for her character. She could bring a friend, but no lawyer, and she was instructed not to tell anyone other than her family the date of her interview. Luckily, for the time being, Edith was exempt from scrutiny because she was married to a British citizen.

By chance, Clara and her son were assigned their hearings on the same day the following week. Uncle Bruno would go with Herman and George promised to take the morning off to accompany Clara. She was consumed by questions. What would the examiners ask? What would she need to prove? What would their judgment be? She was terrified of being sent back to Germany, and she dreaded the idea of being interned, but that was a far better outcome than being deported.

Clara dressed carefully in her traveling suit and put money, a change of underwear, her toothbrush, and a comb in her purse. She would be prepared if she was put in a van and taken to a camp.

No signs were posted at the council building when she and George arrived. The guard at the entrance silently waved them to the lift.

"The second floor on the right," he whispered.

The waiting area was in a small, closed room next to the chambers. She, George, and several others sat on hard, uncomfortable chairs. Clara, her handbag clasped tightly in her lap, perched on the edge of her seat. George frequently reached over and rubbed her shoulder to calm her, though his kind gesture had little effect on her nerves. When her turn came, they were escorted to the adjoining chambers. She was directed to hand over her papers and sit on another hard chair, this one facing the examination committee behind their long table. While the committee members checked her documents, she glanced nervously over her shoulder at George who had been told to sit against the back wall and wait for the committee to call him up if his testimony was needed.

Finally, the man at the center of the table spoke, his voice low and gravelly. "Mrs. Clara Sara Lang. I see you have only arrived in England less than two months ago. Why did you come when our countries were so close to war?"

Clara didn't like that they used the fake middle name the Nazis had given her, but that's what was indelibly in her passport. She wanted to tell him she was Clara Josephine, not Clara Sara which sounded like a children's rhyme, but she realized there would be no profit in correcting these imposing men. Her voice shook as she explained that she was Jewish and things in Germany were dangerous for people like her. The chairman nodded as she answered, choosing her English words carefully. He asked her a few more questions and a couple of the other men asked questions, too. Did she have family in Britain? Did she have family or friends still in Germany? Had she ever been arrested? What organizations had she belonged to in Germany? Did she want to be repatriated? All the questions were easy to answer truthfully, and she began to relax. After about ten minutes of interrogation the chairman smiled.

"We understand that you are a refugee," he said. "You left Germany because you were subject to oppression by the Nazi regime upon racial and religious grounds. Because of these circumstances and the character references and letters from British citizens who vouch for you, we have assigned you to category C. This will allow you to remain at liberty for the duration of your stay in England." He stamped a card, signed it, and gave it to her along with the documents she had brought in. "Keep this card with you at all times," he told her. His voice softened and he added, "You can relax now. You are free to go."

Back at the flat, she immediately phoned Bruno at The Wilderness. Her brother told her Herman had been put into Category B. Bruno assured her that the committee had said it was mainly because he was a male of military age, but the classification did not require he be interned. However, he was not allowed to travel out of greater London and must spend every night at his registered address in Kingston. There would be no more overnight visits to Harcourt Terrace.

MOST DAYS, NEW DIRECTIVES came from the government at Whitehall. The cinemas and theaters had shut down and more children were moved to the country. At night, the dark streets were dangerous as neither cars nor pedestrians could see in the lightless dark. Automobile headlamps and streetlights were covered with cardboard except for a cutaway slit. Torch batteries became difficult to find in the shops. But days and then weeks passed with no further air raid sirens, no planes overhead, and no bombs.

Each morning George turned on the wireless, and it remained on until they all went to bed. There was the morning news, the evening news, and in between music or commentary programs. Clara, Edith, and George did not want to miss any important news of the war, of Germany, or of the British Expeditionary Forces, which were being deployed to the continent in high numbers. Clara pored over the newspaper each day, searching for more details than the wireless offered. In Germany she had tried to avoid the news, but now she found she hungered for details, anything that hinted at how and if she and Albert might be together again.

In early November, Herman received his US visa. The laws regarding his British transit papers and his enemy alien status were clear—he had to leave England. A few days later, a brown envelope arrived for George. Inside was a conscription notice. Clara's family was being ripped apart again.

George was by turns excited and depressed. The day he got the notice in the mail, he waved the letter in front of Edith. "I've been called up," he announced. "They see how valuable my tele-communication know-how is. They've assigned me to the Royal Signal Corps!" He picked up his wife and twirled her around. "Tomorrow, I'll give notice at work and next week I'll be in uniform getting ready to fight Hitler."

When he returned from work the next day, George sunk into his usual armchair near the radio, his elbows on his knees and his head in his hands. Clara was on the divan knitting a small red sweater for Hazel. She watched her son-in-law as the long needles clacked. He was quiet, none of his usual chatter about events at work. Edith came out of the kitchen and saw him slumped in his chair.

"George, sweetheart, are you all right?"

"I've come to my senses, Shorty. I don't want to leave you," he said. His voice was husky and broke as he continued. "The boss said he'd hold my job as long as he can, but I'm afraid this war won't be quick. If we don't defeat Hitler right off, we could be polishing his boots by next summer."

Edith put her arms around her husband and caressed the top of his head. George stood up abruptly.

"Your usual tactics won't make me feel better this time," he said. "We must stop the Nazis. We both know that. But you have no idea what war means. I was just little, but I remember the last one. There'll be hardship and shortages. And bombs sooner or later. How can I leave my family? Who will protect you?"

"We'll be first-rate, darling. Mutti and I will be ducky and we'll protect Hazel. You needn't worry."

"But I will worry!" George's voice was rising. "There won't be my fat pay envelope each week, either. Only soldier's pay from the government, and that's a pittance."

"Sit down, George. Calm down." Edith reached up to her husband's shoulder and tried to guide him back to the chair, but he wouldn't be led. "If need be, I'll get a job again," she said. "Mutti's here now and she can care for Hazel."

George reached out and his large hand wrapped around his wife's arm. Edith winced but made no sound. "I don't want my wife working!" George's voice was rough.

Clara had not seen this side of her son-in-law before. He had been pleasant and helpful since her arrival. But now, his ears were red, his face dark, and Edith seemed to know what could come next.

George pushed his wife away. "Leave me be, woman. Do what a wife is supposed to do and bring me supper."

Clara winced. This reminded her too much of Hugo, but with a touch of physicality added.

After he ate, George went to the bedroom and didn't return even when Hazel started fussing. Finally, Edith put her down in the pram and lulled her to sleep by rocking it back and forth. When the child was quiet, she came over to her mother.

"Can you take the baby into your room tonight?" she asked. "George is unsettled, and the poor mite with her gums hurting wakes up with the slightest noise."

The next morning, George was calm. His glances at Edith overflowed with affection and he snuggled the baby while he sipped his coffee. He rubbed his daughter's small feet and stared at her toes.

"I apologize for last night," he said. "I hope you won't hate me, Clara."

"Nonsense, George. I remember the last war, too, and you're right," she responded. "It upsets everything."

"I didn't mean to upset you, though," he said, his eyes cast down. "I'm glad you're here to help Edith while I'm away."

During the days before he left, George's mood was unpredictable. He sorted through the bills and stridently explained to Edith what must be paid each month. When she reassured him she understood household accounting, that she had gotten high marks in the subject in domestic school, he told her to be quiet and listen so she wouldn't muck it up. That evening, he was nervous and talked incessantly, then sat unmoving for hours, his ear to the wireless.

On his last afternoon home, he dug up all the bulbs from his garden, carefully wrapped them in burlap, and put them in the shed. Later, he stood among the dug-up dirt clods, staring at the starry sky in the blacked-out night. When he came inside, he muttered, "Probably won't get the freesias back in the ground in time." He paced about the living room, then declared he must go to the pub to say goodbye to his mates. He returned late, his gait unsteady. When he bumbled about and slammed the bedroom door, Hazel woke up and cried lustily until Edith put her in the pram and brought her to Clara's room. When George left for training the next morning, Edith and Clara felt a sense of relief.

The newspapers were full of what was being called the Battle of the Atlantic, and finding a ticket for Herman to sail across that ocean to America was difficult. Determined to stop all materials coming from overseas to help England with the war effort, Hitler's U-boats roamed the chilly waters, their torpedoes targeting British and American merchant ships. Several had been sunk. Even ships traveling in convoy were not safe. Though Clara was sad that her son must leave, she was grateful when Bruno found a berth for him on a Japanese steamship, the SS *Fushimi Maru*, sailing to New York. Bruno maintained a shipping contract with the NYK shipping line, and he felt the Japanese company would be a safer way to travel. Japan had a tenuous relationship with England, as well as friendly diplomatic ties to Germany. Bruno was sure the U-boats would not torpedo a Japanese ship.

Once the tickets were bought, time was short. Herman was cleared to stay with his mother and sister in London for two nights before his departure. The day before he was to leave, he confided in his mother.

"I have a date tonight, Mutti. It's important to me." His eyes sparkled with excitement.

"Is it the artist girl?" Clara asked and Herman nodded. "Well, of course you must go." She understood how valuable romantic goodbyes were. He deserved his moment of happiness.

Herman did not return until the early hours of the morning. Clara heard him come in and later heard his tossing and turning on the cot outside her bedroom door. At dawn, he left the flat again and did not come back until little more than an hour before he had to leave for the port. After he had gathered up his luggage, he played with Hazel for a few minutes, nibbled at the breakfast Edith had kept for him, and promised to write.

With his departure time only moments away, he whispered so only Clara could hear. "Mutti, I need you to do me a favor." He produced a small red box from his pocket and showed it to her with a scrap of paper on which he had written an address. "Please post this gift to Molly . . . my artist friend. There's a note for her inside the box. You don't need to worry about any explanation." He seemed to sense the question Clara wanted to ask. "Don't worry. I'm not fool enough to send her a ring," he said. "It's only a little gift so she won't forget me."

Clara hugged him tightly. "I'll mail it first thing tomorrow. It will get to her. Now go, the taxi is waiting. And, Herman, don't forget to send a telegram when you arrive in New York." She watched the black car disappear around the corner and wondered when she would see her son again.

FOR DAYS THE FLAT seemed unnaturally quiet. No stress, but little joy except for what Hazel supplied. The hot summer had turned into a cold, crisp autumn, and now winter was creeping in. The dark nights came earlier and earlier. The blackout curtains had to be drawn before five each afternoon and the sun didn't rise again until after nine in the morning. The endless nights were frigid. In December, ration books were distributed and a bulletin from the Ministry of Food announced that rationing would start in January. Every family must register at their preferred local grocery, butcher, and baker.

"You must come with me, Mutti, when I register our coupon books," Edith announced one afternoon. "I want you to get acquainted with the shopkeepers. In the future, I may need you to help me with the shopping."

Clara and Edith bundled up in coats, scarves, and gloves, maneuvered the perambulator up the steep stairs from the basement flat, and set out under a low, gray sky. Hazel, nestled in a cocoon of blankets, fell asleep, rocked by the bumps of the pavement. The women walked up and down the neighborhood streets, stopping along the way at several shops. Edith introduced her mother and, at each place, registered the two adult and one infant ration books. The butcher was a friendly man with a round face and a spotless white apron. Clara imagined he must have a stack of freshly laundered aprons in back to change into. Other butchers she had known were smeared with blood stains before noon.

The man greeted Edith with a smile and spoke to Clara in halting German. "I learned from my wife," he said. "I found her in Belgium during the last war, and she blessed my life until she passed away last year."

After Clara expressed her condolences, she asked, "Do you know German cuts of meat? And sausages?"

He laughed. "My wife taught me to make bratwurst from meat scraps for our own meals. I don't usually sell my homemade sausages in the shop, but occasionally I share one or two with your daughter." He grinned at Edith who rubbed her tummy and nodded. The butcher turned to Clara. "And for you, Mrs. Lang, of course. You need only ask."

Snow fell thickly during the weeks before Christmas. If it hadn't been for the baby, they might have let the holiday pass without celebration. But it was Hazel's first Christmas. Edith found a tree and Clara made a stollen cake. They felt immensely better as they folded small foil decorations and glued strips of red-and-green colored paper together to form a chain to encircle the tree. Hazel clapped in delight, a grinning English elf in her new red sweater and matching knitted Tam o' Shanter with the pom-pom on top.

On Christmas morning, a set of brightly colored wooden blocks sat stacked under the tree. Best of all, there was a letter from Herman who wrote that he would be in California with his brother by Christmastime.

George returned from training between Christmas and New Year's. He had two days of leave before being shipped over to France to join the Expeditionary Forces. He arrived in his new uniform and proudly strutted about the living room showing off his cap with the badge of the Royal Corps of Signals. He fingered the button-down flap on his uniform pocket.

"Tomorrow I'm off to war!" He danced a quick two-step and embraced Edith. "Come on Shorty, let's go trip the light fantastic.

Who knows when we'll dance again. It's been ages."

Edith silently assessed her mother's willingness to stay with the baby. Clara nodded.

"Go on, you two. Enjoy yourselves. Hazel and I will cuddle away the evening, content as two bunnies in a burrow."

Clara heard the couple's rustling movements when they returned home after midnight, and, in the morning, their door stayed closed long after Hazel was fed, dressed, and playing contentedly on a rug in the middle of the lounge. In the afternoon, Edith went to the station with George, leaving Hazel in her grandmother's care again. When she returned, Edith plunked down on the settee and stretched out her feet.

"I'm knackered," she said, letting out her breath in a long sigh. "My feet are no longer used to all that dancing, but we had a grand time. It turned George quite amorous. He kept me awake most of the night. . . . Sorry, Mutti . . .

To change the subject, Clara asked about the departure at the station.

"It made me cry to see all those men marching off down the platform and onto the train." Edith rubbed her eyes with the back of her hand. "When I think of George going off to fight, I can feel the tears coming on." She shook her head as if to dispel bad thoughts and turned to her mother, her eyes brimming. "What if I never see him again?"

"He'll return, Edith. Your father did. And I have faith that George will, too."

CHAPTER 18

January to June 1940
George

THE NEXT EVENING WAS New Year's Eve, and mother and daughter lingered in the living room after putting Hazel down for the night. Edith leaned against cushions propped into the corner of the sofa, her legs tucked under her, reading a novel. Clara wound a new skein of knitting yarn into a ball. Edith put her finger between the pages she was reading. She stared into the glowing coals in the small fireplace.

"Mutti, I have good news to tell you. Something that will make 1940 a special year, despite the cold and the war and the upcoming shortages."

Clara stopped winding the yarn. "It will have to be magnificent to overcome all those problems," she said.

"Big enough, I think. Hazel will have a companion before summer."

Clara sensed that perhaps Edith's smile was a bit small and weak, but still it was a smile. "How wonderful! I love being a granny. But, what do you feel? I know it can't be the best time with George being away."

Edith confessed that, at first, she had been upset. "But now I find myself pleased by the idea of another baby. A little brother or sister for Hazel. But time is short, Mutti. We must get started on toilet training our little girl." Her eyes shone. "They say the earlier you start, the better . . . and washing and drying diapers for two will ruin my delicate hands." Edith chuckled, then turned serious. "I know you will be the best, most understanding, companion for me. Probably better than George could be. When I was pregnant with Hazel, he was always either clueless or oversolicitous."

1940 BEGAN WITH WHAT turned out to be the coldest winter in forty-five years. The weather was bitter with snow, low gray skies, and an ice storm in January, the nights often well below freezing. The price of coal rose, and the cozy fireplace in the lounge became a luxury both Clara and Edith relished. Several nights in mid-January, it was so cold that they all, including Hazel, ended up in Edith's big bed sharing their body warmth under the double eiderdown.

Rationing began the second week of the year. Early restrictions included bacon, sugar, and butter. By March, milk and all meat, other than organ meats and fish, were rationed.

Daily grocery shopping, which began as an adventure, became a chore. Three coupon books, including Hazel's valuable green one that allowed her to get extra milk, must be checked and the available coupons added up. At each store, the correct coupon needed to be carefully torn out and presented to the shopkeeper along with the shillings and pennies to cover the cost of the food.

Shortages appeared and patience in the long lines was necessary. On one shopping trip, Edith found that the last half-kilo of what she planned for dinner had been bought by a woman ahead in the queue. When she returned home, she dropped her shopping bag on the dining table with a thunk. The noise startled Hazel, who had been crawling around the living room under the watchful eye of her grandmother. Edith seemed unusually tired. She had dark circles under her eyes, and there was no rosy glow on her cheeks.

"Well, it'll be vegetable stew for dinner," Edith said. "The butcher was all out of liver. He shrugged his shoulders and told me even non-rationed variety meats go fast these days." She reached into her shopping bag and held up a small basket of brown mushrooms. "At least I found these." A movement by the couch caught her eye and she turned toward the baby. "Look," she whispered.

Hazel had pulled herself up to stand, a new skill she enjoyed repeatedly. As the two women watched, the child gingerly turned one foot outward, raised her hand from the support of the divan, and wobbled forward three steps. She hesitated, then plopped to the floor. Edith turned to her mother. "She walked! Now let's hope she learns to use the loo as easily."

During the cold months and on into the glory of springtime, Edith grew rounder and rounder. She and her mother established a routine and division of labor that suited them both. Clara, more patient with the long queues, did most of the shopping. Edith, who was a better cook, prepared the meals and, for as long as she could manage, she also handled the laundry, while Clara tackled the hoovering and dusting. Soon Edith's bulging stomach and swollen ankles made it difficult for her to stand for hours at the washing tub, twisting the cumbersome dolly-peg to agitate the clothes and then guiding the heavy, wet linens through the rollers of the mangle to wring the water out. Clara took on most of the laundry chores, giving over the vacuuming to Edith. Always they shared the best job, minding Hazel. While they worked, they listened to music or followed the war news on the wireless.

Clara had not heard from Albert since the first letter the previous summer. The post between Germany and England was suspended for the duration of the war, and there was no way to get mail through unless it was first sent to a neutral country. Clara had not picked up her violin for months. Her mind had tangled Albert's fate with playing the violin, and she doubted she would feel like making music until they were together again.

Letters arrived regularly from California, where Herman had established himself in Los Angeles. George's infrequent letters to Edith hinted that he was in France, but it was hard to tell from his cryptic sentences if the British Expeditionary Forces, which he and the newspapers called the BEF, were engaging the Germans or simply doing training exercises. Edith bought an office-style wall calendar on which she penciled in notes about the war news and imagined where her husband might be. For the first few months, she had to make do with general news of developments in Europe. But as the air warmed up, so did events on the continent and the calendar squares began to fill.

April 9 – Hitler invades Norway & Denmark.

April 10 – Denmark capitulates.

April 12 – Britain takes the Faroe Islands. Yea!

May 8 – Fighting at Maginot Line.

May 10 – Netherlands invaded.

May 11 – Belgium & Luxemburg invaded!

May 14 – Rotterdam bombed.

May 15 – Dutch surrender. Their Queen is in UK.

May 18 – Norwegians holding

May 20 – Germans advance in France. BEF??

As she wrote this last entry on the calendar, Edith shuddered. She turned to her mother, her eyes glistening with held-back tears. "I can't help but wonder where George is in the midst of all this?" she said. "It's been almost two weeks since his last letter when he wrote that he had been assigned to carry messages as a dispatch rider. That means he's no longer safe at headquarters setting up phone lines for the BEF." She wiped her eyes with the corner of her apron. "Now I picture him zooming up and down the back roads of France, from the front lines to headquarters, from the Maginot Line to the coast, always in danger."

Clara knew exactly what Edith was thinking. Even if not actually in combat, George would be surrounded by hazards—land mines on the road, bombs falling from above, hidden Germans in the hedgerows throwing grenades, plus deep ruts and bomb craters that could fling a motorcycle rider into a ditch.

AFTER MAY 20, THE news got progressively worse. The BBC news announcers, more intense each day, read their scripts with gravity. Late in May, a special bulletin from the War Ministry came over the wireless. Edith paused, her hands dripping with dishwater, and moved closer to the radio. She hugged her heavily pregnant belly and listened as the newscaster's voice spread doom. French and Belgian forces were overrun, and King Leopold of Belgium had surrendered his country to the Nazis. British forces were fighting valiantly, but they were cut off on three sides and being steadily pushed back toward the coast. The British High Command would undertake to evacuate the Expeditionary Forces and preserve them to fight Hitler another day.

Clara and Edith listened to the broadcast standing near the radio, their hands clasped tightly together for mutual support. Edith remained stoic, her cheeks dry. She turned to her mother. "What will happen to George? He's out and about and on the roads every day. What if he's away from his unit and they move out? He could be left behind!"

"The job of women in war is to worry." Clara clasped her daughter's hands and squeezed in the gesture she had learned from Albert. "To worry and to wait. There is little more we can do."

"I must do more, Mutti. Perhaps I should find some kind of war work. Or volunteer for ARP."

Clara reached out and stroked Edith's belly, where the new baby lay, still innocent of the upheaval he would be born into. "You must have this baby first. Then we will see what you can do."

"Ha! A couple of foreign women—enemy women even—alone with a toddler and an infant. A lot of help we can be." Edith pulled free from her mother's grasp. "Our new prime minister said we are in for 'blood, toil, sweat, and tears.' It seems those days have arrived."

Both Clara and Edith found it difficult to concentrate on chores. They turned up the volume on the radio so the voices of the newscasters penetrated the entire flat. The daily newspaper was their breakfast companion, but the headlines only intensified their concern.

FLANDERS BATTLE GROWS IN INTENSITY
BEF BATTLING ITS WAY TO COAST
TIRED, HUNGRY, BUT MORALE UNBROKEN

Followed by an article that read, "A grim battle goes on with heavy fighting. There is, in fact, no parallel for the conditions that prevail today in Flanders. Our armies are being hastily evacuated under the full view of the enemy. They fill the roads and stand on the beaches under constant attack from land and from the air."

By the last day of May, photos of evacuated soldiers began appearing in the London newspapers—shattering images of dirty, weary, wounded men struggling up the gangways from battle-ships docked in Dover. Edith could not settle. She paced the flat. She glared at the telephone but it did not ring. She dropped what she was doing for the slightest news bulletin. The next day, a wire-photo of a train car crowded with soldiers, several reaching out to grab apples from women on the platform, filled the front page of the morning paper. The caption indicated the train was heading for London from the Kent Coast.

Edith jumped up from the breakfast table. "I must go," she said. "They're starting to return to London. Perhaps George is with them."

"It'll be like finding a needle in a haystack." Clara could only see the hopelessness of finding George among crowds of soldiers. "Stay here. He'll call as soon as he is able."

"I can't sit quietly and wait." Edith grabbed her coat. "Please, Mutti. Watch Hazel for me." She was out the door before her mother could respond.

The night was dark and the blackout curtains were tightly drawn when her daughter returned. Edith flung herself onto the settee and cradled her bulging abdomen. She looked as weary as the soldiers in the news photos. Clara lifted Hazel from her highchair, sat her on the floor near her mother, and began to untie Edith's shoes. "What happened? Did you see anyone you knew?"

Edith closed her eyes and rubbed them with the heel of her hand. "There were so many trains coming in. I went to St. Pancras and Waterloo and finally to London Bridge Station. That's where the crowds waited to cheer whenever a train arrived with soldiers. There were even kiddies lined up at the kiosk buying sweets to give to the men." She laid her hand across her forehead, too tired to go on.

Clara slowly removed her daughter's shoes and rubbed her feet. Hazel, sensing the somber mood, patted her mother's mountainous tummy gently.

"Baba," she whispered.

Edith opened her eyes and reached out to the little one. "I'll find your daddy, sweetheart. For you and the new baby." She turned to Clara. "I know he's out there somewhere. I won't give up."

Most afternoons, after putting Hazel down for her nap, Edith donned her coat and set off for London Bridge Station. Each evening, she came home fatigued and discouraged. As she nibbled at the warmed-up dinner Clara offered, Edith described her day to her mother. There were always crowds at the stations waving and cheering whenever a train full of soldiers pulled in. Edith would search the faces of the bedraggled soldiers for the one that would light up when he saw her. Everywhere she asked questions, but officials had no time for the concerns of one wife out of thousands clamoring for news.

One evening, Clara showed Edith an article in the *Times* that said trains were coming in from ports other than Dover. The next day, Edith left earlier than usual and returned home even later. She said she had traveled by train all the way to Ramsgate and over to Folkestone. "But I didn't find him," she said, her voice so weary that she could barely speak. "Lots of devastated and wounded soldiers, but no George."

By the end of the first week of June, with still no word from George, Edith heard that the nearby Addison Road Station in Shepherd's Bush was serving as one of the main clearing stations for evacuation trains. Addison Road, only a few underground stops away, was far easier for her to visit.

Each afternoon, she left Clara in charge of her daughter and headed for Shepherd's Bush. "I must be there when the trains come in," she said. "There are volunteers at Addison who hand out cups of hot tea and sweet buns. I can help them. And maybe I can learn where the men are being sent."

On the sixth afternoon, she came home with a look of defeat.

She had learned that many of the men were being sent directly to hospital or to camps along the south coast. "There's a nice lieutenant in charge of sorting incoming troops at the station," she said. "He told me many uninjured, able-bodied men aren't even given leave to visit their families before they are reassigned.

Edith managed a wan smile as she rubbed her belly. "Then he gaped at my bulging shape and swollen ankles and told me to go home and put my feet up! 'If my wife were in your condition,' he told me, 'I'd want her at home, not traipsing about endangering the unborn babe she carried.' He took me by the elbow and steered me to the exit. He virtually ordered me to go home. 'Don't come back,' he said. He's the officer in charge of checking in all the men that come through there, and he promised he would keep his eye open for my George. He promised that if George Collett comes through Addison, he will know it. And he will order him to ring home." She paused, then added, her head downcast. "He said if we don't hear from George in the next few weeks, I should make inquiries with the war department. Only bad news could come from them."

After the weeks of frantic activity and with her due date rapidly approaching, Edith was barely able to drag herself out of bed the next few mornings. "I am grateful for all you do," she told her mother several times during the day.

Later that week, as both Hazel and Edith lay sleeping side by side in the big bed for their afternoon nap, Clara heard the front door open and heavy footsteps in the hall. She rushed out of the kitchen, wiping her palms on her apron, and there he was. George stood in the hallway, slightly stooped, leaning on a crutch, his left foot and ankle wrapped in clean bandages and supported by a splint. But he was alive.

"Where's Edith?" His voice was hoarse.

Clara held her finger to her lips and pointed. George turned, limped to the bedroom, and quietly entered. Later, when she heard the baby fuss, she went in and collected her grandbaby. Edith and George lay spoon fashion, George behind his wife with his long arms encircling her and her baby-filled belly. Both were fast asleep.

Later, in the evening, Edith came out. "He's totally exhausted," she said by way of explanation. "I'll take in a tray."

Clara put Hazel to bed in the pram and wheeled it into her room. While she was washing up in the kitchen, she could hear George in the WC and his shambling footsteps as he returned directly to the bedroom. The sounds of faintly muffled voices and creaking springs came from the room as Clara prepared for bed.

In the small hours of the morning, surrounded by inky darkness, she woke with a start. A sense of unease filled her chest. *Had a noise awakened her?* The luminescent hands on her clock showed it was after 3:00 a.m. Clara sat on the edge of her bed, listening. A whispery sound, like the intake of a breath, urged her to check the hall. Edith stood outside her door, a glass of water in one hand, the other holding up the long skirt of her nightie. Mother and daughter watched as liquid flowed from between Edith's legs and formed a puddle at her feet.

Edith spoke softly. "George had a nightmare," she said. "I was getting him water." A tired smile flitted across her face. "I think this is more water than he's expecting."

Clara turned to the hall telephone. "I'll call the midwife and the hospital."

Edith doubled over as a contraction gripped her.

George came out wide-eyed. "I remember this," he said. "Blimey! This baby is eager to meet his poppa."

George called a taxi, while Edith collected the small valise standing in the corner. Before dawn, Clara was left standing in the hall with Hazel, who fussed and nuzzled in her arms. Late that afternoon, George phoned to announce the birth of a baby boy.

"You have a brother now," Clara whispered in her granddaughter's ear. "For the rest of your life you will be a big sister."

Because of the new baby, George's three-day leave was extended to a fortnight. Clara and her son-in-law were on their own while Edith and baby Michael rested in the lying-in hospital.

George took over much of the cooking and housecleaning, and, though he seldom initiated a conversation these days, Clara always felt his presence in the flat and heard the clump of his crutch as he moved from one room to another. In the afternoon, he took the underground to the lying-in hospital to visit Edith. He returned home with eager descriptions of how greedily baby Michael nursed, how chubby he was, and the wonderful blue of his eyes.

One afternoon, George surveyed the back garden. "It's time to dig for victory," he declared. "Way past time, in fact. It's late in the season. I have no idea what will grow or what to plant!" But he dug up the backyard, turned in leaf mulch he gathered from the nearby cemetery, and planted seeds of radishes and cabbage, starter potatoes, and small plants of rutabaga and butternut and kabocha squash that he had bought from a farm out near Kew Gardens.

In the evenings, after he had sung his daughter to sleep, he sat in a chair he had placed outside near his vegetable patch. The stars glowed above him like pinpricks in a blackout curtain that shut out heaven. He sipped from a bottle of ale until his eyes drooped and his words slurred, then stood and limped into his lonely bedroom. Most nights, in the hours before dawn, George called out in his sleep, names and confused exclamations, his voice loud enough for Clara to hear even though their rooms were separated by the stone-lined wine cellar.

One night, George's nightmares were dreadful. His screams woke Hazel, and Clara could hear him limping up and down the hall trying to soothe the toddler back to sleep. She shrugged into her dressing gown and went into the hall.

"Would you like a cup of tea?" she asked. "Or even better, a glass of warm milk. That would probably soothe both you and Hazel."

"Sounds perfect," he said, his eyes filled with unspoken gratitude. He lowered his head. "I'm sorry I woke you. Even more, I regret waking the little one."

Clara mixed powdered milk with water and warmed it on the stove. She added a drop of vanilla and a drizzle of honey to improve the flavor, then poured the aromatic liquid into two mugs and a nursing bottle. She set the mugs on the table and motioned George over. "Come, let me have Hazel."

The child snuggled into her grandmother's arms, took the bottle with both hands, and ravenously began sucking on the nipple.

George sat down and sipped from his mug of warm milk. "Thanks," he said. "It's delicious. You always know what I need. Probably better for me than ale, too."

Clara could only agree. She nodded and, so as not to disturb the baby, gently lowered herself into a chair across from her son-in-law. "I can't help but hear you having terrible dreams most nights," she said. "It must have been truly harrowing during the evacuation." She paused and wondered if she should go on. "If you're able to talk about it, it might help . . . and I'm willing to listen."

George put his palms over his eyes and shook his head. "I can't get rid of the memories. What I saw! The men dying. The blood."

Clara touched his arm. "It's okay," she whispered. "It's okay to let it out."

George's shoulders heaved, a deep shudder racking his body. For several minutes, they were both quiet. Finally, he began to speak, slowly, as if the words had to claw their way out of his throat.

"In the beginning, when the infantry began to withdraw toward the beaches, the Royal Signals had to keep maintaining communications," he said. "That was our job. A couple of days into it . . . I hadn't slept for days. I don't know when it was. I was given an important message to deliver to the senior naval officer on the beach at Dunkirk.

"I went up and down the roads trying to find a way through. The closer I got to the beach, the more dreadful it became. There were abandoned vehicles all along the road . . . on the verges, even in the middle. And there were suitcases and abandoned prams, too, from the French civilians. And dropped bedrolls and knapsacks from the soldiers. And bodies. God! The road was littered with the bodies of soldiers and civilians . . . even children, laying in heaps like so much rubbish. In the ditches. In the middle of the road. I had to be careful not to run over them." He shuddered and rubbed his eyes with the heels of his hands. "And planes . . . the Luftwaffe roared overhead. And the RAF too. Shooting at the Germans. Bombs exploding. And huge clouds of black smoke towering over the town. It was chaos."

"Did you find the naval officer?"

"Yes, he was overseeing the beaches. There were thousands of men lined up on top of the concrete breakwaters, lines and lines of dark figures stretching out into deep water and scrambling onto boats of all kinds. The sand was littered with abandoned equipment . . . and more bodies. The officer, Captain Tennant, told me I should try to find my unit. That they were up the coast at another beach, Bray or La Panne. It was too difficult to walk along the beach. With the constant strafing and bombing, the beach was a suicide walk. But the roads were a mess, too. Even with the motorcycle, it took me all day to get there. I met another guy from the Signals in a village along the way, and we crouched next to an abandoned personnel carrier to decide what to do. While we were talking, we heard whizzing. The explosion was so close, the force of it shattered the carrier. I yelled at my buddy but couldn't hear my own voice. A jagged piece of metal pierced my leg. I saw the blood on my trousers before I felt the pain. And my buddy . . . Ted. His name was Ted. I had been talking to him one moment then . . . blood everywhere. No arm. No face. Blood and more." George put his head in his arms. His shoulders trembled, and ragged sobs escaped. After a few minutes, he lifted his head and spoke in a raspy whisper. "I tried to pick him up and put him on the back of my motorcycle. But I couldn't balance him. He was dead. One instant we were talking and the next he was dead. I had to leave him."

Clara dared not speak. She waited quietly for her son-in-law to continue. Hazel's eyes drooped, and she no longer sucked on the bottle.

When he was ready, George sipped from his mug and began to talk again. "When I got to La Panne, I couldn't find my unit, but it didn't matter. All of us were lost and separated and desperate. The ships couldn't come in during the daylight anymore because the Luftwaffe was bombing and machine-gunning anything that moved. There were wrecked and grounded ships in the shallows. Men hunkered down in trenches and under abandoned vehicles waiting for night." George paused and a weak smile twisted his lips. "But there was something amazing, too. The Royal Engineers had built a makeshift jetty from the sand out into the water. They had driven vehicles of all kinds—personnel carriers, lorries, jeeps, everything—all out in a long line that stretched into the deep water. They slashed tires to let the air out and weighed down vehicles with sandbags to prevent them from moving when the tide came in. They even lashed planks of wood along the top, from lorry to lorry, so men could walk above the water to where the boats could pick them up. It was amazing to see. And it made us all hopeful. That the engineers could build such a thing amidst all the bombs. It made all of us waiting for the darkness feel like we might have a chance to get to the boats. We did, too. I left my motorcycle on the beach and walked out along those planks and was taken into a small boat that took me to a larger boat. I lost track. I slept most of the way across the channel despite the pain in my leg. Then they took me to hospital."

"You're safe now, George." Clara stood. The cradled baby in

her arms was finally asleep. George's eyes were rimmed in red and filled with such grief that her heart overflowed.

"I'm sorry," he said. "I'm ashamed you had to hear all that. I couldn't bear Edith to see me like this. What kind of man weeps like this?"

"Any man who has experienced what you did," Clara reassured him.

"Please. Don't tell my wife about this. I was distraught tonight. I shouldn't have let all that horror out. You didn't need to hear it, and I don't want to talk about it again. Not ever."

Clara saw the disaster this could cause. She put her hand on her son-in-law's arm. "George, you must—"

"No. Don't you dare tell Edith!" He limped to the hall and brought back the pram. "Put Hazel to bed in this and take her in with you tonight. I don't want to wake her up again. Tomorrow, I'll move her cot over. When Edith returns, the new baby will need to be with us." He glared at Clara. "Tonight never happened. I trusted you. I hope that wasn't a mistake."

CHAPTER 19

June to December 1940
The Blitz

DURING THE DAYS AFTER Edith returned home, the little family tried to ignore the upheaval in Europe—the occupied countries, the fall of Paris and partition of France, and Mussolini's invasion of several North African nations. Closer to home, the channel ports and nearby RAF airfields were being mercilessly bombed by the German Luftwaffe. The BBC continued to issue daily, even hourly, bulletins about what they termed "The Battle of Britain."

George persuaded Edith to rest as long as he was there to help Clara with the household chores. Hazel, at first wary of the tiny life sleeping in a wicker bassinet, quickly took on the protective role of big sister. She hovered at Edith's knee to watch the infant suckle and cruised the flat on her sturdy legs, returning frequently to peer in at Michael nestled in the bassinet. When George returned to duty with his leg only partially healed, he was given an assignment in London and was able to secure permission to spend nights and weekends at home with his family. He could not tell Edith and Clara what his highly secret job entailed, but he dropped hints.

"No need to worry about me if the Germans start bombing London." He rolled his eyes to indicate there was more to it than he could say. "I'll be deep underground doing what I do best for the bigwigs."

Earlier that spring, Edith had received news from Gerti who had married her Swedish boyfriend and returned with him to Sweden. She wrote that she was happily expecting a baby in the fall and that she and her husband were confident Sweden would remain neutral during the war. In June, a letter arrived from Edith's German friend Sophie. She was in an internment camp on the Isle of Man, surrounded by Jewish women, as well as Nazis.

"I feel like such a duck," she wrote. "I don't fit in with either bunch."

Then, in July a letter arrived for Clara with a Portuguese postmark. Inside, there was a short note from a man she had never met and a rough, brown paper envelope with her name and address in Albert's handwriting. Clara's hands trembled as she extracted a single sheet covered with a penciled message. His words were cautious and sprinkled with attempts at humor in hopes of avoiding the censor's black marks. His tactics were only partially successful.

December 12, 1939

My darling Clara, it is with infinite sadness that I must tell you my mother is no longer with me. I am now free to

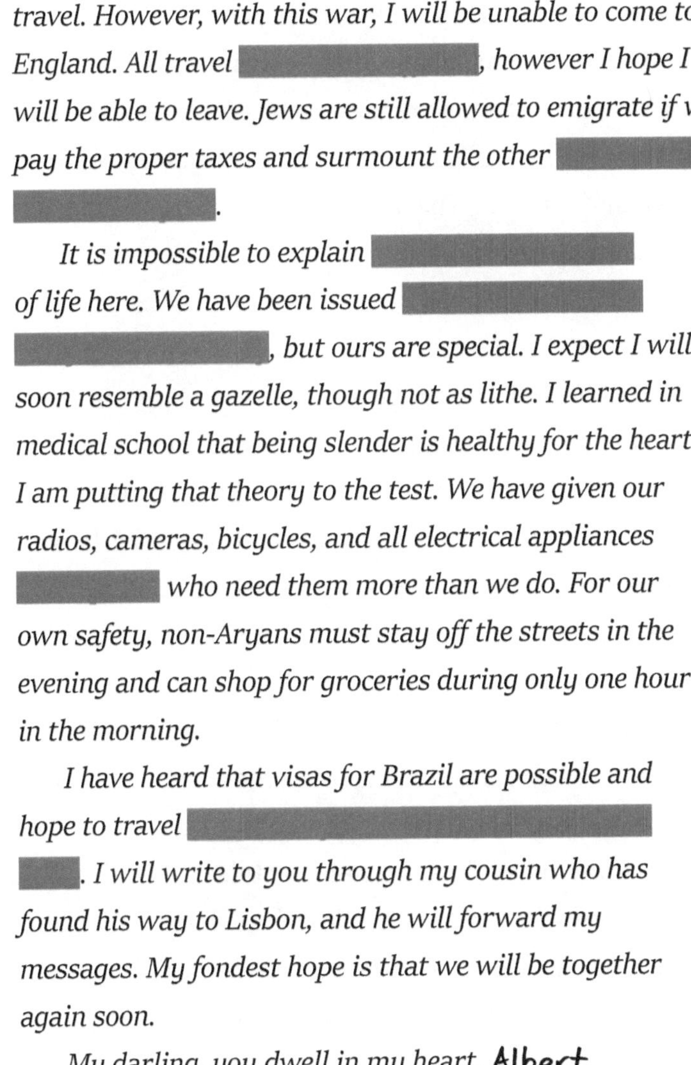

travel. However, with this war, I will be unable to come to England. All travel ██████████████████*, however I hope I will be able to leave. Jews are still allowed to emigrate if we pay the proper taxes and surmount the other* ████████████ ████████████*.*

It is impossible to explain ████████████████ *of life here. We have been issued* ██████████████ ██████████████*, but ours are special. I expect I will soon resemble a gazelle, though not as lithe. I learned in medical school that being slender is healthy for the heart. I am putting that theory to the test. We have given our radios, cameras, bicycles, and all electrical appliances* ████████ *who need them more than we do. For our own safety, non-Aryans must stay off the streets in the evening and can shop for groceries during only one hour in the morning.*

I have heard that visas for Brazil are possible and hope to travel ███████████████████ ████*. I will write to you through my cousin who has found his way to Lisbon, and he will forward my messages. My fondest hope is that we will be together again soon.*

My darling, you dwell in my heart, **Albert**

Clara pressed the letter to her cheek. It had taken more than six months to get to her and no smell of Albert remained. She realized the rough paper was absorbing the dampness of her tears and quickly smoothed it against the cloth of her dress. The note that came with it was brief. Albert's cousin said that he had forwarded the letter immediately after he had received it. His family was waiting for visas to Paraguay, so he didn't know how much longer he would be in Lisbon. Clara sat down immediately and wrote a letter to Albert. The next day, it was in the post on its way to Portugal and from there, she hoped, back to Germany.

In the first week of September, the blare of the air raid siren startled Londoners in the middle of a pleasant Saturday afternoon. Not since the day war had been declared had the piercing cry of the sirens filled the air. Edith, as she had promised herself the year before, calmly pushed the sleeping baby in his pram into the narrow room between the two bedrooms. Clara and George, with Hazel in his arms, followed.

Once the basement wine cellar of a Victorian townhouse that had long since been converted into flats, the windowless room had sturdy, stone-lined walls, perfect for storing wine—or as a bomb shelter. Months before, in anticipation of this day, Edith had accumulated cases of canned food, bottles of water, extra blankets and diapers, their gas masks, a bucket, a deck of cards, magazines, a lantern and a torch, three folding canvas chairs, and other emergency necessities. All these supplies were piled against the wall in a jumble. George lit the lantern, set up the chairs, and made a blanket nest for Hazel. Edith and Clara organized the stacked goods and made a list of what was there. When they could find nothing else to do, they settled into the folding chairs to wait for the raid to end.

The room was chilly, even in the summer. A damp, musty odor wafted through the space, and the lantern cast a dim light that did not reach into the corners. After two hours, the all-clear sounded and they left the old wine cellar feeling disoriented and weary.

While the women prepared a simple meal, George went outside to check the situation.

"Nothing around here," he announced when he came back. "Word is that the bombing was concentrated on the docks and in the East End. There's plenty of smoke off in that direction to confirm it."

A couple of hours later, with Hazel and Michael barely settled for the night, the siren began again, its ululating wail shocking to hear a second time on the same day.

"Bring candles, George," Edith yelled and dashed into the shelter. George followed, a sleeping child in each arm. Two candles stuck out from his pants pocket.

This time, tired and out of sorts from earlier, they had trouble settling down. The baby cried lustily and turned his head away from Edith's breast, while it took more than an hour to cajole Hazel into sleep. After midnight, when the constant, distant crunching of bombs had become little more than background noise, George stood up and paced the room. His long legs stepped over his sleeping daughter and around the pram where the baby lay, his arms flung wide.

"I'm going out," George said. "I can't stand being cooped up any longer."

Ten minutes later he returned. "You ladies must see," he said. "It's quite safe on our street. The bombing is all down in the East End. It must be hell down there, but from here it's quite a sight."

He grasped Edith's hands and pulled her out of the low-slung canvas chair. "Go on, Shorty. You and your mum must see the fireworks. I'll stay with the kiddies."

Clara and Edith slowly climbed up the stairs to the street level, clutching their hands together as the thumping noise intensified. They stood in the middle of Harcourt Terrace, the neighborhood eerie without any glimmer of light from windows, streetlights, traffic signals, or vehicle headlights. A few other neighbors were outside, visible only as moving shadows, black on black in a night darker than tar pitch. The only relief was the glow of stars and a half-moon high above.

Toward the east, the dark sky gradually merged into an orange glow, a kind of midnight sunset. Clara nudged Edith and pointed.

"Fire. The entire East End of London must be ablaze."

Occasional tongues of flame shot up into view. In the near distance, over Battersea Park, barrage balloons bobbed, their shiny skins reflecting golden rather than the usual silver. Dark forms of airplanes like tiny X's passed across the moon and could be seen against the lighter area of smoke and fire haze above the distant London docks. White streaks from searchlights crisscrossed the sky as they pinpointed bombers for British fighter pilots to target. The constant thumping and crunching of exploding bombs beat an ominous tattoo. Clara shivered and wrapped her arms around her shoulders, holding herself together. It was both beautiful and terrifying.

Together, mother and daughter returned to the safe basement for the remainder of the long night. The all-clear siren woke them from a troubled sleep at half-past-four in the morning. The adults left the children sleeping in the shelter and stumbled toward their bedrooms, hoping for a few hours of rest in a comfortable bed before the little ones woke them again.

On Sunday, Edith made a list of things to add to the shelter, and George went out to buy supplies. He returned with a thin, inexpensive mattress, which he flung into the shelter room.

"No torch batteries in any shop," he declared. "We'll have to conserve and only use the torch in an emergency." He held up a black coil of cord and waved it in the air. "But see what I found. An electrical extension cord to run from our bedroom to the shelter! There shall be light the next time the horn blows."

And blow it did. Well before dusk, the siren wailed and for another endless night the three adults and two babies slept in the wine cellar. It was especially uncomfortable for George, whose feet extended far beyond the end of the communal mattress. When the need arose, one or the other would scuttle down to the loo and back as fast as possible. Night after night, and often during the day, the siren wailed, the Luftwaffe ruled the sky, and bombs fell on the city.

George returned home from work with tales of destruction, closed underground routes damaged by bombs, shattered buildings, dusty, homeless people on the streets searching for shelter. Some evenings, the raids began so early he could not make it back and he remained wherever he worked or found shelter in one of the underground tunnels along with hundreds of others.

After weeks of tossing and turning in the wine cellar, Clara's nerves were on edge from lack of proper sleep. Edith was short-tempered with Hazel, for the same reason.

One morning, after hours of daylight raids the previous afternoon and an especially long night raid, Clara went to the lounge, her eyes heavy. She hoped for nothing more than a strong cup of coffee, though she knew her wish was unlikely to be fulfilled.

Edith sat at the dining table, her head in her hands. The brown bottle of "Camp Coffee" stood next to her half-empty cup. Clara poured a portion of the sugary concentrate into another cup, added hot water, and topped it off with canned condensed milk. When she sat down, Edith raised her head, her eyes swollen and red. Clara touched Edith's arm.

"What's the matter? George most likely had to spend the night at work again. I wouldn't worry."

Edith shook her head. She covered her face with her napkin. "It's not George. I'm so stupid . . . stupid to let this happen again."

"What is it, sweetheart?"

"I'm pregnant." Edith's voice was low, and her mother barely understood the words.

"Not so quickly, surely? The baby's barely four months old and still nursing."

Edith took the napkin from her face. "I know. I know. It's simply too stupid. Why am I so fertile? And George is so insistent. When he wakes from his nightmares, I haven't the heart to turn him away." She lowered her eyes. "Mutti, I made him buy condoms, but he hates them."

Clara hesitated to ask but the question hung between them so she voiced it. "What will you do?"

"I don't know. I haven't told George yet. It's not too late to end it, but I'm torn apart. It's difficult to think with all the bombs and so little sleep." They could both hear the baby begin to cry. Edith stood up, wiping her eyes on her sleeve. "I'll get him," she said.

Clara patted her daughter's arm as she passed. "Whatever you decide, I'm here for you."

DAYS PASSED. THERE WERE all the usual things to keep them busy—grocery shopping, washing the mountains of soiled nappies, meal preparation—all between air raids. The nights had turned cold and the vegetables in George's garden shriveled and died. He dug up the few potatoes, harvested the undersized squash and cabbage, and stored them in a cool corner of the shelter.

One afternoon as mother and daughter worked shredding cabbages to make sauerkraut, Clara asked if Edith had made a decision.

She shook her head and muttered, "I don't know. But I've an appointment with a doctor, an obstetrician, next week. I must decide before then."

The attacks by the Luftwaffe had spread throughout the city, targeting areas far beyond the East End and the docks. Central London was gradually being decimated. Westminster Abbey was hit, and Euston Station was severely damaged. Bombs fell all along the Thames River, creeping ever closer to Harcourt Terrace. The terrifying crunch of explosions often reached down to their safe room, and at times the stone floor seemed to tremble and shake.

Most mornings, in the quiet hours between air raids, Clara stood in long queues at the butcher's and grocer's shops.

One day, when the line at the butcher's was especially long, she was blocks from home when the siren blared. She clasped her shopping bag to her chest and ran. Halfway home and out of breath, she ducked into a doorway. Far overhead, an airplane droned across the sky. As she watched, a line of black, egg-shapes dropped from its belly. The bombs fell, down and down, to disappear behind a nearby row of buildings. Immediately a deafening roar assaulted her ears, followed by a strong gust of wind and flying debris. Clara, her eyes closed, and her body curled against the door jamb, wondered if she would die alone on this strange doorstep. But, though covered with dust, she found herself to be unharmed, her limbs still intact. A fire truck careened down the street toward flames shooting from the windows of a nearby office building. She knew she should go to the nearest public street shelter, but the crowded, muddy dugout, filled with strangers, held no appeal. Her daughter and grandbabies—and the safe cellar shelter—were only four blocks away. She would get there or die trying.

As soon as Clara burst into the flat, she knew something was wrong. The lusty cry of the infant filled her ears, which still rang from the explosion. She peered into the dim hallway, strangely dark for midday. She flipped the light switch, but nothing happened. At the far end of the hall, clouds of dust drifted through the broken panes of the lounge door. The baby's cries came from the bedroom. She was about to get him when she saw Hazel. The little girl wobbled across a floor that sparkled with shards of colored glass, toddling toward the spot where the china cabinet had once stood.

"Edith!" she called as she ran and scooped up the child into her arms. "Edith? Where are you?"

"I'm here!"

Her daughter, barely visible, was caught under the large cabinet, her lower body pinned down by the heavy furniture. Clara rushed to Edith's side and carefully inspected her head and neck. There was no blood, only scratches. Hazel struggled and twisted in Clara's arms.

"Are you okay?" she asked.

"I think so." Edith tried to move, then gasped. "But I can't move. I'm pinned down by the cabinet." She waved her free hand toward the hall. "And there's broken glass everywhere. I don't want to end up slashed by our antique crystal." The corner of her mouth twisted as she tried to smile. She turned her head and shifted her shoulders. "I need your help, Mutti. The weight of it is on my stomach and hip . . . and I feel something sharp poking my leg."

Clara put Hazel and Michael together in the pram. "Hazel, my best girl, stay still. You must soothe your brother. Soon, everything will be all right."

She feared lifting the cabinet off her daughter by herself, yet it must be done. What if it shifted? And what of all the broken glass? She knelt next to Edith and stroked her hair. "If I can raise the cabinet enough to wedge something under it, will you be able to get out, do you think?"

Edith nodded. "My arms are free. Maybe I can help push up."

There was a wooden crate in the shelter that they used to store Hazel's collection of books and blocks. Clara dumped the toys on the stone floor; the box seemed strong enough to bear the weight. With Edith pushing with her free arms and Clara lifting on the other side, they managed to raise the cabinet enough so Clara could nudge the wooden box with her foot until it was wedged under the edge of the cabinet. Clara maintained her grip to keep the piece balanced and steady. "Try to move," she told her daughter.

Slowly and carefully, Edith inched her way out from under the furniture. Clara brought over a chair and helped her sit. Edith was covered with dust, scratches, and abrasions. Blood dripped from a large cut on her calf, and she clutched her abdomen in pain.

Clara wrapped a clean dish towel tightly around Edith's leg. "I think you'll need stitches," she said. "I'll find the warden. You need to go to hospital."

Edith winced and wrapped her arms around her abdomen. "Give me Mikey first. I was about to feed him. He must be starving by now."

Clara brought the baby from the pram and lowered him carefully into Edith's lap. The child, his face red and his cheeks wet with tears, latched onto his mother's breast and curled into her arms. Clara gazed at the strange sight of her daughter nursing her infant surrounded by glass and overturned furniture, then went to search for the air raid protection warden.

The all-clear signal wailed as she headed for the ARP headquarters. Before she had gone two blocks, she found the warden on the street, checking up on his neighborhood. He promised to send an ambulance but warned that there were others with more serious injuries.

"Now go home and do your best to keep your daughter calm," he said. "That's the best way to help."

In the evening, moments after Edith was whisked away by two ambulance girls, George arrived home. The hall was still littered with broken glass. Clara sat at the table spooning porridge into Hazel's mouth while crooning to Michael who slept peacefully in the pram. She lifted her head when her son-in-law came into the parlor, a worried expression on his face. "Edith's been taken to hospital," she said.

"Only a cut that needs stitching, I think. She'll be fine . . ." Before she finished, he turned and rushed out again, still in his uniform.

Clara sighed. She would deal with the glass in the hall later. But later did not come until the next morning. First there was another nighttime raid and hours alone with the children in the cave-like shelter.

George returned not long after she had swept up the last of the glass. Clara could see he'd had a difficult night. His eyes were red-rimmed and his complexion almost gray. He grabbed her shoulders so tightly she winced with pain. "The baby is gone. I didn't even know there was a baby and now it's gone." He flung her away and turned. "I have to get a fresh shirt and go back to work," he said. "Tonight, I'll go directly to St. Stephen's Hospital . . . if I can get there." Within minutes he was gone.

Clara leaned against the wall and took a deep breath. She didn't dare sit down. She wasn't sure she would be able to get up again. She was on her own. With George tired and agitated, it was probably for the best. She did not see George again until he brought Edith home three days later.

THE ROUTINE BEGAN AGAIN. Shopping amid the rubble, washing nappies, counting coupons and preparing meals from limited supplies. Nights, they slept like pilchards in a can on the thin mattress in the shelter. George came home less often and sometimes he reeked of ale.

One evening, as Clara and Edith lay on the mattress waiting to see if George would appear, Clara whispered, "You must be heartbroken about the baby. It's always a sad thing to lose a wee one."

"No Mutti, it was my choice in the end." She grasped her mother's hand. "By the time I got to the hospital, the contractions had stopped and there was no spotting." Edith rolled over to face Clara. "The doctor came in and found me crying. 'No need to cry,' he told me. 'The baby's doing well. A strong heartbeat,' he said. I burst into sobs. I was hysterical. 'That's the trouble,' I told him, 'I can't have another baby now.' I explained about George's nightmares and his being in the army and the two little ones at home. I admitted that the cabinet didn't fall over all by itself."

Clara gasped but Edith continued unchecked. "He said he could help me if I was positive it was what I wanted and if my husband consented. George was shaken but he said yes, just like last time. The doctor made the arrangements and before morning it was done. He wrote miscarriage on the charts."

Clara was stunned, but she wasn't surprised. Edith must have been more desperate than she had realized. "I'm sure your decision was for the best," she said. "We'll be all right. Together we'll be okay."

Edith turned onto her back and stared at the ceiling, her arms behind her head. "George is a good man, Mutti. But it's hard to anticipate how he'll react. He can be gentle one minute and mean the next. And the war. The bombing. I couldn't bear to bring a new life into this chaos."

As the months passed slowly, Clara's days were filled with worry and chores. Keeping track of coupons became more difficult as more and more items were added to the ration list. In July, tea was put on ration, as well as margarine and other cooking fats. The government's national milk program came as a relief. At least with two children under five and a nursing mother in the family, there was enough milk allotted to them for an occasional creamed soup or a soothing custard. Without any regularity, Bruno's driver brought an envelope containing a fifty-pound note from her brother. Clara knew that he was unable to offer more as his thermos-flask factory had been retooled to produce war material and his profits were greatly reduced. Clara visited his estate near Wimbledon periodically, and he generously loaded her bags with freshly harvested vegetables from his garden and eggs laid that morning by his hens. But her sister-in-law's welcome was always restrained, and she only saw Nelda smile if Hazel and the baby came along for the visit. One of the few bright notes these days were the letters from Herman. Occasionally he even inserted a few American dollars ". . . to help out with the kiddies," he wrote.

Clara noticed her daughter becoming restless and frustrated. Hazel's unrelenting cheerfulness seemed to grate on her mother. The child, at almost two, was running around and constantly underfoot. Michael was a quiet baby and undemanding, but he was starting to crawl, and he didn't like being contained in the pram or behind the corral of dining chairs they sometimes set up. Clara, with her kindergarten-teacher experience, was adept at entertaining and calming the little ones. Clara took over most of the childcare, while Edith, who relished the time out of the house, returned to the long lines that went with grocery shopping. She continued to do most of the cooking, declaring it a creative outlet. She carefully budgeted her coupons and shillings and put together tasty dishes that featured lots of vegetables and sausages or small, tough cuts of meat.

George's assignment in central London ended and he reported to a headquarters in Richmond, which was even closer to home. He had been promoted to corporal and the Signal Corps sent him all over the home counties to set up telephone lines and new communication systems at requisitioned hotels, estates, and factories that would now be used by the army. Though he was frequently away for days at a time, he always came home on the weekends when he worked in the garden, made small improvements in the shelter, and helped with the children.

Even with his promotion, George's army pay remained less than he had earned as an engineer with the post office, and, despite wartime controls, they worried about meeting the monthly rent for their comfortable flat. Christmas was approaching and new, store-bought toys and gifts were out of the question. Using fabric remnants, Edith stitched a cloth doll for Hazel and a small, stuffed horse for Michael. The three adults agreed that the best Christmas gift for all of them would be a second mattress for the shelter. Without waiting for the holiday, George bought a gently used mattress at a salvage sale and proudly brought it home. For the first time, he was comfortable during air raids and Clara had a bed of her own, separate from the married couple.

On an evening when George was away for an assignment, the nightly air raid found Clara and Edith in the shelter as usual. The familiar thump of bombs rumbled through the stone walls, and the sleeping children nestled together in the pram. Clara, always busy, stitched strands of yarn to the head of the ragdoll Edith had finished. The little horse sat atop her knitting basket, waiting patiently for his mane. Edith finished folding a stack of cloth diapers and set them to one side.

"What would you think if I went back to work?" she asked. "Could you manage the kiddies on your own if I were gone a few days a week?"

Clara paused in her sewing. "Sounds like you have something in mind. What is it?"

"I met a lady in the grocer's queue today. I've seen her around before and we got to chatting." Edith's words came out in a rush. "She told me that she's planning to move out to her sister's near Towcester to get away from the bombs. She said she was giving notice the day after tomorrow, before she leaves for her Christmas visit. She's one of the housekeeping managers at the new Cumberland Hotel over by Hyde Park. When she heard about my experience, she asked if I was interested in her job."

"Seems you're interested. Do you think you can qualify for a manager's position?"

"I don't see why not. I have excellent reference letters from all my previous employers and my certificate from the domestic school. And Betty, she's the lady . . . she said she'd recommend me. Please say you agree and are willing to care for the kiddies."

"Of course, I will happily care for the children. But you must promise not to oversleep on your off days and leave me with all the housework, too."

Edith stood and hugged her mother. "Of course not. Don't worry! Betty says she shares with another manager and only works four days a week. I promise we'll be a team whenever I'm at home. And the extra wages will be such a help!"

"How will you convince George? He may not be pleased."

"Mum's the word until I know for sure I've got the job," Edith answered. "Why upset him if there's no reason? If I get it, I'll promise him an occasional chop for dinner with the extra money. That should soften him up. Besides, I have other methods to get my way with him."

"Be careful with that," Clara said. "You get pregnant far too easily."

Edith grinned. "Don't worry, Mutti. Remember that doctor who helped me at the hospital? I saw him again and he fitted me for a diaphragm. George doesn't even know, and it seems to work." She waved her hand toward the ceiling. "Once these bombs let up, I'll phone Betty and let her know I want the job."

CHAPTER 20

1941
It Keeps On

EDITH BEGAN WORK AT the Cumberland Hotel right after New Year's. At least half of the large housekeeping staff were Jewish refugees who, like herself, had come to London on work visas. Their backgrounds were varied, their previous lives nothing like their circumstances now. Business was slow due to the constant air raids, and only half the rooms were occupied so the work wasn't difficult. Most of the guests who braved the city were important men who worked at Whitehall or in other government offices and returned on the weekend to the country homes where their wives and children lived full time. During the nighttime raids, it was up to housekeeping to keep the guests in the basement shelter supplied with pots of hot tea, bottles of spirits, trays of late-night snacks, and extra blankets for friends who had missed the last train out of the city.

Edith came home from work brimming with stories about the Cumberland. She was delighted with all the modern features of the hotel, built less than ten years before. There was an air purification system that supplied constant, fresh, cool, filtered air. Every room had its own bathroom and telephone. Besides the eight floors of rooms, there were five floors below ground level filled with offices, mechanical rooms, kitchens, and, for the guests, two restaurants, a bar, a banquet room, a tailor's shop, even a hairdresser and a barber, and of course, the shelter.

"Can you imagine?" Edith told her mother. "The whole hotel is soundproof and quiet. No street noise coming in. No loud bells to call housekeeping and jangle our nerves. We have a system of lights that show where we are needed."

The only downside was Edith's schedule of three and a half days back-to-back. The first two days were routine, but her third day was Saturday, and she was given the shift from noon until nine at night. The next day, her half day, she had to be at the hotel by seven in the morning. At first, she chose to stay that abbreviated night at the staff annex next door to the hotel, a kind of rooming house for the employees. But when she didn't come home Saturday night, George spent Sunday afternoon demanding her attention and complaining about a wife who worked rather than caring for her family. As another frigid winter settled over London, Edith struggled home every Saturday night, through the blackout darkness, hoping the bus could get through the cratered and rubble-strewn streets, that the bombs fell on the other side of London, or that the all-clear would wail.

In February, on a Saturday night when the temperature dipped below minus 17 degrees Celsius, Edith arrived home close to midnight, her coat and woolen scarf sodden, ice crusted on her lashes.

The all clear had not yet sounded when she let herself in the front door and stumbled into the shelter. Clara and George were awake playing cards. Relief was obvious in their expressions when she appeared. She removed her mittens and rubbed her blue fingers.

"Bloody weather," she swore. "The bus couldn't get through past Queen's Gate, and I had to walk from there. Took me near forty minutes what with the snow and the dark. The bombs are falling way off to the south, so I ignored them. But I slipped on a patch of ice out there and almost broke my ankle." George stood and Edith lowered herself into the chair he had vacated. She took off her wet shoes and rubbed her toes. "God, my feet hurt," she said.

George poured her a cup of hot tea from the thermos. "This will make you feel better," he said. "And I'll warm you up more later."

Her husband stood over her, a glint in his eye. "Not tonight, George. I'm dead tired."

Clara watched silently as George bent down and took Edith's face in both his hands, his thumbs caressing her cheeks. "Come on, Shorty. I've waited for you all night, and now I want a cuddle with my wife."

Edith swatted his hands away and gulped down the warm tea. George leaned against the stone wall, his arms folded across his chest as he appraised her. Clara sensed an argument coming. Privacy was an almost unknown luxury these days, and she tried not to interfere in small squabbles between Edith and George. She turned away, took off her dressing gown, slipped under the covers on her single mattress, and lay on her side facing the other wall. This was an intimate marital issue. She needed to stay out of it. Yet she sensed all the sounds and the words like daggers.

She could hear the muted rustling of Edith undressing. The swish of her uniform as she lifted it over her head. Clara heard the creak of the canvas chair and knew her daughter was rolling down those cotton lisle stockings she detested. She would drop her slip, unhook her bra, and reach for her nightie. Clara heard a muted sigh. She knew the mattress called to her daughter, but she could sense George's tense mood. Edith's voice was irritated.

"George, let me sleep tonight. I must be up at five-thirty and go back to work."

"Bollucks to that, sweetie. I want you tonight. It's been weeks, thanks to the bloody bombs. Let's go to the bedroom and have a cuddle."

Clara cringed. George seemed to have fallen into one of his agitated and unstable moods. Ever since his return from France, they had come without warning and they made him unreasonable.

"I'll be home tomorrow afternoon, George." Edith's tone was cajoling. "Can't it wait till tomorrow afternoon when we have more time and there's no raid on?" George only grunted in response. Edith continued to speak soothingly. "George, tomorrow. I promise. We can cuddle tomorrow."

Clara heard a scuffling sound. Edith's voice rose a pitch to a loud hiss. "Stop it, George. Put me down. Not tonight! I want to sleep."

Clara opened her eyes. George, his long arms around Edith's waist, had lifted her off the floor and was carrying her out the door, down the hall, and toward their bedroom.

"Put me down! You're hurting me, George!"

Clara heard another grunt, this time from the hall. Then noises that ended with a thump, the swish of bare feet on carpet, the clump of heavy footsteps, the slam of the front door, and the turn of the key in the lock. *Well, good riddance to him,* Clara thought, assuming George had left in an angry huff as he had done so often before. Seconds later, the sound of banging on the front door startled her. Her daughter's muffled voice came from outside.

"Let me in, George! Let me in. It's cold out here."

Nothing. No words from George. No second click of the lock.

Minutes passed. More banging on the wooden door.

"George, you bloody knobhead! I'm only in my nightie. Let me in or I'll freeze out here."

No answer from George. No movement.

"George! Let me in! George, I'm sorry. Pity me, George!" All interspersed with pounding and drawn-out minutes of silence. Hazel slept through it all, but Michael was starting to stir, tossing and rubbing his eyes.

Clara sat up. Should she interfere? The argument had become serious, but she was torn. She hesitated to upset the balance within their close-knit family. All her life she had been taught to accept a man's authority over his wife. And her experiences with Hugo had conditioned her to think of a man's anger as normal. But this was different. Her daughter would be in danger of frostbite or pneumonia if forced to stay outside for even an hour.

Finally, Clara could stand it no longer. She tiptoed into the dark hall. It was empty. She peeked into the front bedroom. George lay curled up on top of the quilts on the bed. She understood that her son-in-law suffered from his frequent psychic torment and visions of the horrors of Dunkirk. Sometimes he lost control and, at those times, became agitated and jumpy. She must use caution and gentle persuasion. She touched his shoulder, and his eyes snapped open.

"George, be reasonable. You can't leave Edith out there. She'll freeze."

He sat up, his legs hanging over the edge of the bed. He shook his head but didn't stand. "Come on, George. Let her in before she ends up with pneumonia."

George's hard expression frightened his mother-in-law. "She deserves to freeze," he said. "She's freezing me out, more and more." He let a long breath out from the depth of his lungs. "But I'll do it for you, Clara. I don't want you upset. I'd never want that. It's for you; I'll let her in." He walked slowly to the front door and turned the key in the lock. Then he returned to the bedroom and shut himself in, alone.

Clara led her daughter into the stone room, wrapped her like a mummy in a blanket, and lay down beside her. They were both too tired to speak. Clara lay awake, staring into the darkness. She could feel Edith's body tremble from the cold and despair that shook her. Finally, Clara fell asleep. She half-felt Edith get up and vaguely heard snuffling and sucking as the baby nursed. Then she drifted back to sleep. She awoke to Hazel's high-pitched voice.

"Granny, Granny wake up. I'm hungry." Both Edith and George were gone.

When Edith returned, first making sure her husband was not at home, she collapsed onto the bed in the front bedroom, curled up under the eiderdown, and fell asleep. Later that evening, with George still not home, Edith, Clara and the two children settled into the shelter for another night as bombs fell on London. Hazel was soon asleep in a nest of blankets, the thrum of distant explosions too familiar to keep her awake.

"Mutti, I'm sorry about last night," Edith said, the baby at her breast. "I wish you didn't have to see and hear all that. I regret you had to get involved."

Michael's sucking noises and baby snuffles were beautiful to Clara's ears. She patted her daughter's hand. "It's not for you to apologize . . . but I worry about George. His moods are erratic. His anger comes from a hidden place he can't control." She hesitated to fully betray George's trust. She had promised to keep his tales of Dunkirk to herself. "And now he's the one out in this freezing weather."

Edith pushed a strand of hair behind her ear. "He's probably at the barracks or on the couch at a pub buddy's flat." The baby had fallen asleep, and she stroked his head gently. "Or sleeping it off with a woman in her flat."

Clara was astounded by these words spoken so casually.

"I only suspect," Edith said. "That's his way of dealing with stress, and if not me, another woman will turn up sooner or later."

"I hope not," Clara whispered. "It would be an unpleasant repetition of family history." She turned and smoothed the covers over her dreaming granddaughter. "Put the baby in the pram now. There's hot Ovaltine in the thermos tonight. I made it with real milk. That should give you strength and help us both sleep better." She poured the beverage into two mugs. They sat in the sling-back, folding chairs and sipped the hot, malty, chocolate milk until their eyes drooped.

George returned two evenings later, a distant and subdued man. During the nightly air raids, he avoided the shelter. He slept in the front bedroom by himself and left early for Richmond. He couldn't meet Edith's eyes with his own, but he went out of his way to help with the children. On Saturday when Edith was at work, he helped Clara peg up the wet laundry. As they stood side by side among the lines that crisscrossed the hall on rainy wash days, George turned to his mother-in-law.

"I regret my behavior this last week," he said. "I'm going to try harder."

"You must, George. If you could only tell Edith what troubles you before . . . before you get angry."

"I can't tell her about all that!" His voice was suddenly abrasive like sandpaper, and Clara involuntarily stepped back. George rubbed his eyes. "I still have terrible nightmares," he said, his voice under control again. "I sleep with a pillow over my head to muffle my voice if I call out in my sleep."

"Oh no! You mustn't worry about us hearing." His solution made her think of being smothered. "You need to talk to someone. Maybe a doctor? Is there no army psychologist?"

"Listen, Clara. I've talked to my commanding officer. I've asked to be put back on active duty. I want to join the fighting in North Africa." He paused and turned back to the line and pegged another diaper. "I may as well go," he said. "I'm no use here."

Clara wrapped her arms around the man's waist and hugged him tightly, but she could think of nothing to say.

LATER IN FEBRUARY, CLARA was caught up in her own misery again. Another letter arrived from Lisbon. The note from Albert's cousin said he and his family were leaving for Paraguay the next week, but the Portuguese widow they had been boarding with had become a trusted friend. She would continue to forward letters. Albert's words were on lined school paper with penciled math problems on the back. Again, it had taken forever to reach her.

November 3, 1940

Darling Clara,

Please excuse this pre-used paper. It was all I could find today, yet I longed to write to you. Perhaps this letter will find you. I fear many of my letters are not reaching you and think the same fate meets the letters you send. I think of you each day and believe our letters are out there, perhaps blowing on the wind and speaking to each other.

We hear much news of the war. I read ██████████ ████████████████ *to England and London will fall. I pray you are safe. We also hear* ████████████████ ██████████████████████████ *Warsaw. I cannot write my* ████████████*.*

I have been unable to ████████████ *and begin to lose hope regarding getting a visa. I write constantly to the remaining consulates in Germany.*

My days are filled trying to keep my friends well. Our low-calorie diet is not as good for health as I had hoped. I play my cello daily and think of you. I can say no more beyond that I will continue to love you for as long as my heart beats.

Yours Forever, **Albert**

When she finished reading, Clara's chest ached. Albert's words revealed a depth of despair that was unusual for him. She immediately wrote him a letter and posted it to the widow in Lisbon. She searched her memory for anyone else she knew who lived in a neutral country and could forward mail to Germany. She sent copies of the letter and a plea to forward it to a lady she had once met in Switzerland, her sister in New York, and Edith's friend Gertie in Sweden. She went to the offices of the Jewish aid organization again and asked if they had any information about refugees who might have made it to Portugal or Sweden. She registered her name and address and gave them Albert's name. She could think of nothing else. She could only wait and hope.

The British Expeditionary Forces had been fighting in North Africa since Italy declared war on Britain the preceding June. Things had been going well for them until General Rommel arrived in Libya to take over as commander of the German Afrika Corps. By late March, the British and the German armies were engaged in a fierce campaign in the heat of the North African desert. Even the Royal Signals were losing men. Radio operators and communication specialists were constantly on the move as the army was pushed back and dispatch riders careened from one outpost to another across the sands. Messages in their saddlebags, the men fell to bullets, dehydration, and blowing sand. Reinforcements were needed. George received his requested reassignment to active duty and left to join a regiment in Egypt.

CLARA AND EDITH WERE on their own again with the children, food scarcity, and the Blitz. Edith's job increased Clara's share of the household work, and she missed George's help. But her daughter's connection to the hotel brought benefits, too. Restaurants were off-ration, and Edith got in the habit of eating her evening meals at the inexpensive staff canteen in the Cumberland annex. This left more coupons available for family meals at home. However, as scarcity grew, more and more foods were added to the list of rationed items. In March, jam was put on ration. In May, cheese joined the list and the only cheese available was an almost tasteless variety called "Government Cheddar." Potatoes were the only vegetable in abundance and the government encouraged the consumption of "potatoes at every meal." The children didn't mind the constant mashed potatoes, potato pancakes, and potato soup, but it was difficult to get them to swallow the free cod-liver oil the government issued to youngsters. Edith learned to mix it with the special children's ration of bottled orange juice. Hazel made a face when she drank the bitter orange drink, but at least she didn't spit it out.

One sunny weekend, Clara and Edith planted three rows of cabbage, squash, and carrot seeds and a few herbs in the garden and hoped they would grow without George's expert help.

On the second weekend in May, the bombing began early and continued relentlessly all night. The moon was full, and the Thames River was at low ebb tide, conditions that made the city an easy target for German bombers. Clara was home alone with the children while Edith worked her back-to-back double shift at the hotel. Loud sirens and deafening explosions seemed to come from all four sides and the cellar trembled. Dust and dirt sifted out between the stones of the walls and the ceiling as Clara cowered with her grandchildren in the shelter.

After the long night trapped in the dark, narrow room with the children, Clara felt claustrophobic the next morning. When she opened the blackout curtains, she could see the May sunshine glittering off broken glass in the streets. The sky was blue, and the Luftwaffe was gone. She would take the children for a walk. After breakfast she struggled to lift the pram up to the sidewalk, then returned to carry Michael up the stairs. Hazel, a big girl at almost two and a half, clung to the lowest section of handrail and climbed up one step at a time behind her.

Clara pushed the pram carefully along the rutted pavement. Hazel clung tightly to the edge of her grandmother's skirt with one hand and sucked the fingers of her other.

On some streets, they walked past bomb craters and rubble, while on others, red, double-decker buses trundled along, passengers filling every seat and hanging on to the overhead straps. Only three blocks from Harcourt Terrace, two houses were destroyed. One home had lost its roof, and the chimney lay in the street, little more than a pile of bricks. Its neighbor stood completely open on one side, the entire outer wall missing, exposing the rooms open to view like a dollhouse. The street was dotted with torn clothing, a single shoe, and cracked dinnerware. Hazel gazed up at the private rooms on display.

"Look Granny. A loo."

Clara nodded. She wondered where the people had been. Were they safe or had they been blown to bits like the chimney? Hazel let go of Clara's skirt and trotted ahead to where a headless doll lay among bits of plaster wallboard.

"Poor dolly," she said and stroked the doll's neck.

"Put it down, sweetheart. And stay close beside me. You mustn't run off like that."

As they moved farther down the street, Hazel kept turning back to check on the broken doll, which she had gently placed on a large chunk of rubble. "Granny, the dolly is lonely."

"Come on, Hazel. Let's go to the big park you like. There will be grass for you to roll in and flowers." Though the far corner of Brompton Cemetery was pockmarked with bomb craters, most of the park-like burial ground was still undamaged. Clara thought this was perhaps the only green area left in London that hadn't been dug up and turned into a vegetable garden.

She pushed the carriage along the lanes between the headstones until they found a little slope covered in grass and dandelions. Hazel ran about till she had a bouquet of yellow puffballs. She brought them over to where Clara relaxed on a sunny bench, Michael, sitting up proudly in the pram next to her. He reached out his chubby fingers when he saw Hazel, and she waved the bouquet out of her brother's reach, then gave the flowers to him. The baby sneezed loudly and dropped the blossoms onto the ground, but Hazel didn't notice. She was back at the hill, rolling down it like a blond log in a dress.

Clara took an alternate route on the return home. It was probably best not to go by the lonely, headless doll. They passed St. Stephen's Hospital where Michael had been born and Clara was sad to see that a nearby explosion had blown the roof off one wing. Black soot stained the remaining windows below.

Around the corner, an entire block of buildings had taken a direct hit from a high explosive bomb. At least ten buildings had been reduced to a heap of rubble, wall fragments and steel girders jutting at odd angles, smoke and steam rising through the stones. An ambulance waited, the lady attendants standing near the cab, one holding a stretcher on end. Rescue crews and firemen clustered around a gaping black crevice in the middle of the wreckage. They were moving chunks of debris as fast as they could, passing the bits back along a line of workers in a frantic effort to clear the entrance. Clara caught her breath. *There must be people trapped underneath.*

She could see the ARP warden talking to a tall, thin, young woman in a business suit. Clara pushed the pram along the road, as far away from the rescue efforts as she could manage. Hazel clung again to her skirt. Suddenly she felt a sharp tug. "Look, Granny. Lady in knickers."

Across the street, the young woman now stood in her underwear, her clothing neatly folded on the fender of the ambulance. Clara could not move. As she watched, the ARP warden handed the young woman a small bundle, which she stuffed into her bra. Two burly firefighters picked her up, grasped her firmly by the ankles, and lowered her headfirst down into the narrow opening between two large slabs of broken concrete.

At her knees, Hazel tugged again at her skirt. "Granny. Funny game. Where is lady?"

There must be someone clinging to life down under all that rubble, Clara thought. *They were trying to help. But why had the woman been pulled into the rescue efforts? Perhaps she was the only one slim enough to be lowered into the dark and dangerous hole. What had she tucked into her bra? Food? Water? Painkillers?* Clara did not know what to say to her granddaughter. She knew she could not tell her the truth—that she thought someone was dying under the piles of stone and concrete.

She gathered Hazel into her arms. For long minutes, she hugged her silently. "The lady is all right, sweetie." She pointed to the firefighters and the two stocking-clad feet they held over the entrance to hell. "See, the firemen are holding her feet."

As they watched, the men lifted the young woman up and out of the hole and set her gently on the ground. She turned toward the rubble, leaned over, and vomited. Hazel buried her face in her grandmother's neck. "Lady make sick. Bad game," the child said.

Mein Gott! What had the young woman seen? Mangled bodies? Dying children? Whatever she had seen in that abyss, it was the stuff of nightmares. Clara forced herself to move. She clung to Hazel and pushed the pram down the street and away from what would become a recurring vision of horror on sleepless nights.

THAT TERRIBLE WEEKEND TURNED out to be the last night of bombing for many weeks. The Germans switched their lethal attention toward Russia. Of course, there were a few nights when German planes droned overhead and dropped their deadly payloads, but most of the air raids concentrated on the south coast, RAF landing fields, and industrial cities farther north. Clara and Edith were thankful to sleep in their own beds again and enjoy a warm meal cooked in the kitchen and eaten at the table.

On a morning when Edith didn't have to rush off to work, Clara and her daughter listened to the wireless as they sipped ersatz coffee. Hazel, sitting atop a stack of books on a regular chair, made a mess of her porridge and nibbled small squares of toast, while Michael, now king of the highchair, wielded a spoon that dribbled applesauce. Clara sat beside him and periodically wiped his chin. Edith counted coupons and schillings in preparation for a morning of shopping and standing in lines. After the news finished, she paused in her counting to listen to her favorite morning program, the "Kitchen Front." A quick, five-minute show, it offered ration information, hints about how to stretch and substitute different foods, and "low coupon" recipes. When the program was over, Edith stood up and gathered her shopping bags.

"I wonder what will be rationed next," she said. "Whatever it is, it will mean more lines."

The next morning, while they ate breakfast, the president of the Board of Trade announced on the radio that starting that day of June 1st, clothing, most fabric, and shoes would be rationed.

"Every man, woman and child will be entitled to sixty-six clothing coupons per year," he explained.

Ration books would include a detailed explanation of how many coupons would be needed to purchase specific items of clothing. Clara looked down at her worn skirt. Though Edith had made her a couple of blouses and a two-piece dress in the two years since she had fled Germany, she had not added much to her meager wardrobe. She may have waited too long.

June also brought egg rationing. Even the unpopular dried egg powder was rationed, and the "Kitchen Front" filled several broadcasts with advice on how to reconstitute powdered eggs and use them in baking. With George gone, the garden was a sad affair, and they harvested only a few undersized cabbages, some runty carrots, and two bright-orange squash. By the end of the summer, heating coal was rationed. Clara knew they would feel it in the coming winter, but her thoughts were more on the postman's daily rounds.

Any day that brought a letter from Herman was a sunny day. Occasionally there was a postcard from Fred's wife and in early summer, a package arrived filled with almonds, raisins, and dried apricots, all grown in California, which surely must be a paradise.

July brought Edith a letter from Sophie, who had been released from the internment camp. She was returning to London again and had a job promised as a night waitress at the Lyons' Corner House on Tottenham Court Road, close to the Cumberland Hotel. Edith was overjoyed.

"I'll have a girlfriend again," she told Clara. "Sophie can easily join me at the staff canteen on my lunch break and have a ration-free sandwich on my account. I can't wait to see her again!"

But it was the hope of a letter from Albert that kept Clara running to check the carpet below the mail slot each afternoon. Finally, in August, a letter with a Portuguese postmark fell through the slot. This letter was even shorter than usual and covered with so many black lines from the censors, it was difficult to read. All she could make out besides his declarations of love was a hint that he was walking more due to prohibitions against using public transportation and something about a yellow star to decorate his jacket sleeve. She couldn't tell if he had received any of her letters and had no idea if he was still trying to get a visa.

In October, suddenly it no longer mattered what Albert might be trying to do. The BBC news reported that the Third Reich had forbidden any further emigration of Jews from Germany. They had closed the door firmly. All Jews who lingered in Germany were well and finally trapped.

The next month, Clara received another letter from Lisbon. When she tore open the envelope, there was no penciled message from Albert. Inside there was only a letter from the Portuguese widow. She explained that they were hearing rumors of many changes in Germany. Refugees who managed to cross the Pyrenees on foot and make their way to Portugal told stories of the liquidation of many Judenhäuser in German cities. There were whispers that German Jews were being put on eastbound trains headed for forced labor or worse.

For months, Clara's violin had stood untouched in its case in the corner. Slowly she took out the slim, curved instrument and caressed its polished surface. She picked up the bow and slid it across the strings, but she could think of nothing except the eight bars of Mozart's poignant *Lacrimosa*. She would not play a requiem. She ran her finger down the strings, then returned the instrument to its case and shoved it far under her bed next to her suitcase.

I cannot play again, she thought. *I am overcome with sadness to even touch it.* She lay down on the bed and her tears soaked into her pillow. Her fingers touched the floor, and she sensed the empty air under her bed, her hope surrounded by darkness. "He is somewhere," she whispered, the sound of the spoken words a comfort. "I know he is still somewhere."

CHAPTER 21

1942
The Yanks Are Coming

1941 ENDED WITH A shock and a hooray. The shock was the news of Pearl Harbor. On December 7, the Japanese bombed Hawaii, a territory of the United States. The hooray was that America had finally joined the war and England no longer felt alone in its fight against the enemy.

The previous fall, Herman had written that he had been drafted into the US Army and, in his New Year's letter, he described how he had finished his basic training only days before Pearl Harbor was attacked. Now Clara and Edith had two men in uniform to worry about. And, always in Clara's heart, the ever-present longing for Albert, lost in the maelstrom of Nazi-dominated Europe.

Yet, as women had always done in times of war, they carried on.

Early in the year, all processed food, including canned meats and fish, canned vegetables, rice, and lentils, as well as both canned and dried fruit, were rationed. Edith's efforts to create tasty meals became more and more difficult as the lines grew longer. Her cooking skills were stretched to breaking. In February, soap was rationed. How was one to wash nappies with limited soap? Or bathe properly? Because of coal shortages, they were urged to limit the use of hot water, and Edith drew a five-inch mark on the side of the clawfoot tub to show the maximum depth allowed per bath. Edith's extra earnings allowed them to use their ration coupons on better cuts of meat when such things could be found. Counting each shilling, they carefully paid the monthly rent. Once in a while, Edith splurged on some small luxury. To help reduce shopping time and relieve the need for trudging along with heavy grocery bags, she bought a used bicycle fitted with a large basket. Astride this two-wheeled extravagance, she gained a sense of freedom and was able to pedal from one shop to another in half the time. The bomb-free nights made it possible to spend a few hours after dinner baking or sewing clothing for the growing children and occasionally relaxing with a book.

On a cold evening in February, Clara and Edith sat cozily in the lounge, their feet propped up on footstools in front of the fireplace. The chunks of coal, judiciously placed in the firebox, had fallen into embers, casting a warm, amber glow into the room. Edith's favorite band played on the BBC and she leaned against pillows in the corner of the divan, a book in her lap.

On the other side of the hearth, Clara unraveled one of George's old jumpers, winding the kinked yarn into a loose ball. She surveyed the comfortable scene and couldn't help but smile. What a contrast to last winter when they huddled every night in the cold and drafty stone shelter.

"Isn't this lovely?" she said. "For a few hours I'm able to imagine the war doesn't exist."

Edith looked up from the pages of her book. "Yes, for the moment," she said, "everything is rosy. Kind of like in the story I'm reading."

"What is it?" Clara asked. It had been years since she read anything for the pure pleasure of the experience.

Edith turned the cover to show her mother the title. "*Clothes-Pegs*. It's British slang for fashion models." She put her hand behind her head and thrust out her chin in a semi-reclining imitation of a strutting model. "It's nothing more than a simple Cinderella romance. Working-class girl falls in love with Lord, and so on. But for me it's fun. All about a fashion atelier, dress design, and modeling. But the best thing is that though the story takes place in London and the main characters are a contemporary, working-class family, there is no mention of the war, or bombs, or rations. And the girl's mother is sweet, too. Like you."

Clara laughed. "Are you buttering me up, my dear?"

"Well, kind of. I've made friends with one of the seamstresses in the tailor shop at the hotel. A girl named Rachael. She's the one who loaned me the book."

"Yes and . . .?"

"The thing is, Rachael told me the owner of the tailor shop at the Cumberland has a bigger tailor and dressmaking boutique with an established clientele. She says they're having trouble getting experienced seamstresses, what with all the girls going to factories and war work where the pay is better."

Clara raised her eyebrows. "And? Please get to the point. Which I've guessed."

"Mutti, I've talked to the owner and told him about my dress-making classes in Germany and that I can cut my own patterns and all. He offered me a job at the boutique. The pay's a shilling less per hour than I make at the Cumberland, but he wants me to work five days a week, so the weekly will be a bit more. And Mutti, no late nights, no weekends, and doing work I actually love."

"Sounds to me like you've made up your mind. Where's the shop?"

Edith grinned. "A few blocks closer, but also near Hyde Park. Not far from Harrod's department store! Please say you'll mind the kiddies during the day. I can be home in time to prepare dinner, and Mr. Mazur said that once I've proven myself, he might let me take work home. I told him I have a good, German sewing machine."

Clara could see that Edith was excited and the only thing for her to do was agree. Her daughter was not one to stay in the same job for long. Probably a year was her limit. Clara should have known this was coming.

WITHIN A FORTNIGHT, EDITH was working weekdays at the dressmaker's shop. She was even more enthusiastic about it than she had once been about the Cumberland Hotel. The Thread and Thistle was an upscale place that designed and created custom dresses and suits for women with money to spend—the wives and daughters of titled men, government officials, and the bigwigs of commerce. They displayed a few samples of their designs in the window and allowed customers to purchase these premade dresses at the end of the season, but the Thread and Thistle specialized in custom clothing made to order for their clients. The coming of clothing rationing had changed the nature of their business. Now an exact number of coupons must be collected for any garment they sold—a dress was eleven coupons, a blouse five, a winter coat eighteen! Each item of clothing right down to knickers and socks had a coupon value in addition to the price. Knowing his regular clients had plenty of money but the same sixty-six coupons per year as everyone else, Mr. Mazur allowed them to bring in yardage, which required fewer coupons than a finished garment, outdated clothing to restyle, as well as stored-away table linens or curtains to be made into frocks. At the shop, the charge for labor to make and create garments was high, but the work required no precious coupons, which could then be saved for shoes or lingerie.

Clara quickly understood from her daughter's more even temper and ready smile that the new job was exactly what had been needed. With Edith so blithe, Clara didn't mind doing the full load of housework and childcare five days a week. Again, saddled with the tiresome and frustrating daily shopping, she now tackled these expeditions with a toddler and a rambunctious three-year-old in tow. Hazel loved to help her granny and delighted in chatting with whoever stood next to them in the slow-moving lines. Clara and her talkative companion fit right in, and the ladies they met almost daily became friends, though no one gave away their personal secrets about a butcher who had received portions of beef almost free of gristle or a grocer with a stock of eggs or onions, both rare culinary treasures.

The shelves of the shops were sparsely stocked, and Clara was often unable to find all the items her daughter scrawled on a scrap of paper. Sometimes she simply bought what was available and Edith had to make do. Carrots and potatoes were praised by the Ministry of Food through the anthropomorphic Potato Pete and Dr. Carrot, ever-present, cartoon-like characters who appeared on posters, in newspaper ads, and were constantly mentioned on the "Kitchen Front." Even the children were getting tired of eating spuds and Edith tried to make them more interesting by adding curry powder or fresh herbs. Arriving on ships from America, canned Spam was the newest treat, and both Hazel and Michael gobbled up a concoction of diced potatoes and the greasy, salty chopped pork, a dish Edith named American Hash.

Worse was the bread situation. Due to wheat shortages, white bread was banned at the beginning of the year, as well as white flour. Only National Loaf made with fortified, whole-meal flour was available. Bakers were restricted to selling the heavy, gray loaves unsliced the same day it was baked. Because of the paper shortage, the bread came unwrapped, resulting in bread that was often dry and crumbly. The children would only eat the gritty bread if it was toasted and spread with drippings or soaked in milk. Despite the myriad shortages, Edith somehow managed to make meals palatable.

At the Thread and Thistle, Edith became a favorite of the clients, who appreciated her personal interest in their appearance. She measured carefully, was an expert at fitting and repairs, and offered suggestions on how to make an outfit more attractive. She was soon assigned to help the most favored customers. A few of the ladies brought Edith past issues of their women's magazines and Edith brought home copies of *Britannia & Eve* and *British*

Vogue to study. She clipped articles and photos and pasted them into a notebook she called her Idea Book.

One Saturday, Clara heard Edith sifting through the wardrobe in her room. Later, she came into the kitchen where Clara was washing up after breakfast.

"Look at this," she said. She held up one of George's suits on a wooden hanger. "George hasn't worn this since before the war." She rubbed the fabric between her fingers and held it out for Clara to touch. "Feel how soft it is, Mutti. And lightweight enough for summer."

Clara rubbed the gray, wool flannel cloth between her fingertips. "What do you have in mind?"

Edith grinned. "I need a more professional outfit to wear to work now that I'm making clothes for wealthy ladies. Mr. Mazur expects his head dressmakers to dress well." She took the jacket from the hanger and put it on. The coat hung down past her knees and the sleeves fell inches below her fingertips. She held the pants level with her chin, the cuffs grazing the floor, and laughed. "There's probably enough fabric here for a suit for me and a pair of big boy shorts to put away for Mikey for next year."

Clara appreciated the comic image of her daughter wearing George's jacket. "Maybe enough for a skirt for Hazel, too!' she said.

Edith couldn't wait to start. She sat at the dining table and carefully began to pick the stitches out of the seams of the suit. It was slow work and after several hours, Edith's fingers began to cramp. While the children napped that afternoon, Edith set up a corner of the wine cellar as a sewing room and Clara finished the picking job. When Edith was preparing dinner, Clara washed the fabric gently in cold water and, the next morning when the cloth was almost dry, Edith pressed each piece. Using ideas from her scrapbook, she cut out a pattern from newspaper and laid the paper shapes on the clean wool. She began to sew that evening and didn't stop until shortly before midnight. The new suit was completed the next weekend and Edith wore it proudly to work the following day.

When she returned home after work, Edith couldn't contain her happiness. She strutted once around the lounge pretending to be a fashion model. Hazel and Michael clapped their hands.

"Pretty Mommy," Hazel chirped.

Michael stood on his feet, tottered over, and hugged his mother's knee.

"Did Mr. Mazur like it?" Clara asked.

Edith picked up her son and, though the modern, narrow style of her skirt offered little to flare out, she twirled around with him in her arms. "He loved it!" She twirled again and set the giggling toddler on the floor. "He's asked me to make dress samples. My own designs!"

After dinner, with the two children tucked in bed, Edith explained her boss's offer. There was a new mandated style of clothing that was being called Utility clothing. "Not a romantic name," she said, "but that's what the government is calling it." The clothing had to be made from specified fabrics that were sturdy and long wearing, but she found the colors and patterns cheerful enough. The rules that governed the styles were strict. The government had set up standardized sizes for factory-made Utility garments. The length and width of skirts, the size of lapels, and the number of pleats and pockets were all limited to reduce the yardage and labor needed. No zippers or elastic, limited buttons, no leather for belts, no lace or frills. The Board of Trade was encouraging classic style and proper fit. To make Utility clothing popular with buyers, they had hired well-known fashion designers to create examples that would be showcased the coming summer. She showed Clara a copy of the *Picture Post* with the actress Deborah Kerr modeling Utility clothes.

"Mr. Mazur believes these classic styles will be all the rage for the duration of the war," she said. "He's asked me to produce a sample dress, a suit, and a coat in the Utility style. He's sure our ladies will want to be patriotic and wear the new styles, but they won't want to settle for factory-made, off-the-rack clothes. And Mutti, he says I should work at home on Fridays to keep my designs a secret. When they're finished, I'll get a bonus."

From then on Edith was in her element. She sketched a few ideas and took them to her boss to be approved. He supplied the fabric she needed, and she set to work, pumping the treadle of her sewing machine for hours most nights and all day Friday. Clara thought the frock Edith created was especially becoming, its narrow skirt enhanced by an inverted pleat from hip to hem on each side and the neckline and short sleeves accented with contrasting binding.

One Sunday morning, Clara enticed Edith away from her sewing. "You could use a break, and the children need country air," she said. "Let's take the train out to Kingston and visit Bruno. We can take the children for a foraging expedition around the grounds and maybe to the park, too." Though the children were far too big for the pram, Edith bundled them both into it and they all set off on the train. They headed to Bushy Park first to scout in the sunny spots for wild strawberries they could give Nelda as a gift. To their surprise, American soldiers stood sentry at the gate and would not allow them to enter. They could see construction work was going on in the park—buildings rose among the trees and soldiers walked the path-ways carrying ladders and pushing wheelbarrows filled with bricks.

Hazel ran up to the gate and pointed. "Look, Mummy, that man has a black face."

"Yes, sweetie, he's an American soldier. We have Black sol-diers, too, from Jamaica and Africa, even from India where Poppa was born." Edith turned to her mother. "The girls at work say the Black American soldiers have come to construct new airfields and bases for the US Army," she said. "They whisper that these men are marvelous dancers."

Luckily, Bruno's estate with its extensive grounds offered plenty of shady woods where wild garlic grew and sunny spots with strawberries, chickweed, and leafy dandelion plants. They gave half the collected strawberries to Nelda and Bruno and filled the pram with vegetables from his garden and a jar of honey from his beehives. On the way home, Michael curled up around the bags of produce, while Hazel skipped along holding her granny's hand.

That evening, as they munched on leafy greens and freshly picked cucumbers, they were grateful for Bruno's garden and his generosity.

For several days after the visit to the country, Clara noticed Edith was often distracted from her chores. Her feet slowed their rhythmic pump of the treadle or her hands stilled as she scrubbed the potatoes for dinner.

One evening Clara walked up behind her daughter as she stood over the wash tub, the dolly-peg motionless in her hands. When her mother touched her shoulder, Edith startled.

"You were miles away," Clara said. "Why so dreamy?"

"Nothing really." Edith ducked her head and furiously began to agitate the nappies in the tub.

"Come on, now. There's something that keeps dragging your mind away."

"Mutti, I simply miss the fun times. Dancing. Going out of an evening. You know?" She turned to Clara and for a moment her eyes sparkled. "The girls at the Thread and Thistle keep talking about this new American dance. Very jazzy. They call it the jitter-bug. They say the guy sometimes swings his partner over his shoulder!"

Clara reached over and massaged Edith's neck. "I know how you love to dance," she said. "Maybe, after you get your sewing project for Mr. Mazur finished and your Utility designs are set up in the window at the shop, you and Sophie can plan an evening out. You've worked so hard. You'll deserve a celebration."

At the end of the month, Edith begged her mother to watch the children so she could go to a dance club. Soon, she and Sophie were out most Saturday evenings.

Clara enjoyed the quiet time with her grandchildren. They built towers on the floor and pushed together the big pieces of Hazel's cardboard puzzle. Clara taught them German nursery rhymes and read them poems from *A Child's Garden of Verses*. As long as they had a sweet at the end, the children were content with simple meals, and they happily splashed together in five inches of water at bathtime. After the little ones were in bed, Clara sat with her feet up and nibbled on a sandwich made with National Bread, thinly spread with margarine and filled with a few slices of liver sausage or the butcher's homemade bratwurst.

THE MONTHS WENT BY, one after another.

In July, sweets and chocolate joined the list of rationed items and the children took it hard. In August, sweet biscuits were rationed. Clara and Edith felt this as they must now limit themselves to one cookie on alternate nights with their evening tea. By the fall, it seemed that almost all foods were rationed and most unrationed items like onions, fish, variety meats, and fresh fruit were in ever shorter supply. The only foods they could count on were potatoes, carrots, cabbage, parsnips, prunes, canned milk, whole-meal flour, the tasteless Government Cheddar, and their own garden herbs.

Letters from Herman arrived regularly, though they were less frequent now that he was in the army. In his most recent letter, mailed from Fort Lewis in the state of Washington, he wrote:

An American soldier must be a citizen to be allowed to fight overseas. With a recommendation from Uncle Walter, my application was expedited. I am now a US citizen!

Letters from George, who had never been a diligent correspondent, dribbled in. His messages were short and didn't disclose much, though they knew he was in North Africa where

Montgomery was fighting back the Germans, and he was "*riding a motorcycle daily.*"

Edith's Utility clothing designs were a hit with Mr. Mazur's customers and her workdays were busy creating stylish dresses for his wealthy clients. On weekends, she cooked and helped with cleaning, laundry, and mending.

As December approached, the days and nights remained mild compared to the last three freezing winters. Hazel and Michael snuggled in their cots next to Edith's bed, while their mother and grandmother relaxed comfortably in the lounge despite the closely rationed coal available to burn in the fireplace. Edith held her darning egg, one of Hazel's small socks stretched over it as she carefully wove threads to close a hole in the heel. Clara's knitting needles clacked rhythmically, a small blue mitten gradually growing as she worked.

"I think it's time for another foraging trip with the children to The Wilderness," Clara told Edith. "We can go on our own during the week while you're at work."

Edith's darning needle paused among the frayed threads of the heel of Hazel's sock. "What shall we do for the upcoming holiday?" The question seemed to have come from nowhere. "Can you get some greenery to decorate the house for Christmas? I've missed the decorated tree the last few years. I'd be thankful for even one pine bough."

"I think I remember Bruno has holly bushes behind his house. He'll let us cut a few branches to put on the mantel." Clara's imagination expanded as she thought of what they might find on her brother's estate. "And maybe I can find late Chantrelle mushrooms, too . . . and some fresh greens. I hope his chickens are laying and we can get a half-dozen extra eggs."

Edith sighed. "We must hoard our food coupons to be able to buy treats for Christmas dinner. The children won't think it's a real Christmas without presents. What shall we do about that?"

Clara held up her knitting. "How about blue mittens with a matching cap for Mikey? Shall I do pink or yellow for Hazel? Or what about gay stripes to use all the bits of yarn from other projects?"

"Colorful stripes are a splendid idea for our chatterbox," Edith said. "I'll unpick that pair of George's blue trousers and make a pinafore dress for Hazel and a one-piece suit for Mike. And perhaps I can find a picture book or some small toy for each of them at Harrods one afternoon after work."

Clara could tell her daughter had more than presents on her mind. Her round, questioning eyes betrayed her. "Mutti, wouldn't it be lovely to have company for Christmas day? There are lots of people with no family around."

Clara agreed. Christmas at home in Germany had always included guests, as well as the extended family. "Who do you have in mind?"

"Well, Sophie, of course." Edith paused and Clara watched her gather courage to go on. "And Mutti . . . Sophie and I have made some friends at the nightclub where we go dancing. A couple of American soldiers who keep turning up at the same place we go. They're awfully nice blokes and their families are far away."

Clara wasn't at all sure having soldiers for Christmas was a good idea, but Edith seemed eager. While she cast about for the best response, Edith continued.

"I'd want someone to ask George for dinner when he is far from home. Wouldn't you want a family to invite Herman?"

"Well, that's not a fair comparison. Of course, we'd want George and Herman to enjoy the holiday, but American soldiers . . . I don't think George would like that idea."

"But Mutti, Herman is an American soldier! And one of these guys—one of the ones I want to invite—he's Jewish and from New York where your sister Ida lives."

Clara wondered if this Jewish young man would be interested in a family Christmas. But Edith was determined, and, after all, it was her home. Clara hadn't thought about it for months, but it was possible her US visa would arrive sometime in the coming year, and she would have to leave for America. Perhaps it would be beneficial for her to get to know a couple of Americans.

By the holiday, the flat was decked out in festive regalia. The mantel was laden with sprigs of holly, red berries scattered among the leaves, and candles set in a row. Edith had created silver ornaments from the lids of tin cans, which she cut into star shapes and hung out of the reach of the children because of their sharp edges. Clara and the children glued together loops and loops of newspaper strips to make paper chains that hung from the curtain rod and formed swags across the blackout drapes covering the French doors to the garden.

On Christmas afternoon, Sophie arrived accompanied by the two young men dressed in warm overcoats and trim, well-pressed uniforms. They tipped their forage caps when they were introduced. Nathan was tall, with dark curly hair.

"I'm from the Bronx, ma'am," he said. "I understand you have a sister in New York. I hope she finds it welcoming."

The other soldier was introduced as "Red Burgess, from Virginia." He had a shock of bright auburn hair, freckles across his nose, and a wedding ring. He presented Clara with two cans of Spam and a jar of peanut butter, a thing she had never seen before.

Nathan handed Edith a book tied with a blue ribbon. "I hope you will enjoy this," he said. "It's *The Great Gatsby* by one of our best American novelists. It takes place not far from where I grew up, though the characters are rich folks, nothing like my family." He smiled as Edith took the novel from his hand and led the way into the sitting room.

The dining table was spread with one of the stored, fancy tablecloths. Settings of the Rosenthal china, unused since its arrival from Germany, and their best flatware were arranged around the table. Edith had spent hours in the kitchen preparing a meal planned around the treasures her mother had brought back from The Wilderness.

The meal began with small bowls of potato soup topped with a swirl of emerald-green, sorrel-enriched cream. She had added chopped Chanterelles to minced beef along with diced onion, breadcrumbs, and an egg from one of Bruno's hens and formed it all into a loaf. When it was baked, she covered the whole thing with a creamy, mashed mix of swedes and potatoes and slipped it back into the oven until the outside was hot and crisp. She sprinkled the loaf with chopped parsley and a few cowberries so when she presented it at the table, it resembled a Yule log. She filled a crystal bowl with tangy and sweet chutney made from more cowberries and set the ruby-colored offering on the table. Edith opened one of the cans of Spam and fried the meat in its own juices until a golden-brown crust developed. The children's eyes lit up when their mother placed a platter of juicy pork slices on the table.

"You must thank our American guests," she told them.

Hazel released a stream of, "Thank you, thank you, thank you," until Red laughed out loud.

The feast ended with carrot-infused raisin cookies and a pudding made with canned apricots, a bonus resulting from a month of careful coupon counting.

Satiated after the ample meal, they all moved to the lounge. Edith apologized for the lack of coffee when she brought out the tea tray.

"Well, we are in England," Nathan said, his smile spreading across his handsome face. "Tea is what we expect here. We can get plenty of muddy coffee at the base."

Red sat on the carpet and built a tower of blocks with Hazel while Sophie sat nearby with Michael on her lap, keeping him from knocking the structure over. Clara asked Nathan about his family, and he spoke about his parents, his grandmother who spoke more Russian than English, and his younger sister, an ambitious student who studied chemistry in high school. While he talked, Clara couldn't help noticing how often his eyes drifted toward Edith who listened raptly, her face filled with delight.

It was almost the children's bedtime when the Americans and Sophie finally insisted they must leave. Nathan stood and shook Clara's hand.

"I've had such a lovely time, Mrs. Lang. Even knowing my parents would be shocked to see me celebrating the Christmas holiday, I loved it all. And your daughter is a splendid hostess, not to mention a superb cook." He smiled at Edith in the natural, open way that seemed to be part of his personality. "Truly," he said. "Best meal I've had since I left home." He took two Hershey chocolate bars from the inner pocket of his overcoat and gave one to each of the children. "You must save these for tomorrow," he said. "Your mom will scold me if you eat them before bedtime."

Hazel danced around the room chanting, "Boxing Day candy. Boxing Day candy." Michael stared at the shiny brown paper. His fingers fiddled with the loose edges of the wrapping until Hazel grabbed the candy away and made another round the length of the hall waving both bars over her head.

Nathan's grin stretched across his face, exposing a dimple in one cheek. "Slow down, little one, and bring the chocolate to your mom so she can put it away until tomorrow." He turned to his coat again and stuck one arm in a sleeve. Suddenly an exaggerated expression of surprise crossed his face. "Red, my man," he said. "We almost forgot. We've brought a gift for the ladies, too." He playfully hunted through the pockets of his greatcoat, until, with a flourish, he produced two packages of nylon stockings. He presented one to Edith and the other to Clara. "From Red and me to thank you for such a delightful afternoon." Edith glowed and stretched to kiss both men lightly on the cheek.

Sophie pulled another packet of stockings from her handbag and flaunted it, as gay as Hazel with the chocolate.

"Me too," she said, then turned and hugged Red who blushed, his ears turning as scarlet as his hair.

Clara was embarrassed by the men's intimate gift. Besides, where would she wear such valuable stockings?

CHAPTER 22

1943
Independence

AFTER THREE AND A half years of war, all of Britain was feeling battle fatigue. Tempers were sometimes as short as supplies. Husbands like George had been gone too long, leaving their wives and girlfriends to face bombing and hardships without the support of their men. And now the Americans were showing up in droves. The situation was like an undetonated bomb waiting to explode.

Though she had enjoyed visiting with the young men from America, Clara couldn't shake the unease she felt for Edith. She remembered well what she had read in her daughter's youthful diaries. She remembered her weakness for romance, attention, and tall men. Nathan was undoubtably charming and there was no longer any need for Edith to protect her virginity. Her marriage to George had been rocky when he was last at home and now her husband had been away for almost two years. It was only a matter of time before Edith did something reckless.

Clara ran possible conversations through her mind. She didn't want to disrespect her daughter's adulthood. She knew that treating her like an errant teenager would only cause trouble. She remembered all too well how Edith had reacted when she was forbidden to write to Charlie. But as a mother, Clara felt it was important to remind Edith of the risks to her marriage, her children, even to Nathan's feelings.

On an evening in mid-January, when Clara had finally decided she must speak about her concerns, the air raid siren wailed for the first time since the previous spring. Her resolve totally forgotten, she turned to Edith, the question of what to do hanging in the air between them. Must they go to the uncomfortable wine cellar again? Would it be another spate of constant nights of bombing? The very thought of night after night in the cold shelter made them weary, yet they knew they must take refuge for the sake of the little ones. They stood, resolutely gathered up the sleeping children, and went to the stone-walled room, now more of a sewing workshop than a shelter. They had to push aside the sewing machine before they could unroll the mattresses, set up the canvas chairs, and turn on the lamp.

"Dear God," Edith said, "I hope this isn't the start of another Blitz."

The noise outside had a new tempo, faster, more high-pitched and insistent, while the familiar thud and crunch of bombs exploding seemed far away. The children, so large now that one of Hazel's legs was flung over the side of the pram, curled together and slept soundly through the noise.

"Let's go up and have a look," Edith said. "Remember how beautiful it was way back during the first raid."

Outside, occasional planes droned high overhead, though the explosions of bombs were far to the south. The familiar white searchlights marked the enemy, but now there were more lights in the night sky. Bright, fiery-orange streaks traveled across the darkness. They came from high places nearby and from roofs in the distance beyond the Thames, and they synchronized with the deafening *ack-ack* of anti-aircraft guns. As they watched the deadly trails in the distance, one hit a gnat-like speck in the sky. Immediately the dark spot burst into a ball of flame and Clara watched as the dying airplane spiraled down, leaving a trail of fire and one lone parachute floating behind.

As she stood mesmerized by the death spiral, a loud zing and crash hit the metal railing behind her. Suddenly she was aware of black shards falling from the sky, pieces of metal, hot and lethal falling randomly into the street.

Edith grabbed her. "We have to get inside!" Her daughter tugged her down the stairs and they stood under the overhang above their door. "Shrapnel," Edith said. "It's the broken bits from our own shells. Our anti-aircraft defenses have more than doubled during the last year. I read about the danger months ago, but I forgot." She shuddered. "They warned to stay inside, even if the bombs were far away."

The next morning, Clara went out to the place where she had stood the night before. Only a few feet from where she had been, she found a jagged piece of metal lying on the pavement. She picked it up and gingerly passed her fingers over the rough surface. The piece, smaller than her palm, weighed about half a kilo and its edges were sharp. If it had struck her, it could have killed her. She carried the iron fragment downstairs and set it on top of her dresser. There was more than one way to die in this war. Her personal piece of shrapnel would be a reminder that death could come at any moment. She understood all over again why Edith would want to grab happiness while she could.

When the air raid siren blared the following night, Clara slipped the rough metal talisman into the pocket of her housecoat. As the bombs exploded in the distance and her knitting needles twisted yarn into a small sweater, she felt the weight of the shrapnel in her pocket and understood her mortality. Though there were only three air raids that week, nothing like the previous year, it was the night the shrapnel fell that she would remember. Clara vowed to waste no time on fear—from now on she would make each day count. She needed to broaden her world, to do something besides keep her daughter's house and care for her grandchildren.

First, she volunteered as a fire watcher. After a short training session, she spent one night a week on the roof of the tallest building in the neighborhood, keeping watch for fires started by incendiary bombs. Her partner, Mr. Bray, was a taciturn man who seldom spoke, but he was friendly enough and always arrived with a thermos of hot coffee to share. She never asked where he was able to get such good, strong coffee, and he did not volunteer the information.

Over the next three months, there was only one other air raid in London, and it was far to the east. No fire or bombs came to Chelsea or Earl's Court or anywhere else she could see from her lookout station. Clara spent her fire-watching nights knitting and watching the dark shapes of buildings, the black vacancies filled with rubble like pox on the cityscape. On the street below, an occasional bus passed by, their partially covered headlamps casting a slit of yellow light. This sedentary job, though it was important to the safety of the home front, did not satisfy her need to expand her world. One evening as Clara sipped from a mug of hot coffee, she asked Mr. Bray about his life.

"During the day," he said, "I collect things for recycling. Paper, metal, rags, even fat. Fat's important, you know. They use it to make explosives."

"That must be hard work, and it can't bring in enough for you to get by."

He chuckled. "Don't need much. I'm alone. No kiddies and my wife's long gone. Not dead, simply gone. On the nights I'm not here, I clean a half-dozen government offices. That gets me extra benefits." He raised his mug in a gesture of salute. "Cleaning is good work, especially now with all the young ones off to factories and the army. I like to come into a messy place and leave it better than the way I found it."

"I never had to clean even my own home until the Nazis changed my life, but I've found I like housekeeping," Clara said. "I understand the pleasure one can get from making a space clean and neat. It settles the mind." This was the longest conversation she'd ever had with Mr. Bray. "I'm Clara," she said.

He stuck out his hand. It was calloused and rough, but his grip was warm, not too limp and not too strong. "Harold," he said. "Now we are on a first-name basis, we must be friends. It's good to have a friend during these times." After that he lapsed into silence again.

Clara didn't forget what Harold had said about cleaning. The next Saturday afternoon, she went into the shelter room to talk to Edith while she sewed. Clara settled into a canvas chair and watched the easy flow of fabric as her daughter pushed it under the rhythmical stitching of the needle.

Clara picked up her current knitting project and began another row—knit, purl, knit, purl. The repetitive motion calmed her. "Edith, I've been thinking lately. It can't be much longer before my visa from America will be granted. I'll have to leave, whether I want to or not."

Her daughter paused in her work and her feet stopped pumping the treadle. "Oh, Mutti, no. It could be months yet."

"Yes, probably. But surely sometime in the next year. Whenever it comes, I'll have to go to California and live with Fred and Bonnie. The idea scares me a bit. You know how Fred can be, and I don't know his wife at all. Often, she seems almost cold. Other times, she seems friendly enough—though probably very shy. It's hard to tell when all she ever sends are postcards."

"Everything will be fine, Mutti. I'm sure Bonnie will welcome you. And there's your American granddaughter to get to know. And a new baby on the way, too." Edith began to slowly work the treadle again and push the fabric under the needle. "I hope the visa doesn't come for a long time yet," she said. "I can't bear to think how greatly I'll miss you. And Hazel and Mike will be lost without their granny."

"Yes . . . but, whenever I must go to California . . . and I also hope it won't be for a long while, I'd like to have money of my own. I want to find some work and earn a few pounds."

"What can you do? You've only ever run a kindergarten, and the Brits won't accept your German certification."

"I was thinking of housecleaning. I heard a few ladies in one of the queues talking about how difficult it is to find a housekeeper these days. The young girls don't want that kind of work anymore. But I wouldn't mind cleaning. I've had plenty of practice the last few years."

"Have you considered how we would manage here if you go off to work? There's the kids and everything else."

Clara took a deep breath. The next bit was the most difficult because it could cut into Edith's earnings. "I thought maybe you could take the kiddies to Sophie's a couple of days a week. She works nights and she loves the children. She might do it for a new frock or a coat. Or you could pay her a shilling now and then. I'd only want to work maybe three or four days a week. Weekends would work for me, though most people don't like help underfoot on the weekends."

"Well, maybe. I don't know." Edith's face was somber. "Mutti, cleaning is hard work. What would you use for references? And technically you are not allowed to take employment. Remember the paper you signed with your transit visa?"

Clara knit a complete row before continuing. "I've thought about the visa bit and I don't know that it's valid anymore now that I'm on an Enemy Alien Class C permit. Anyway, I'll ask to be paid in cash . . . what do they call it? Under the table? I'll have to see." She looked up from her knitting. "Maybe I can talk to those ladies I met in line. I can make up a notecard with my name and phone number. Or I can post notices in shop windows. I know the butcher would let me. What I do know for sure is that I don't want to be completely dependent on Fred when I get to California."

Edith answered slowly. "It might work. I could ask around. One of our regulars at the Thread and Thistle might need a cleaner. It might be quite pleasant working in a house in Mayfair or Kensington—a place like our home on Bernardstrasse."

Clara laughed. "Nothing that grand, I should think. A few middle-class homes nearby would be all I could handle."

Once Sophie agreed to babysit, Clara posted notices. Edith found a customer who had a townhouse in Belgravia and was thrilled to have a trustworthy housekeeper who would come on an occasional Saturday or Sunday.

"I stay at our country estate most of the time," she told Edith. "But I come into the city for a week or ten days now and then. Your mother could open our house up and prepare it for us."

WITHIN A SHORT TIME, Clara cleaned three houses a week and was on call for weekends with Lady Broadmoor, the Thread and Thistle customer. Her weekly jobs were scheduled on Monday, Wednesday and Friday mornings. On Mondays and Wednesdays, Edith took the children to her friend's flat, and Clara picked them up before lunch to give Sophie time to sleep before her night shift at the Corner House. The other job was on Friday mornings when Edith could be home. Edith and Clara organized their grocery shopping carefully and were able to get by with only three days a week. Clara and the children shopped on Tuesdays and Thursdays, while Edith took over the Friday shopping.

Clara learned to navigate the bus system and the underground to get to her jobs in South Kensington and Chelsea. On the days she worked, she set off with a clean housedress and a head scarf folded in a shopping bag. She enjoyed dusting and hoovering, even scrubbing the kitchen counters, the bathroom fixtures, and mopping the floor. Because of soap rationing, it was not always easy to get the tile clean, but she learned on the "Kitchen Front" how to make a solution out of vinegar and baking soda that did an adequate job. As she worked, scrubbing other people's bathrooms, she often thought of how different her life turned out from what she had expected as a child. She had grown up in a mansion surrounded by sisters, aunts, uncles, cousins, and loving parents while the servants did all the cooking and cleaning, driving and dressmaking. There was even a governess until her youngest sister turned fourteen. With no chores to do, she had been able to learn English and French and to play the piano and violin.

Now she spent her days cleaning, ironing, mending, doing laundry, shopping, and caring for children. Her hands were roughened and red and her only quiet moments were spent knitting. Yet surprisingly, she was as content as she had been during those childhood years and certainly happier than she had been during her marriage. The only sadness in her life was worrying about Albert and missing him.

The days she liked best were when Lady Ester Broadmoor called to say she and her husband were coming to stay at the townhouse. With the key she had been given, Clara let herself into the elegant Edwardian townhome and removed the dustcovers from the furniture. The rooms usually didn't need deep cleaning, only a bit of dusting and hoovering, plus polishing all the furniture till it shone and the rooms were filled with the scent of lemon oil. It was also her job to make sure a large Chinese vase in the sitting room was filled with flowers, and the refrigerator was stocked with wines, cheese, and chops for which Lady Ester sent coupons and a list of shops where she had accounts.

When the Broadmoors returned to the country, Clara went back to their city house to cover the furniture, throw out the wilted flowers, clean the bathrooms, and send the dirty linens to a commercial laundry. The kitchen, always cleaned at the end of the stay by the cook they brought with them, was left spotless and Clara only had to check the refrigerator for perishables. Lady Ester had given her strict instructions to take away anything that might spoil. When she returned to Harcourt Terrace, her shopping bag was often filled with delicacies—ends of real cheese, a precious orange, a few slices of roast beef or ham, or the remnants of an apple pudding.

Spring flew by and the hot days of summer arrived. From the bus window on her way to work, Clara noticed how many American soldiers filled the sidewalks. The military base they had seen being built near The Wilderness was now complete, and on weekends the young men in their immaculate, tailored uniforms seemed to be everywhere, from Kingston to Chelsea.

Edith continued to go out to dance clubs on Saturday evenings. She stayed in the flat only long enough to help with the supper washup. She dressed carefully in a stylish outfit, her one pair of dress shoes, and the new nylon stockings Nathan kept bringing her. Her hair was always carefully combed, her lips bright red with fresh lipstick, and her cheeks pink with makeup. Before eight, she was out the door on her way to meet Sophie. She came home long after Clara was asleep and didn't wake up until well past breakfast on Sunday.

The first thing Edith did when she got up was rinse out her stockings in cool water and a drop of precious soap. She rolled the nylons up in a towel, then carefully pegged them on a line that hung over the bathtub. When Clara asked her why she washed them after each use, Edith told her, "*Britannia & Eve* described this as the best way to ensure nylon stockings last and keep looking their best."

Nathan, who had been billeted in central London at Christmas, was now assigned to Camp Griffiss at Bushy Park. On the few weekends when Edith hadn't gone dancing on Saturday, he was sure to come by on Sunday afternoon for tea. He always brought gifts from the Post Exchange at the camp—chewing gum or chocolate bars for the children, Spam, soap, Nescafe, or peanut butter, and usually a special treat of nylons or lipstick for Edith. Clara knew that he was the strongest lure that drew Edith to the clubs, but she was sure there were probably other Americans her daughter flirted with if Nathan wasn't beside her. All of this made Clara uneasy. She was finding it more and more difficult to stay quiet about her concerns.

Then the thing she feared happened. One Saturday night, Edith did not come home. She called in the morning, said not to worry, that she would be home before noon, but she gave no explanation. When she arrived at the flat, she put on her dressing gown and went straight to the bathing room to rinse out her stockings. It had been a hot August morning, and the children were cranky. Clara fed them an early lunch and put Michael down for his nap in the shelter, the coolest room in the house.

When her stockings were hung and drying in the warm air, Edith sat at the kitchen table and sipped a cup of strong tea.

Hazel leaned on her mother's knee, her little face worried. "Mommy, where were you?"

"I was dancing, my best girl. I was dancing the night away."

"In the morning, too?"

"Yes, Hazel. Now go look at your picture books in the stone room. Even if you're too big for a nap, it's rest time."

Clara brought her daughter a slice of bread spread with peanut butter and honey, now a family favorite, and sat down at the table. "Edith, staying out all night can lead to trouble. What were you thinking?"

"I was dancing and lost track of time. That's all. We slept an hour in the lobby of the Cumberland and, when they chased us out, we went to the Corner House for breakfast."

"You can lie to Hazel, if you want. But don't lie to me. We've shared too much, and I know you."

"Mutti, I'm telling the truth. But if you don't believe me, I may as well do what you're imagining. A hotel room would certainly be more comfortable than the chairs in the hotel lobby."

"You think you're smart with your diaphragm. That you won't get pregnant again. But what about your family? Do you think of George? He's fighting for you and the children—to protect you from Hitler and Mussolini. He's counting on you to stay loyal, to be here waiting for him when he returns."

Edith stood up and slammed her cup onto the saucer. "I doubt he's staying loyal all the time. I'll bet he has a girl in Tobruk and another in Cairo and a third in Tunisa somewhere."

Clara knew she had started a conversation that would not end well. Why had she done it? "You don't know that for sure, Edith! Anyway, men are different. They think they have the right."

"Well, I want the right to enjoy myself, too. I'm tired of the dark nights. The endless potatoes. No new clothes for the kids. My only fun is going to the clubs. Nathan is a good dancer and he's a gentleman. I want to be happy again. And if I decide to do something more, I'll do that too!" Edith turned and stalked toward her bedroom, leaving the peanut butter toast untouched.

"Let me know when Mike wakes up. I'll take my children on a bicycle ride. I can dance and keep my family together."

CHAPTER 23

Decisions

WHEN EDITH RETURNED FROM her outing with the children, her attitude was frosty. She heated up a can of Spam, fried potatoes, and sliced cabbage for a salad. She and Clara ate the simple meal silently, while Hazel filled the void with her chatter.

"Granny, we had so much fun. We went on Mommy's bicycle! Mikey got to ride in the front basket. I had to sit behind mommy. I hung on tight! My hair almost blew off, we went so fast."

Edith's anger persisted. Days went by when she hardly spoke to her mother, and she never asked for help. Clara automatically did what she had always done. She kept the flat tidy, washed up after meals, shopped, took care of the children when she wasn't working, and picked them up from Sophie's on the days she was. She missed her daughter's cheerful news about the ritzy clients at the Thread and Thistle and their comfortable companionship in the evenings. At night, after the children were tucked in bed, Edith went to the shelter to sew or to her room to read. On Saturday night, she left right after supper and she did not return until well after midnight.

On Sunday morning, Clara could stand it no longer. When she saw Edith putting the children's outdoor shoes on their feet, she took off her house slippers and slipped on her walking shoes. "Edith, may I come out with you?"

Edith glanced up from tying Michael's shoes. "We're going on the bike."

"Couldn't we all walk together like we used to do? The weather is beautiful today. The sun is out. Please Edith, I've missed you."

"Mutti, I don't know." Her face softened. "I've been angry. I don't like being treated like a child . . . or a liar. But I've missed you too." She sighed. "I'm sorry it took me so long to cool off." She turned to the children, her smile gentle. "Come on, we're off for a walk to Brompton Cemetery. Mikey darling, take Granny's hand."

"Can we pick dandelions?" Hazel asked.

"They will be nothing but puffballs this late in the summer," Edith told her. "Maybe we can find daisies. Or some of that yummy wild garlic."

As they walked, they passed the bombed site where Clara and Hazel had seen the rescue teams at work on a similar excursion two years before. All the large pieces of rubble had been removed and the area was nothing more than a vacant space dotted with stones, the remnants of a concrete wall along one side. Among the stones, the earth was dug up and Clara saw rows of shiny cabbage heads, the red leaves of beet plants, and sprawling vines with baby squash forming. The place that had given her frightening dreams was now a victory garden.

Clara vowed to keep her worries about her daughter's personal life to herself. Edith was an adult, and she would ask if she wanted her mother's opinion. Clara was glad her daughter had put aside her anger and they again worked side by side as a team. She would not jeopardize the peace with unsolicited advice a second time.

As the summer wound to a close, the blue skies were frequently marred by thunderclouds and the air hung hot and humid. Clara and Edith moved their folding canvas chairs to the garden and after the children were in bed, they sat in the shade cast by the wall of the house. Clara's blouse clung stickily to her back, and she fanned herself with a folded newspaper page. Edith was reading an article titled, "How to Look After Your Bicycle" in *Britannia & Eve.*

"Isn't that a queer article for a woman's magazine," Clara commented.

"Women have to take care of everything themselves now," Edith said. "What with all the men elsewhere. And I see more and more women riding bicycles, even in the posh neighborhoods. It must be the gasoline shortage that gets them on two wheels." She thumbed through the magazine and held up a page with a series of little drawings and the title, "No Maid? No Matter?"

"Look Mutti," she said. "Here's an article that is more lady-oriented. But it could put you out of work! See, under this picture it says a good housewife, 'scrubs kitchen tabletops with salt and water, or with Parazone, a liquid bleaching agent.'"

Clara chuckled. "I'd like to see that article when you're finished reading about bicycle maintenance. I could use a few labor-saving tips."

Edith laid the magazine in her lap and turned to her mother. "There's something I need to tell you," she said. "Nathan has invited me for a long weekend on the upcoming bank holiday. He has friends stationed in Dorset and they've told him it's lovely. And he's been able to get a jeep for the three days." She held her mother's eyes and continued. "I've said yes. I intend to go. I promise I won't give my heart away, but I need this, Mutti. I'm only twenty-six. I need to remember how it feels to be young and loved by a man." She paused. Clara waited. Her mind was full of objections she was determined not to voice. "I hope you'll be able to stay with the children," Edith concluded.

Clara hesitated. It was hard for her to simply say yes, though she knew in the end she would agree. "What if Lady Broadmoor decides to come to town for the holiday? Then I'll have to work on Saturday and again on Monday evening or Tuesday to set the townhouse right. I can't take Mike and Hazel to such a posh home."

Edith had a ready answer for that possibility. "If you can't stay with them, Sophie will keep the children. She said Red will help. He would even watch the kids at night when she works, if necessary."

Clara nodded. Edith had made up her mind. She would go to Dorset with Nathan. Nothing would stop her. "We'll work it out, Sophie and I. If Lady Ester doesn't need me, Sophie needn't do anything."

The last weekend in August was the hottest since Clara had lived in London. Lady Broadmoor, who almost never came into town in the summer, did not come on the bank holiday. Clara had the entire long holiday weekend for herself and the children. The weather was simply too hot to stay in the city. She telephoned her brother and asked if they could come to visit for three days. She had never done that before and, though Bruno was surprised, he said he would be delighted to have their company. It was a perfect time to come, as Nelda was visiting her sister in the Lake district. He warned that meals would be simple as he had given the house-keeper and the cook the weekend off.

"We'll have a lovely time," he said. "All picnics and games and Edith's splendid humor."

Clara knew it would disappoint Bruno, but she didn't want him to be surprised. "It will only be the two children and myself," she said. "Edith has gone to Dorset with friends for the weekend."

The days at The Wilderness were glorious. The children, dressed in cotton shorts and shirts, ran barefoot on the grassy grounds, up and down the hills, circling the trees. One day, Bruno took them out in a rowboat on his pond, and they dangled their fingers in the cool water. Another day, he took them to the hen-house, and they collected enough eggs for Clara to make four small omelets for supper. They ate their meals picnic-style on the porch. Bruno's cook had left him an ample supply of boiled eggs, leftover roast beef, potato salad, and a rice pudding made with canned, condensed milk. They harvested tomatoes, cucumbers, lettuce, and scallions from the garden and feasted on summer vegetable sandwiches. Neither Hazel nor Michael had any memory of such bounty. They fell asleep curled together on the big guest bed, their tummies full and their heads awash in pleasant dreams.

After the children were asleep, Clara and Bruno sat companionably in his library. They finished off his last bottle of port and talked about Nuremburg and their far-flung family, now spread across the globe. Bruno told her how he had become a manufacturer when he realized the banking business was too sedentary for him. He hinted that his factory struggled to find the best way to meet wartime needs and still make a profit.

"I can't wait until we are able to return to our pre-war production," he said. "In a nation of working-class tea drinkers, the thermos business was a good one."

Clara thought that this was probably the first time she had actually sat down with Bruno to talk. Her strongest childhood memory of him was watching his straight figure board the train at the Nuremburg Bahnhof as he headed for England to work in a branch of their father's bank. She had been barely ten years old as she stood on the platform, surrounded by the crowd that was her family, waving but with no sense that she would miss the young man who was her elder brother and who she hardly knew. On this impromptu long weekend, brother and sister finally connected.

Clara, the children in tow, returned to London on Monday afternoon with a bag full of fresh produce and a joyful heart. She had not wasted any time worrying about Edith.

Her daughter arrived home on Monday night after the children were in bed and Clara was in her nightclothes.

"I'll tell you everything tomorrow at dinner," Edith said. "I'm simply knackered and must get some sleep."

She went to her room and closed the door. The following evening, the children, still in high spirits from their weekend in the country, showed their mother their tanned arms and toes. Michael displayed scratches on his arms while he stuffed the juicy blackberries he had picked into his mother's mouth.

Hazel told a long story about riding in a boat and seeing a fish jump out of the water.

"But we couldn't go fishing," she said with a sad face. "Uncle had no fishing pole." She put her hands one on each of her mother's cheeks. "Where were you, Mommy?"

"I was at a lovely village in the country with some friends," she told Hazel. "We walked on the beach and there were tall cliffs that came right down to the sand. We saw American soldiers climbing up the cliffs on ropes. It was exciting to watch."

"What were they doing that for, Mommy?"

Edith caught her mother's eye and shook her head. "Playing games, sweet girl. For the joy of it."

Once the child was safely settled and surrounded by her picture books, Edith told her mother more. "Nathan and I stayed in a pretty, little inn in a village," she said. "We met his friend at the local pub on Saturday, but when we walked along the coast on Monday morning, there were a lot of American soldiers gathered near the cliffs. There were airmen, but also other groups. Nathan told me not to tell anyone what I saw. I probably shouldn't have said anything to Hazel. Thank goodness she's not in school yet to blab to her friends."

Clara had no idea what would be safe to ask. She simply said, "I hope your vacation was all you hoped for."

"And more! Nathan is such a wonderful guy. It's difficult not to fall in love with him."

"You must be careful—"

"I know, Mutti. I know. He says he expects to be transferred to Dorset in the next few months. That will make it so we can't see each other as often. It's probably for the best. I need to think. I'm torn by my choices. Mutti, I do have a choice."

"What do you mean? What choice?"

"We both know my marriage to George wasn't always the best. Even before he went to Europe, things weren't perfect. He could be nasty jealous sometimes. And rough, too. Then after he came back, after Dunkirk, it was so much worse. Remember the time he locked me out and you had to beg him to be reasonable?"

Clara nodded. It was an effort to stay quiet and simply listen.

"Nathan is so kind and considerate. He reminds me of my Charlie . . . long ago. And he says he loves me, too, like Charlie did. But, despite all his faults, I care for George. And he's the father of my children. But he's been gone so long." Tears had started to hang on Edith's bottom lashes. She swiped them away with her knuckles. "The war makes figuring out what's right difficult. George is gone and Nathan is here. But Nathan is an American. And what am I? A German? A refugee? George's wife. The mother of two British children. I have no idea what I'll feel when this war is over. When George returns, will I want to be married to him? Do I want to uproot my children and move to America? Nathan hasn't mentioned marriage. I have no idea what he might want."

"I've thought of divorce, Mutti. I thought of it when I was locked outside in the freezing cold. In England, divorce is for rich people and actresses. The women I work with every day would never consider leaving their husbands. It's just not done! And war can change everything in a split second. Nathan will be part of any Allied invasion of Europe. Then he will be gone too! He could die in battle. George could be killed too. They could both die." The tears flowing down her cheeks had become unstoppable. "Oh, Mutti. I have no idea what to do."

Clara handed her daughter a handkerchief and she blew her nose into it. Her cheeks still damp, she shook her head. "I don't know how to decide. Mutti, how can I decide?"

"When you know what do, that's the right time," Clara said. Her daughter had asked her opinion, but she had to admit that she had no idea how to make this kind of choice in the middle of a war. Men were gone for years at a time. Countless men now lay dead on the battlefield and would never come home. How could one know what life would be like when it was all over? "I think you're right not to choose when you're confused. Life is unpredictable during a war. Take one day at a time, I think." She took Edith's hand. "But you must not get pregnant. That would force you into a choice."

"I know. I know. I won't. I've told Nathan about the diaphragm, but I make him use a condom too." She smiled weakly. "Double safe," she said. "And he understands how important this is."

"Edith, you are being so honest. I need to tell you something too. I promised George I wouldn't tell you, but I think you should know."

"What? What secret do you have with George?

"George saw terrible things during the Dunkirk evacuations. When you were in the hospital with Michael, he told me a lot. He cried while he told me."

"What happened to him? What did he see?"

"The details are his to share, not mine. He said he would never tell you because he didn't want you to see his weakness. But be open and listen if he changes his mind. What you need to know is Dunkirk changed him. In the last war they called it shell shock. I think now they call it battle fatigue. Probably during every war the doctors come up with a name for what happens to a man's mind when he experiences traumatic horrors. By any name it's devastating. Difficult for the soldier, difficult for the family. And almost impossible to treat. I don't think it ever goes away. Though I hope, for George's sake, the terrors and memories will gradually become less vivid. Now he's at war again. Who knows what new horror he may be living through."

"Yet he asked to go back into action! Why did he do that?"

"Perhaps he felt it would be easier to be with men who've had similar experiences. He understood how his night terrors and his tempers made you miserable. I think he needed to get away." She took Edith into her arms and hugged her. "All I ask, sweetheart, is that you take what I've told you into account when you think about your future and what is best for your family."

They were so close that Clara could feel her daughter's ragged breath.

"I will," Edith whispered. "I promise." She eased out of her mother's arms. "But there must be limits. If he tries to take me by force again, or if he hits me even once . . . He's not hit me yet, but he's come so close. Mutti, if that happens, I won't stay with him. No matter what he's been through." She straightened her shoulders and wiped the tears away with her palms. "For the children's sake, I would have to leave him. I would have to ask for a divorce."

CHAPTER 24

Letters and Endings

IN THE BEGINNING OF September, four letters arrived for Clara, one after the other. The first was from Herman, with a postmark from the state of Maryland. His news was cryptic. He said he was sworn to secrecy and prohibited from disclosing anything about his new assignment.

> *All I can tell you is that I am slated to go to officer training.*
> *If I do well (and I will), I'll graduate as a lieutenant.*

An actual letter rather than a postcard came the same day from her daughter-in-law in California. The message was short, but tucked between the folded stationery was a photograph of Clara's two American granddaughters, a curly-haired girl of about five awkwardly cradling a chubby, bald infant dressed in diapers and an undershirt. Clara rubbed her fingertip across the shiny photo. How she longed to hug these girls, yet doing so would mean leaving Hazel and Michael who filled the empty center of her heart.

The third letter arrived the next day, this one from the Portuguese widow. She wrote that refugees from Germany continued to straggle into Lisbon and one of them had brought news of a place called Theresienstadt. This man told of a ghetto-labor camp in Czechoslovakia where many of the Jews removed from Germany had been transported. Before he escaped that place, the man had seen trains filled with Jews leaving Theresienstadt, headed to camps in Poland rumored to specialize in starvation and mass killing. The widow wrote that the man could not account for one Jew among thousands. There was no way to know if Clara's friend was in Theresienstadt or far worse, transported to Poland. The news shattered any hope Clara had of reuniting with Albert until the war ended . . . and she doubted she would ever find him alive.

She had no time to grieve. The following day, the fourth letter dropped through the mail slot. This one came in an official envelope stamped with the symbol of the US government. The formal letter inside informed her that her visa to enter the United States had been approved and she must come to the US Embassy in London to pick it up. She knew she would have to leave England as soon as the British Home Office was notified of her US visa. If she overstayed, she would be living in the United Kingdom illegally.

The following days were frantic with paperwork and preparations. She gave notice to her employers that she would no longer come to clean. She sent a telegram to Fred to let him know she would soon be on her way. A telegram came back from California:

"We welcome your arrival."

She contacted Bruno and asked him if he could help her find passage to America. He reminded her that since Pearl Harbor, a Japanese line was out of the question. He would see what he could find. Her best bet might be a Canadian shipping line that would sail to Halifax rather than New York. She visited the offices of the Central British Fund for German Jewry and pleaded for help understanding the maze of rules and paperwork, as well as aid finding a ship. A volunteer at the CBF said he would do what he could. He told Clara that the shipping lanes had moved into the far North Atlantic where there were fewer German U-boats. After unloading their cargo of war material, food, and Canadian or American soldiers, most ships gathered near the ports along the north coast or in Ireland until a convoy could be formed for the return trip. The volunteer warned Clara that once transportation was found, she must be prepared to leave immediately. When the time came, they would allocate funds to help with the expenses of immigration.

Clara knew it was time to think of packing her luggage. She laid out her clothing. What should she take? She had one dress she had purchased, and the few things Edith had made for her. The long-sleeved dresses from Germany were no longer stylish, but they would last for a while more. They had been superior quality to begin with and she had seldom worn them in London. The skirts she had brought from home four years before were worn thin and one had a stain on the back. Her travel suit was frayed at the sleeve edges and the hem. Her summer jacket was faded, and the elbows were almost gone. The elastic in her corsets was stretched beyond usefulness, and her underwear was so thin from constant washing that they might fall apart at any moment. She stared at her wardrobe hopelessly.

Edith came into the room. She fingered the clothing arranged on her mother's bed. "Perhaps I can help with this," she said. "I don't want you going to Fred dressed like a destitute refugee."

"Please. I know you can make sense of this jumble." Clara pulled her clothing ration book out of her dresser drawer. "I have a few coupons left for this year, but I need your advice on how to best use them."

Together mother and daughter went through Clara's wardrobe, one piece at a time. They set aside blouses, dresses, and a nightgown that were in good shape. Besides two German sweaters, she had a new one she had knit last winter and two pairs of hand-knitted knickers. She would take these, though they laughed at the idea of woolen underwear in warm and sunny California.

Edith examined the skirts and the travel suit. "I can combine the best sections of fabric from the three skirts and make one skirt with contrasting panels," she said. "There should be enough bits left to put edging around the sleeves and collar of the jacket. That will look quite stylish." She turned to the summer dresses her mother had brought from home; both were threadbare. "These frocks are almost worn through. They're as soft as handkerchiefs. Do you want to take them with you?"

Clara shrugged. Maybe she could wear them when she was helping Bonnie around the house. "I'll need warm weather clothes in California," she said.

"I'll figure out something. Maybe you can buy a lightweight dress when you get there. Do you think they have clothes rationing in the US?" Edith held up the worst of the two old dresses. Pinpoints of light revealed holes in the bodice, though most of the skirt was okay. "What about new knickers? The fabric is soft. And I'll find one of George's shirts that will do. That should get you a couple of pairs of knickers. You can pack the other dress to wear around the house." With these decisions made, she inspected Clara's light flannel jacket. "I think with decorative patches on the elbows and a packet of dye, we can make this acceptable," she said.

Clara counted her clothing coupons. They agreed she should use them to buy a new corset, two bras, and a pair of shoes. Edith twirled her mother's gray felt hat on her hand. The brim drooped and the ribbon was soiled. "I think we can freshen this up so it suits," she said. "A new ribbon and fresh black netting should do it. Maybe a feather?"

One Saturday, they took the children to the clothing exchange in Nottinghill. Besides finding used clothing that fit Michael and Hazel in exchange for a bag of outgrown items, they donated Clara's heavy winter coat and a pair of George's flannel trousers in exchange for a lady's summer coat and a short-sleeved, cotton frock for Clara.

When they returned home, Edith went to the linen chest and poked about until she found the banquet tablecloth. She spread it on the table and called her mother over. "I should have thought of this before," she said. "I'm never going to have a table this big or enough food to fill it. If you agree, I think we should cut this cloth up and make you another summer dress. I hear its summer all year where Fred lives."

Clara ran her palm across the smooth fabric. She remembered the dinners in Germany, the table laid with porcelain and silver, the friends and family gathered around, the wine, the serious discussions, the laughter. It was all long gone. She touched a blurred pink stain and remembered how one of her guests had spilled a glass of burgundy wine. The lady had been embarrassed but Clara had laughed, telling the friend it was no matter, that's what tablecloths were for. Later she rubbed the stain with salt, but the faint color of wine remained.

"We'll dye the cloth blue, your favorite color, and you'll not see that blot again." Edith measured the cloth by stretching it from the tip of her nose to her fingertips several times. "There's almost three, extra wide, meters here. Plenty for a dress, plus another blouse for you or rompers for Hazel and Mike."

"Use the extra for the children. When I miss them, I'll imagine we're wearing matching outfits."

With so many plans, Edith spent every spare minute sewing. Clara lived in her housecoat while her daughter remodeled her wardrobe. She laundered the clothing she would take and folded everything carefully.

As the women worked, the wireless filled the room with popular band music, now Edith's favorite. One evening, they both sat in the lounge, their hands busy with sewing tasks. Edith hemmed the tablecloth dress with small stitches, and Clara's needle closed the recurring holes in a basket of children's socks. Lou Preager's band finished its rendition of "We'll Meet Again," and Clara half listened to the news that came on after. Things had finally improved for the British. Now they were fighting with their allies in southern

Italy. The newscaster's voice changed in pitch, and she heard the words "convoy in the North Atlantic." Clara's needle paused in midair. She held her breath to listen.

"A double convoy of sixty-five merchant ships accompanied by nineteen warships, crossing from Liverpool to Halifax and New York, was attacked for three consecutive days by a German submarine wolfpack near Greenland. Losses are heavy."

Clara felt she could not breathe. *What of the sailors and servicemen adrift in the icy waters, of the sinking ships, of the U-boats lurking below? Soon I'll be making the same journey, across the same cold sea.*

Clara tried to forget what she had heard. There was nothing to be done. She could not delay her departure. By early October, there was little left to do besides wait for word of a berth and a ticket. Clara spent as many hours as she could with Edith and the children. She would need these joyful memories to nourish her soul.

During that waiting time, she was surprised to receive a letter from California, her address typed in all capital letters and a return address that read, "Frederick M. Lang." She had not received a letter from her oldest son since her first year in London. She carefully slit the envelope open. Inside was a single typed sheet with an almost illegible signature at the bottom.

Dear Mother, Bonnie and I and the girls are
pleased you will finally come to live with us
in sunny California. Though you are welcome
here, there is one condition I insist on: You
must never mention our Jewish background.

My life here is good and I am content.
However, there are places and groups in this
great country that are pleased with Hitler's
racial policies. Bonnie and her family are
originally from the southern part of the
United States, a region that has many who fit
that category, not least of which is my own
father-in-law. Though California is relatively
free of these problems, and our small town on
the Pacific coast is home to many artists and
freethinkers, one can never know when a change
will occur. We know how fast this can happen.
We saw it in Germany.

You must understand that your welcome
here is contingent on maintaining my secret.
You must promise that when asked, you will
say only that our family left Germany because
we disagreed with Hitler's policies. You
must never refer to yourself or any of our
relatives as Jewish. If you can promise this,
I will welcome you with open arms.

I hope you will send another telegram with
more details of your trip and when you will
arrive.

Your son, *Frederick*

Clara wadded up the letter in her fist. It was no more friendly
than a notice from a lawyer. Was this the cold, secretive life she

would need to lead in her son's home? She sat on the edge of the bed and stared at the crumpled paper. She had no choice. She had to go. She would have to agree to Fred's conditions. She smoothed the letter out on her lap and set it on the top of her dresser. The scored and marred paper reminded her of how few choices she had.

Two days later, the CBF representative called to say they had found her a cabin on a ship leaving Liverpool in six days. It would be part of a convoy to Nova Scotia. The Central British Fund for German Jewry would help her arrange transport to the port. She must come to the office to pick up her tickets and a travel stipend. In four days, Clara would have to catch a train north.

SHE HAD HEEDED THE CBF warning that she must be prepared to leave on short notice and her packing was almost complete. The brown leather suitcase, the same case she had packed so carefully on the last day she had seen Albert, was full. At least on this journey she would not have to hide her few pieces of jewelry.

Edith had given her the old suitcase she had carried in 1936.

"It's not very classy," she said. "But it should hold together."

Clara carefully folded the rest of what she would take, wrapped her shoes in a cloth bag, and arranged them in the second case. Edith brought in the new blue dress made from the tablecloth and held it up.

"What do you think?" she said.

"Oh Edith! It's quite lovely. Too beautiful for a middle-aged lady. Where did you find the lace? And such a wide, flared skirt! How did you dare? Isn't all that frivolous and against the rules?"

"Never mind the rules! Our designers have made dresses like this for export. The rules for exports are different . . . less strict. I guess the government is greedy for the income from American fashionistas." Edith went to her sewing space, brought back a copy of *Vogue* magazine, flipped through the pages, and opened it to a two-page spread. There, pictured alongside an off-the-shoulder ball gown with a full skirt and satin rose on the sash, was a day dress similar to the one Edith had made for her. The headline read, "British Designer, Edward Molyneux, Sends Stunning Collection to America for the Upcoming Season."

Clara was astounded. "Who knew?" she said. "You are amazing, my dear."

"Thanks, Mutti." She gently folded the blue dress and laid it on top of Clara's suitcase. "You will be dressed as well as any of our clients at the Thread and Thistle. And Fred will be proud to have such a stylish mother." Edith dashed to the kitchen. "Wait, there's something else." She returned with a freshly laundered and ironed apron. "You must take this as well," she said. "Bonnie needs to know you have come to help, not to be waited on."

Later that evening, Clara retrieved her violin case from under the bed. She set it next to her packed suitcases in the corner. She was unsure how she felt about bringing her violin with her now that all hope of reuniting with Albert was an illusion. Yet she knew she couldn't bear to leave it behind. Besides, Edith would worry if her mother abandoned her instrument.

The afternoon before Clara was to leave, a postcard from Bonnie slid through the mail slot. On one side was a picture of a wide beach, cerulean waves edged with a ripple of white and colorful beach umbrellas dotting the sand. A sailboat stood out in the water and a golden cliff in the distance was topped with the silhouettes of palm trees. On the other side of the card, opposite her name and the Harcourt address, Bonnie had written, "I'm thrilled we will finally meet. California awaits you with open arms." She seemed to have no idea about Fred's letter or the secret it hid. The glossy postcard and her daughter-in-law's message uplifted Clara's spirits.

In the morning, Sophie came over to stay with the children, allowing Edith to go with her mother to Euston Station. Tears streamed down Clara's cheek as she crouched in the hall, repeatedly hugging her grandbabies. Michael, now a chubby three-year-old, patted her cheeks. "Don't cry, Granny. Don't cry. You're going on a train ride!"

Hazel understood that there was more to her grandmother's departure than a simple train ride. Her eyes were filled with tears. She wrapped her little arms around Clara and hung on.

"I love you, Granny. Don't go."

Clara gathered both children into her arms for one final embrace. "I must go, my darlings. I'll miss you terribly. I'll write you long letters and your mommy will read them to you."

The train station was full of British and American service men who clogged the smoke-filled platforms and chatted amongst themselves. Edith helped Clara find a compartment occupied by a woman traveling with two small children. She hoisted Clara's two suitcases, the violin, and a sack lunch into the overhead luggage rack and hugged her mother until they heard the train whistle announcing imminent departure.

"I love you, Mutti," she said.

When she finally fled to the stairs and jumped down to the platform, the train had begun to inch forward. Clara pressed her face to the window for a last glimpse of her daughter. Edith stood wiping away tears with one hand and waving with the other. Clara kissed her fingertips and pressed them to the glass as her daughter disappeared into the smoke and steam of the station.

THE JOURNEY WAS LONG and exhausting. They were frequently shuttled to a sidetrack to allow the passage of freight trains rushing to London. A gray, blackout dusk enveloped Liverpool when they arrived. On the way to the harbor, she could see bomb-damaged buildings from the taxi window. She stayed the night in a refugee hotel booked by the CBF and the next morning boarded the ship. If all went well, the convoy would form up that evening and they would sail out across the north Atlantic.

Her ship, ironically named *Eros*, was a refrigerated fruit carrier owned by the Cunard Line. It rode high on the water, its holds almost empty with no fresh produce being sent out of Britain. Clara couldn't help but imagine boxes of satin ball gowns and wide-skirted party dresses like the ones she had seen in the magazine layout stashed in the spaces below decks. The ship had only ten passengers and five of them were stateless persons like herself, whose welcome in Britain had expired. She shared a tiny, double bunk space with Eva, a shy Jewish girl of twelve whose parents slept in an adjoining cabin. The family had lived in Birmingham since they fled Lithuania three years before. They also had recently received their long-awaited visas and planned to start a new life in America.

The ten passengers ate dinner with the ship's officers, sat huddled against the cold in deck chairs, and read or played cards in the tiny passenger salon.

One night, feeling stifled in the cabin and unable to sleep, Clara took her violin from its case, bundled up in a sweater and her coat, and went out onto the deck.

A half moon hung in the sky and the sea was the color of steel. In the distance, she could barely make out the forms of the other ships in the convoy—nine merchant vessels, two American destroyers, a British frigate, and two corvettes, strung out like a line of beads across the horizon. Clara wondered if German U-boats waited deep beneath the surface aiming torpedoes at the silent ships.

The air was frigid, and Clara hugged her violin to her chest. It had been a long time since she had played it. Slowly she raised the instrument to her chin and plucked the strings. Her fingers were so cold and stiff they hurt. She raised the bow and moved it along the strings, the music mournful and subdued. Gradually a melody began to form, the notes drifting across the water, swallowed by the night.

As she played, Clara sensed movement. In the dark shadow of the ladder to the bridge, her cabin mate stood wrapped in a blanket, the white hem of her nightgown flapping in the wind.

"Eva, I'm sorry if I woke you when I left."

"I couldn't sleep, either. I hope you don't mind that I followed you, Mrs. Lang."

Clara walked back and held out her arm. "Come, let's stand together to stay warm."

Eva offered her half the blanket, and they stood shoulder to shoulder gazing at the sea.

"You play beautifully," Eva whispered. "It reminded me of life at home before the war."

Clara nodded. Music was part of her remembered life too. "Do you like music then?" she asked.

"Oh, yes, Mrs. Lang. Ever so much. When I was seven, I started to learn to play the violin. I longed to play as well as you do and one day to perform with an orchestra." Eva released a deep sigh before she spoke again. "My violin was lost when we fled our home. In Birmingham, we hadn't enough money for lessons. Poppa says in Canada things will get better."

Eva was so earnest. She reminded Clara of herself at the same age. "Would you like entirely free private lessons while we are together on the ship?"

"Oh, yes! Please!"

"Then we'll begin tomorrow morning if your parents agree. But now we must return to our cabin before we turn into icicles."

FOR THE REMAINDER OF the two-week passage, Clara and Eva sat together in the salon mornings and afternoons and played music. Clara was surprised to see how well her young pupil remembered. Her fingers were agile, and she had a musical ear. Clara would play a few bars, then hand the violin to Eva. The girl would quickly reproduce the notes. Before the end of the voyage, she played entire pieces from memory. Clara gave her pointers on how to improve her tone, perfect the smoothness of transitions, and maintain tempo. Clara had no doubt that if Eva was able to continue practicing and learning, she would one day play in an orchestra.

After supper on the night before the ship docked in Halifax, Clara strode to the stern, one hand deep in her coat pocket, the other clutching the handle of her violin case. Fred's letter demanding secrecy was folded in one of her pockets and her fist clenched around the paper as she withdrew it. She set the violin on the deck and slowly tore the paper into strips. She stretched her hand over the edge of the gunwale and released the fragments into the wind. They twisted and spiraled and fell slowly toward the churning water in the ship's wake.

She walked back along the deck toward the salon. The full moon cast a silver path across the flat water, and, on the horizon, the dark shape of Nova Scotia was little more than a line in the distance. She lifted her violin from its case and tucked her cheek onto the smooth chinrest. She raised her bow and began to play the violin part of Mozart's Requiem Mass. Her heart flew to Albert and her bow faltered. For a moment, she almost threw the violin into the sea, but she couldn't do it. Slowly her hand again moved the bow across the strings. Clara let the sad sounds envelop her and her spirit rose with the music.

Clara felt a gentle tug on her coat and saw Eva at her side.

"Your music is sad," Eva said. "Mother and I came out to see if you are all right."

Clara turned. Eva's mother waited in the shadows.

Clara motioned with her hands. "Come and join us, Mrs. Daviots. The sea is like mercury tonight. Like liquid silver."

Clara returned her violin to its case and set it at her feet. The two women, with Eva between them, stood and gazed across the water into the surrounding night. The dark was pierced by pinpricks of light—a sailor's lantern, a flashing Morris code light from one of the other merchant ships, miniscule dots of light on the distant shoreline, and the stars above.

Clara picked up her violin and held it out to her student. "Eva, I want you to have this. I know you will take it all the way to an orchestra one day."

"Truly? You give it to me, Mrs. Lang?"

Clara nodded. Eva grasped the handle of the violin case, the warmth of her hand touching Clara's cold fingers.

"No, it is too extravagant." Eva's mother brushed away a single tear as she faced Clara. "You have done so much for Eva. She cannot take your violin."

"But she must. It is exactly what I want." Clara felt light; her heart had found the right solution. "Eva is our future. We are the past. I want my violin to carry music into the future. It is a way to defy Hitler. Eva will do that for all of us."

The next morning, Clara stood at the top of the gangway and watched Eva follow her parents down the steep stairs. The violin case in her grip, her feet firmly on the North American wharf, her young pupil turned and waved. Holding Eva's gaze, Clara stepped onto the gangway and set one foot in front of the other.

October 1946

WHEN THE MAIL ARRIVED, Edith recognized the blue envelope and the slanting penmanship immediately. The postmark was German, but the letter had originally been mailed care of Mrs. Atkinson who had forwarded it to Harcourt Terrace. Edith stuffed it into her bra and walked back into the parlor.

"Nothing of interest this afternoon," she said. "Only these two adverts."

George glanced up from the newspaper and grunted. Edith dropped the flyers on the dining table and retreated into the kitchen. As she prepared supper, her hand frequently slid over her left breast to feel the stiff paper hidden there. She would read the letter later.

As soon as the meal was finished, the dishes washed, and the children tucked safely in bed, George turned to her.

"I'll just nip out to the pub," he said. "Only one pint with my mates and I'll be back. I promise."

For once Edith was happy to hear her husband's frequent re-frain. When she heard the slam of the front door and George's heavy footsteps climbing the stairs to the street, Edith pulled the letter out from its soft hiding place. She stared at the blue enve-lope. Her heart thrummed in her chest as if she were eighteen years old again.

She ripped open the envelope and pulled out a single sheet of blue paper. Charlie's familiar handwriting covered both sides.

My darling Edith,

I hope this letter finds you. I only have your first address in England and hope someone will know how to get my letter to you.

It has been ten years. Years of war and hardship and separation, but I still think of you every day. I waited as I promised I would. My love for you has never wavered. Finally, with the war over, I dare to hope we might be reunited.

Because I refused to join the National Socialist Party, I lost my job as soon as the Olympic project was finished. For a while I worked on the autobahn. The workers I supervised were mostly political prisoners from labor camps, sometimes even women and young boys. Later, once the war was in full swing, I was conscripted into the army and sent to the East. My engineering skills kept me away from the front lines and busy repairing bridges and roads. I was released from the military last spring and have been cleared of Nazi association by the Americans who occupied Meiningen for a time. However, the Russians will be taking over Thuringia soon and the Americans will leave. We will be part of the Soviet sector, which is not good news. We will have to see what happens.

My father passed away while I was on the Eastern Front. It was difficult for my aging mother to handle the privation and upheaval at the end of the war on her own. I am glad to be home again and able to help her as our country starts to recover. Much of our town was destroyed by Allied bombs in the final days of the war, but the park where we walked and the hillsides leading to the Schloss remain as they were. These places are filled with memories of you and happier times.

Please write to me and tell me how you are. I pray each day that you were not injured during the bombing of London. I hope you are safe and happy. I long to hold you—to press you to my chest, our hearts beating in unison as they once did.

Please write to me if you receive this letter. I remember well how your letters lit up my days so many years ago. The world has finally regained its balance, and we are free to be together again. I hope that is what you want as much as I do.

You will always have my heart, Charlie

Tears streamed down Edith's cheeks. She thought of the simple locket with the hand-drawn heart inside. She had stopped wearing it years before, and it lay hidden in a drawer of her jewelry box, along with the one letter her mother had brought and the hand-painted birthday card.

Charlie's wish to hold her was impossible to grant. She shook her head, wiped her cheeks, and slipped the letter into her bra again. She needed to think before she wrote to him.

Later that night, when George snored quietly in inebriated sleep, Edith eased out from under the blankets. She pulled a sweater over her nightie, took up her jewelry box, the letter now hidden there along with the other mementos, and carried it out to the dark dining room. She switched on the overhead light and lay the letter on the table, running her palm over the words Charlie had written. She opened the drawer of the box and reached her fingers inside, touching the locket that nestled there. Edith slipped the necklace over her head and held the locket in the warm palm of her hand as she reread Charlie's letter. She read it two times. She removed the early love letter and the card and stared at them. She had reread them so often over the years that she knew them by heart. Finally, she opened the stationery box she kept in the sideboard and selected a piece of creamy paper. Edith stared at the blank sheet. *How could she write the words that needed to be said?* She picked up her fountain pen and began.

Dear Charlie,

Your letter, when it arrived in the post today, caught me by surprise and your words brought back many memories.

Of course, I am happy to know you are alive and unharmed after this awful war. I too have survived without a scratch. We have both been lucky. There are millions who cannot say the same.

I told you I would build a new life in England and that you should forget me. It breaks my heart that you did not heed my words. I am no longer the young girl you loved. I barely remember her myself.

I am a grown woman now and a different person altogether, more serious and less prone to romantic notions. I am the wife of an Englishman who fought in Normandy, suffered the evacuation of Dunkirk, and later returned to the North African front. He, like all of us, has been changed by the war, but still, he is my husband. Now that he is home after four years away, we are rebuilding our life together. For what he has suffered and the love he has given me, I owe him my best effort to be a good wife.

We have two children, a girl who is seven and a boy aged six. Both are full on English children who speak not a word of German, love cricket and the king. Most of all, I must do what is best for my children who are deeply rooted in British soil. Even if I wanted to return to Germany, the country that rejected me so cruelly (and I do NOT want to return!), I must remain in England for my children.

This will be my only letter to you. I have written it in the dark of night while my husband sleeps, and I will not commit this act of disloyalty again. Please understand. You must do as I asked in 1936. You must make a life for yourself that does not include me. I hope you will find happiness. Our time of love is past and cannot be recovered.

You will forever remain dear to my heart's memories, Edith

When she had finished writing, Edith slipped the folded page into an envelope, carefully wrote out Charlie's address, licked the flap, and sealed it. She put the letter into her handbag. She would mail it on her way to work in the morning.

Edith stood and carried the two letters, the old and the new, to the kitchen sink. Slowly she tore both of Charlie's letters and their blue envelopes into strips, letting them fall onto the wet porcelain. She struck a match and dropped it onto the pile of paper bits. The small flame caught and flared up, turning the paper into curling ashes. She turned on the water tap and washed the gray-black ash down the drain.

Edith stood in the parlor watching the dark night sky gradually lighten into dawn. She slipped the locket chain over her head and returned the keepsake, along with the birthday card, both things too precious to part with, to her jewelry box. She carried it back to the bedroom and set the box on her dresser. She slid between the bedcovers, lying next to her husband. George shifted in his sleep and his long arm encircled her shoulder. Edith felt his warmth and her body relaxed. She had made a home, and she would keep what she had made.

TIMELINE

1933

January 3	Hitler appointed Chancellor of Germany.
July 14	Nazi Party made only legal political party in Germany.

1934

May 9	Edith's eighteenth birthday. Her older brother, Friedel, gives her the diary.
July 12	Friedel sails from Bremmerhaven to New York.
August	Edith starts at the domestic school.
September	Edith meets Charlie.

1935

Summer	Edith graduates from domestic school.
	Edith goes with her cousin to work at Jewish summer camp.
July 20	Hugo dies and Edith returns to Meiningen for her father's funeral.
August	Herman is sent to Suhl to attend business school.
Fall	Edith attends dressmaking school in Aschaffenburg.
September 15	The Nuremberg Laws are passed, including the Law for the Protection of German Blood and German Honor.

1936

Winter	Edith works for the Jewish family in Erfurt.
Spring	Edith goes to Berlin to see Charlie.
	Edith emigrates to the United Kingdom.

1937

Summer	Clara and Edith enjoy a vacation together in the Bavarian mountains.
December 25	Edith meets George Collett.

1938

March 12	Clara goes to London.
	Edith has abortion.
	Germany annexes Austria: the Anschluss.
April	Edith and George marry.
	Friedel/Fred marries in California.
	Clara starts shipping furniture and art to London and California.
May	Edith and George visit Meiningen for their honeymoon.
August 17	All Jews in Germany must take either the male name of Israel or the female name of Sara.
November 9-10	Kristallnacht: Herman returns to Meiningen to hide in Clara's apartment.

1939

February 3	Hazel is born to Edith and George.
March 3	Herman leaves for England where he lives with Uncle Bruno and Aunt Nelda.
	Clara meets Albert.
April	Edith, George, and the infant, Hazel, visit Clara in Meiningen.
	Clara begins reading Edith's diary.
Summer	Clara and Albert become lovers.
August	Clara flees to England.
September 1	Germany invades Poland.
September 3	Britain declares war with Germany.
Late October	George is conscripted and goes to France with the British Expeditionary Force.
November 18	Herman leaves London and sails for the United States.

1940

January 8	Food rationing begins in Britain.
May 26 to June 4	The evacuation of British troops from Dunkirk and other ports in Normandy, France.
June 12	George returns home and his son Michael is born.
	George is stationed in London and assigned to a secret project.

September 7	The Blitz begins.
	London experiences fifty-seven consecutive nights of heavy bombing.
November	Edith starts work as hotel housekeeper.

1941

March	George is assigned to North African front.
May 11	End of the heaviest bombing of London.
June 4	Start of clothing rationing in Britain.
December 7	Japanese attack Pearl Harbor.
December 8	United States and Britain declare war on Japan.
	America is in the war.

1942

February	Edith starts job at the Thread and Thistle.
Spring	Edith starts designing Utility style dresses for the Thread and Thistle.
Late Summer	Edith goes dancing and meets Nathan.
December 25	Christmas dinner with American GIs.

1943

Early Spring	Clara starts to work as a house cleaner.
August	Edith goes on Bank Holiday weekend with Nathan.
	Clara and the children visit Bruno.
September	Clara gets her US visa.
October	Clara sails from Liverpool with a convoy heading for America.

1946

October	Edith receives letter from Charlie.

Author's Note

My first novel, *Immigrant Soldier*, was based on the World War II experiences of my uncle, Herman Lang. His story grabbed me and would not let me go. Herman's Jewish blood branded him in Nazi eyes, forced him to flee his homeland, and landed him in the U.S. Army where he was trained to interrogate German prisoners of war.

Though the story was gripping—a combination of a coming-of-age story, an immigrant tale, and a wartime adventure—I found that writing from the point-of-view of a young man was sometimes an out-of-body experience. As a woman (at the time in my late seventies), my experience of male emotions and attitudes came to me, at best, second hand, from my father, various boyfriends, my husband, and my son. And my knowledge of the military was almost nonexistent.

During the months I spent researching and writing that first novel (okay, let's be honest . . . the years!) the idea of writing a woman's story always bubbled below the surface and thoughts of the women from *Immigrant Soldier* kept circling my mind. My grandmother Clara (Herman's mother) and my aunt Edith (Herman's sister) spoke to me, begging me to write about them.

But I was unsure how to make their quieter story work as a novel. My two women relatives did nothing unusual in any big heroic sense. They were not spies or resistance fighters, ambulance drivers or code breakers. They did not suffer in concentration camps or hide in basements, sewers, or forests. Yet, I knew instinctively that they represented something important—women who waited, made do, worked hard, worried about their loved ones, and protected their children. They were the strength behind the heroes. I also came to understand that in many small and quiet acts, Clara and Edith were heroes, too.

Though my grandmother and I adored each other, under her son's stricture of silence, she did not tell me of her life in Germany. Finally in her last years, after I discovered on my own about our Jewish heritage and came to understand the terrors of the Holocaust, she shared a few tantalizing glimpses of her previous life.

I interviewed my aunt Edith while doing the research for *Immigrant Soldier,* and in the autumn of 2023, I pulled out the transcript and reread it. Though Edith recounted in detail her young love for Charlie and how she met Sophie and George, much of the rest of her life story was forgotten as she eagerly showed me old family photographs of long-dead relatives. But she told me enough to start the ideas churning.

I have often told readers that *Immigrant Soldier* is about 90 percent true and the plot line is based entirely on Herman's memories shared with me over many days of interviews. I realized at once that because I had less primary material, *Ashes and Ruins* would be more fictionalized than my earlier work. I would need to stretch my imagination. Fortunately, this time, I was telling the story of a mother blessed by a strong relationship with her daughter and was able to cull the depths of my own experiences.

Questions about time and place led me to copious amounts of research, including a trip to London and correspondence with the city archives in Meiningen, Germany.

Readers of *Immigrant Soldier* will notice some differences between the two stories, most noticeably the appearance of a significant new character, Cousin Rikka. This unpleasant woman appeared in early drafts of Herman's story but was removed because she was of little importance in his life. Obviously, her role in family dynamics had a huge impact on both Clara and Edith and, for that reason alone, she had to be brought back. As a character, she also acted as a villain who our brave heroines could vanquish.

Regarding the question of how much is true, something readers are always interested in understanding, I offer the following:

- From what Herman told me, documents, and the little bits my grandmother shared before she died, I know how the family celebrated Christmas, why Rikka (not her real name) came to live with the family, where and how Clara discovered her dead husband, what she wrote on his death certificate, that she kicked Rikka out after Hugo's death, how much she was able to ship out of Germany, that she fell in love with Albert (a fictitious name), how her friend warned her to leave Germany, that Fred insisted on secrecy regarding their Jewishness, and the name and type of ship on which Clara traveled to America.

- When I interviewed Edith in 2000, she told me about her shunning by the students at the domestic school and her role at the graduation fashion show, her trip to Berlin to "seduce" Charlie, her first job in London, her friendship with Sophie, how she met George, both abortions, and being locked out of the house in subzero temperatures in her nightie.

Snippets of truth aside, *Ashes and Ruins* is a work of fiction. I hope readers will find its strength does not lie in what is true, but in how it depicts the evolving relationship between a mother and daughter, the quiet heroism of women on the home front, and the step-by-step escalation of anti-Semitic laws in Nazi Germany. As I wrote about Edith and Clara, I realized PTSD and a woman's right to choose, two issues with current significance, were also part of their story. It is my hope that these themes make *Ashes and Ruins* both universal and relevant to today's readers.

Kathryn Lang-Slattery
Laguna Beach, California

Acknowledgments

This book could not have been written without the help of a myriad of readers, editors, advisors, librarians, officials, history professors, the internet, and my ever-supportive family and friends.

During early research, I was aided by two women in Germany. Special thanks to Andrea Tischer of the Department of Culture in Meiningen and Dr. Iris Helbing who is responsible for research on Jewish history in that city. Both of these women graciously answered my countless emails, responded to my questions, and sent me documents and photos.

A special thank you to Silke Turner, who answered my "Nextdoor" notice asking for someone who could translate German into English. She came to my home in the wee hours of the morning to help me place a phone call to the Archives of the City of Meiningen and make the first contact with Andrea Tischer. Silke also translated several documents for me and skimmed an entire German book to see if it contained a specific bit of information I was researching. I am grateful for her invaluable help.

Thanks also to Dr. Joachim Hahn of Alemannia-Judaica who attempted to find evidence of the grave markers for Hugo and his mother. Unfortunately, the Meiningen Cemetery was heavily damaged by bombs at the end of the war and nothing could be found. Sharone of the World Jewish Relief sent me copies of the cards showing Edith, Herman, and Clara's registrations with the organization in London, primary documents that confirmed family lore.

The staff of the British Library helped me with patience and led me to important documents and books. The librarians of the London Archives found my relatives' names in the 1939 census and allowed me to pore over the color-coded maps of bomb destruction in the neighborhood where my characters lived. These professionals made my days of research in London exciting and fruitful.

I will forever be grateful to my English cousins for their support and encouragement. Even in her final days, Hazel shared some of her childhood memories with me, and her daughter Louise allowed me to look over her mother's treasured photo album and take pictures of several pages. Michael Collett welcomed me into his home, shared memories, showed me the water-stained side table, and most helpfully, drew me a rough sketch of the layout of the Harcourt Terrace basement apartment where he lived until the age of sixteen. My time with these cousins will always be treasured. Their memories helped me feel a part of the story.

Various authors offered advice and insight to me along the way. I want to especially thank Wolf Gruner for his willingness to correspond with me. His book, *Resisters, How Ordinary Jews Fought Persecution in Hitler's Germany,* allowed me to see Clara's simple actions as her personal resistance to tyranny.

Several other books also offered understanding that enabled me to write a better book. The following are only a few of the books that guided my writing: *The Twisted Road to Auschwitz: Nazi Policy toward German Jews 1933–1939* by Karl A. Schleunes; *Between Dignity and Despair: Jewish Life in Nazi Germany*, by Marion A. Kaplan; *Before the Holocaust: Antisemitic Violence and the Reaction of German Elites and Institutions during the Nazi Takeover* by Hermann Beck; *Millions Like Us: Women's Lives During the Second World War* by Virginia Nicholson; *Collar the Lot!: How Britain Interned and Expelled Its Wartime Refugees* by Peter and Leni Gillman; *Fashion on the Ration: Style in the Second World War*, by Julie Summers; *Wartime: Britain 1939-1945 by* Juliet Gardiner; and *Love, Sex and War Changing Values, 1939-45*, by John Costello.

As usual, I have beta readers to thank as well: Ricki Older, Donna Feeney, Lesley Danziger, Lee Kuchera, and Shannon Zingel. Special thanks to Lesley Danziger for fact-checking the British section. For her invaluable help in rooting out errors, whether typos, glitches, or misspellings, I thank my friend Barbara Miller. She has an acute ability to find tiny problems. And finally, special thanks to Michele Orwin for stepping in at the end of the project for a final, and important, manuscript proofread.

To my indomitable editor, Lorraine Fico-White, for her support, suggestions, and tireless answering of questions, I extend my fullest gratitude. She always guides me to my best writing.

Last, but not least, for their help in the preparation of a beautiful book, special thanks to Lorie DeWorken, book designer par excellence, and to Cole Waidley for his help creating the book cover, an arduous task because he must work with an author who fancies herself an artist, too.

Every book is a group endeavor. I have many thanks to extend and if I have forgotten anyone, I sincerely apologize. Please know that any forgetfulness is not based on lack of appreciation.

DISCUSSION QUESTIONS FOR YOUR BOOK GROUP

- The author uses personal diary entries to reveal Edith's youthful personality. Did you enjoy reading the diary segments? What did you find interesting about Edith and her thoughts as a young woman?

- Did you learn anything about the early Nazi years in Germany that you hadn't known before or found surprising? What? Did any information change your perspective?

- Edith falls deeply in love with Charlie. What do you think attracted her most to this man? What do you think attracted him to her?

- Were you surprised by how much Clara was able to ship to her children? What was her motive for doing this? What made this unusual act possible for Clara?

- As she is preparing to emigrate, Clara meets Albert and falls in love for the first time. Did you see parallels between Clara's love story and Edith's? How were their experiences similar and how were their stories different?

- Edith travels all the way to Berlin to have a special night with Charlie. Did you sympathize with her reasons for making this trip? How did you feel about the way her trip ended?

- After she meets George, Edith soon finds herself pregnant. Could you understand her decision to have an abortion? Could you have done the same? Why or why not?

- When George returns from Dunkirk, he suffers from nightmares and is more emotionally volatile. With today's understanding, did you realize this was probably caused by war trauma (PTSD)? Do you have any personal experience with people suffering from PTSD and, if so, did you find the depiction of the syndrome to be accurate?

- To maintain her relationship with her daughter, Clara had to learn to treat Edith as an adult. This is often a difficult transition for a parent. Do you think Clara successfully made the adjustment?

- The author uses letters to show what is happening to characters far from London. What do you think it was like to wait for months to get news from loved ones? Do you or does anyone you know still write letters to communicate with family or friends? Have you ever received a letter that was so important to you that you saved it in a special place?

- Fred insists that Clara never mention their Jewish heritage when she comes to California. Why do you think he made this demand? How do you think it made Clara feel?

- Did you find the ending of *Ashes and Ruins* satisfying? Why or why not?

ALSO BY K. LANG-SLATTERY

Immigrant Soldier: The Story of a Ritchie Boy

Wherever the Road Leads: A Memoir of Love, Travel, and a Van

Children's books published under the name of Katie Lang-Slattery:

Tagalong Caitlin

Caitlin's Buddy

Caitlin's Party

Learn more about the author and her books at:
https://klangslattery.com
https://kathrynslattery.substack.com

9 798986 201313